Mary Higgins Clark is the author of twenty-three bestselling novels and a memoir. She lives with her husband in Saddle River, New Jersey

Praise for **Mary Higgins Clark**

'Clark plays out her story like the pro that she is . . . flawless' *DAILY MIRROR*

'Should come with a warning: start in the evening and you'll be reading late into the night. This one is well worth the lost sleep' *USA TODAY*

'Mary Higgins Clark is a master plotter, seeding [her stories] with crimes, clues and psychopathic quirks that pay off' *NEW YORK TIMES*

'One of the best storytellers ever. Yes, you won't put it down' LARRY KING

'The suspense lasts right to the end of the book' *LEICESTER MERCURY*

'There's something special about Clark's thrillers, and it's not just the gentleness with which the bestselling writer approaches her often lurid subject matter . . . special above all is the compassion she extends to her characters. Grace, charm and solid storytelling' *PUBLISHERS WEEKLY*

'Ms Clark is a natural-born storyteller . . . she taps into some elemental fear that really gives you the willies' *NEW YORK TIMES*

'As well-oiled as a fine-tuned engine' *NOTTINGHAM EVENING POST*

'Another cracking tale from the ex-president of the Mystery Writers Club of America' *HELLO*!

'An instant classic . . . superbly plotted'
LOS ANGELES TIMES

'Gripping' *BOLTON EVENING NEWS*

'The "Queen of Suspense" is renowned for her fast-moving prose and dazzling plot twists; this latest title does not disappoint' *GOOD BOOK GUIDE*

Also by Mary Higgins Clark,
from Pocket Books UK

Second Time Around
Daddy's Little Girl
On the Street Where You Live
Before I Say Goodbye
We'll Meet Again
All Through the Night
You Belong to Me
Pretend You Don't See Her
My Gal Sunday
Moonlight Becomes You
Silent Night
Let Me Call You Sweetheart
Remember Me
Weep No More, My Lady
Stillwatch
A Cry in the Night
The Cradle Will Fall
A Stranger is Watching
Where are the Children?

Non-fiction
Kitchen Privileges

With Carol Higgins Clark
He Sees You When You're Sleeping
Deck the Halls

MARY HIGGINS CLARK

NIGHT-TIME IS MY TIME

POCKET BOOKS

LONDON • SYDNEY • NEW YORK • TORONTO

First published in Great Britain by Simon & Schuster UK Ltd, 2004
This edition published by Pocket Books, 2005
An imprint of Simon & Schuster UK Ltd
A Viacom Company

1 3 5 7 9 10 8 6 4 2

Simon & Schuster UK Ltd
Africa House
64–78 Kingsway
London WC2B 6AH

www.simonsays.co.uk

Simon & Schuster Australia
Sydney

A CIP catalogue record for this book is available from
the British Library

ISBN 0-7434-8959-4
EAN 9780743489591

Typeset by SX Composing DTP, Rayleigh, Essex
Printed and bound in Great Britain by
Cox & Wyman Ltd, Reading, Berkshire

Acknowledgments

I am frequently asked if the longer I write, the easier it gets. I wish that were true, but it simply isn't. Each story is a new challenge, a new landscape to fill with characters and events. That is why I am so grateful to those same people who are always there for me, especially when I'm beginning to wonder if I really can tell the tale the way I hope to tell it.

Michael Korda has been my editor ever since my first suspense fiction novel thirty years ago. He has been friend, mentor, and editor par excellence for three decades. Senior editor Chuck Adams has been part of our team for the last dozen years. I am grateful to both of them for everything they do to guide this writer along the way.

My literary agents, Eugene Winick and Sam Pinkus, are true friends, good critics, and great supporters. I love them. Dr. Ina Winick brings her psychological expertise to assist me on the workings of the human mind.

Lisl Cade, my publicist and dear friend, is always there for me.

Many thanks to Michael Goldstein, Esq., and Meyer Last, Esq., for their valuable assistance in answering my queries about adoption law and procedure.

Again and always a tip of the hat to Associate Director of Copyediting, Gypsy da Silva, and her team: Rose Ann Ferrick, Anthony

Newfield, Bill Molesky, and Joshua Cohen, and to Detective Richard Murphy and Sgt. Steven Marron, Ret., for their continuing support and guidance.

Agnes Newton, Nadine Petry, and Irene Clark are always in my corner on my literary journeys.

The special joy is that after the story is told, I celebrate with my nearest and dearest, the children and grandchildren and, of course, "Himself," my marvelous husband, John Conheeney.

And now I hope you, my valued readers, enjoy the goings-on at a deadly twentieth class reunion in the beautiful Hudson Valley.

For Vincent Viola, a proud West Point graduate,

and his lovely wife, Theresa,

with affection and friendship.

NIGHT-TIME IS MY TIME

The definition of an owl had always pleased him: A night bird of prey . . . sharp talons and soft plumage which permits noiseless flight . . . applied figuratively to a person of nocturnal habits. *"I am The Owl," he would whisper to himself after he had selected his prey, "and night-time is my time."*

1

It was the third time in a month he had come to Los Angeles to observe her daily activities. "I know your comings and goings," he whispered as he waited in the pool house. It was one minute of seven. The morning sun was filtering through the trees, causing the waterfall that spilled into the pool to sparkle and shimmer.

He wondered if Alison could sense that she had only one minute more of life on earth. Did she have an uneasy feeling, perhaps a subconscious urge to skip her swim this morning? Even if she did, it wouldn't do her any good. It was too late.

The sliding glass door opened, and she stepped onto the patio. Thirty-eight years old, she was infinitely more attractive than she had been twenty years ago. Her body, tanned and sleek, looked good in the bikini. Her hair, now honey blond, framed and softened her sharp chin.

She tossed the towel she was carrying onto a lounge chair. The blinding anger that had been simmering inside him escalated into rage, but then, just as quickly, was replaced by the satisfaction of knowing what he was about to do. He had seen an interview in which a daredevil stunt diver swore that the moment before he began to dive, knowing that he was risking his life, was an indescribable thrill, a sensation he needed to repeat over and over again.

For me it's different, he thought. The moment before I reveal myself to them is what gives me the thrill. I know they're going to die, and when they see me, they know, too. They understand what I am going to do to them.

Alison stepped onto the diving board and stretched. He watched as she bounced softly, testing the board, then positioned her arms in front of her.

He opened the door of the pool house just as her feet lifted from the board. He wanted her to see him when she was in midair. Just before she hit the water. He wanted her to understand how vulnerable she was.

In that split second, their eyes locked. He caught her expression as she plunged into the water. She was terrified, aware that she was incapable of flight.

He was in the pool before she had surfaced. He hugged her against his chest, laughing as she flailed about, kicking her feet. How foolish she was. She should simply accept the inevitable. "You're going to die," he whispered, his voice calm, even.

Her hair was in his face, blinding him. Impatiently he shook it away. He didn't want to be distracted from the pleasure of feeling her struggle.

The end was coming. In her craving for breath, she had opened her mouth and was gulping water. He felt her final frantic effort to break away from him, then the hopelessly feeble tremors as her body began to go limp. He pressed her close, wishing he could read her mind. Was she praying? Was she begging God to save her? Was she seeing the light that people who have experienced a near-death event claim to have seen?

He waited a full three minutes before he released her. With a satisfied smile he watched as her body sank to the bottom of the pool.

It was five minutes after seven when he climbed out of the pool, pulled on a sweatshirt, shorts, sneakers, a cap, and dark glasses. He had already chosen the spot where he would leave the silent reminder of his visit, the calling card that everybody always missed.

At six minutes past seven he began to jog down the quiet street, another early morning fitness buff in a city of fitness buffs.

2

Sam Deegan had not intended to open the file on Karen Sommers that afternoon. He'd been fishing through the bottom drawer of his desk in search of the packet of cold pills he vaguely remembered having stashed there. When his fingers touched the well-worn and troublingly familiar folder, he hesitated and then, with a grimace, pulled it out and opened it. When he looked at the date on the first page, he realized that he had been subconsciously intending to find it. The anniversary of Karen Sommers' death was Columbus Day, twenty years ago next week.

The file ought to have been kept with the other unsolved cases, but three successive Orange County prosecutors had indulged his need to keep it at his fingertips. Twenty years ago Sam had been the first detective to arrive in response to the frantic phone call from a woman screaming that her daughter had been stabbed.

Minutes later, when he had arrived at the house on Mountain Road in Cornwall-on-Hudson, he had found the victim's bedroom crowded with shocked and horrified onlookers. One neighbor was bent over the bed uselessly trying to administer mouth-to-mouth resuscitation. Others were attempting to pull the hysterical parents away from the heartbreaking sight of their daughter's brutalized body.

Karen Sommers' shoulder-length hair was spilling onto the pillow. When he yanked the would-be rescuer back, Sam could see the vicious stab wounds in Karen's chest and heart that must have caused instant death and had drenched the sheets with her blood.

He remembered his initial thought had been that the young woman probably never even heard her attacker enter her room. She probably never woke up, he reflected, shaking his head as he opened the folder. The mother's screams had attracted not only neighbors but a landscaper and delivery man who were on the premises next door. The result was a thoroughly compromised crime scene.

There had been no signs of forced entry. Nothing was missing. Karen Sommers had been a twenty-two-year-old first-year medical student who surprised her parents by coming home for an overnight visit. The logical suspect was her ex-boyfriend, Cyrus Lindstrom, a third-year law student at Columbia. He admitted that Karen had told him she wanted both of them to start seeing other people, but he also insisted that he had agreed it was a good idea because neither one of them was ready for a serious commitment. His alibi—that he had been asleep in the apartment he shared with three other law students—was verified, although all three roommates admitted they had gone to bed by midnight and therefore did not know whether or not Lindstrom had left the apartment after that time. Karen's death was estimated to have taken place between two and three in the morning.

Lindstrom had visited the Sommers house a few times. He knew a spare key was kept under the fake rock near the back door. He knew that Karen's room was the first one to the right off the back staircase. But that wasn't proof that in the middle of the night he had driven fifty miles from Amsterdam Avenue and 104th Street in Manhattan to Cornwall-on-Hudson and killed her.

"A person of interest"—that's what we call people like Lindstrom today, Sam reflected. I always thought that guy was as guilty as sin. I could never understand why the Sommers family stood by him. God, you'd have thought they were defending their own son.

Impatiently, Sam dropped the file on his desk, got up, and walked to the window. From his perspective he could see the parking lot, and he remembered the time a prisoner on trial for murder had overpowered a guard, dropped out the window of the courthouse, raced across the lot, mugged a guy getting into his car, and driven away.

We got him in twenty minutes, Sam thought. So why in twenty years can't I find the animal who killed Karen Sommers? For my money, it's still Lindstrom.

Lindstrom was now a high-powered New York criminal attorney. He's a master at getting the murdering bums off, Sam thought. Appropriate, since he's one of them.

He shrugged. It was a rotten day, rainy and unusually cold for early October. I used to love this job, he thought, but it's not the same anymore. I'm ready to retire. I'm fifty-eight years old; I've been at police work most of my life. I should just take the pension and run. Lose a little weight. Visit the kids and spend more time with the grandkids. Before you know it, they'll be in college.

He had a vague sense of a headache brewing as he ran a hand through his thinning hair. Kate used to tell me to stop doing that, he thought. She said I was weakening the roots.

With a half smile at his late wife's unscientific analysis of his approaching baldness, he went back to his desk and stared down again at the file marked "Karen Sommers."

He still regularly visited Karen's mother, Alice, who had moved to a condominium in town. He knew it comforted her to feel that they were still trying to find the person who had taken her daughter's life, but it was more than that. Sam had a feeling that someday Alice would mention something that had never occurred to her as being important, something that would be the first step toward finding out who had gone into Karen's room that night.

That's what has kept me in this job the last couple of years, he thought. I wanted so much to solve this case, but I can't wait any longer.

He went back to his desk, opened the bottom drawer, and then hesitated. He should let it go. It was time to put this folder with the other unsolved cases in the general file. He'd done his best. For the first twelve years after the murder, he'd gone to the cemetery on the anniversary. He'd stayed there all day, hidden behind a mausoleum, watching Karen's grave. He'd even wired the tombstone to catch anything a visitor might say. There'd been some cases where killers had been caught because they'd paid an anniversary visit to their victim's grave, even talking about the crime to their victim.

The only people who ever came to Karen's grave on the anniversary were her parents, and it had been a gut-wrenching intrusion of privacy to hear them reminisce about their only daughter. He'd given up going there eight years ago, after Michael Sommers died and Alice came alone to stand at the grave where her husband and daughter were now resting side by side. That was when he walked away, not wanting to be a witness to her grief. He'd never gone back.

Sam stood up and put the Karen Sommers file under his arm, his decision made. He wouldn't look at it again. And next week, on the twentieth anniversary of Karen's death, he'd put in his retirement papers.

And I'll stop by the cemetery, he thought. Just to let her know how sorry I am that I didn't do better by her.

3

It had taken nearly seven hours to drive from Washington through Maryland, Delaware, and New Jersey to the town of Cornwall-on-Hudson.

It was not a trip Jean Sheridan enjoyed making—not so much because of the distance, but because Cornwall, the town in which she had grown up, was filled with painful memories.

She had promised herself that no matter how persuasively charming Jack Emerson, the chairman of their twentieth high school reunion committee, attempted to be, she would plead work, other commitments, health—anything to avoid being part of it.

She had no desire to celebrate her graduation twenty years ago from Stonecroft Academy, even though she was grateful for the education she'd received there. She didn't even care about the "Distinguished Alumna" medal she'd be receiving, despite the fact that the scholarship to Stonecroft had been a stepping-stone to the scholarship to Bryn Mawr and then the doctorate at Princeton.

But now that a memorial for Alison had become part of the reunion schedule, it was impossible for her to refuse to attend.

Alison's death still seemed so unreal that Jean almost expected the phone to ring and hear that familiar voice, the words clipped and rushed as though everything had to be said in the space of ten seconds: "Jeannie. You haven't called lately. You've forgotten I'm alive. I hate you. No, I don't. I love you. I'm in awe of you. You're so damn smart. There's a premiere in New York next week. Curt Ballard is one of my clients. An absolutely terrible actor, but so gorgeous nobody cares. And his latest girlfriend is coming, too. You'd faint if I even whispered her name. Anyhow, can you make it next Tuesday, cocktails at six, the film, then a private dinner for twenty or thirty or fifty?"

Alison always did manage to get that kind of message across in about ten seconds, Jean thought, and Alison was always shocked when ninety percent of the time Jean couldn't drop everything and race to New York to join her.

Alison had been dead almost a month. Impossible as that was to believe, the fact that she might have been the victim of foul play was unbearable. But during her career she had made scores of enemies. No one got to head one of the largest talent agencies in the country without being hated. Besides, Alison's rapier-like wit and biting sarcasm had been compared to the stinging utterances of the legendary Dorothy Parker. Was someone whom she had ridiculed or fired been angry enough to kill her? Jean wondered.

I like to think that she had a fainting spell after she dove into the pool. I don't want to believe that anyone held her under the water, she thought.

She glanced at the shoulder bag beside her on the passenger seat, and her mind raced to the envelope inside it. What am I going to do? Who sent it to me and why? How could anyone have found out about Lily? Is she in trouble? Oh, God, what shall I do? What *can* I do?

These questions had caused her weeks of sleepless nights ever since she had received the report from the laboratory.

She was at the turnoff that led from Route 9W to Cornwall. And near Cornwall was West Point. Jean swallowed over the lump in her throat and tried to concentrate on the beauty of the October afternoon. The trees were breathtaking with their autumn colors of gold and orange and fiery red. Above them, the mountains, as always, were serenely calm. The Hudson River Highlands. I'd forgotten how beautiful it is here, she thought.

But of course that thought led inevitably to the memory of Sunday afternoons at West Point, sitting on the steps of the monument on an afternoon such as this. She had begun her first book there, a history of West Point.

It took ten years to finish, she thought, mainly because for a long time I simply couldn't write about it.

Cadet Carroll Reed Thornton, Jr., from Maryland. Don't think about Reed now, Jean warned herself.

The turn from Route 9W onto Walnut Street was still an automatic reaction rather than a considered decision. The Glen-Ridge House in Cornwall, named after one of the town's large boardinghouses of the mid-nineteenth century, was the hotel chosen for the reunion. There had been ninety students in her graduating class. According to the latest update she'd received, forty-two of them were planning to attend, plus wives and husbands or significant others, and children.

She hadn't had to make any of those extra reservations for herself.

It had been Jack Emerson's decision to have the reunion in October rather than June. He'd done a poll of the class and determined that June was when their own kids were graduating from high school or grammar school, making it more difficult for them to get away.

In the mail she'd received her ID badge with her senior class picture on top and her name emblazoned under it. It had come with the schedule of events for the weekend: Friday night, opening cocktail party and buffet. Saturday, breakfast buffet, tour of West Point, the Army-Princeton football game, and then cocktail party and black-tie dinner. Sunday was supposed to have concluded the reunion with a brunch at Stonecroft, but after Alison's death it had been decided to include a morning memorial service in her honor. She had been buried in the cemetery adjacent to the school, and the service would be at graveside.

In her will, Alison had left a large donation to the scholarship fund at Stonecroft, which was the primary reason for the hastily planned memorial ceremony.

Main Street doesn't feel very different, Jean thought as she drove slowly through the town. It had been many years since she'd been here. The summer she graduated from Stonecroft, her father and mother had finally split, sold the house, and gone their separate ways. Her father was now managing a hotel in Maui. Her mother had moved back to Cleveland where she had been raised and had married her high school sweetheart. "My biggest mistake was not marrying Eric thirty years ago," she'd gushed at the wedding.

And where does that leave me? That was the thought that ran through Jean's mind at that moment. But the breakup had at least meant the merciful end of her life in Cornwall.

She resisted the impulse to detour to Mountain Road and drive past her old home. Maybe I will sometime over the weekend, she thought, but not now. Three minutes later she was pulling into the driveway of the Glen-Ridge House, and the doorman, a professionally warm smile creasing his face, was opening the door of the car and saying, "Welcome home." Jean pushed the button for the trunk and watched as her garment bag and suitcase were scooped up.

"Go right to the check-in desk," the doorman urged. "We'll take care of the luggage."

The hotel lobby was clubby and warm, with deep carpeting and comfortable groupings of chairs. The front desk was to the left, and diagonally across from it Jean could see that the bar was already filling with pre-cocktail party celebrants.

A banner over the front desk welcomed the Stonecroft reunion class.

"Welcome home, Ms. Sheridan," said the clerk, a man in his sixties. His smile revealed glistening white teeth. His badly dyed hair exactly matched the finish on the cherry wood desk. As Jean gave him her credit card, she had the incongruous thought that he might have cut a chip from the desk to show his barber.

She wasn't ready to deal with any of her old classmates yet and hoped she could get to the elevator without being stopped. She wanted to have at least a quiet half hour while she showered and changed, before she had to put on her badge with the picture of the frightened and heartbroken eighteen-year-old girl she had been, and join her former classmates at the cocktail party.

As she took the room key and turned, the clerk said, "Oh, Ms. Sheridan, I almost forgot. I have a fax for you." He squinted at the name on the envelope. "Oh, sorry. I should be calling you Dr. Sheridan."

Without replying, Jean ripped open the envelope. The fax was from her secretary at Georgetown: "Dr. Sheridan, sorry to bother you. This is probably a joke or mistake, but I thought you'd want to see it." The "it" was a single sheet of paper that had been faxed to her office. It read, "Jean, I guess by now you've verified that I know Lily. Here's my problem. Do I kiss her or kill her? Just a joke. I'll be in touch."

For a moment Jean felt unable either to move or think. Kill her? Kill her? But why? Why?

He had been standing in the bar, watching, waiting for her to come in. Over the years he'd seen her picture on her book jackets, and every time he did, it was a shock to see that Jeannie Sheridan had acquired such a classy look.

At Stonecroft she'd been one of the smart but quiet ones. She'd even been nice to him in an offhand sort of way. He'd started to really like her until Alison told him how they'd all made fun of him. He knew who "they" were: Laura and Catherine and Debra and Cindy and Gloria and Alison and Jean. They used to sit at the same table at lunchtime.

Weren't they cute? he thought as the bile rose in his throat. Now Catherine and Debra and Cindy and Gloria and Alison were gone. He'd saved Laura for last. The funny part was that he still wasn't sure about Jean. For some reason he wavered about killing her. He still remembered the time when he was a freshman and had tried out for the baseball team. He'd been cut right away and had started to cry, those baby tears that he never could hold back.

Crybaby. Crybaby.

He'd run off the field, and a little later Jeannie had caught up with him. "I didn't make the cheerleader squad," she said. "So what?"

He knew she had followed him because she felt sorry for him. That's why something told him that she hadn't been one of the ones who made fun of him for wanting to take Laura to the prom. But then she had hurt him in a different way

Laura had always been the prettiest girl in the class—golden blond, china blue eyes, great body, noticeable even in the Stonecroft skirt and blouse. She was always sure of her power over the guys. The words "come hither" had been meant for her to utter.

Alison had always been mean. As a writer for the school paper, her "Behind the Scenes" column was supposed to be about school activities, but she always managed to find a way to take a dig at someone, like in a review for the school play when she'd written, "To everyone's surprise, Romeo, a.k.a. Joel Nieman, managed to remember most of his lines." Back then the popular kids thought Alison was a riot. The nerds stayed away from her.

Nerds like me, he thought, savoring the memory of the look of terror on Alison's face when she saw him coming toward her from the pool house.

Jean had been popular, but she hadn't seemed like the other girls. She'd been elected to the student council, where she'd been so quiet you'd think she couldn't talk, but anytime she opened her mouth, whether there or in class, she always had the right answer. Even then she'd been a history buff. What surprised him was how much prettier she was now. Her stringy light brown hair was darker and fuller, and cut like a cap around her face. She was slim, but not painfully thin anymore. Somewhere along the way she'd also learned how to dress. Her jacket and slacks were well cut. Wishing he could see the expression on her face, he watched as she shoved a fax into her shoulder bag.

"I am the owl, and I live in a tree."

In his head he could hear Laura imitating him. "She has you down pat," Alison had screeched that night twenty years ago. "And she told us you wet your pants, too."

He could imagine them all making fun of him; he could hear their shrill gales of mocking laughter.

It had happened way back in the second grade when he was seven years old. He'd been in the school play. That was his line, the only thing he had to say. But he couldn't get it out. He'd stuttered so much that all the kids on stage and even some of the parents began to snicker.

"I ammm th-th-the ooooowwwwwlllll, and, and I livvvvve in aaaaaa . . ."

He never did get the word "tree" out. That was when he burst out crying and ran off the stage holding the tree branch in his hand. His father had slapped him for being a sissy. His mother had said, "Leave him alone. He's a dopey kid. What can you expect? Look at him. He's wet his pants again."

The memory of that shame mingled with the imagined laughter of the girls and swirled in his head as he watched Jean Sheridan get into the elevator. Why should I spare you? he thought. Maybe Laura first, then you. Then you can all have a good laugh at me, all of you together, in hell.

He heard his name being called and turned his head. Dick Gormley, the big baseball hero of their class, was standing beside him in the bar, staring at his ID. "Great to see you," Dick said heartily.

You're lying, he thought, and it's *not* great to see you.

4

Laura had barely put her key in the door of the room when the bellman appeared with her luggage: a garment bag, two large suitcases, and an overnight satchel. She could sense what the man was thinking: *Lady, the reunion lasts for forty-eight hours, not two weeks.*

What he said was "Ms. Wilcox, my wife and I used to watch *Henderson County* every Tuesday night. We thought you were great in it. Any chance it will be coming back?"

Not the chance of a snowball in hell, Laura thought, but the man's obvious sincerity gave her a much-needed lift. "Not *Henderson County*, but I've done a pilot for Maximum Channel," she said. "It's scheduled to go on the air after the first of the year."

Not the truth, but close to the truth. Maximum had okayed the pilot and announced it was optioning the series. Then two days before she died, Alison had phoned. "Laura, honey, I don't know how to tell you this, but there's a problem. Maximum wants someone younger to play Emmie."

"Younger?" she had shouted. "For God's sake, Alison, I'm thirty-eight. The mother in the series has a twelve-year-old daughter. And I look good. You know I do."

"Don't yell at me," Alison had shouted back. "I'm doing my best to convince them to keep you. As for looking good, between laser-surgery and botox and face-lifts, everybody in this business looks good. That's why it's so hard to cast anyone as a grandmother. Nobody looks like one anymore."

We agreed to come to the reunion together, Laura thought. Alison told me that, according to the list of classmates who'd responded yes, Gordon Amory would be here, and apparently he just bought into Maximum. She said that he had enough influence to help me keep the job, assuming he could be convinced to use his power.

She had pushed and pushed Alison to call Gordie right away and make him force Maximum to accept her for the role. Finally Alison had said, "First of all, don't call him Gordie. He hates it. Second, I was trying to be tactful, something as you well know I rarely trouble to be. I'll say it straight. You're still beautiful, but you're not much of an actress. The people at Maximum think this series could turn out to be a real hit, but not with you in it. Maybe Gordon can change their minds. You can charm him. He had a crush on you, didn't he?"

The bellman had gone down the hall to fill the ice bucket. Now he tapped on the door and came back in. Without even thinking, Laura had already opened her purse and pulled out a twenty-dollar bill. His fervent "Thanks so much, Ms. Wilcox," made her wince. Once again she had played the big shot. Ten bucks would have been plenty.

Gordie Amory had been one of the guys who'd had a really big crush on her when they were at Stonecroft. Who'd have guessed that he'd end up such a big shot? God, you never know, Laura thought as she unzipped the garment bag. We should all have a crystal ball to look into the future.

The closet was small. Small room. Small windows. Dark brown carpet, brown upholstered chair, bedspread in tones of pumpkin and brown. Impatiently, Laura pulled out the cocktail dresses and evening suit she'd carried in the garment bag. She already knew that she'd wear the Chanel tonight. Go for glitter. Knock them dead. Look successful, even if you are behind in your taxes and the IRS has a lien on the house.

Alison had said that Gordie Amory was divorced. Her final advice rang in Laura's ears: "Look, honey, if you can't talk him into using you in the series, maybe you can get him to marry you. I understand he's mighty impressive. Forget what a nerd he was at Stonecroft."

5

"Anything else I can do for you, Dr. Sheridan?" the bellman asked.

Jean shook her head.

"You feel all right, Doctor? You look kind of pale."

"I'm fine. Thank you."

"Well, you just let us know if there's anything we can do for you."

At last the door closed behind him, and Jean could sink down on the edge of the bed. She had jammed the fax into the side panel of her shoulder bag. Now she grabbed it and reread the cryptic sentences: "Jean, I guess by now you've verified that I know Lily. Here's my problem. Do I kiss her or kill her? Just a joke. I'll be in touch."

Twenty years ago Dr. Connors had been the physician in Cornwall to whom she had confided her pregnancy. He had reluctantly agreed with her that involving her parents would be a mistake. "I'm going to give up the baby for adoption no matter what they say. I'm eighteen, and it's my decision. But they'll be upset and angry and make my life even more miserable than it is," she had said, weeping.

Dr. Connors told her about the couple who had finally given up hope that they would have their own child and who were planning to adopt. "If you're sure you're not going to keep the baby, I can promise you they will give it a wonderful, loving home."

He had arranged for her to work in a nursing home in Chicago until the baby was due. Then he flew to Chicago, delivered it, and took the baby from her. The following September she began college, and ten years later learned that Dr. Connors died of a heart attack after a fire consumed his medical offices. Jean had heard that all his records were lost.

But perhaps they weren't lost. And if not, who found them, and why after all these years is that person contacting me? Jean agonized.

Lily—that was the name she'd given to the baby whom she'd carried for nine months and then had known for only four hours. Three weeks before Reed's graduation from West Point and hers from Stonecroft, she had realized she was pregnant. They had both been frightened but agreed that they would get married immediately after graduation.

"My parents will love you, Jeannie," Reed had insisted. But she knew he was worried about their reaction. He admitted that his father had warned him about getting serious with anyone until he was at least twenty-five. He never got to tell them about her. A week before graduation he'd been killed by a hit-and-run driver on the West Point campus who'd been speeding along the narrow road on which he was walking. Instead of watching Reed graduate fifth in his class, General, now retired, and Mrs. Carroll Reed Thornton accepted the diploma and sword of their late son in a special presentation at the graduation ceremony.

They never knew they had a granddaughter.

Even if someone had salvaged the record of her adoption, how would he or she have gotten close enough to Lily to take her hairbrush, with long, golden strands of her hair still caught in its bristles? Jean wondered.

That first terrifying communication had contained the brush and a note telling her to "Check the DNA—it's your kid." Stunned, Jean had submitted strands from the lock of hair she had kept from her baby, along with her own DNA sample and strands from the brush to a private DNA laboratory. The report had unequivocally confirmed her worst fears—the hairs on the brush had come from her now nineteen-and-a-half-year-old daughter.

Or is it possible that the wonderful, caring couple who adopted her know who I am, and this is a buildup to asking me for money?

There had been a lot of publicity when her book about Abigail Adams became a best-seller and then a very successful film.

Let it be only about money, Jean prayed as she stood up and reached for the suitcase that it was time to unpack.

6

Carter Stewart threw his garment bag on the bed. Besides underwear and socks, it contained a couple of Armani jackets and several pairs of slacks. On impulse he decided to go to the first night party in the jeans and sweater he was wearing.

In school he'd been a scrawny, untidy kid, the child of a scrawny, untidy mother. When she did remember to throw clothes in the washer, as often as not she was out of detergent. Then she'd toss in bleach, ruining whatever garments were in the machine. Until he started hiding his clothes from her and then laundering them himself, he'd gone to school in slightly soiled or freakish-looking attire.

Being too dressed up when he first met his former classmates might bring on remarks about how he used to look. Now what would they see when they looked at him? Not the shrimp he'd been most of the high school years but now of average height with a disciplined body. Unlike some of the others he'd spotted in the lobby, he had no gray strands in his full head of well-barbered dark brown hair. His ID showed him with shaggy hair and his eyes almost shut. A columnist had recently referred to his "dark brown eyes that suddenly flicker with a hint of yellow flames when he is angry."

Impatiently he looked around the room. He'd worked in this hotel the summer of his junior year at Stonecroft. He'd probably been in this dumpy room any number of times, carrying room service trays to businessmen, to ladies on a tour of the Hudson Valley, or to parents visiting their kids at West Point—or, he thought, even to trysting couples who were sneaking away from their homes and families. I could always spot those, he thought. He used to smirk and ask those couples, "Would this be a honeymoon?" when he brought up their breakfasts. The guilty expression on their faces had been priceless.

He'd hated this place then and he hated it now, but since he was here, he might as well go downstairs and start the backslapping, "great-to-see-you" ritual.

Making sure he was carrying the piece of plastic that passed for a room key, he left the room and walked down the corridor to the elevator.

The Hudson Valley Suite where the opening cocktail party was being held was on the mezzanine floor. When he stepped off the elevator, he could hear the electronically enhanced music and the voices trying to yell above it. There looked to be about forty or fifty people already gathered there. Two waiters with trays holding glasses of wine were standing at the entrance. He took a glass of the red and sampled it. Lousy merlot. He might have guessed.

He started into the suite, then felt a tap on his shoulder. "Mr. Stewart, I'm Jake Perkins, and I'm covering the reunion for the *Stonecroft Gazette*. May I ask you a few questions?"

Sourly, Stewart turned and looked at the nervously eager redheaded kid standing inches away from him. The first thing you learn when you want something is not to get in the other guy's face, he thought irritably as he tried to step back and felt his shoulders brush against the wall. "I would suggest we step outside and find a quiet spot unless you can read lips, Jake."

"That's not my talent, I'm afraid, sir. Outside is a good idea. Just follow me."

After a split second's consideration, Stewart decided not to abandon the wine. Shrugging, he turned and followed the student down the corridor.

"Before we begin, Mr. Stewart, may I tell you how much I enjoy your plays. I want to be a writer myself. I mean, I guess I am a writer, but I want to be a successful one like you."

Oh, God, Stewart thought. "Everyone who interviews me says the same thing. Most, if not all of you, won't make it."

He waited for the expression of anger or embarrassment that usually followed that statement. Instead, to his disappointment, the baby-faced Jake Perkins smiled cheerfully. "But I will," he said. "I'm absolutely sure of that. Mr. Stewart, I've done a lot of research on you and the others who are being honored. You all have one thing in common. The three women were achievers when they were here, but not one of you four men created much of a stir at Stonecroft. I mean, in your own case, I couldn't find a single activity listed in your yearbook, and your marks were only mediocre. You didn't write for the school paper or—"

The nerve of this kid, Stewart thought. "In my day, the school paper was amateurish even for a school paper," he snapped, "as I'm sure it still is. I was never athletic, and my writing was restricted to a personal journal."

"Is that journal the basis for any of your plays?"

"Perhaps."

"They're all pretty dark."

"I have no illusions about life, nor did I have any when I was a student here."

"Then would you say that your years at Stonecroft were not happy?"

Carter Stewart took a sip of the merlot. "They were not happy," he said evenly.

"Then what brought you back to the reunion?"

Stewart smiled coldly. "The opportunity to be interviewed by you. Now if you'll excuse me, I see Laura Wilcox, the glamour queen of our class, getting out of the elevator. Let's see if she recognizes me."

He ignored the sheet of paper that Perkins was trying to hand him.

"If you'd just give me one minute more, Mr. Stewart. I have a list here that I think you'll find of great interest."

Perkins studied the back of Carter Stewart's lean frame as he walked with swift strides to catch up with the glamorous blonde now walking into the Hudson Valley Suite. Nasty to me, Perkins thought, jeans and sweater and sneakers to show his contempt for everyone here who's all duded-up for the night. He's not the kind to show up just to collect some crummy, meaningless medal. So what really brings him here anyhow?

It was the question he'd ask in the last sentence of his article. He'd already done plenty of research on Carter Stewart. He'd started writing in college, offbeat one-act plays that were performed by the drama department and that led to a postgraduate stint at Yale. That was when he dropped his first name, Howard—or Howie, as he'd been called at Stonecroft. He had his first Broadway hit before he was thirty. He was reputed to be a loner who escaped to one of his four homes around the country when he was working on a play. Withdrawn, unpleasant, perfectionist, genius—those were some of the words used to describe him in articles. I have a few others I could add, Jake Perkins thought grimly. And I will.

7

It took Mark Fleischman longer than he had expected to drive from Boston to Cornwall. He had hoped to have a couple of hours in which to walk around the town before having to face his former classmates. He wanted to have a chance to figure out the difference between his perception of himself as it had been when he was growing up there and the reality, as he understood it, of who he was now. Am I hoping to exorcise my own demons? he wondered.

As he drove with maddening slowness down the congested Connecticut Turnpike, he kept thinking of the statement he'd heard that morning from the father of one of his patients: "Doctor, you know as well as I do that kids are cruel. They were cruel in my day, and they haven't changed. They're like a pride of lions stalking the wounded prey. That's what they're doing to my kid now. That's what they did to me when I was his age. And you know what, Doctor? I'm a pretty successful guy, but when I go to an occasional reunion at my prep school, in ten seconds I'm not the CEO of a Fortune 500 company. I'm back to feeling like the clumsy nerd everyone else had fun picking on. Crazy, isn't it?"

As the car once again slowed to a crawl, Mark decided that, in hospital terminology, the Connecticut Turnpike was in a constant state of intensive care. There was always a huge construction project going on somewhere along the way, the kind of project that meant cramming three lanes into only one, causing inevitable traffic jams.

He found himself comparing the turnpike problems to problems he saw in patients, such as the boy whose father had come in for the conference. The child had attempted suicide last year. Another kid, ignored and tormented as he had been, might have gotten a gun and turned it on his classmates. Anger and hurt and humiliation were squeezed together and forced into one outlet. Some people tried to destroy themselves when that happened; others tried to destroy their tormentors.

A psychiatrist who specialized in adolescents, Mark had an advice and call-in television program that had recently become syndicated. The response had been gratifying. "Tall, lanky, cheerful, funny, and wise, Dr. Mark Fleischman brings a no-nonsense approach to helping solve the problems of that painful rite-of-passage called adolescence"—that's what one critic had written about the show.

Maybe I can put it all behind me after this weekend, he thought.

He hadn't taken time for lunch, so after he finally got to the hotel, he went into the bar and ordered a sandwich and a light beer. When the bar suddenly began to fill up with reunion attendees, he quickly got his check, left half the sandwich uneaten, and made his way up to his room.

It was a quarter of five, and the shadows were heavy and closing in. For a few minutes he stood at the window. The knowledge of what he had to do weighed heavily on him. But after that, I'll put it all behind me, he thought. The slate will be clean. Then I really will be able to be cheerful and funny—and maybe even wise.

He felt his eyes begin to moisten and abruptly turned from the window.

Gordon Amory went down in the elevator with his ID in his pocket. He would slip it on when he got to the party. For now, it was amusing to stand unrecognized by his former classmates and glance at their names and pictures as, floor by floor, they got into the elevator.

Jenny Adams was the last one to get on. She'd been a bovine kid, and while she had slimmed down some, she was still a big woman. There was something unmistakably small-town suburban in the cheap brocade suit and off-the-pushcart costume jewelry she was wearing. She was accompanied by a burly guy whose beefy arms were straining the seams of his too-tight jacket. Both were smiling broadly and said a general hello to the occupants of the elevator.

Gordon did not reply. The half-dozen others, all wearing their tags, sent out a chorus of greetings. Trish Canon, whom Gordon remembered as being on the track team and who was still beanpole thin, squealed, "Jenny! You look marvelous!"

"Trish Canon!" Jenny's arms flew around her former classmate. "Herb, Trish and I used to pass each other notes in math. Trish, this is my husband, Herb."

"And my husband, Barclay," Trish said. "And—"

The elevator stopped at the mezzanine. As they stepped out, Gordon reluctantly took out his ID and put it on. Expensive plastic surgery had made sure that he no longer looked like the weasel-faced kid in the school picture. His nose was now straight, his formerly heavy-lidded eyes now wide. His chin was sculpted, and his ears lay flat against his head. Implants and the artistry of a top colorist had transformed his formerly thin and drab brown hair into a thick chestnut mane. He knew he was now a handsome man. The only outward manifestation of the tortured kid he had been was that in moments of great stress he could not stop himself from biting his nails.

The Gordie they knew doesn't exist, he told himself as he started toward the Hudson Valley Suite. He felt a tap on his shoulder and turned.

"Mr. Amory."

A baby-faced, redheaded kid with a notebook was standing next to him.

"I'm Jake Perkins, a reporter for the *Stonecroft Gazette*. I'm interviewing the honorees. Could I just have a minute of your time?"

Gordon managed a warm smile. "Of course."

"May I begin by saying that you've changed a lot in the twenty years since your senior picture."

"I guess I have."

"You already owned the majority share of four cable television channels. Why did you buy into Maximum?"

"Maximum has a reputation for strong family programming. I decided it would round out our ability to reach a segment of the audience I wanted in our entertainment portfolio."

"There's been buzz about a new series and a rumor that your former classmate Laura Wilcox may be the star. Is that true?"

"There has been no casting yet on the series you mention."

"Your crime and punishment channel has been criticized as being too violent. Do you agree?"

"No, I do not. It offers genuine reality, not those made-up ludicrous situations that are the bread and butter of the commercial networks. Now if you'll excuse me."

"One more question, please. Would you just glance at this list?"

Impatiently, Gordon Amory took the sheet of paper from Perkins.

"Do you recognize those names?"

"They seem to be some of my former classmates."

"They are five women, members of this class, who have died or disappeared during these twenty years."

"I didn't realize that."

Perkins pointed. "I was astonished when I began my research. It started with Catherine Kane nineteen years ago. Her car skidded into the Potomac when she was a freshman at George Washington University. Cindy Lang vanished when she was skiing at Snowbird. Gloria Martin was an apparent suicide. Debra Parker piloted her own plane, and six years ago it crashed, killing her. Last month, Alison Kendall drowned in her pool. Wouldn't you say it would be fair to call this a hard luck class, and maybe do a program on your network about it?"

"I would prefer to call it a 'tragedy-ridden' class, and, no, I would not want to do a program about it. Now if you'll excuse me."

"Of course. Just one more question. What does receiving this medal from Stonecroft mean to you?"

Gordon Amory smiled. It means I can say a pox on your house. In spite of the misery I endured here, I've made it big—that's what he thought. Instead he said, "It is the fulfillment of my dream to be considered a success in the eyes of my classmates."

8

Robby Brent had checked into the hotel on Thursday afternoon. He'd just finished a six-day engagement at the Trump Casino in Atlantic City where his famous comedy act had drawn its usual large audience. It made no sense to fly home to San Francisco only to come right back, and he hadn't felt like staying in Atlantic City or stopping in New York.

It had been a satisfactory decision, he decided as he dressed for the cocktail party. He reached in the closet for a dark blue jacket. Putting it on, he looked at himself critically in the mirror on the closet door. Lousy lighting, he thought, but he still looked okay. He'd been compared to Don Rickles, not only because of his swift-paced comedy act, but because of his appearance as well. Round face, shiny dome, a bit stocky—he could understand the comparison. Still, his looks hadn't stopped women from being attracted to him. Post Stonecroft, he added to himself, definitely post Stonecroft.

He still had a couple of minutes before it was time to go down. He walked over to the window and looked out, thinking about how yesterday, after he'd checked in, he'd walked around town, picking out the homes of the kids who, like him, were honorees at the reunion.

He'd passed Jeannie Sheridan's house. He'd thought about how a couple of times the cops had been called by the neighbors because her parents were scuffling with each other in the driveway. He had heard they divorced years ago. Probably lucky they had. People used to predict that one or the other would end up getting hurt during one of their fights.

Laura Wilcox's first house was right next to Jeannie's. Then her father inherited some money, and the family moved to the big house on Concord Avenue when they were sophomores. He remembered walking past Laura's first house when he was a kid, hoping she'd happen to come out so he could start a conversation with her.

A family named Sommers had bought Laura's house. Their daughter had been murdered in it. They'd sold it eventually. Most people don't hang around a place where their kid has been stabbed to death. That had been on Columbus Day weekend, he reflected.

The invitation to the reunion lay on the bed. He glanced at it. The names of the honorees and their bios were included in the packet. Carter Stewart. How long after Stonecroft did it take him to drop being called Howie? Robby wondered. Howie's mother had called herself an artist and was always seen around town with her sketch pad. Occasionally she'd persuade the art gallery to show some of her stuff. Really bad, Robby remembered. Howie's father had been a bully, always whacking him around. No wonder his plays were so dark. Howie used to run out of the house and hide from his old man in the neighbors' backyards. He may be successful, but inside he has to be the same sneak who used to peep in people's windows. Thought he got away with it, but I caught him a couple of times. He had a crush on Laura so intense it practically oozed from his pores.

As did I, Robby admitted, sneering down at the picture of Gordie Amory, the plastic surgery kid. Mr. Cover Boy himself. Yesterday, during his walk, he'd looked up Gordie's house and saw that it had been totally renovated. Originally an odd shade of blue, it was now twice the size and sparkling white—like Gordie's new teeth, Robby thought.

Gordie's first house had burned down when they were juniors. The joke in town was that it was the only way it could be thoroughly cleaned. Gordie's mother had kept the place looking like a pigpen. A lot of people thought that Gordie deliberately set the fire. I wouldn't have put it past him, Robby thought. He was always weird. Robby reminded himself to call Gordie "Gordon" when they met at the cocktail party. Over the years he'd run into him a few times—uptight as they come and another one who'd been crazy about Laura.

So was Mark Fleischman, the other guy being honored. At school Mark had never said boo to anyone, but you got the feeling there was a lot going on inside him. He'd always been in the shadow of his older brother, Dennis, who'd been an all-around big man at Stonecroft, top student, outstanding athlete. Everyone in town knew him. He'd been killed in a car accident the summer before their class began its freshman year. Different as day and night, the two brothers. It was well known around town that if God had to take one of their sons, Mark's parents would have preferred that he and not Dennis had been chosen. He had so much resentment built up inside him that it's a wonder the top of his head didn't come off, Robby thought grimly.

He reached for his room key, finally ready to face the crowd below, and then opened the door of his room. I either disliked or hated just about all of my classmates, he thought. Then why did I accept the invitation to come here? He pushed the button for the elevator. I'll get plenty of new material for the act, he promised himself. There was another reason of course, but he quickly pushed it out of his mind. I won't go there, he thought as the elevator door opened. At least not now.

9

As they arrived at the cocktail party, Jack Emerson, the chairman of the reunion committee, invited the honorees to step into the alcove at the end of the Hudson Valley Suite. A florid-faced man with the look of a drinker, indicated by the broken capillaries in his face, he was the only member of the class who had elected to stay in Cornwall and therefore was in place to do hands-on planning for this weekend. "When we introduce the class individually, I want to save you and the others for last," he explained.

Jean walked into the alcove in time to hear Gordon Amory observe, "Jack, I gather that we have you to thank that we're the ones to be honored."

"It was my idea," Emerson said heartily. "And you deserve it, one and all. Gordie, I mean Gordon, you're an outstanding figure in cable television. Mark is a psychiatrist with a reputation for being an expert in adolescent behavior. Robby is an outstanding comedian and mimic. Howie, I mean Carter Stewart, is a major playwright. Jean Sheridan—oh, here you are, Jean, so good to see you—is a dean and professor of history at Georgetown, and now she's a best-selling author. Laura Wilcox was the star of a long-running sitcom. And Alison Kendall became head of a major talent agency. As you know, she would have been the seventh recipient. We'll send her plaque to her parents. They are very pleased to know that she is being honored by her graduating class."

The hard luck class, Jean thought with a stab of pain as Emerson rushed over to plant a kiss on her cheek. That had been the term that school reporter Jake Perkins had suggested when he'd grabbed her for an interview. What he'd told her had been a shock. I lost track of everyone except Alison and Laura after graduation, she remembered. The year Catherine died, I was in Chicago, supposedly choosing to work for a year before college. I knew that Debby Parker's plane crashed, but I didn't know about Cindy Lang and Gloria Martin. And only last month, Alison. Dear God, we all used to sit at the same table.

And now only Laura and I are left, she thought. What kind of karma is hanging over us?

Laura had phoned to say she'd meet her at the party. "Jeannie, I know we were talking about getting together earlier, but I'm not nearly ready. I have to make an entrance with all flags flying," she'd explained. "My object for the weekend is to woo and win Gordie Amory so that I can play the lead in his new TV series."

Instead of being disappointed, Jean realized she had been relieved. The respite had given her time to phone Alice Sommers, who had been their next-door neighbor years ago. Mrs. Sommers now lived in a townhouse near the parkway. The Sommerses had moved to Cornwall about two years before their daughter Karen was murdered. Jean never forgot the time when she'd been picked up at school by Mrs. Sommers. "Jean, why don't you come shopping with me?" she'd suggested. "I don't think you should go home right now."

That day she'd been spared the cringing embarrassment of seeing a squad car in front of her house and her parents being handcuffed. She never knew Karen Sommers well. Karen had been in Columbia Medical School in Manhattan, and the Sommerses kept an apartment in Manhattan. That was where they spent time with their daughter. In fact, until the night of her death, Karen had rarely come to Cornwall.

We've always kept in touch, Jean thought. When they came to Washington, they always called to invite me to dinner. Michael Sommers had died years ago, but Alice had learned about the reunion and called to say that Jean must come over for a ten o'clock breakfast before the scheduled visit to West Point.

In the time she might have visited with Laura, Jean had made up her mind. Tomorrow when she saw Alice, she would tell her about Lily and show her the faxes and the original letter with the hairbrush and strands of Lily's hair. Whoever knew about the baby must have seen Dr. Connors' records, she thought. It has to be someone who was around here at that time or who knew someone from around here who could get hold of the records. Alice might help me find the right person to talk to in law enforcement here. She had always said that they were still trying to find her Karen's murderer.

"Jean, it's good to see you again." Mark Fleischman had been speaking to Robby Brent, but now he came over to her. "You look lovely, but upset. Did that kid reporter grab you?"

She nodded. "Yes, he did. Mark, I was shocked. I didn't know about anyone's death except Debby's and then, of course, Alison's."

Fleischman nodded. "Neither did I. In fact, I hadn't heard about Debby. I've never bothered with any of the stuff that came from Stonecroft until Jack Emerson contacted me."

"What did Perkins ask you?"

"Specifically, he wanted to know if since none of the five died together in some sort of multiple accident, wouldn't I, as a psychiatrist, find that many deaths in so small a group an unusually high number? I told him I didn't have to look up anything to know that the number was out of the ball park. Of course it was."

Jean nodded. "He told me that according to his research, that kind of statistic is much more likely to happen in wartime, but he said there are examples of families or classmates or members of a team that seem to be jinxed. Mark, I don't think it's jinxed. I think it's eerie."

Jack Emerson had overheard. The smile he'd worn while listing their accomplishments vanished and was replaced by a look of irritated concern. "I asked that Perkins kid to stop showing that list around," he said.

Carter Stewart came into the alcove with Laura Wilcox in time to hear Emerson. "I can assure you, he's showing it around," he said shortly. "My suggestion to anyone who has not yet been pounced upon by that young man is to tell him you do not wish to see it. It worked for me."

Jean was standing to the side of the entry, and Laura did not spot her when she walked in. "OK if I join you?" she joked. "Or have I wandered into the men's club by mistake?"

Smiling, she moved from one man to the other, closely examining their tags, then kissing each one of them on the cheek. "Mark Fleischman, Gordon Amory, Robby Brent, Jack Emerson. And, of course, Carter, whom I used to know as Howie and who hasn't kissed me yet. You all look marvelous. You see, there's the difference. I was at my peak at sixteen, and after that it was all downhill. You four and Howie, I mean Carter, were just starting up the hill in those days."

Then she spotted Jean and rushed to embrace her.

It was the icebreaker they needed. Mark Fleischman could see the notable relaxation as polite expressions became amused smiles and the better wines they'd put aside for the honorees began to be sipped.

Laura's still a knockout, he thought. Thirty-eight or -nine like the rest of us, but could pass for thirty. The cocktail suit she was wearing was clearly pricey, very pricey. The television series she'd been on had been cancelled a couple of years ago. He wondered how much work she'd had since then. He knew she'd had a messy divorce, with claims and counterclaims; he'd read about it on Page Six of the *New York Post.* He smiled to himself as she kissed Gordie a second time. "You used to have a crush on me," she teased him.

Then it was his turn. "Mark Fleischman," she said breathlessly. "I swear you were jealous when I was dating Barry Diamond. Am I right?"

He smiled. "Yes, you're right, Laura. But that was a long time ago."

"I know, but I haven't forgotten." Her smile was radiant.

He had once read that the Duchess of Windsor had the capacity to make every man she spoke to feel like the only man in the room. He watched as she turned to another familiar face.

"I haven't forgotten either, Laura," he said quietly. "Never for one *minute* have I forgotten."

10

It amused him to note that at the cocktail party Laura was, as usual, the center of attention, even though she was the least deserving of all the honorees. On the television series that had been the one feather in her cap, she had played a shallow blonde who only cared about the person she saw reflected in the mirror. The ultimate in typecasting, he thought.

There was no denying that she still looked damn good, but she was enjoying that final bloom before the change begins to take place. Already there were fine lines around her eyes and mouth. He remembered that her mother had that same papery skin, the kind that ages fast and hard. If Laura lived another ten years, even plastic surgery could only do so much for her.

But of course, she wasn't going to live another ten years.

Sometimes, even for months at a time, The Owl retreated to a secret spot deep inside him. During those times he was almost able to believe that all the things The Owl had done had been a dream. Other times, though, like now, he could feel it living inside him. He could see The Owl's head, its dark eyes surrounded by pools of yellow. He could feel how its talons grasp the limb of a tree. He could feel the touch of its soft velvety plumage, causing him to shiver inwardly. He could feel the rush of air beneath its wings as it swooped down on its prey.

Seeing Laura had brought The Owl rushing from its perch. Why had he waited so long to come to her? The Owl demanded to know, but he was afraid to answer. Was it, he wondered, because when Laura and Jean were finally destroyed, The Owl's power over life and death would vanish with them? Laura should have been dead twenty years ago. But that mistake had liberated him.

That mistake, that accident of fate, had transformed him from the stuttering crybaby—"I ammm th-th-the oooooowwwwwlllll and I livvvvve in aaaa . . ."—into The Owl, the predator, powerful and unflinching.

Someone was studying his ID, a guy with glasses and thinning hair, dressed in a reasonably expensive dark gray suit. Then the man smiled and held out his hand. "Joel Nieman," he said.

Joel Nieman. Oh, sure, he had been Romeo in the senior play. He was the one Alison had written about in her column: "To everyone's surprise, Romeo, a.k.a. Joel Nieman, managed to remember most of his lines."

"Did you give up on acting?" The Owl asked, smiling back.

Nieman looked surprised. "You have a good memory. I thought the stage could do without me," he said.

"I remember the review Alison wrote about you."

Nieman laughed. "So do I. I was going to tell her she did me a favor. I took up accounting, and it was a better way to go. Terrible shame about her, isn't it?"

"Terrible," The Owl agreed.

"I read that initially there was some question of a possible homicide investigation, but the police now pretty much believe that she passed out as she hit the water."

"Then I think the police are stupid."

Joel Nieman's expression became curious. "You think Alison was *murdered?*"

The Owl realized suddenly that perhaps he looked and sounded too vehement. "From what I read, she made a lot of enemies along the way," he said carefully. "But who knows? The police are probably right. That's why they always say that no one should go swimming alone."

"Romeo, my Romeo," a voice squealed.

Marcy Rogers, who had been Juliet in the school play, was tapping Nieman's shoulder. He spun around.

Marcy still wore her chestnut hair in a mass of tangled curls, but now it was highlighted with random streaks of gold. She struck a theatrical pose. "And all the world shall be in love with night."

"I can't believe it. It's Juliet!" Joel Nieman exclaimed, beaming.

Marcy glanced at The Owl. "Oh, hi." She turned back to Nieman. "You've got to meet my real life Romeo. He's over at the bar."

Dismissal. Just the way he'd always experienced it at Stonecroft. Marcy hadn't even bothered to look at his ID. She simply wasn't interested in him.

The Owl looked around. Jean Sheridan and Laura Wilcox were standing next to each other on the buffet line. He studied Jean's profile. Unlike Laura, she was the kind of woman who got better looking as she aged. She looked decidedly different, although her features certainly hadn't changed. What had changed was her poise, her voice, the way she held herself. Oh, sure, her hair and clothes made a difference, but the change in her was more interior than outward. Growing up, she had to have been embarrassed by the way her parents carried on. A couple of times the cops had been exasperated enough to cuff them.

The Owl walked over to the buffet line and picked up a plate. He realized that he was beginning to understand his ambivalence toward

Jean. During the years at Stonecroft, a couple of times, such as when he didn't make the football team, she'd gone out of her way to be nice to him. In fact, in the spring of senior year he'd actually considered asking her for a date. He had been sure she wasn't going out with anyone. Sometimes, on warm Saturday nights, he would hide behind a tree in lovers' lane and wait for the cars to drive there after the movies. He never saw Jean in one of them.

Positive thoughts aside, it was too late to change course now. Only a couple of hours ago, seeing her come into the hotel, he'd finally made up his mind to kill her, too. At this moment he understood why he had made that irrevocable decision. His mother used to say "still waters run deep." Jeannie may have acted nice to him a couple of times, but she was probably just like Laura underneath, snickering about the poor dope who had wet his pants and cried and stuttered.

He helped himself to salad. And so what if she hadn't been in lovers' lane with one of the jerks in their class, he reflected. Instead, Miss "Butter-Wouldn't-Melt-in-Her-Mouth" Jeannie had been romancing a West Point cadet—he knew all about that.

Fury lashed through him, alerting him that soon he would have to release The Owl.

He skipped the pasta, selected poached salmon and green beans with ham, and looked around. Laura and Jean had just settled at the honoree table. Jean caught his eye and waved him over. Lily looks just like you, he thought. The resemblance is really striking.

The thought sharpened his hunger.

11

At two o'clock, Jean gave up the attempt to sleep, turned on the light, and opened a book. But after reading for an hour and realizing that she had not absorbed one word, she restlessly put the book down and turned off the light again. Every muscle in her body felt wired and taut, and she had the beginning of a headache. She knew that the effort to socialize all evening, despite the constant gnawing worry that Lily might be in danger, had exhausted her. She realized that she was counting the hours until ten o'clock when she would visit Alice Sommers and tell her about Lily.

The same thoughts kept racing through her mind. In all these years I've never mentioned her to a soul. The adoption was private. Dr. Connors is dead, and his records were destroyed. Who could have found out about her? Is it possible that her adoptive parents know my name and have kept track of me? Maybe they told someone else, and that person is the one contacting me now. But *why?*

The window facing the back of the hotel was open, and the room was getting cold. After a moment's debate Jean sighed and pushed back the covers. If I have any hope of getting some sleep, I'd better close it, she thought. She got out of bed and padded across the room. Shivering as she cranked in the open panel, she happened to glance down. A car without its lights on was pulling into the self-parking area of the hotel parking lot. Curious, she watched as the figure of a man stepped out and began walking quickly toward the back entrance of the hotel.

His coat collar was up, but when he opened the door to the lobby, his face was clearly visible. Turning away from the window, Jean thought, I wonder what in the name of God one of our distinguished dinner partners found to do until this hour of the night.

12

The call came into police headquarters in Goshen at 3:00 A.M. Helen Whelan of Surrey Meadows was missing. A single woman in her early forties, she had last been seen by a neighbor. Whelan had been walking her German shepherd, Brutus, at or about midnight. At 3:00 A.M. a couple living a few blocks away at the edge of the county park were awakened by the howling and barking of a dog. They investigated and found a German shepherd trying to struggle to its feet. It had been savagely beaten on the head and back with a heavy instrument. A woman's size seven shoe was found on the road nearby.

At 4:00 A.M., Sam Deegan had been called in and assigned to the team of detectives investigating the disappearance. He stopped first to talk to Dr. Siegel, the veterinarian who had treated the wounded animal. "My guess is that he was knocked out for a couple of hours by the blows to his head," Siegel told Deegan. "They came from something about the size and weight of a tire iron."

Sam could visualize the scenario. Helen Whelan had let her dog off the leash for a run in the park. Someone seeing her standing alone in the road had tried to drag her into a car. The German shepherd had rushed to protect her and had been beaten senseless.

He drove to the street where the animal had been found and began ringing doorbells. At the fourth house an elderly man claimed he heard a dog barking frantically at about 12:30 A.M.

Helen Whelan was, or had been, a popular physical education teacher at Surrey Meadows High. Sam learned from several fellow teachers that her habit of walking her dog late at night was well known. "She was never nervous about it. She'd tell us that Brutus would be dead before he'd let anyone hurt her," the principal of her school said sadly.

"She was right," Sam told him. "The vet had to put Brutus down."

By ten o'clock that morning he could see that this case was not going to be an easy one to solve. According to her distraught sister who lived in nearby Newburgh, Helen had no enemies. She had been seeing a fellow teacher for several years, but he was on a sabbatical in Spain this semester.

Missing or dead? Sam was sure that anyone who had so savagely injured a dog would have no mercy on a woman. The difficult investigation would begin, and he would commence his share of it in Helen's neighborhood and at her school. There was always the chance that one of the weirdo teenagers the schools were spitting out today held a grudge against her. From her picture he could tell that she was a very attractive woman. Maybe some neighbor had fallen in love and been rejected.

He only hoped it wouldn't turn out to be one of those random crimes, committed by a stranger on a stranger, whose only fault was to be in the wrong place at the wrong time. That kind of crime was the hardest to investigate, and often went unsolved, something he hated.

That train of thought inevitably brought him to Karen Sommers.

But her death wasn't hard to *solve*, Sam thought; it was only hard to *prove*.

Karen's killer was Cyrus Lindstrom, the boyfriend she dumped twenty years ago—of that he was sure. But as of next week, when I turn in my papers, I'll be off that case, Sam reminded himself.

And I'll be off yours, too, he thought, as with compassionate eyes he studied a recent picture of blue-eyed, auburn-haired Helen Whelan, who was now officially listed as "missing, presumed dead."

13

Laura had been tempted to sleep in and save her energy for the pre-game luncheon at West Point, but when she awoke on Saturday morning, she changed her mind. Her goal of romancing Gordie Amory had achieved only middling success at the dinner after the cocktail party. The honorees had sat together, and Jack Emerson had joined them. At first Gordie was quiet, but eventually he had warmed up some and even paid her a compliment. "I think every guy in our class had a crush on you at some point, Laura," he said.

"Why past tense?" she had teased.

His answer had been promising: "Why indeed?"

And then the evening provided an unexpected bonus. Robby Brent told the group that he'd been asked to do a situation comedy on HBO and he liked the script. "The public is finally getting sick of all the reality shows," he said, "and is ready to laugh. Think about the classic comedies: *I Love Lucy, All in the Family, The Honeymooners, The Mary Tyler Moore Show.* They had real humor, and, trust me, real humor is about to make a comeback." Then he'd looked at her. "You know, Laura, you really ought to read for the part of my wife. I have a feeling you'd be good."

She wasn't sure if he was kidding, since Robby made his living as a comic. On the other hand, if he *wasn't* kidding and if she didn't get to first base with Gordie, it might be yet another chance at grabbing the golden ring—perhaps her last chance.

"Last chance." Unintentionally, she whispered the words aloud. They gave her a funny, queasy feeling. All night she'd had troubled dreams. She'd dreamt of Jake Perkins, that pushy kid reporter who'd handed out the list of the girls who used to sit at their lunch table at Stonecroft and who had died since then. Catherine and Debra and Cindy and Gloria and Alison. Five of them. She'd dreamt that, one by one, he was crossing their names off the list, until now only she and Jeannie were still alive.

Separately we both stayed close to Alison, she thought, and now we're the only two left. Even though we lived next door to each other in school, Jeannie and I weren't enough alike to ever be really close. She's too nice. She never made fun of the guys the way the rest of us did.

Stop it! Laura warned herself. Don't think about a jinx or a curse. You have today and tomorrow to catch the golden ring. With one word from his newly sculpted lips, Gordie Amory could keep her on the series for Maximum. And suddenly Robby Brent was another one of the group who could make things happen. If he wasn't just pulling her leg about the series and if he decided he wanted her in his show, she'd have a real chance at the part. And I'm good at comedy, Laura told herself. Darn good.

And then there was Howie—no, Carter. He could open doors for her as well if he wanted to. Not in his plays, of course. God, they were all not only depressing but impossible to figure out. His artistic obscurity, however, didn't make him less powerful when it came to helping her career.

I wouldn't mind being in a hit play, she thought wistfully. Although, now that Alison was dead, she needed a new agent, too.

She glanced at her watch. It was time to get dressed. She knew she had lucked out with her choice of an outfit to wear for the day at West Point—the blue Armani suede with a Gucci scarf would be perfect for the chilly day that was forecast. According to the weather report, the temperature would only reach the low fifties.

An outdoor girl, I'm not, Laura thought, but since everybody says they're going to the game, I'm not missing it.

Gordon, she reminded herself as she tied the scarf. Gordon, not Gordie. Carter, not Howie. At least Robby was still Robby, and Mark was still Mark. And Jack Emerson, the Donald Trump of Cornwall, New York, hadn't decided to be known as Jacques.

When she went down to the dining room, she was disappointed to see that only Mark Fleischman and Jean were at the honorees table.

"I'm just having coffee," Jean explained. "I'm meeting a friend for breakfast. I'll catch up with you at lunch."

"You'll go to the trooping of colors and the game?" Laura asked.

"Yes, I will."

"I never went up there much," Laura said. "But you did, Jeannie. You were always a history buff. Didn't one of the cadets you knew pretty well get killed before graduation? What was his name?"

Mark Fleischman took a sip of coffee and watched as Jean's eyes clouded with pain. She hesitated, and he clamped his lips firmly together. He had been about to answer for her. "Reed Thornton," she said. "Cadet Carroll Reed Thornton, Jr."

14

The most difficult week of the year for Alice Sommers was the one leading up to the anniversary of her daughter's death. This year it had been particularly hard.

Twenty years, she thought. Two decades. Karen would be forty-two years old now. She'd be a doctor, probably a cardiologist. That had been her goal when she started medical school. She'd probably be married and have a couple of children.

In her mind, Alice Sommers could see the grandchildren she had never known. The boy, tall and blond, like Cyrus—she had always believed that he and Karen would end up together. The one thing about Sam Deegan that really upset her was his unshakable belief that Cyrus had caused Karen's death.

And what about their daughter? She would have looked like Karen, Alice had decided, fine-boned, with blue-green eyes and jet black hair. Of course, she would never really know.

Turn back the clock, Lord. Undo that terrible night. It was a prayer she had uttered thousands of times over the years.

Sam Deegan had told her that he didn't believe Karen ever woke up when the intruder came into her room. But Alice had always wondered. Had she opened her eyes? Had she sensed a presence? Had she seen an arm arcing over the bed? Had she felt the terrible thrusts of the knife that had taken her life?

It was something she could talk about to Sam, although she had never been able to express it to her husband. He had needed to believe that his only child had been spared that instant of terror and pain.

All this had been running through Alice Sommers' mind for days. On Saturday morning when she awoke, the heaviness and pain was lifted at the thought that Jeannie Sheridan was coming to see her.

At ten o'clock the bell rang. She opened the door and embraced Jean with fierce affection. It felt so good to hold the young woman in her arms. She knew her welcoming kiss was for Karen as well as Jean.

Over the years she had watched Jean evolve from the shy, reticent sixteen-year-old she had been when they became neighbors in Cornwall to the elegant, successful historian and writer she was now.

During the two years they'd lived next to each other before Jean graduated from high school, went to work in Chicago, and then went to Bryn Mawr, Alice had learned to both admire and pity the young girl. It seemed incredible that she was the child of her parents, people so caught up in their own contempt for each other that they never could see what effect their public brawls were having on their only child.

Even then she had shown so much dignity, Alice thought, as she held Jean out to inspect her and then hugged her again. "Do you realize it's been eight months since I've seen you?" she demanded. "Jeannie, I've *missed* you."

"I've missed you, too." Jean looked at the older woman with deep affection. Alice Sommers was a pretty woman with silver hair and blue eyes that always held a hint of sadness. Her smile, though, was warm and quick. "And you look wonderful."

"Not bad for sixty-three," she agreed. "I decided to stop supporting the hair salon, so what you see now is the real thing."

Arms linked, they walked from the vestibule to the living room of the townhouse. "I just realized, Jeannie, that you've never been here. We've always gotten together in New York or Washington. Let me show you around, starting with my fabulous view of the Hudson."

As they walked through the townhouse, Alice explained, "I don't know why we stayed in the house so long. I'm so much happier here. I think Richard felt that if we moved, in some way we'd be leaving Karen behind. He never got over losing her, you know."

Jean thought about the handsome Tudor-style house that she had admired so much when she was growing up. I knew it like the back of my hand, she thought. I was in and out of it when Laura lived there, and then Alice and Mr. Sommers were always so nice to me. I wish I had known Karen better. "Did anyone I might have known buy the house?" she asked.

"I don't think so. The people who bought it from us were from upstate. They sold it last year. I understand the new owner did some renovating and is planning to rent it furnished. A lot of people think that Jack Emerson is the real buyer. The rumor is that he's been picking up a lot of property in town. He has certainly come a long way from the kid who used to sweep out offices. He's quite the entrepreneur now."

"He's chairman of the reunion."

"And the driving force behind it. There's never been this much hoopla over a twentieth anniversary at Stonecroft." Alice Sommers shrugged. "But at least it got you here. I hope you're hungry. Waffles and strawberries are the breakfast menu."

It was over their second cup of coffee that Jean took out the faxes and the envelope with the brush and showed them to Alice, and told her about Lily. "Dr. Connors knew a couple who wanted a baby.

They were patients of his, which means they must have lived in this area. Alice, I don't know whether to go to the police or get a private investigator. I don't know what to do."

"You mean you had a baby at age eighteen and never told anyone about it?" Alice reached across the table and took Jean's hand.

"You knew my mother and father. They'd have had a shouting match about whose fault it was that I got into trouble. I might as well have distributed flyers around town with the news."

"And you've never told anyone?"

"Not one single soul. I had heard that Dr. Connors helped people adopt babies. He wanted me to tell my parents, but I was of age and he said he had a patient who had learned she could not have a child. She and her husband were planning to adopt, and they were absolutely wonderful people. When he spoke to them, they immediately said they'd be thrilled to have the baby. He got me a job in the office of a nursing home in Chicago, which gave me the cover of being able to say that I wanted to work for a year before I entered Bryn Mawr."

"I remember how proud we were when we heard about your scholarship."

"I left for Chicago right after we graduated. I needed to get away. And it wasn't just because of the baby. I needed to grieve. I wish you could have known Reed. He was so special. I guess that's why I've never married." Tears welled in Jean's eyes. "I've never felt that way about anyone else." She shook her head and picked up the fax. "I thought of going to the police with this, but I live in Washington. What could they do? *'Do I kiss her or kill her? Just a joke.'* This isn't necessarily a threat, is it? But it stands to reason that whoever adopted Lily was living in this area because she was a patient of Dr. Connors. That's why I believe if I go to the police it should be in this town, or at least in this county. Alice, what do you think?"

"I think you're right and I know exactly the right person to contact," Alice said firmly. "Sam Deegan is an investigator for the district attorney's office. He was there the morning we found Karen and has never closed the file on her death. He's become a good friend. He'll find a way to help you."

15

The bus to West Point was scheduled to leave at ten. At nine-fifteen, Jack Emerson left the hotel and made a quick trip home to pick up the necktie he had forgotten to pack. Rita, his wife of fifteen years, was reading the newspaper as she sipped coffee at the breakfast table. When he came in, she looked up indifferently.

"How's the great reunion going, Jack?" The sarcasm that tinged every word she uttered to him was particularly apparent in her greeting.

"I would say it's going very well, Rita," he said amicably.

"Is your room comfortable at the hotel, or do you know?"

"The room is as comfortable as rooms at the Glen-Ridge get. Why don't you join me there and see for yourself?"

"I think I'll pass." Her eyes dropped back to the newspaper, dismissing him.

For a moment he stood looking at her. She was thirty-seven years old, but not one of those women who got better as she aged. Rita had always been reserved, but along the way her narrow lips had acquired an unattractive sullen droop. When she was in her twenties and her hair was loose around her shoulders, she had been genuinely attractive. Now, with her hair drawn tightly back and pinned in a French knot, her skin seemed taut. In fact, everything about her looked pinched and angry. Standing there, Jack realized how thoroughly he disliked her.

It infuriated him that he felt the need to explain his presence in his own home. "I don't have the tie I'll want for the dinner tonight," he snapped. "That's why I stopped by."

She put the paper down. "Jack, when I insisted that Sandy go to boarding school instead of your beloved Stonecroft, you must have known something was in the wind."

"I believe I did." Here it comes, he thought.

"I'm moving back to Connecticut. I've rented a house in Westport for the next six months or so until I see what I want to buy. We'll work out visitation for Sandy. In spite of the fact that you're a rotten husband, you've been a reasonably decent father, and it's better if we keep our separation amicable. I know exactly what you're worth, so let's not waste too much money on lawyers." She stood up. "Hail fellow, well met—jovial, wisecracking, community-minded, smart businessman, Jack Emerson. That's what a lot of people say about you, Jack. But even besides the womanizing, there's a lot festering inside of you. Out of idle curiosity I'd be interested to know what it is."

Jack Emerson smiled coldly. "Of course I knew that when you insisted on sending Sandy to Choate you were beginning your move back to Connecticut. I debated about trying to talk you out of it—that is, for ten seconds I debated. Then I celebrated."

And guess again if you think you know what I'm worth, he added mentally.

Rita Emerson shrugged. "You always said that you had to have the last word. You know something, Jack? Underneath what passes for veneer, you're still the same tacky little janitor who resented pushing mops after school. And if you don't play fair in the divorce, I might have to tell the authorities you confessed to me that you arranged to have that fire set in the medical building ten years ago."

He stared at her. "I never told you that."

"But they will believe me, won't they? You worked in that building and knew every inch of it, and you wanted that property for the mall you were planning. After the fire you were able to buy it cheap." She raised an eyebrow. "Run along and get your school tie, Jack. I'll be on my way out of here in a couple of hours. Maybe you can pick up one of your fellow classmates and have a real reunion here tonight. Be my guest."

16

The sense of finally beginning to take action gave Jean a measure of peace. Alice Sommers had promised to call Sam Deegan and try to arrange a meeting for Sunday afternoon. "He often stops by on Karen's anniversary anyhow," she said.

I don't have to go home tomorrow, Jean thought. I can stay at the hotel for at least a week. I'm good at research. Maybe I can find someone who worked in Dr. Connors' office, a nurse or secretary who can tell me where he registered the births of the babies whose adoptions he handled. Maybe he kept copies of his records elsewhere. Sam Deegan could help me find out how to get them, assuming they exist.

Dr. Connors had taken the baby from her in Chicago. Was it possible he had registered her birth there? Had the adoptive mother traveled with him to Chicago, or had he taken Lily back to Cornwall himself?

Anyone in the reunion group who was driving separately to West Point had been told to park in the lot near the Thayer Hotel. Jean felt a lump in her throat as she drove through the gate onto the grounds of the academy. As she had so often in the past few days, she thought of the last time she had been there, at the graduation of Reed's class, when she watched his mother and father accept his diploma and sword.

Most of the Stonecroft group were on tours of the Point. They were scheduled to meet at twelve-thirty for lunch at the Thayer. Then they would watch the trooping of colors before going to the game.

Before joining the others, Jean headed for the cemetery to visit Reed's grave. It was a long walk through the grounds, but she welcomed the time for reflection. I found so much peace here, she thought. What would my life have been like if Reed had lived, if my daughter were with me now, not somewhere with strangers? She had not dared go to Reed's funeral. It had taken place on her graduation day from Stonecroft. Her mother and father had never met Reed and knew virtually nothing about him. There was no way to explain that she could not go to her own graduation.

She walked past Cadet Chapel, remembering the concerts she had attended there, at first alone and then later a few times with Reed. She walked past the monuments that bore names emblazoned in history, as she wended her way to section 23 and stood in front of the headstone that bore his name, Lt. Carroll Reed Thornton, Jr. There was a single rose propped against the headstone with a small envelope attached to it. Jean gasped. Her name was written on the envelope. She picked up the rose and tore the card from the envelope. Her hands began to tremble as she read the few words it contained: "Jean, this is for you. Knew you'd stop by."

On the walk back to Thayer she tried to compose herself. It almost has to mean that someone at the reunion knows about Lily and is playing this cat-and-mouse game with me, she thought. Who else would have known I was going to be here today and would anticipate that I'd go to Reed's grave?

There are forty-two from our class here, she thought. That narrows the field of who might be contacting me from anyone in the world to one of forty-two. I'm going to find out who it is and where Lily is. Maybe she doesn't know she's adopted. I won't interfere with her life, but I need to know that she's all right. I'd just like to see her once, even from a distance.

Her footsteps quickened. There was only today and tomorrow to try to see everyone face-to-face, to try to learn who had been in the cemetery. I'll talk to Laura, she thought. She doesn't miss anything. If she was on the tour that included the cemetery, she might have noticed something.

The moment she stepped inside the room reserved for the Stonecroft luncheon, Mark Fleischman came up to her. "The tour was really interesting," he said. "I'm sorry you missed it. I'm ashamed to say that even when I was living in Cornwall, the only times I came down to West Point were to jog. But you were here pretty often in senior year, weren't you? I mean, I remember you wrote some articles about it for the school paper."

"Yes, I was," Jean said carefully. A kaleidoscope of memories rushed through her mind. Sunday afternoons in spring, walking down the footpath at Trophy Point and settling on one of the benches to write. The pink granite benches had been donated to the Point by the class of 1939. She could recite the words inscribed on them: DIGNITY, DISCIPLINE, COURAGE, INTEGRITY, LOYALTY. Even the lettering on those benches made me realize the pettiness of the life my parents were leading, she thought.

She wrenched her attention back to Mark. "Our leader, Jack Emerson, has decreed that the honorees are supposed to mingle and sit anywhere today" he was saying, "which is going to pose a problem for Laura. Did you notice how she's been spreading her charms? She was flirting with our television executive, Gordon, our playwright, Carter, and our comedian, Robby, at the dinner table last night. On the bus she was sitting next to Jack Emerson and making a fuss over *him*. He's become quite the real estate magnate, I gather."

"You're the one specializing in adolescent behavior, Mark. Laura always went for the guys who were successful. Don't you think that carries through into adulthood? And, anyhow, she might as well concentrate on those four. Her ex-boyfriends, such as Doug Hanover, are either not here or have their wives in tow." Jean had to sound amused.

Mark was smiling, but as she studied him, Jean saw a change in his expression, a tightening in his eyes. You, too? she wondered. And she realized that it was disappointing to think that Mark had been another one to have a crush on Laura, and maybe even still had one. Well, she wanted to have a chance to talk to Laura, and if he wanted to be with her, too, that was fine. "Let's sit with Laura," she suggested. "I always did in school." For a moment the image of the lunch table at Stonecroft surfaced vividly in her mind. She saw there Catherine and Debra and Cindy and Gloria and Alison.

And Laura and me.

And Laura . . . and me . . .

17

The Owl had expected that the disappearance of a woman in Surrey Meadows, New York, would not be reported in time to make the Saturday morning papers but was pleased that it was featured on both the radio and television. Before and after breakfast, as he soaked his arm, he watched and listened to the reports. The pain in his arm emanated from where the dog had sunk his teeth; he considered it a punishment for his carelessness. He should have noticed the leash in the woman's hand before he stopped the car and grabbed her. The German shepherd had appeared out of nowhere, leaping onto him, snarling as it attacked. Fortunately, he was able to grab the tire jack that he always kept on the front seat when he went on that kind of outing.

Now Jean was sitting across the luncheon table from him, and it was obvious that she had found the rose at the grave. He was sure she was hoping that Laura had noticed who in their group might have been carrying the flower or had slipped away during the cemetery tour. He wasn't worried. Laura hadn't noticed anything. He'd stake his own life on that. She'd been too busy trying to figure out which of us she had the best chance of using. She's broke and desperate, he thought triumphantly.

The accident of learning about Lily all those years ago had made him realize all the many ways in which it was possible to have power over other people. Sometimes it amused him to use that power. Other times, he just waited. His anonymous tip to the IRS three years ago had caused the audit of Laura's finances. Now she had a lien on her house. Soon it wouldn't matter anymore, but he had the satisfaction of knowing that even before he killed her, she had been worried about losing her home.

The idea of contacting Jean about Lily had only surfaced when he happened to meet the adoptive parents of her daughter. Even though I was ambivalent about killing Jean, I wanted to make her suffer, he thought, without regret.

Leaving the flower on the headstone had been a stroke of genius. At the lunch table in Thayer, he had seen the distress in Jean's eyes. At the trooping of the colors before the football game, he made it his business to sit next to her. "It's a marvelous sight, isn't it?" he'd asked her.

"Yes, it is."

He knew she was thinking about Reed Thornton.

The Hellcats drum and signal corps was marching past the stand where they were sitting. Take a good look, Jeannie, he thought. Your kid is the one on this end in the second row.

18

After they got back to the Glen-Ridge House in Cornwall, Jean made it her business to go up in the elevator with Laura and to follow her down to her room. "Laura, honey, I need to talk to you," she said.

"Oh, Jeannie, I've just got to have a hot bath and rest," Laura protested. "Tours of West Point and going to a football game may be all very well, but I'm not one for spending hours outdoors. Can we get together later?"

"No," Jean said firmly. "I need to talk to you now."

"Only because you're such a good friend," Laura said with a sigh. She slipped the plastic key into the lock. "Welcome to the Taj Mahal." She opened the door and flipped the light switch. The lamps at the side of the bed and on the desk went on, casting uncertain light on the room already falling into shadows from the late afternoon sun.

Jean sat on the edge of the bed. "Laura, this is really important. You went to the cemetery as part of your tour, didn't you?"

Laura began to unbutton the suede jacket she had worn to West Point. "Uh-huh. Jeannie, I know you used to go up there a lot when we were at Stonecroft, but this is the first time I went through the cemetery. God, when you think of all the famous people who are buried there. General Custer. I thought they'd figured he messed up that attack he led, but now I guess, thanks to his wife, they've decided he was a hero. Standing at his grave today I thought of something you told me a long time ago, that the Indians called Custer 'Chief Yellow Hair.' You always managed to come up with things like that."

"Did everyone go on the tour to the cemetery, Laura?"

"Everyone on the bus did. Some of the people who brought their kids had their own cars, and they kind of did their own tour. I mean, I saw them wandering off by themselves. When you were a kid, did you want to look at tombstones?" Laura hung up her jacket in the closet. "Jeannie, I love you, but I have got to lie down. You should, too. Tonight's our big night. We get the medal or the plaque or whatever it is we get. You don't think they'll make us sing the school song, do you?"

Jean got up and put her hands on Laura's shoulders. "Laura, this is important. Did you notice if anyone on the bus was carrying a rose, or did you see anyone take out a rose in the cemetery?"

"A rose? No, of course not. I mean I saw some other people putting flowers on some of the graves, but no one from our crowd. Who in our group knew someone who's buried there well enough to bring flowers?"

I should have known, Jean thought. Laura wasn't paying attention to anyone who wasn't important to her. "I'll get out of your way," she promised. "What time are we due downstairs?"

"Seven o'clock cocktails, dinner at eight. We get our medals at ten o'clock. Then tomorrow it's just the memorial service for Alison and the brunch at Stonecroft."

"Are you going right back to California, Laura?"

Impulsively, Laura hugged Jean. "My plans are not yet definite, but let's say I may have a better option. See you later, honey."

When the door closed behind Jean, Laura pulled her garment bag out of the closet. As soon as the dinner was over, they would slip away. As he had said, "I've had enough of the hotel, Laura. Have an overnight bag ready, and I'll put it in my car before dinner. But keep your mouth shut. It's nobody's business where we stay tonight. We'll make up for you not realizing how great I was twenty years ago."

As she packed a cashmere jacket to wear in the morning, Laura smiled to herself. I did tell him that I definitely want to go to Alison's memorial, but I didn't care if we skipped brunch.

Then she frowned. He'd replied, "*I* wouldn't dream of missing Alison's memorial," but of course he meant we'd be there together.

19

At three o'clock in the afternoon, Sam Deegan was surprised to receive a phone call from Alice Sommers. "Sam, are you by any chance free this evening to go to a black-tie dinner?" she asked.

Sam hesitated out of pure astonishment.

"I realize this is absolutely no notice," Alice said apologetically.

"No, not at all. The answer is that, yes, I'm free, and I do have a tuxedo hanging in my closet, cleaned and pressed."

"There's a gala tonight honoring some of the graduates of the twentieth reunion class at Stonecroft. People in town were asked to buy seats for the dinner. The whole thing is really a fund-raiser for the new addition they want to put on Stonecroft. I wasn't planning to go, but there's someone being honored I want you to meet. Her name is Jean Sheridan. She used to live next door to me, and I'm very fond of her. She has a serious problem and needs some advice, and my original plan was to ask you to stop by tomorrow to talk to her about it. Then I decided it would be lovely to be there when Jean receives her medal, and . . ."

Sam realized that Alice Sommers' invitation had been impulsive, and she was becoming not only apologetic but perhaps was even regretting having made the phone call.

"Alice, I would enjoy going very much," he said emphatically. He did not tell her that he had been at work since 4:30 A.M. on the Helen Whelan case and had just returned home, planning to go to bed early. A nap of an hour or two will take the edge off, he thought. "I was planning to stop by tomorrow," he added.

Alice Sommers knew what he meant. "Somehow I expected that you would. If you can make it at seven at my place, I'll give you a drink first, then we'll start over to the hotel."

"It's a date. See you later, Alice." Sam hung up and sheepishly realized he was inordinately pleased to receive the invitation; then he considered the reason for it. What kind of problem could Alice's friend, Jean Sheridan, be having? he wondered. But no matter how serious, it couldn't compare with what had happened to Helen Whelan early this morning as she was walking her dog.

20

"This really is a big to-do, isn't it, Jean?" Gordon Amory asked.

He was sitting to her right, on the second tier of the dais where the honorees had been placed. Below them, the local congressman, the mayor of Cornwall-on-Hudson, the sponsors of the dinner, the president of Stonecroft, and several trustees were observing the packed ballroom with satisfaction.

"Yes, it is," she agreed.

"Did it occur to you to invite your mother and father to this grand occasion?"

If there had not been a wry note in Gordon's voice, Jean would have been angry, but at his touch of humor, she responded in kind. "No. Did it occur to you to invite *yours*?"

"Of course not. As a matter of fact, you've probably noticed that not one of our fellow honorees seems to have brought a beaming parent to share this moment of triumph."

"From what I understand, most of our parents have moved away. Mine were gone the summer I graduated from Stonecroft. Gone and split, as you may know," Jean added.

"As are mine. When I consider the six of us sitting here, supposedly the pride of our graduating class, I've decided that of all of us, Laura was probably the only one who enjoyed growing up here. I think you were quite unhappy, as was I, as were Robby and Mark and Carter. Robby was an indifferent student in a family of intellectuals, and was always being threatened with the loss of his scholarship to Stonecroft. Humor became his armor and his retreat. Mark's parents let the world know that they wished his brother had been spared, and that Mark had been the son who died. His reaction was to become a psychiatrist treating adolescents. I wonder if he has been trying to treat the adolescent inside."

Physician, heal thyself, Jean thought, and suspected that Gordon might be right.

"Howie, or Carter as he insists on being called, had a father who used to whack him and his mother around," Gordon continued. "Howie stayed out of the house as much as possible. You knew that he used to be caught peeking in windows. What was he trying to do, get a glimpse of normal home life? Don't you think that might be why his plays are so dark?"

Jean decided to sidestep that one. "That leaves you and me," she said quietly.

"My mother was a slovenly housekeeper. You may remember that when our house caught on fire, the joke in town was that that was the only way to really clean it. I now have three homes and confess to being positively obsessed with the need for cleanliness in every one of them, which is why my marriage failed. But then, that was a mistake from the beginning."

"And my mother and father had public brawls. Isn't that what you're remembering about me, Gordon?" She knew that was exactly what he was thinking.

"I was remembering how easily kids get embarrassed and that with the exception of Laura, who was always the golden girl of our class, you and Carter and Robby and Mark and I had a tough row to hoe. We certainly didn't need our parents to make it harder for us, but one way or the other, they all did. Look, Jean, I wanted to change so much, I got myself a whole new face. But when the chips are down, I sometimes wake up to find I'm still Gordie the nerd, the dopey-looking kid it was fun to pick on. You've made a name for yourself in academic circles, and now you've written a book that is not only critically acclaimed but a best-seller. But who are you inside?"

Who indeed? Inside, I'm still too often the needy outsider, Jean thought, but she was saved from answering when Gordon suddenly smiled boyishly and said, "One should never get too philosophical over dinner. Maybe I'll feel differently after they hang that medal on me. What do you think, Laura?"

He turned to speak to her, and Jean turned to Jack Emerson who was on her left.

"That seems to be an intense discussion you've been having with Gordon," he observed.

Jean noted the naked curiosity on his face. The last thing she wanted to do was continue with him the conversation she had been having with Gordon. "Oh, we were just gossiping about growing up here, Jack," she said glibly.

I was so unsure of myself, she thought. I was so thin and awkward. My hair was stringy. I was always waiting for my mother and father to start blasting at each other again. I felt so guilty when they told me that the only reason they were staying together was for *my* sake. All I wanted to do was grow up and get as far away as possible. And I did.

"Cornwall was a great place to grow up," Jack said heartily. "Never could understand why more of you didn't settle here or at least buy a country retreat for yourselves around here, now that you're all so successful. Incidentally, if you ever decide you want one, Jeannie, I have some properties listed that I can promise you are little jewels."

Jean remembered that Alice Sommers had told her the rumor was that Jack Emerson was the new owner of Alice's former home. "Any in my old neighborhood?" she asked.

He shook his head. "No. I'm talking about places with drop-dead river views. When can I take you around and show them to you?"

Never, Jean thought. I'm not coming back here to live. I just want to get out of here. First, though, I have to find out who is contacting me about Lily. It's just a hunch, but I'd stake my life that that person is sitting in this room right now. I want this dinner to be over so that I can meet Alice and the detective she has brought here tonight. I have to believe that somehow he will be able to help me find Lily and remove any threat to her safety. And when I am sure that she is well and happy, I need to go back to my adult world. Being here for twenty-four hours has already made me realize that, for better or for worse, whatever I have become was because of the life I led here, and I have to make peace with that.

"Oh, I don't think I'm in the market for a home in Cornwall," she told Jack Emerson.

"Maybe not now, Jeannie," he said, his eyes twinkling, "but I bet that someday soon I'll find a place for you to stay. In fact, I'm *sure* of it."

21

At these dinners the honorees are usually introduced in increasing order of importance, The Owl thought sardonically as Laura's name was called. She was the first to receive her medal, jointly presented by the mayor of Cornwall and the president of Stonecroft.

Laura's garment bag and small suitcase were in his car. He'd sneaked them down the backstairs, out the service entrance, and into the trunk without being observed. As a precaution he'd broken the light over the service entrance and worn a cap and jacket that could vaguely have passed for a uniform if anyone happened to see him, even from a distance.

Predictably, Laura looked beautiful. She was wearing a gold dinner gown that, as the well-worn saying went, "left nothing to the imagination." Her makeup was flawless. Her diamond necklace was probably fake but looked good. Her diamond earrings might be genuine. They were probably the last, or near the last, of the jewelry she'd received from her second husband. A little talent, helped by her spectacular good looks, had given Laura her fifteen minutes of fame. And, face it, she had an engaging personality—that is, if you weren't on the receiving end of her trashing.

Now she was thanking the mayor, the president of Stonecroft, and the dinner guests. "Cornwall-on-Hudson was a wonderful place to grow up," she gushed. "And the four years at Stonecroft were the happiest of my life."

With a thrill of anticipation, he imagined the moment when they got to the house, when he closed the door behind her and saw the terror begin to come into her eyes, the moment when she understood that she was trapped.

They were applauding Laura's speech, and then the mayor was announcing the next honoree.

Finally it was over, and they could get up to leave. He sensed that Laura was looking at him, but he did not meet her glance. They had agreed that they would mingle for a little while, then go to their rooms separately while everyone was saying good night. Then she would meet him at the car.

The others would be checking out in the morning and driving in their own cars to the memorial service at Alison's grave, and then on to the farewell brunch. Laura wouldn't be missed until then, and the supposition might easily be that she'd simply had enough of the reunion and had headed home early.

"Congratulations are in order, I suppose," Jean said, resting her hand a few inches above his wrist. She had touched the deepest and most ragged of the dog bites. The Owl felt a spurt of blood from the wound dampen his jacket and realized that the sleeve of Jean's royal blue dinner gown was in contact with it.

With a tremendous effort he managed not to give any hint of the pain that shot through his arm. Obviously Jean did not realize what had happened, and she turned to greet a couple in their early sixties who were approaching her.

For an instant, The Owl thought of the blood that had dripped onto the street when the dog bit him. DNA. It concerned him that it was the first time he'd ever left physical evidence behind—except, of course, for his symbol, but over the years everyone everywhere had missed that. In a way he'd been disappointed by their stupidity, but in another way he'd been glad. If the deaths of all those women were linked, it would make it harder for him to continue. *If* he chose to continue after Laura and Jean.

Even if Jean realized the spot on her sleeve was blood, she wouldn't have any idea where it had come from and how she had come in contact with it. Besides, no detective, not even Sherlock Holmes, would connect a spot on the sleeve of an honoree of Stonecroft Academy with blood found in the street twenty miles away.

Never in a million years, The Owl thought, dismissing the idea as absurd.

22

From the moment she met Sam Deegan, Jean understood why Alice had spoken so highly of him. She liked his looks: a strong face enhanced by clear dark blue eyes. She also liked the warmth of his smile and his firm handshake.

"I told Sam about Lily and about the fax you received yesterday," Alice said, her voice low.

"There's been another one," Jean whispered. "Alice, I'm so frightened for Lily. I almost couldn't make myself come down to dinner. It's been so hard to try to make conversation when I don't know what may be happening to her."

Before Alice could reply, Jean felt a tug on her sleeve as a cheery voice cried, "Jean Sheridan. My, how happy I am to see you! You used to baby-sit for my kids when you were thirteen."

Jean managed a smile. "Oh, Mrs. Rhodeen, it's so good to see you again."

"Jean, people want to talk to you," Sam said. "Alice and I will go over and get a table in the cocktail lounge. Join us as soon as you can."

It was fifteen minutes before she could break away from the local people who had attended the dinner and who remembered her growing up or who had read her books and wanted to talk to her about them. But at last she was with Alice and Sam at a corner table where they could speak without being overheard.

As they sipped the champagne Sam had ordered, she told them about the flower and note she had found in the cemetery. "The rose couldn't have been there long," she said nervously. "It almost has to have been put there by someone in the reunion group who knew I was going to West Point and was sure I'd stop at Reed's grave. But why is he or she playing this game? Why these vague threats? Why not come out with the reason for being in touch with me now?"

"May I be in touch with you now?" Mark Fleischman asked pleasantly. He was standing at the empty chair beside her, a glass in his hand.

"I was looking to ask you to have a nightcap, Jean," he explained. "I couldn't find you, then I spotted you over here."

He saw the hesitation on the faces of the people at the table, and acknowledged to himself that he had expected it. He had been perfectly aware that they were in a serious discussion, but he wanted to know whom Jean was with and what they were talking about.

"Of course, join us," Jean said, trying to sound welcoming. How much did he overhear? she wondered as she introduced him to Alice and Sam.

"Mark Fleischman," Sam said. "*Dr.* Mark Fleischman. I've seen your program and like it very much. You give darn good advice. I especially admire the way you handle teenagers. When they're your guests, you have a way of letting them vent their feelings and feel comfortable about doing it. If more kids opened up and got decent advice, they would realize they were not alone and their problems wouldn't seem so overwhelming."

Jean watched as Mark Fleischman's face brightened with a pleased smile at the obvious sincerity of Sam Deegan's praise.

He was so quiet as a kid, she thought. He was always so shy. I never would have guessed that he'd end up a television personality. Was Gordon right that Mark became a psychiatrist specializing in adolescents because of his own problem after his brother's death?

"I know you grew up here, Mark. Do you still have family in town?" Alice Sommers asked.

"My father. He's never moved from the old homestead. Retired, but does a lot of traveling, I gather."

Jean was startled. "At dinner, Gordon and I were talking about the fact that none of us has roots here anymore."

"I don't have roots here, Jean," Mark said quietly. "I haven't been in touch with my father in years. Although he clearly must realize from all the publicity about this reunion and the fact that I'm here as one of the honorees, I haven't heard from him."

He caught the note of bitterness that had crept into his voice, and was ashamed of it. What made me open up like that to two perfect strangers and to Jeannie Sheridan? he wondered. I'm supposed to be the listener. "Tall, lanky, cheerful, funny, and wise, Dr. Mark Fleischman" was how they introduced him on TV.

"Perhaps your father is out of town," Alice suggested softly.

"If he is, then he's wasting a lot of electricity. His lights were on last night." Mark shrugged, then smiled. "I *am* sorry. I didn't mean to pour out my soul. I came barging over here because I wanted to congratulate Jean on her remarks at the podium. She was sweet and natural and thankfully made up for the antics of a couple of our fellow honorees."

"And so did you," Alice Sommers said heartily. "I thought Robby Brent was absolutely out of order and that Gordon Amory and Carter Stewart sounded downright bitter. But if you're going to congratulate Jeannie, be sure to mention how lovely she looks."

"I seriously doubt that with Laura up there, anybody noticed me," Jean said, but she realized how pleased she was by Mark's unexpected compliment.

"I'm sure everyone noticed you and would agree you look lovely," Mark said as he stood up. "I also wanted to be sure to tell you that it's been good to see you again, Jeannie, in case we don't get a chance to visit tomorrow. I'll go to Alison's memorial service, but I may not be able to stay for the brunch."

He smiled at Alice Sommers and extended his hand to Sam Deegan. "I've enjoyed meeting you. Now I see a couple of people I want to catch in case I miss them in the morning." With long strides he was across the room.

"That man is very attractive, Jean," Alice Sommers said emphatically. "And it's obvious that he has an eye for you."

But that may not be the only reason he dropped by, Sam Deegan thought. He'd been watching us from the bar. He wanted to know what we were talking about.

I wonder why it was so important to him.

23

The Owl was almost out of the cage. He was separating from it. He could always tell when total separation was taking place. His own kind, gentle self—the person he might have become under different circumstances—began to recede. He heard and saw himself smiling and joking and accepting the kisses on the cheek from some of the women in the reunion group.

And then he slipped away. He could feel the velvety softness of his plumage when, twenty minutes later, he sat in the car waiting for Laura. He watched as she slipped out the back entrance of the hotel, taking care to look around and avoid running into anyone. She had even been smart enough to wear a hooded raincoat over her gown.

Then she was at the car door, opening it. She slid onto the seat beside him. "Take me away, honey," she said laughing. "Isn't this fun?"

24

Jake Perkins stayed up late to write his report about the banquet for the *Stonecroft Academy Gazette*. His home on Riverbank Lane looked over the Hudson, and he valued that view as he valued few things in his life. At age sixteen he already considered himself something of a philosopher as well as a good writer and a keen student of human behavior.

In a moment of profound thinking, he had decided that the tides and currents of the river symbolized to him the passions and moods of human beings. He liked to get that kind of depth into his news stories. He knew, of course, that the columns he wanted to write would never get by Mr. Holland, the English teacher who was the adviser and censor of the *Gazette*, but to amuse himself, Jake wrote the column he wished he could print before he got down to the one that he'd submit.

> The somewhat shabby ballroom of the stuffy Glen-Ridge House was somewhat brightened with blue and white Stonecroft banners and centerpieces. The food was predictably dreadful, beginning with what passed for a seafood cocktail followed by filet mignon done to a crisp, yet only slightly warm, pan-roasted potatoes that could have been

lethal weapons, and wilted string beans almondine. Melted ice cream with chocolate sauce completed the chef's attempt at gourmet dining.

The townspeople supported the event by turning out to honor the graduates, all of whom were once residents of Cornwall. It is generally known that Jack Emerson, the chairman and driving force behind the reunion, has a purpose behind his effort not connected with embracing his fellow classmates. The banquet was also the kickoff for the building project at Stonecroft, a new addition that will be erected on land presently owned by Emerson and built by the contractor acknowledged to be in Emerson's pocket.

The six honorees were seated at the dais together with Mayor Walter Carlson, Stonecroft president Alfred Downes, and trustees . . .

Their names don't matter in this version of the story, Jake decided.

Laura Wilcox was the first to receive the Distinguished Alumna medal. Her gold lamé dress had most of the men in the assembly unaware of what she was babbling, something to the effect of how happy her life had been in this town. Since she had never come back and since no one could ever picture the glamorous Ms. Wilcox strolling down Main Street or stopping by for a tattoo at our recently opened tattoo emporium, her remarks were greeted with polite applause and a few whistles.

Dr. Mark Fleischman, psychiatrist and now television personality, gave a low-key, well-received address in which he cautioned parents and teachers to build up their kids' morale. "The world will be happy to beat them down," he said. "It's your job to make them feel good about themselves even while you give them appropriate limits."

Carter Stewart, the playwright, gave a two-level speech in which he said he was sure that the townspeople and the students who have become prototypes for many of the characters in his plays were present at the banquet. He also said that contrary to Dr. Fleischman's remarks, his father believed in the old chestnut that to spare the rod was to spoil the child. He then thanked his late father for having been that kind of parent because it gave him a dark view on life which has served him well.

Stewart's remarks were greeted with nervous laughter and little applause.

Comedian Robby Brent broke up the audience with his vividly funny imitation of the teachers who were always threatening to fail him, which would have caused him to lose his scholarship to Stonecroft. One of those teachers was present and smiled gamely at Brent's merciless parody of her gestures and mannerisms and dead-on imitation of her voice. But Miss Ella Bender, the rock of the mathematics department, was close to tears as Brent devastated the audience with a perfect parody of her high-pitched tone and nervous giggle.

"I was the last and dumbest of the Brents," Robby concluded. "You never let me forget it. My defense was humor, and for that I thank you."

He then blinked his eyes and puckered his lips exactly as President Downes blinks his eyes and puckers his lips, and handed him a check for $1, his contribution toward the building fund.

Then, as the audience gasped, he yelled, "Just kidding," and waved a check for $10,000, which he ceremoniously handed over.

Some in the audience thought he was sidesplittingly funny. Others, like Dr. Jean Sheridan, were distressed by

Brent's antics. She was later overheard telling someone that she did not believe humor should be cruel.

Gordon Amory, our cable television czar, was next to speak. "I never made any team I tried for at Stonecroft," he said. "You can't imagine how hard I prayed that I'd get just one chance to be a jock—which proves the old adage, 'Be careful what you pray for. You may get it.' Instead I became a television addict, then began analyzing the stuff I was watching. Before long, I realized I could tell why some programs or specials or situation comedies or docudramas worked and why others were worthless. That was the beginning of my career. It was founded on rejection, disappointment, and pain. And, oh yes, before I leave, let me set a rumor to rest. I did not deliberately set fire to my parents' home. I was smoking a cigarette and did not notice after I turned off the television and went up to bed that the live butt had slipped behind the empty pizza box my mother had left on the couch."

Before the audience had time to react, Mr. Amory then presented a check for $100,000 to the building fund and joked to President Downes, "May the great work of molding minds and hearts at Stonecroft Academy continue well into the future."

He might as well have been saying go jump in a lake, Jake thought, remembering how Amory had settled at his place on the dais with a self-satisfied smile.

The last honoree, Dr. Jean Sheridan, spoke about growing up in Cornwall, the town that had been the enclave of the wealthy and the privileged nearly 150 years ago. "As a scholarship student, I know I received a superb education at Stonecroft. But outside the school grounds there was another learning place, in this town and countryside. Here and in the area around us, I acquired an appreciation of history that has shaped my life and career. For that I am eternally grateful."

Dr. Sheridan did not say that she was happy here, or mention that all the old-timers would remember her parents' domestic disputes that enlivened the town, Jake Perkins thought, or that she was known to break down and cry in class after some of her parents' more publicized episodes.

Well, tomorrow's the end of it, Jake thought as he stretched and walked over to the window. The lights from Cold Spring, the town across the Hudson, were less visible since a fog was setting in. Hope it lifts tomorrow, Jake thought. He'd cover the memorial service at Alison Kendall's grave and then catch a movie in the afternoon. He had heard that the names of the four other graduates who had died were also going to be read at the memorial.

Jake went back to his desk and looked at the picture he'd dug out of the files. In an almost unbelievable twist of fate, all five of the dead graduates had not only shared the luncheon table in senior year with two of the honorees, Laura Wilcox and Jean Sheridan, but they had died in the order in which they were seated.

Which means Laura Wilcox is probably next, Jake thought. Can this be just a bizarre coincidence, or should someone be looking into it? But that's crazy. Those women died over a period of twenty years, in totally different ways, all across the country. One of them was even skiing when she must have gotten caught in an avalanche.

Fate, that's what it was, Jake concluded. Nothing but fate.

25

"I'm planning to stay on for a few extra days," Jean told the front-desk clerk who answered the phone on Sunday morning. "Will that be a problem?"

She knew it wouldn't be a problem. All the other reunion guests would undoubtedly be on their way home after the brunch at Stonecroft, so there'd be many empty rooms.

Although it was only eight-fifteen, she was already up and dressed and had sipped the coffee and juice and nibbled at a muffin from the continental breakfast she had ordered. She had arranged to go back to Alice Sommers' house after the Stonecroft brunch. Sam Deegan would be there, and they would be able to talk without fear of interruption. Sam had told her that no matter how private the adoption was, it had to have been registered, and a lawyer must have drawn up papers. He had asked Jean if she had a copy of the document she had signed, giving up her rights to the baby.

"Dr. Connors didn't leave me any papers," she explained. "Or maybe I didn't want to have any reminder of what I was doing. I really don't remember. I was numb. I felt as if my heart was being torn out of my body when he took her from me."

But that conversation had opened another avenue of thought. She had been planning to go to the nine o'clock Mass at St. Thomas of

Canterbury on Sunday morning, before the memorial service for Alison. St. Thomas had been her parish when she was growing up, but in talking to Sam Deegan, she had remembered that Dr. Connors had been a parishioner there as well. In the midst of one of her sleepless periods during the night, it had occurred to her that it was at least possible the people who adopted the baby had been parishioners of St. Thomas as well.

I told Dr. Connors that I wanted Lily to be raised Catholic, she remembered. And if the adoptive parents were Catholic and were members of St. Thomas of Canterbury at that time, it would have made sense for Lily to be baptized there. If I could look at the records of baptisms between late March and mid-June of that year, it would be a start in searching for Lily.

When she woke at six, it was to feel tears running down her cheeks and to hear herself whispering the prayer that now was becoming a part of her subconscious: "Don't let anyone hurt her. Take care of her, please."

She knew that the office of the church wouldn't be open on Sunday. Even so, maybe this morning, after Mass, she could talk to the pastor and make an appointment to see him. I've got to feel as though I'm doing *something*, she thought. Maybe there's even a priest who was at the parish twenty years ago and who might just remember a parishioner adopting a baby girl at that time.

A sense of something imminent, a growing certainty that Lily was in immediate danger, had become so strong that Jean knew she could not go through the day without taking some kind of action.

At eight-thirty she went downstairs to the parking lot and got in her car. It was a five-minute drive to the church. She had decided that the best time to speak to a priest was after Mass when he would be standing outside, greeting people as they exited.

She started to drive to Hudson Street, realized she was at least twenty minutes early, and impulsively turned the car toward Mountain Road to look at the house where she had grown up.

The house was almost halfway up the winding street. When she had lived there, the exterior had been brown siding with beige shutters. The people who owned the house now had not only enlarged it but refinished it with white shingles and a forest green trim on the shutters. The new owner obviously understood how trees and plants could frame and beautify a relatively modest home. It looked almost jewel-like in the early morning mist.

The brick and stucco house where the Sommerses had lived also looked well cared for, Jean thought, even though it was obvious no one was living there now. The shades were drawn in all the windows, but the trim was freshly painted, the hedges neatly clipped, and the long bluestone walkway from the front door to the driveway was new.

I always loved this house, she thought as she stopped the car for a better look. Laura's father and mother kept it up when they lived there, and then the Sommerses did as well. I remember when we were nine or ten, Laura said that she thought our house was ugly. I thought the brown was ugly, too, but I wouldn't give her the satisfaction of admitting it. I wonder if she would approve of it now.

Not that it mattered. Jean turned the car around and began to drive down the hill toward Hudson Street. Laura never deliberately meant to hurt me, she thought. She was taught to be self-centered, and I don't think, in the long run, it's done her much good. The last time I talked to Alison, she said that she was trying to get Laura a job on a new sitcom, but that it was tough to make it happen.

She said that Gordie—then she laughed and changed it to Gordon—could make it happen but that she didn't think he would, Jean recalled. Laura has always been the golden girl. It was almost pathetic to see her playing up to all the guys, even, for God's sake, to Jack Emerson. There's something downright *unattractive* about him, she thought with a shiver. What makes him so certain that I'll buy a house around here someday?

Earlier it had looked as though the mist would clear, but in the way of October weather, the clouds had become stronger and the mist was now a wet, cold drizzle. Jean realized that it was the same kind of weather as the day when she realized she was pregnant. Her mother and father had been having another of their arguments, although this one ended in what passed for peace. Jean was going to college on a scholarship. There was no need for them to have to put up with each other anymore. They had done their duty as parents, and now it was time for them to lead their own lives.

Put the house on the market—with luck, they'd be rid of it by August.

Jean thought of how she had come silently down the stairs, slipped out of the house, and walked and walked and walked. I didn't know what Reed would say, she thought. I did know that he would feel he had betrayed his father's expectations for him.

Twenty years ago Reed's father had been a lieutenant general stationed at the Pentagon. That was one of the reasons we never mingled with his classmates, Jean thought. Reed didn't want it to get back to his father that he was seriously dating anyone.

And I didn't want him to meet my parents.

If he had lived and we had married, would it have lasted? It was a question she had asked herself many times in the last twenty years, and she always came to the same answer: It would have lasted. In spite of his family's disapproval, in spite of the fact that it probably would have taken me years to get the education I knew I had to have, it would have lasted.

I knew him such a short time, Jean thought as she drove into the church parking lot. I'd never even had a boyfriend before him. And then one day when I was sitting on the steps of the monument at West

Point, he sat down beside me. My name was on the cover of the notebook I'd brought with me. He said, "Jean Sheridan," and then he said, "I like Stephen Foster's music, and do you know what song I'm thinking of now?" Of course I didn't, and he said, "It begins like this: 'I dream of Jeannie with the light brown hair . . .'"

Jean parked the car. Three months later he was dead, she thought, and I was carrying his child. And when I saw Dr. Connors in this church and remembered having heard that he handled adoptions, it was like a gift, telling me what to do.

I need a gift like that again.

26

Jake Perkins figured the number of mourners at Alison Kendall's grave at less than thirty. The others had all elected to go directly to the brunch. Not that he blamed them. The rain was picking up. His feet were sinking into the soft, muddy grass. There's nothing worse than being dead on a rainy day, he thought, and hoped he'd remember to jot down that bit of wisdom later.

The mayor had skipped this event, but President Downes, who had already extolled the generosity and talent of Alison Kendall, was now offering a generic prayer that was sure to satisfy everyone except an out-and-out atheist, if one happened to be present.

She may have been talented, Jake thought, but it was her generosity that has us out here risking pneumonia. I know one person who *didn't* risk it. He looked around to be sure he had not missed Laura Wilcox, but she definitely wasn't there. All the other honorees were present. Jean Sheridan was standing near President Downes, and there was no question she was genuinely sad. A couple of times she dabbed at her eyes with a handkerchief. Everyone else in the group looked as if they wished Downes would wrap it up quickly so they could get inside and have a Bloody Mary.

"We remember also Alison's classmates and friends who have been called home," Downes said soberly: "Catherine Kane, Debra

Parker, Cindy Lang, and Gloria Martin. This graduating class of twenty years ago produced many great achievers, but also never before has one class known such great loss."

Amen, Jake thought, and decided he would definitely use the picture of the seven girls at the lunch table with his story on the reunion. He already had the caption—Downes had just handed it to him: "Never before has one class known such great loss."

At the beginning of the ceremony a couple of students had handed a rose to each of the people who came to the memorial service. Now, after Downes concluded his remarks, one by one everyone placed the rose at the foot of the tombstone and started to walk across the cemetery to the adjacent school grounds. The farther they got away from the grave, the faster they moved. Jake could read their minds: "Well, thank God that's over. I thought I'd freeze."

The last one to leave was Jean Sheridan. She stood there, looking not just sad but deep in thought. Jake noticed that Dr. Fleischman had stopped and was waiting for her. Sheridan reached down and touched Alison's name on the tombstone, then turned, and Jake could see that she seemed glad to see Dr. Fleischman. They began to walk toward the school together.

Before he could stop her, the sophomore who was handing out the roses had given him one. Jake wasn't much for ceremonies, but he decided to leave his rose with the others. As he was about to put it down, he noticed something on the ground. He bent down and picked it up.

It was a pewter lapel pin in the shape of an owl, about an inch long. Jake could see at a glance that it wasn't worth more than a couple of bucks. It looked like something a kid or some nature lover who was on a crusade to save owls might wear. Jake was about to toss it away, then changed his mind. He brushed it off and put it in his pocket. It would soon be Halloween. He'd give it to his kid cousin and tell him that he had dug it out of a grave just for him.

27

Jean was disappointed that Laura had not bothered to attend the memorial service for Alison, but she also realized that she was not surprised. Laura had never put herself out for anyone, and it was silly to think that she might begin at this stage of her life. Knowing Laura, she wasn't going to stand out in the cold and rain—she'd go directly to the brunch.

But by the time the brunch was half over and Laura had not appeared, Jean felt the beginning of deep unease. She confided that feeling to Gordon Amory. "Gordon, I know you were talking to Laura a lot yesterday. Did she say anything to you about not showing up today?"

"We talked at lunch yesterday and at the game," he corrected. "She was campaigning to get me to make her the lead in our new sitcom. I told her that I never interfere with the people I hire to cast my programs. When she continued to persist, I rather unkindly emphasized that I never made exceptions, particularly for minimally talented school chums. At that point she used a rather unladylike expression and turned her charms on our insufferable chairman, Jack Emerson. As you may know, he has been bragging about his considerable financial assets. Also, last night he gleefully announced that his wife had just left him, so he was fair game for Laura, I guess."

Laura seemed to be in wonderful spirits at dinner, Jean thought. And she was fine when I tried to talk to her in her room before dinner. Did anything go wrong later last night? Or did she just decide to sleep in this morning?

I can at least check on that, she thought. She was sitting next to Gordon and Carter Stewart at the luncheon table. With a murmured "Back in a minute," she walked between the rows of tables, taking care not to make eye contact with anyone. The brunch was being held in the auditorium. She slipped into the corridor that led to the homeroom of the freshman class and dialed the hotel.

Laura did not answer the phone in her room. Jean hesitated and then asked to be switched to the front desk. She identified herself and asked if by any chance Laura Wilcox had checked out. "I'm a little concerned," she explained. "Ms. Wilcox was supposed to meet a group of us and hasn't shown up."

"Well, she hasn't checked out," the clerk said genially. "Why don't I send someone up to see if she's overslept, Dr. Sheridan. But you take the blame if she gets mad."

He's the guy whose hair matches the top of the desk, Jean thought, recognizing both the voice and the tone. "I'll take responsibility," she assured him.

As she waited, Jean glanced around the corridor. God, I feel as though I never left this place, she thought. Ms. Clemens was the homeroom teacher when we were freshman, and my desk was the second seat in the fourth row. She heard the door from the auditorium open and turned to see Jake Perkins, the reporter from the school newspaper.

"Dr. Sheridan." The clerk's voice had lost its jocular tone.

"Yes." Jean realized she was gripping the phone. Something's wrong, she thought. *Something's wrong.*

"The maid went into Ms. Wilcox's room. The bed hasn't been

slept in. Her clothes are still in the closet, but the maid did notice that some of her toiletries that were on the vanity are gone. Do you think there's a problem?"

"Oh, if she took some things with her, I would say not. Thank you."

That's all Laura would need, Jean thought, for me to be asking questions about her if she went off with somebody. She pushed the button on the cell phone to end the call and snapped the cover closed. But who would she have been with? she wondered. If Gordon was to be believed, he had brushed her off. He said that she'd been flirting with Jack Emerson, but she certainly hadn't neglected Mark or Robby or Carter, either. Yesterday at lunch she was joking with Mark about how successful his show was and saying that maybe she should go into therapy with him. I heard her telling Carter she'd love to do a Broadway show, and later she was in the bar with Robby for a nightcap.

"Dr. Sheridan, may I have a word with you?"

Startled, Jean spun around. She'd forgotten about Jake Perkins. "I'm sorry to bother you," he said unapologetically, "but I wonder if you can tell me if Ms. Wilcox is planning to show up here today."

"I don't know her plans," Jean said, smiling dismissively. "Now I really must get back to the table."

Laura probably got friendly with one of the guys at the dinner last night and went to his place with him, she thought. If she hasn't checked out, she's bound to show up at the hotel later.

Jake Perkins studied Jean's expression as she passed him. She's worried, he thought. Could it be because Laura Wilcox didn't show up? My God, is it possible that she's missing? He pulled out his own cell phone, dialed the Glen-Ridge House, and asked for the front desk. "I have a flower delivery for Ms. Laura Wilcox," he said, "but I was asked to make sure that she hadn't checked out."

"No, she hasn't checked out," the clerk told him, "but she didn't stay here last night, so I'm not sure when she'll be back to pick up her bags."

"Was she planning to stay through the weekend?" Jake asked, trying to sound indifferent.

"She was supposed to check out by two. She ordered a car to take her to the airport at two-fifteen, so I don't know what to tell you about your flowers, sonny."

"I guess I'll check with my customer. Thanks."

Jake turned off his cell phone and slipped it back into his pocket. I know exactly where I'm going to be at two o'clock, he thought—I'll be in the lobby of the Glen-Ridge, waiting to see if Laura Wilcox is there to check out.

He started to walk back down the corridor to the auditorium. Suppose she never *does* show up, he thought. Suppose she just disappears. If she does . . . He felt a thrill of nervous anticipation shoot through him. He understood what it was—a newsman's nose for a hot story. It's too big for the *Stonecroft Academy Gazette*, Jake thought. But the *New York Post* would love it. I'll get the lunch table picture enlarged and have it ready to run with the story. He could see the headline: "Hard Luck Class Claims Another Victim." Pretty good.

Or maybe even, "And Then There Was One." Even better!

I took a couple of really good pictures of Dr. Sheridan, he thought. I'll have them ready to show the *Post* as well.

As he opened the door of the auditorium, the first lines of the school song were being sung by the assembled guests. "We hail thee, dear Stonecroft; the place of our dreams . . ."

The reunion of the twentieth-anniversary graduates was over at last.

28

"I guess this is good-bye, Jean. It's been good to see you again." Mark Fleischman was holding his card in his hand. "I'll give you mine if you'll give me yours," he said, smiling.

"Of course." Jean dug into her bag and pulled a card out of her wallet. "I'm glad you were able to make the brunch after all."

"I am, too. When do you leave?"

"I'm staying at the hotel for a few days more. A little research project." Jean tried to sound casual.

"I tape some shows in Boston tomorrow. Otherwise I'd stay and ask you to join me for a quiet dinner tonight." He hesitated, then bent down and kissed her cheek. "Again, as people say, it's been good to see you."

"Good-bye, Mark." Jean caught herself before adding, "Give me a call if you plan to be in Washington." For an instant their hands lingered together, then he was gone.

Carter Stewart and Gordon Amory were standing together, saying final good-byes to the dispersing classmates. Jean walked over to them. Before she could speak, Gordon asked, "Have you heard from Laura?"

"Not yet."

"Laura's unreliable. That's another reason her career has tanked.

She has a history of keeping people waiting, but Alison had been moving heaven and earth to get her a job. Too bad that Laura couldn't remember that today."

"Well . . ." Jean decided not to agree or disagree. She turned to Carter Stewart. "Are you heading back to New York, Carter?"

"As a matter of fact, I'm not. I'm checking out of the Glen-Ridge and into the Hudson Valley Hotel across town. Pierce Ellison is directing my new play. He lives only ten minutes away in Highland Falls. We need to go over the script together, and he suggested we could work quietly at his place if I stayed over a few days. I'm not staying at the Glen-Ridge, though. They haven't spent a nickel on improvements at that place in fifty years."

"I can vouch for that," Amory agreed. "I have too many memories of being a busboy and then a room-service waiter there. I'm heading over to the country club. Some of my people are coming in. We're looking for a corporate headquarters in this area."

"Talk to Jack Emerson," Stewart said sarcastically.

"Anyone but him. My people have lined up some places for me to see."

"Then this may not be good-bye," Jean said. "We may be bumping into one another in town. Whether or not, it's been good to be with you."

She did not see Robby Brent or Jack Emerson, but didn't want to wait any longer. She had agreed to meet Sam Deegan at Alice Sommers' home at two o'clock, and it was nearly that time now.

With a final smile and a murmured good-bye to the classmates she passed on the way out, she walked quickly to the parking lot. As she got into her car, she looked across the school grounds to the cemetery. The unreality of Alison's death hit her again. It seemed so strange to leave her here on this cold, wet day. I used to tell Alison that she should have been born in California, Jean thought as she turned the key in the ignition. She hated the cold. Her idea of heaven was to get out of bed in the morning, open the door, and go for a swim.

That was what Alison was doing the morning she died.

It was the thought that accompanied Jean as she drove to Alice Sommers' home.

29

Carter Stewart had reserved a suite at the new Hudson Valley Hotel near Storm King State Park. Perched on the side of the mountain overlooking the Hudson, with its center building and twin towers, it reminded him of an eagle with outstretched wings.

The eagle, symbol of life and light and power and majesty.

The tentative title for his new play was *The Eagle and the Owl.*

The owl. Symbol of darkness and death. Bird of prey. Pierce Ellison, his director, liked the title. I'm not sure, Stewart thought, as he pulled up at the entrance of the hotel and stepped out of the car. I'm just not sure.

Is it too obvious? Symbols are meant to be noted by the profound thinker, not served on a platter to the Wednesday matinee bridge club. Not that that group rushed to buy tickets to his plays.

"We'll take care of your bags, sir."

Carter Stewart pressed a five-dollar bill into the doorman's hand. At least he didn't say, "Welcome home," he thought.

Five minutes later, a scotch from the mini-bar in his hand, he was standing at a window in his suite. The Hudson was brooding and restless. Only mid-afternoon in October and there was already a winter feel in the air. But at least, thank God, the reunion was over. I even quite liked seeing a few of those people again, Carter thought, if only to remind me of how far I've come since I left there.

Pierce Ellison felt that they needed to strengthen the character of Gwendolyn in the play. "Get someone who really is a ditsy blonde," he'd been urging. "Not an actress *playing* a ditsy blonde."

Carter Stewart chuckled aloud as he thought of Laura. "My, my, how she would have fit the bill," he said aloud. "I'll drink to that, even though in one hundred thousand years it would never have happened."

30

Robby Brent had not missed the fact that many of his former classmates shunned him after his speech at the dinner. A few others had paid him the barbed compliment of saying that he was a marvelous mimic, even if he had been a little hard on their old teachers and the principal. It also got back to him that Jean Sheridan said humor should not be cruel.

All of which was intensely satisfying to Robby Brent. Miss Ella Bender, the math teacher, had apparently been seen crying in the ladies room after the dinner. You seem to forget, Miss Bender, how frequently you reminded me that I didn't have one-tenth the ability for higher mathematics that my brothers and sisters did. I was your whipping boy, Miss Bender. The last and least of the Brents. And now you have the nerve to be offended when I show your prissy ways and unfortunate habit of frequently licking your lips with your tongue. Too bad.

He had hinted to Jack Emerson that he might be in the market to invest in property, and Emerson had buttonholed him after the brunch. Emerson was a blowhard in a lot of ways, Robby thought as he turned into the Glen-Ridge driveway, but he did make sense when they talked about real estate and the advisability of investing in this area.

"Land," Emerson had expounded. "Around here it does nothing but go up in value. Taxes are low when it's undeveloped. Sit on it for twenty years, and you'll be worth a fortune. Get in on it before it goes out of sight, Robby. I have a few listings on some fabulous parcels, all with views of the Hudson, and some of them waterfront. They'll knock your socks off. I'd buy them myself, but I have plenty. Don't want to make my kid too rich when he grows up. Stay over and I'll take you around tomorrow."

"It's the land, Katie Scarlett, it's the land." Robby grinned, remembering the bewildered look on Emerson's face when he quoted that line from *Gone With the Wind* to him. But then he'd latched onto it when he explained that what Scarlett's father meant was that land was the basis for security and wealth.

"Gotta remember that, Robby. That's great and it's true. Land is real money, real value. Land doesn't go away."

Next time I'll try a quote from Plato on him, Robby thought as he stopped the car at the entrance to the Glen-Ridge. Might as well let the valet do the parking today, he thought. I'm not going anywhere until tomorrow, and then I'll be in Emerson's car.

Jack Emerson should only know how much property I already have, he thought. W. C. Fields used to leave money in banks in towns all over the country, wherever he was performing. I buy undeveloped land all over the country and then have it posted with NO TRESPASSING signs.

All my life growing up, I lived in a rented house, he thought. Even back then, those intellectual wizards, my mother and father, couldn't scrape together enough money for a down payment on a real home. Now, besides my home base in Vegas, if I wanted, I could build a house on my property in Santa Barbara or Minneapolis or Atlanta or

Boston or the Hamptons or New Orleans or Palm Beach or Aspen, to say nothing of acres and acres in Washington. Land is my secret, Robby thought smugly as he walked into the lobby of the Glen-Ridge.

And land holds my secrets.

31

"I was at the cemetery this morning," Alice Sommers told Jean. "I could see the Stonecroft group at the memorial service. Karen's grave isn't terribly far from where Alison Kendall is buried."

"Not as many people attended as I would have expected," Jean said. "Much of the class went directly to the breakfast."

They were sitting in the cozy den of Alice Sommers' townhouse. She had started the fire, and the leaping flames not only warmed the room but elevated their spirits as well. It was clear to Jean that Alice Sommers had been weeping for a long time. Her eyes were swollen and puffy, but there was an expression of peace on her face that had not been there yesterday.

As though she could read her thoughts, Alice said, "You know, as I told you yesterday, the days leading up to the anniversary are the worst. I go over every minute of that last day, wondering if there was something we could have done to keep Karen safe. Of course, twenty years ago we didn't have an alarm system. Now, most of us wouldn't dream of going to bed without setting an alarm in the house."

She reached for the teapot and refilled their cups. "But now I'll be okay again," she said briskly. "In fact, I've decided that retirement may not be such a good thing. One of my friends has a flower shop and needs help. She's asked me to work for her a couple of days a week, and I'm going to do it."

"That's a great idea," Jean said sincerely. "I remember how beautiful your garden always looked."

"Michael used to tease me by saying that if I spent as much time in the kitchen as I did in the garden, I'd be a world-class chef," Alice said. She glanced out the window. "Oh, look, here's Sam. Right on time, as always."

Sam Deegan scraped his feet carefully on the mat before he rang the bell. He had stopped at Karen's grave on his way to meet Jean, then had found himself almost unable to say that he had to give up trying to find her killer. Something kept blocking the apology he had planned to offer her. Finally he had said, "Karen, I'm retiring. I have to. I'll talk your case over with one of the young guys. Maybe somebody smarter than I am can nab the guy who hurt you."

Alice was opening the door before his finger touched the bell. He did not comment on her swollen eyes, but gripped both her hands in his. "Let me just be sure I don't track mud into the house," he said.

He was at the cemetery, Alice thought gratefully. I know he was. "Come on in," she told him. "Don't worry about a speck or two of dirt." There was something so strong and reassuring about Sam, she thought as she took his coat. I was so right when I asked him to try to help Jean.

He had brought a notebook with him, and after greeting Jean and accepting the offer of a cup of tea from Alice, he got down to business. "Jean, I've been doing a lot of thinking. We have to take seriously that whoever is writing you about Lily may be capable of hurting her. He was near enough to her to pick up her hairbrush, so it may be someone in the family who adopted her. He—and understand, it could just as easily be a *she*—may intend to try to extort money from you, which as you point out would be almost a relief. But that kind of situation could go on for years, too. So it's clear we've got to find this person as fast as possible."

"I went to St. Thomas of Canterbury this morning," Jean said, "but the priest who said Mass was one who only comes in on Sundays. He said I should go to the rectory office tomorrow and see the pastor about looking at the baptismal records. Since then I've been thinking about it. He might be pretty wary about opening them to me. He might think this is just my way of trying to find Lily."

She looked directly at Sam. "I'll bet that thought occurred to you."

"When Alice told me about it, it did occur to me," Sam said frankly. "Having met you, though, I absolutely believe that the situation is exactly as you describe it. But you're right—the priest would have to be very careful, which is why I think it should be me going to him instead of you. He'd probably be a lot more willing to talk to me if he knows of an adopted baby who was baptized at that time."

"I've thought of that, too," Jean said quietly. "You know, for these twenty years I've wondered if I shouldn't have kept Lily. It wasn't all that many generations ago that an eighteen-year-old with a baby was the norm. Now that I have to find her, I realize that if I could see her even from a distance, I'd be satisfied." She bit her lip. "Or at least I think I'd be satisfied," she said softly.

Sam looked from Jean to Alice. Two women who, each in a different way, had lost a child. The cadet was about to graduate and be commissioned. If he had not been killed in that accident, Jean would have married him and kept her baby. If Karen had not happened to come home for an overnight visit twenty years ago, Alice would still have her, and probably have grandchildren as well.

Life never has been fair, Sam thought, but some things we can try to make better. He hadn't been able to solve Karen's murder, but at least maybe he could help Jean now.

"Dr. Connors had to have worked with a lawyer to handle the

adoption papers," he said. "Somebody is sure to know who that lawyer was. Does his wife or family still live around here?"

"I don't know," Jean said.

"Well, we'll start with that. Did you bring the hairbrush and faxes with you?"

"No, I didn't."

"I'd like to get them from you."

"The brush is one of those small ones that you carry in a purse," Jean said. "It's the kind you can get in a drugstore. The faxes don't have anything to identify the source, but of course you can have them both."

"When I speak to the pastor, it will help if I have them."

Jean and Sam left a few minutes later. They arranged that he would follow her in his car to the hotel. From the window, Alice watched them go, then reached in the pocket of her sweater. This morning she had found a trinket on Karen's grave that had undoubtedly been dropped by a child. When she was little, Karen had loved stuffed animals and had a variety of them. Alice thought of the owl that had been one of her favorites, as with a wistful smile she looked down at the inch-long pewter owl she was holding in the palm of her hand.

32

Jake Perkins sat in the lobby of the Glen-Ridge House, watching as the last of the reunion celebrants checked out and headed back to their private lives. The welcoming banner was gone, and he could see that the bar was empty. No last good-byes, he thought. By now they're probably all sick of one another.

The first thing he had done when he arrived was stop at the front desk and verify that Ms. Wilcox had not yet returned to check out, and that she had not cancelled the car that was to take her to the airport at two-fifteen.

At two-fifteen he watched as a uniformed driver came into the lobby and went to the desk. Jake rushed to stand next to him and hear for himself that the man expected to pick up Laura Wilcox.

At two-thirty the driver left, obviously disgruntled. Jake overheard his comment that it was too damn bad he hadn't been told that she wasn't going, because he could have had another job, and not to bother to call him the next time she needs a ride.

At four o'clock, Jake was still in the lobby. That was when Dr. Sheridan returned with the older man she'd been talking to after the dinner. They went directly to the front desk. She's asking about Laura Wilcox, Jake thought. His hunch was right—Laura Wilcox was missing.

He decided it wouldn't hurt to try to get a statement from Dr. Sheridan. He reached her side in time to hear the man she was with say, "Jean, I agree. I don't like the look of it, but Laura is an adult and has the right to change her mind about checking out of the hotel or catching a plane."

"Excuse me, sir. I'm Jake Perkins, a reporter for the Stonecroft paper," Jake broke in.

"Sam Deegan."

It was clear to Jake that his presence was not welcomed by either Dr. Sheridan or Sam Deegan. Get right to it, he thought. "Dr. Sheridan, I know you were concerned that Ms. Wilcox didn't show up for the brunch, and now she has missed her car to the airport. Do you think that anything may have happened to her—I mean, given the history of the women at your old lunch table at Stonecroft?"

He saw the startled glance Jean Sheridan gave to Sam Deegan. She hasn't told him about the lunch table group, Jake thought. He didn't know who this guy was, but it would be interesting to test his reaction to what Jake was now sure was a breaking story. He pulled out the picture of the girls at the lunch table from his pocket. "You see, sir, this was the group at Dr. Sheridan's lunch table in their senior year at Stonecroft. Over these twenty years since they graduated, five had died as of last month. Two of them were killed in accidents, one was a suicide, and one disappeared, supposedly caught in an avalanche in Snowbird. Last month, the fifth one, Alison Kendall, died in her swimming pool. From what I read, it seems to be a possibility that it was not an accidental death. Now Laura Wilcox seems to be missing. Don't you think that this is a pretty bizarre coincidence?"

Sam took the picture, and as he studied it, the expression on his face became grim. "I don't believe in coincidence of this magnitude," he said brusquely. "Now if you'll excuse us, Mr. Perkins."

"Oh, don't worry about me. I'm going to wait around to see if Ms. Wilcox shows up. I'd like to have a final interview with her."

Ignoring him, Sam took out his card and handed it to the desk clerk. "I want a list of the employees who were on duty last night," he said, his voice commanding and forceful.

33

"I thought I'd be gone by now, but I had a whole bunch of messages waiting for me when I got back from the brunch," Gordon Amory explained to Jean. "We're shooting one episode of our new series in Canada, and some major problems have developed. I've been on the phone the last two hours."

His bags at his side, he had come up to the front desk as the clerk was showing Sam the worksheets of the hotel employees. Then he studied Jean's face. "Jean, is something wrong?"

"Laura is missing," Jean said, hearing the tremor in her own voice. "She was supposed to have been picked up at two-fifteen to go to the airport. The bed in her room wasn't slept in, and the maid said that some of her toiletries seem to be gone. Maybe she just decided to stay with someone and is perfectly all right, but she was so definite about being with us this morning that I'm terribly worried now."

"She was certainly definite about being at the brunch when she was talking to Jack Emerson last night," Gordon said. "As I told you, she was pretty cool to me after I told her she didn't have the faintest chance of being cast in the upcoming series, but in the bar after dinner I overheard what she said to Jack."

Sam had been listening to their conversation. He turned to Gordon and introduced himself. "We have to realize that Laura Wilcox is an adult. She has every right in the world to go off by herself or with a friend, and to change her mind about checking out. Nevertheless, I think it would be wise to follow up and see if anyone, either a hotel employee or a friend, knew her plans."

"I'm sorry to have kept you waiting, Mr. Amory," the clerk said. "I have your bill ready."

Gordon Amory hesitated, then looked at Jean. "You think something may have happened to Laura, don't you?"

"Yes, I do. Laura was very close to Alison. She simply wouldn't deliberately skip the memorial, no matter what plans she had for last night."

"Is my room still free?" Amory asked the clerk.

"Yes, of course, sir."

"Then I'm going to stay at least until we know more about Ms. Wilcox." He turned to Jean, and for an instant, even in the midst of her concern about Laura, she was struck by the realization of what a handsome man Gordon Amory had become. I used to feel so sorry for him, she thought. He was a pathetic loser back then, and look what he's made of himself.

"Jean, I know I hurt Laura last night, and it was lousy of me—kind of a payback, I guess, for the way she used to brush me off when we were kids. I could have promised her a part even if it wasn't the lead in that series. I have a feeling she may be desperate. That could explain why she didn't show up this morning. I bet she'll be back with or without an explanation for where she's been, and when she is, I'm going to offer her a job. And I'm going to hang around to do it personally."

34

Jake Perkins stayed in the lobby of the Glen-Ridge, watching as, one after another, the employees who had been on duty Saturday night went into the small office behind the desk and talked to Sam Deegan. When they came out, he managed to buttonhole enough of them to learn that they got the impression that Deegan was also going down the list and phoning anyone who was off today but had been around last night.

The upshot from what he heard was that no one had seen Laura Wilcox leave the hotel. The doorman and the valet parkers were absolutely certain that she had not left by the front door.

He correctly guessed that the young woman in a maid's uniform might be the one who cleaned Laura's room. When she emerged from talking to Deegan, Jake followed her across the lobby, jumped in the elevator behind her, and got off at the fourth floor with her. "I'm a reporter for the Stonecroft newspaper," he explained as he handed her his card, "and I'm also a stringer for the *New York Post.*" Close to the truth, he thought. Before much longer, I will be.

It wasn't hard to get her talking. Her name was Myrna Robinson. She was a student at the community college and worked part-time at the hotel. She's kind of naïve, Jake thought smugly as he observed her absolutely thrilled expression at the excitement of having been questioned by a detective.

He opened his notebook. "What exactly did Detective Deegan ask you, Myrna?"

"He wanted to know if I was sure that some of Laura Wilcox's cosmetics were missing and I told him I was absolutely positive," she confided breathlessly. "I said, 'Mr. Deegan, you have no idea how much stuff she managed to get on top of that skinny vanity in the bathroom, and half of it's gone. I mean, things like cleanser and moisturizer and a toothbrush and her cosmetic bag.' "

"The kind of stuff any woman carries when she goes away overnight," Jake said helpfully. "What about clothes?"

"I didn't talk about clothes to Mr. Deegan," Myrna said hesitantly. Nervously she twisted the top button on her black uniform dress. "I mean, I told him I was sure one of her suitcases was missing, but I didn't want him to think I was nosey or anything, so I didn't mention that her blue cashmere jacket and slacks and ankle-top boots weren't in the closet."

Myrna was about Laura's size. Dollars to doughnuts she had been trying on the clothes, Jake thought. A suit and slacks were missing—probably what Laura planned to wear to the memorial service and brunch. "You told Mr. Deegan about a suitcase that isn't in her room?"

"Uh-huh. She brought a lot of luggage with her. Honest, you'd think she was on a round-the-world trip. Anyway, the smaller suitcase wasn't there this morning. It was different from the others. It's a Louis Vuitton—that's how I noticed it wasn't there. I love that pattern, don't you? So distinctive. The two big ones she had are creamy-colored leather."

Jake prided himself on his ear for French, so he winced inwardly at Myrna's pronunciation of "Vuitton." "Myrna, is there any chance I could get a look at Laura's room?" he asked. "I swear I won't touch a thing."

He had gone too far. He could see an alarmed expression replace the excitement on her face. She looked past him down the corridor, and he could read her thoughts. If the housekeeper ever caught her bringing someone into a guest's room, she'd be fired. Quickly he backtracked. "Myrna, I shouldn't have asked you that. Forget it. Listen, you have my card. It would be worth twenty bucks to me if you take my number and give me a call if you hear anything about Laura. How about it? Want to be a girl reporter?"

Myrna bit her lip as she considered the offer. "It's not the money," she began.

"Of course not," Jake agreed.

"If you put the story in the *Post*, I'd have to be an unnamed source."

She's smarter than she looks, Jake thought, as he nodded eagerly. They shook hands on the deal.

It was nearly six o'clock. When he went back to the lobby, it was almost deserted. Jake went up to the desk clerk and inquired if Mr. Deegan had left the hotel.

The clerk looked tired and distressed. "Look, sonny, he's gone, and unless you want to rent a room, I'd suggest you go home, too."

"I'm sure he asked you to let him know if Ms. Wilcox returns or if you hear from her," Jake suggested. "May I give you my card? I became friendly with Ms. Wilcox during the course of the weekend, and I'm concerned about her, too."

The clerk took the card and studied it. "Reporter for the *Stonecroft Academy Gazette* and writer-journalist-at-large, huh?" He tore the card in half. "You're too big for your breeches, sonny. Do me a favor and get lost."

35

The body of Helen Whelan was discovered at 5:30 P.M. on Sunday afternoon in a wooded area in Washingtonville, a town about fifteen miles from Surrey Meadows. The discovery was made by a twelve-year-old boy who was cutting through the woods, taking a shortcut to his friend's home.

Sam got the message as he was finishing his interviews of the employees at the Glen-Ridge House. He called Jean in her room. She had gone upstairs to phone Mark Fleischman, Carter Stewart, and Jack Emerson, in the hope that one of them might have known Laura's plans. She had already seen Robby Brent in the lobby, and he had disclaimed any knowledge of where Laura might be.

"Jean, I have to go," Sam explained. "Have you reached anyone yet?"

"I talked to Carter. He's very concerned but has no idea where Laura might be. I told him that Gordon and I are having dinner, and he's going to join us. Maybe if we can make a list between us of the people Laura seemed to be spending time with, we might come up with something. Jack Emerson isn't home. I left word on his answering machine. Same with Mark Fleischman."

"That's about the best you can do for the moment," Sam said. "Our hands are legally tied. If no one has heard from her by tomorrow, I'll try to get a search warrant to go through her room and see if she left any indication of where she might have gone. Otherwise, sit tight."

"You will go over to the rectory in the morning?"

"Absolutely," Sam promised. He snapped closed his phone and hurried out to his car. There was no point in telling Jean that he was on his way to the crime scene where another woman who had disappeared had been found.

Helen Whelan had been struck with a blow on the back of her head and then had been stabbed repeatedly. "He probably hit her from behind with the same blunt weapon that he used on the dog," Cal Grey, the medical examiner, told Sam when he arrived at the crime scene. The body was in the process of being removed, and under floodlights investigators were combing the roped-off area for possible clues to the killer. "I can't be sure until I do the autopsy, but it looks to me as if the injury to her head might have knocked her out. The stab wounds happened after he got her here. One can only hope that she didn't know what was happening to her."

Sam watched as the slender body was lifted into a body bag. "Her clothes don't look disturbed."

"They're not. My guess is that whoever grabbed her brought her directly here and killed her. She still has the dog's leash around her wrist."

"Hold it a minute," Sam snapped to the attendant who was opening the stretcher. He squatted down and felt his feet sink into the muddy ground. "Let me have your flashlight, Cal."

"What do you see?"

"There's a smear of blood on the side of her slacks. I doubt she got it from the wounds in her chest and neck. My guess is that the killer was bleeding pretty heavily, probably from a dog bite." He straightened up. "Which means he may have needed to go to an emergency room. I'll get an alert out to all the hospitals in the area to report any dog bites they may have treated over the weekend or that may come up in the next few days. And make sure the lab runs tests on the blood. I'll meet you back at your place, Cal."

On the drive to the medical examiner's office, the waste of the life of Helen Whelan hit Sam with intensity, catching him in the pit of his stomach. It happened whenever he encountered this kind of violence. I want that guy, he thought, and I want to be the one who cuffs him. I hope to God that wherever that dog bit him, he's in misery right now.

That train of thought gave him another idea. Maybe he's too smart to go to an emergency room, but he'll still have to take care of that bite. It's like looking for a needle in a haystack, but it might be worth notifying all the pharmacies in the area to watch out for someone buying items such as peroxide and bandages and antibacterial ointments.

But if he's smart enough to avoid a hospital, he's probably smart enough to shop for stuff like that in one of the big drugstores where there's a long line at the cash register and no one is paying attention to what's in the basket except to scan it.

Still, it's worth a try, Sam decided grimly, remembering the smiling picture of Helen Whelan he had seen in her apartment. She was twenty years older than Karen Sommers had been, he thought, but she died the same way—savagely stabbed to death.

The mist that had come and gone all day had turned into a driving rain. Sam frowned as he switched on the windshield wipers. There couldn't be any connection between those cases, though, he thought. There hadn't been a similar stabbing in this area in twenty years. Karen had been in her home. Helen Whelan had been outside walking her dog. But, then again, was it possible that some maniac had been lying low all these years?

Anything was possible, Sam decided. Please let him have gotten careless, he thought. Let him have dropped something that would lead us to him. Hopefully we'll have his DNA. That must be his blood on the dog's whiskers and maybe also the smear on her slacks.

Arriving at the medical examiner's office, he pulled into the parking area, got out of his car, locked it, and went inside. It was going to be a long night and a longer day tomorrow. He had to see the pastor at St. Thomas and persuade him to open the records of baptisms that had taken place nearly twenty years ago. He had to get in touch with the families of the five women from Stonecroft who had died in the order in which they sat at the lunch table—he needed to know more about the details of their deaths. And he needed to find out what had happened to Laura Wilcox. If it weren't for the deaths of the other five from her class, I'd say she just took off with a guy, he thought. From what I understand she's pretty lively and has never been without a man for long if she can help it.

The medical examiner and the ambulance with Helen Whelan's body arrived seconds behind him. Half an hour later Sam was studying the effects that had been removed from the body. Her watch and a ring were her only jewelry. She had probably not been carrying a handbag because her house key and a handkerchief were in the pocket on the right side of her jacket.

Lying on the table next to the house key was one other object: a pewter owl a little over an inch long. Sam reached for the tweezers that the attendant had used in handling the keys and the owl, picked up the owl and examined it closely. The unwinking eyes, cold and wide, met his gaze.

"It was way down in the pocket of her slacks," the attendant explained. "I almost missed it."

Sam remembered there had been a pumpkin outside the door of Helen Whelan's garden apartment and a paper skeleton in a box in the hall that she must have been planning to hang up somewhere. "She was decorating for Halloween," he said. "This was probably part of the stuff she had. Bag everything, and I'll take it to the lab."

Forty minutes later, he was watching as the clothing of Helen Whelan was checked under a microscope for anything that might help identify her killer. Another attendant was examining the car keys for fingerprints.

"These are all hers," he commented, as with tweezers in his hand he reached for the owl. A moment later he said, "That's funny. There aren't any fingerprints on this thing, not even smudges. How do you figure that one? It didn't walk into her pocket. It had to have been put there by someone wearing gloves."

Sam thought for a minute. Had the killer left the owl deliberately? He was sure of it. "We're keeping this quiet," he snapped. Taking the tweezers from the attendant, he picked up the owl and stared at it. "You're going to lead me to this guy," he vowed. "I don't know how yet, but you *will.*"

36

They had agreed to meet at seven o'clock in the dining room. At the last minute Jean decided to change into dark blue slacks and a light blue sweater with a floppy wide collar that she had bought at an Escada sale. All day she had been unable to shake off the chill of the cemetery. Even the jacket and slacks she had been wearing seemed to retain the cold and dampness she had felt there.

Ridiculous, of course, she told herself as she touched up her makeup and brushed her hair. While standing in front of the bathroom mirror, she paused for a moment, holding the brush and staring at it. Who had been so close to Lily that he or she had managed to take her brush from her home or handbag, she wondered.

Or was it possible that Lily managed to trace me and is punishing me for giving her up? Jean asked herself, agonized by the thought. She's nineteen and a half now. What kind of life has she led? Have the people who adopted her been the wonderful couple Dr. Connors described to me, or did they turn out to be bad parents once they had the baby?

But instinct immediately told Jean that Lily wasn't playing games to torment her. This is someone else, someone who wants to hurt *me.* Ask for money, she pleaded silently. I'll give you money, but don't hurt *her.*

She looked back into the mirror and studied her reflection. Several times she had been told that she resembled the *Today* show host Katie Couric, and she felt flattered at the comparison. Does Lily look like me? she wondered. Or is she more like Reed? Those strands of hair are so blond, and he used to joke that his mother said his hair was the color of winter wheat. That means she has his hair. Reed's eyes were blue and so are mine, so she certainly has blue eyes.

This line of speculation was familiar territory. Shaking her head, Jean laid the brush on the counter, turned off the bathroom light, reached for her purse, and went down to meet the others for dinner.

Gordon Amory, Robby Brent, and Jack Emerson were already at the table in the nearly empty dining room. As they stood up to greet her, she was aware of the marked contrast in the way they looked and dressed. Amory was wearing a cashmere open-necked shirt and expensive tweed jacket. He looked every inch the successful executive. Robby Brent had changed from the cableknit sweater he had worn to the brunch. To Jean, the turtleneck shirt he was wearing now emphasized his short neck and squat body. A hint of perspiration on his forehead and cheeks gave him a glistening appearance that she found offputting. Jack Emerson's corduroy jacket was well cut, but cheapened by the red-and-white-checked shirt and bright multicolored tie he wore. The thought went through her mind that with his fleshy florid face, Jack Emerson embodied the old anti-Nixon political ad with the slogan "Would you buy a used car from this man?"

Jack pulled out the empty chair beside his own and patted her arm as she stepped around it. In a reflex action, Jean stiffened and pulled her arm away from him.

"We've ordered drinks, Jeannie," Emerson told her. "I took a chance and ordered a chardonnay for you."

"That's fine. Are you guys early, or am I late?"

"We're a bit early. You're exactly on time, and Carter isn't here yet."

Twenty minutes later, as they were debating whether or not to order, Carter arrived. "Sorry to keep you waiting, but I didn't expect another reunion quite this soon," he observed dryly as he joined them. He was now wearing jeans and a hooded sweatshirt.

"None of us did," Gordon Amory said in agreement. "Why don't you order a drink, and then I suggest we get down to the reason we're here now."

Carter nodded. He caught the waiter's eye and pointed to the martini Emerson was drinking. "Continue," he said to Gordon, his tone dry.

"Let me start by saying that after some consideration, I believe and hope that our concern for Laura may be unnecessary. I remember hearing that a few years ago she accepted an invitation to visit some big bucks guy, who shall be nameless, at his Palm Beach estate, and she reportedly left in the middle of a dinner party to go away with him on his private plane. That time, as far as anyone could gather, she didn't even bother to bring her own toothbrush, never mind her cosmetics."

"I don't think anyone returned to Stonecroft in a private plane," Robby Brent observed. "In fact, I think from the looks of some of them, they probably backpacked to get here."

"Come on, Robby," Jack Emerson protested. "A lot of our graduates have done mighty well. That's why quite a few of them have bought property around here for an eventual second home."

"Let's skip the sales pitch for tonight, Jack," Gordon said irritably. "Listen, you have big bucks, and you're the only one, as far as we know, who has a house in town and could have invited Laura to join you for your own quiet reunion."

Jack Emerson's already florid face darkened. "I hope that's supposed to be funny, Gordon."

"I don't want to displace Robby as our comedian in residence,"

Gordon said as he helped himself to an olive from the dish the waiter had placed on the table. "Of course I was joking about you and Laura, but not about the sales pitch."

Jean decided it was time to try to redirect the conversation. "I left a message for Mark on his cell phone," she said. "He called me back just before I came downstairs. If we haven't heard from Laura by tomorrow, he's going to rearrange his schedule and come back."

"He always had a thing for Laura when we were kids," Robby observed. "I wouldn't be surprised if he still does. He made it a point to sit next to her on the dais last night. He even changed place cards to make it happen."

So that's why he's rushing back, Jean thought, realizing she had read too much into his phone call. "Jeannie," he had said, "I want to believe that Laura is okay, but if anything has happened to her, it could mean that there is a terrible pattern to the loss of the girls at your lunch table. You've got to realize that."

And I assumed he was worrying about me, she thought. I was even thinking of telling him about Lily. Since he's a psychiatrist, I thought maybe he'd have some insight into what kind of person is contacting me about her.

It was a relief when the waiter, a slight, elderly man, began passing out menus. "May I tell you our specials for this evening?" he asked.

Robby looked up at the waiter with a hopeful smile. "Can't wait," he murmured.

"Filet mignon with mushrooms, filet of sole stuffed with crabmeat . . ."

When he had finished the recitation, Robby asked, "May I ask you a question?"

"Of course, sir."

"Is it a habit of this establishment to make last night's leftovers today's specials?"

"Oh, sir, I assure you," the waiter began, his voice flustered and apologetic, "I've been here forty years, and we're very proud of our cuisine."

"Never mind, never mind. Just a little humor to lighten the table talk. Jean, you first."

"The caesar salad and rack of lamb, medium-rare," Jean said quietly. Robby isn't just sarcastic, she thought; he's nasty and cruel. He likes to hurt people who can't strike back, people like Miss Bender, the math teacher at the dinner last night, and now this poor guy. He talks about Mark having a crush on Laura. But no one had a bigger crush on her than he did.

Suddenly, a disquieting thought occurred to her. Robby's made a lot of money now. He's famous. If he invited Laura to meet him somewhere, she would go, I know she would. Jean was aghast to realize that she was seriously considering the fact that Robby might have lured Laura away and then harmed her.

Jack Emerson was the last to order. As he handed the menu back to the waiter, he said, "I promised some friends that I'd drop in for a nightcap, so I think it would be a good idea to start discussing who we think Laura might have paid a lot of attention to over the weekend." He shot a glance at Gordon. "Besides you, of course, Gordie. You were at the top of her A-list."

Dear God, Jean thought, they'll all be at each other's throats if this keeps up. She turned to Carter Stewart. "Carter, why don't we start with you. Any suggestions?"

"I saw her talking a lot to Joel Nieman, better known as the Romeo who forgot half his lines in the school play. His wife was here only for the cocktail party and dinner Friday night, then went home. She's an executive with Target and was flying to Hong Kong Saturday morning."

"Don't they live somewhere around here, Jack?" Gordon asked.

"They live in Rye."

"That's not that far away."

"I was talking to Joel and his wife at the party Friday night," Jean said. "He doesn't look at all like the kind of guy who would ask Laura to go home with him the minute his wife is out of town."

"He may not look like it, but I happen to know he's had a couple of girlfriends," Emerson said. "Also that he was damn near indicted for some shady deals his accounting firm was involved in. That's why we passed on making him an honoree."

"How about our missing honoree, Mark Fleischman?" Robby Brent asked. "He may be, as his introduction at the dinner quoted, 'tall, lanky, cheerful, funny, and wise,' but he also was hanging around Laura every minute he could. He broke his neck rushing to sit next to her on the bus to West Point."

Jack Emerson finished his martini and signaled the waiter for a refill. Then he raised his eyebrows. "Just occurred to me. Mark would have a place to invite Laura. I know for a fact that his father's out of town. I met Cliff Fleischman in the post office last week and asked him if he was coming to see his son honored. He told me he had long-standing plans to visit some friends in Chicago but that he'd give Mark a call. Maybe he offered him the house. Cliff won't be back till Tuesday."

"Then I think Mr. Fleischman must have changed his mind," Jean said. "Mark told me that he'd passed his old house and there were a lot of lights on. He didn't say anything about hearing from his father."

"Cliff Fleischman leaves a bunch of lights on whenever he's away," Emerson replied. "His house was burglarized when he was on vacation about ten years ago. He blamed it on the fact that it was so dark. He said it was a dead giveaway that there was no one home."

Gordon broke off a bread stick. "I got the feeling Mark was estranged from his father."

"He is, and I know why," Emerson said. "After Mark's mother died, his father gave up the housekeeper, and she came to work for us for a while. She was a real gossip and gave us the lowdown on the Fleischmans. Everybody knew that Dennis, the older son, was the apple of his mother's eye. She never got over losing him, and blamed Mark for the accident. The car was at the top of that long driveway, and Mark was always pestering Dennis to teach him to drive. Mark was only thirteen and wasn't allowed to start the car unless Dennis was with him. That afternoon he'd started it and then forgotten to put on the parking brake before he left the car. When the car started to roll down the hill, Dennis never saw it coming."

"How did she find out?" Jean asked.

"According to the housekeeper, one night shortly before she died, something happened and she turned completely against Mark. He didn't even come to her funeral. She cut him out of her will, too; she had big bucks from her mother's family. Mark was in medical school at that time."

"But he was only thirteen years old at the time of the accident," Jean said in protest.

"And always jealous of his brother," Carter Stewart said quietly. "You can bet that. But maybe he has been in touch with the father, and maybe he still has a key to the house, and maybe he knew the father was away."

Did Mark lie about having to go back to Boston? Jean wondered. He went out of his way to stop at the table in the bar when I was with Alice and Sam to tell us about walking past his father's house. Could he still be right here in town with Laura?

I don't want to believe that, she acknowledged to herself, as Gordon Amory volunteered, "We're all assuming that Laura went *with* someone. It's also possible she went *to* someone. We're not that far from Greenwich and Bedford and Westport, where a lot of her celebrity friends have homes."

Jack Emerson had brought a list of the people who attended the reunion. In the end, they decided that each of them would take names to call, explain why they were concerned, and ask for their thoughts as to where Laura might have gone.

When they left the dining room, after promising to be in touch in the morning, Carter Stewart and Jack Emerson headed for their cars. In the lobby, Jean told Gordon Amory and Robby Brent that she was going to stop at the desk.

"Then I'll say good night," Gordon told her. "I still have some phone calls to make."

"It's Sunday night, Gordie," Robby Brent said. "What could be so important it can't wait till morning?"

Gordon Amory stared at Robby's deceptively innocent face. "As you know, I prefer to be addressed as 'Gordon,'" he said quietly. "Good night, Jean."

"He is so full of himself," Robby said as he watched Gordon walk across the lobby and press the button for the elevator. "I bet he goes up and turns on the television. Tonight's the opening of a new series on one of his channels. Or maybe he just wants to look in the mirror at his pretty new face. Honest to God, Jeannie, that plastic surgeon must be a genius. Remember what a dorky-looking kid Gordie used to be?"

I don't care why he's going up to his room, Jean thought. I just want to check to see if by any chance Laura has phoned and then go up to bed myself. "More power to Gordon that he was able to turn his life around. He had a pretty nasty time growing up."

"Like all of us," Robby said dismissively. "Except of course, for our missing beauty queen." He shrugged. "I'm going to grab a jacket and go out for a while. I'm a health nut and except for a couple of walks, I haven't had any exercise all weekend. The gym in this place is the pits."

"Is there anything about this town or this hotel or the people you've been meeting that isn't the pits in your opinion?" Jean asked, not caring if her voice sounded sharp.

"Very little," Robby said cheerfully, "except for you, of course, Jeannie. I was sorry to see that you looked kind of upset when we talked about Mark hanging around Laura this weekend. For the record, I could see that Mark was playing up to you, too. He's a hard guy to figure out, but then most psychiatrists are more nuts than their patients. If Mark did release the brake on the car that killed his brother, I wonder if consciously or unconsciously it was deliberate. After all, it was his brother's new car, a gift from Mommy and Daddy for graduation from Stonecroft. Think about that."

With a wink and a wave of his hand he was on his way to the bank of elevators. Furious and humiliated that he had so correctly diagnosed her reaction to the comments about Mark and Laura, Jean walked over to the desk. The clerk on duty was Amy Sachs, a small soft-voiced woman with short graying hair and oversized glasses that hung loosely over the bridge of her nose.

"No, we definitely have not heard from Ms. Wilcox," she told Jean. "But a fax came in for you, Dr. Sheridan." She turned and reached for an envelope on the shelf behind the desk.

Jean felt her mouth go dry. As she told herself that she should wait and read the contents upstairs, she ripped open the envelope.

The message it contained consisted of eight words: LILIES THAT FESTER SMELL FÅR WORSE THAN WEEDS.

Lilies that fester, Jean thought. *Dead lilies.*

"Is anything wrong, Dr. Sheridan?" the mousy clerk asked anxiously. "I hope that isn't bad news."

"What? Oh . . . no . . . it's quite all right, thank you." In a daze, Jean made her way upstairs, went to her room, opened her purse, and ransacked her wallet for Sam Deegan's cell phone number. His terse, "Sam Deegan" made her realize that it was nearly ten o'clock and that he might have been asleep. "Sam, I probably woke you up—"

"No, you didn't," he interrupted. "What is it, Jean? Did you hear from Laura?"

"No, it's Lily. Another fax."

"Read it to me."

Her voice trembling, she read the eight words to him. "Sam, that's a quote from a Shakespeare sonnet. He's referring to dead lilies. Sam, whoever sent this is threatening to kill my child." Jean heard the rising hysteria in her voice as she cried, "What can I do to *stop* him? What can I *do?*"

37

She probably had the fax by now. He still didn't know why he enjoyed taunting Jean, especially now that he had decided he was going to kill her. Why twist the knife by threatening Meredith, or Lily, as Jean called the girl? For nearly twenty years his secret knowledge of her birth and of her adoptive parents had been one of those little facts that seem useless, like gifts that cannot be returned but will never be taken from the shelf.

It was only when he met her parents at a luncheon last year and realized who they were that he had made it his business to be friendly with them. In August he had even invited them to spend a long weekend with him and to bring Meredith who was home on vacation with them. That was when the idea of taking something that would be proof of her DNA occurred to him.

The opportunity to steal her brush had been handed to him on a platter. They were all at the pool, and her cell phone rang while she was brushing her hair after a swim. She answered the call and walked away to talk privately. He slipped the brush into his pocket and then began circulating among his other guests. The next day he sent the brush and the first message to Jean.

The power of life and death—so far he had exercised it over five of the lunch room girls as well as over many other women, chosen at random. He wondered how soon it would be before they found the body of Helen Whelan. Had it been a mistake to leave the owl in her pocket? Until now he had left his symbol hidden, unobtrusive, unnoticeable. Like last month, when he had slipped one of them into a kitchen drawer in the pool house where he had waited for Alison.

The lights in the house were off. He took the night vision glasses from his pocket, put them on, put his key in the lock, opened the back door, and went inside. He closed and locked the door and walked through the kitchen to the back staircase, then padded noiselessly up the stairs.

Laura was in the bedroom that had been hers before her family moved to Concord Avenue when she was sixteen. He had tied her hands and feet and put a gag on her mouth. She was lying on top of the bed, her gold evening gown glittering in the dark.

She had not heard him come into the room, and when he bent over her, he could hear her terrified gasp. "I'm back, Laura," he whispered. "Aren't you glad?"

She tried to shrink away from him.

"I ammmm an owwlllll annnnd I livvvvve in in in a tree," he whispered. "You thought it was funny to mimic me, didn't you? Do you think it's funny now, Laura? Do you?"

With the night glasses, he could see the terror in her eyes. Whimpering sounds came from her throat as she shook her head from side to side.

"That's not the right answer, Laura. You do think it's funny. All of you girls think it's funny. Show me you think it's funny. Show me."

She began to shake her head up and down. In a quick movement, he untied the gag. "Don't raise your voice, Laura," he whispered. "No one will hear you, and if you do cry out, I will hold this pillow over your face. Do you understand me?"

"Please," Laura whispered. "Please . . ."

"No, Laura I don't want you to say 'please.' I want you to mimic me, giving my line onstage, and then I want you to laugh."

"I . . . I ammmm an owl annnd I lllivvve livvvvve innnnn aaaa treeee."

He nodded approvingly. "That's the way. You're a very good mimic. Now pretend that you're with the girls at the lunch table and giggle and snicker and cackle and laugh. I want to see how amused all of them were after you ridiculed me."

"I can't . . . I'm sorry . . ."

He lifted the pillow and held it over her face.

Desperately, Laura began to laugh, shrill, high-pitched, hysterical bleating sounds. "Ha . . . ha . . . ha . . ." Tears spilled from her eyes. "Please . . ."

He put his hand over her mouth. "You were about to use my name. That is forbidden. You may only call me 'The Owl.' You will have to practice imitating the girls being amused. Now I am going to untie your hands and let you eat. I brought you soup and a roll. Wasn't that good of me? Then I will permit you to use the bathroom.

"After that, when you are back in a safe sleep position, I am going to dial the hotel on my cell phone. You will tell the desk clerk that you are with friends, that your plans are indefinite, and to hold your room for you.

"Do you understand that, Laura?"

Her answer was barely audible: "Yes."

"If you attempt in any way to seek help, you will die immediately. You do understand that?"

"Y-e-s."

"Very well."

Twenty minutes later the computerized answering system at the Glen-Ridge House was responding to a caller who had pushed "3" for reservations.

The phone at the front desk rang. The clerk picked it up and identified herself. "Front desk, Amy speaking." Then she gasped. "Ms. Wilcox, how good to hear from you. We've all been so concerned about you. Oh, your friends will be so happy to hear that you've called. Of course we'll hold the room for you. Are you sure you're all right?"

The Owl broke the connection. "You did that very well, Laura. Some stress in your voice, but that's natural, I suppose. Maybe you do have the makings of an actress." He tied the gag over her mouth. "I'll be back eventually. Try to get some sleep. You have my permission to dream about me."

38

Jake Perkins knew that the clerk who had booted him out of the Glen-Ridge went off duty at 8:00 P.M. That meant he could go back to the hotel anytime after eight and hang around the desk with the other clerk, Amy Sachs, to see if anything had developed.

After dinner with his parents, who were enthralled with his account of what was going on at the hotel, he went over the notes he would be giving to the *Post.* He had decided to wait until the morning to call the newspaper. By then Laura Wilcox would have been missing a full day.

At ten o'clock he was back at the Glen-Ridge, entering the deserted hotel lobby. You could fly a plane through this place and not hit anyone, he thought as he walked to the front desk. Amy Sachs was there.

Amy liked him. He knew that. Last spring when he had been covering a luncheon for Stonecroft, she had said he reminded her of her kid brother. "The only difference is Danny is forty-six and you're sixteen," she'd said, then she'd laughed. "He always wanted to be in publishing, too, and in a way I guess he is. He owns a trucking company that delivers newspapers."

Jake wondered how many people realized that under her timid, anxious-to-please exterior, Amy had a good sense of humor and was pretty sharp.

She welcomed him with a timid smile. "Hi, Jake."

"Hi, Amy. Just thought I'd stop by and see if you'd heard from Laura Wilcox."

"Not a word." Just then the phone at her elbow rang, and she picked up the receiver. "Front desk, Amy speaking," she whispered.

Then as Jake watched, Amy's face changed and she gasped, "Oh, Ms. Wilcox . . ."

Jake leaned over the desk and motioned to Amy to hold the receiver away from her ear so that he could listen, too. He caught Laura saying that she was with friends, her plans were indefinite, and to please hold her room for her.

She doesn't sound like herself, he thought. She's upset. Her voice is trembling.

The conversation lasted only twenty seconds. When Amy replaced the receiver, she and Jake looked at each other. "Wherever she is, she's not having a good time," he said flatly.

"Or maybe she's just hung over," Amy suggested. "I read an article about her in *People* magazine last year, and it said she'd been in rehab for a drinking problem."

"That would explain it, I guess," Jake agreed. He shrugged. So much for my big story, he thought. "Where do you think she went, Amy?" he asked. "You were on duty all weekend. Did you notice her hanging around with anyone specially?"

Amy Sachs' oversized glasses wiggled when she frowned. "I saw her arm in arm with Dr. Fleischman a couple of times," she said. "And he was the first to check out Sunday morning, even before that brunch at Stonecroft. Maybe he'd left her sobering up somewhere and was anxious to get back to her."

She opened a drawer and took out a card. "I promised that detective, Mr. Deegan, that I'd phone him if we heard from Ms. Wilcox."

"I'm on my way," Jake said. "I'll see you, Amy." With a wave of his hand he started for the front door as she dialed. He went outside, stood indecisively on the pavement, walked halfway to his car, and then returned to the desk.

"Did you reach Mr. Deegan?" he asked.

"Yes. I told him that I'd heard from her. He said that was good news and to let him know when she actually comes back for her bags."

"That's what I was afraid of. Amy, give me Sam Deegan's number."

She looked alarmed. "Why?"

"Because I think Laura Wilcox sounded scared rather than hung-over, and I think Mr. Deegan should know that."

"If anyone finds out I let you listen in on her call, I'll lose my job."

"No, you won't. I'll say I grabbed the receiver when you mentioned her name and turned it so I could hear, too. Amy, five of Laura's friends are dead. If she's being held against her will, she may not have much time, either."

Sam Deegan had barely hung up after speaking to Jean when he received the telephone call from the Glen-Ridge clerk. His immediate reaction was that Laura Wilcox was a remarkably selfish woman to have missed her friend's memorial service, worried her other friends, and cost the limousine driver another fare by not cancelling. But even that reaction had been tempered by the unsettling fact that there was something suspicious about the vague story she had told the clerk and the clerk's assessment that she had sounded either nervous or hungover.

Jake Perkins' follow-up phone call cemented that impression, especially since Jake was emphatic that he thought Wilcox sounded frightened. "Do you agree with Ms. Sachs that it was exactly ten-thirty when Laura Wilcox called the hotel?" Sam asked him.

"At exactly ten-thirty," Jake confirmed. "Are you thinking of tracing it, Mr. Deegan? I mean, if she used her cell phone, you'd be able to trace the area where the call was made, isn't that right?"

"Yes, that's right," Sam said irritably. This kid was a know-it-all. But he was only trying to be helpful, so Sam was inclined to cut him some slack.

"I'll be happy to continue to keep my ear to the ground for you," Jake said, his voice now cheerful. The thought that Laura Wilcox might be in danger and that he was assisting the investigation to locate her filled him with a feeling of importance.

"Do that," Sam said, then reluctantly added, "and thanks, Jake."

Sam pushed the end button on his phone, sat up, and swung his legs out of the bed. He knew that at least for the next few hours there was no question of sleep. He had to let Jean know that Laura had been in contact with the hotel, and he had to get an order from a judge to look at the hotel's telephone records. He knew that the Glen-Ridge had caller ID. When he got the phone number, he would subpoena the phone company to find out the name of the subscriber and the locale of the antenna that had carried the call.

Judge Hagen in Goshen was probably the nearest judge in Orange County authorized to issue the order. As he dialed the district attorney's office to get Hagen's phone number, Sam realized it was some measure of the level of his own unease about Laura that he was now planning to disturb the sleep of a notoriously cantankerous judge rather than wait until morning to start trying to trace the missing woman.

39

Jean had set the volume of her cell phone at the highest level, afraid that when she went to bed she might miss a call. Sam had suggested that whoever was contacting her about Lily might go one step further and call her. "Hang on to the idea that this may be all about money," he said. "Somebody wants you to believe that Lily is in danger. Let's hope his next move might be to speak to you. If he does, we can trace the call."

He had managed to calm her down somewhat. "Jean, if you let yourself get paralyzed with worry, you're going to be your own worst enemy. You tell me that you confided to no one that you had a baby and that in Chicago you were known by your mother's maiden name. But somebody found out nonetheless, and that may have happened recently or it may have happened nineteen and a half years ago when the baby was born. Who knows? You've got to help yourself now. Try to remember if you saw anyone in Dr. Connors' office when you consulted him, maybe a nurse or secretary who figured out why you were there and who was nosey enough to find out where your baby was taken. Don't forget, you've become a celebrity now, with your best-selling book. Your new contract with your publisher was brought up during your interviews. My bet is that somebody who has access to Lily has decided to blackmail you by threatening her. I'll go to see the pastor of St. Thomas in the morning, and you start making a list of anyone you got friendly with at that time, especially anyone who might have had access to your records."

Sam's calm reasoning had the effect of snapping Jean's growing panic. After she said good-bye to him, she sat at the desk with a pen and notepad and wrote on the first page: DR. CONNORS' OFFICE.

His nurse had been a cheerful heavyset woman of about fifty, she remembered. Peggy. That was her name. Her last name was Irish and began with a K. Kelly . . . Kennedy . . . Keegan . . . It will come to me, I know it will, she thought.

It was a beginning.

The sharp ring of her cell phone made her jump. She glanced at the clock as she picked it up. It was almost eleven. Laura, she thought. Maybe she's come back.

Sam's message that Laura had called the desk clerk should have been reassuring, but Jean heard the concern in his voice. "You're not sure that she's all right, are you?" she asked.

"Not yet, but at least she did call."

Which means that she's still alive, Jean thought. That's what he's saying. She chose her words carefully. "Do you think that for some reason Laura may not be able to come back here?"

"Jean, I meant for this call to reassure you about Laura, but I guess I'd better level with you. The fact is that two people who heard the call have confirmed that she sounded distressed. Laura and you are the only two lunch table girls still alive. Until we know exactly where she is and who she's with, you've got to be very, very careful."

40

She knew he was going to kill her. It was only a question of when. Incredibly, after he left, she had fallen asleep. Light was flickering through the closed blinds, so it must be morning. Is it Monday or Tuesday? Laura wondered as she tried not to become fully awake.

Saturday night when they'd gotten here, he had poured champagne for them and toasted her. Then he'd said, "Halloween is coming soon. Want to see the mask I bought?"

He was wearing the face of an owl, each enlarged eye with a wide black pupil set in a sickly yellow iris, and edged with tufts of grayish down that darkened into deep brown around the pointed beak and narrow mouth. I laughed, Laura remembered, because I thought that was what he was expecting. But I could sense then that something had happened to him—he had changed. Even before he took off the mask and grabbed my hands, I knew I was trapped.

He dragged her upstairs, tied her wrists and her ankles together, and covered her mouth with a gag, being careful to leave it loose enough to be sure she didn't choke. Then he tied a rope across her waist and fastened it to the frame of the bed. "Did you ever read *Mommie Dearest?*" he'd asked. "Joan Crawford used to tie her kids to the bed to make sure they didn't get up at night. She called it 'safe sleep.' "

Then he'd made her begin to recite the line about the owl in the tree, the line from that grade school play. Over and over again he made her say it, and then he made her imitate the girls at the lunch table, laughing at him. And each time, she could see the murderous anger building in his eyes. "You all laughed at me," he said. "I despise you, Laura. The sight of you revolts me."

When he left her, he deliberately put his cell phone on the top of the dresser. "Just think, Laura. If you could reach this phone, you could call for help. But don't do it. The cords will tighten if you try to open them. Take my word for it."

She had tried anyway, and now her wrists and ankles were throbbing with pain. Her mouth was parched. Laura tried to moisten her lips. Her tongue touched the rough cloth of the sock he had taped over her mouth, and she felt bile rise in her throat. If she got sick, she would choke. Oh, God, please help me, she thought, panicking as she fought back the wave of nausea.

The first time he reappeared, there was some light in the room. It must have been Sunday afternoon, she figured. He untied my wrists and gave me soup and a roll. And he let me go to the bathroom. Then he came back a long time later. It was so dark, it must have been night. That was when he had me make the phone call. Why is he *doing* this to me? Why doesn't he just kill me and get it over with?

Her head was clearing. As she tried to move her wrists and ankles, the dull throbbing became intense pain. Saturday night. Sunday morning. Sunday night. It had to be Monday morning now. She stared at the cell phone. There was no way she could reach it. If he let her call anyone again, should she try to shout his name?

She could imagine the pillow muffling the sound before it escaped her throat, imagine the pillow pressing over her nostrils and mouth, choking life from her. I can't, Laura thought. I can't. Maybe if I don't upset him, someone will realize that I may be in trouble and try to find me. They can trace calls from cell phones. I *know* they can. They can find out who owns his phone.

That hope was the only chance she had, but it gave her the faintest trickle of relief. Jean, she thought. He intends to kill her, too. They say people can project thoughts. I'm going to try to send mine to Jean. She closed her eyes and imagined Jean as she had looked at the dinner, dressed in her royal blue evening gown. Moving her lips under the tape, she began to say his name aloud. "Jean, I'm with him. He killed the other girls. He's going to kill us. Help me, Jean. I'm in my old house. Find me, Jean!" Over and over she whispered his name.

"I forbade you to use my name."

She had not heard him come back. Even with the gag over her mouth, Laura's scream broke the silence of the room that had been hers for the first sixteen years of her life.

41

Monday morning, around dawn, Jean finally drifted off into a heavy but fitful sleep in which vague, undefined dreams of urgency and helplessness pulled her to momentary consciousness. But when she became fully awake, she was shocked to see that it was almost nine-thirty.

She considered ordering room service, then vetoed the idea of having even a continental breakfast in this room. It felt cramped and depressing, and the gloomy colors of the walls, bedspread, and window drapery made her long for her comfortable home in Alexandria. Ten years ago, in an estate sale, she had bought a seventy-year-old Federal-style, two-story house that had been owned by the same recluse for forty years. It had been dirty and neglected and cluttered, but she had fallen in love with it. Her friends had tried to dissuade her, saying such an undertaking was a bottomless pit of financial woes, but now they confessed that they'd been wrong.

Beyond mouse droppings, peeling wallpaper, the soiled carpet, dripping sinks, and the filthy stove and refrigerator, she had seen the high ceilings, oversized windows, and generous rooms, and the spectacular view of the Potomac that was then obscured by overgrown trees.

She'd gone for broke, buying the house and having the roof replaced. After that she had done the minor repairs herself, scrubbing and painting and wallpapering. She'd even sanded the parquet floors that had been an unexpected bonus, discovered when she pulled up the ragged carpet.

Working on the house was therapeutic for me, Jean thought as she showered, washed her hair, and toweled it dry. It was the place I dreamed of living in when I was growing up. Her mother had been allergic to flowers and plants. With an unconscious smile, she thought of the conservatory off her kitchen where every day fresh flowers bloomed.

The colors she had used throughout the house were those that to her meant cheer and warmth: yellows and blues and greens and reds. Not a single beige wall, her friends joked. The advance on her last contract had made it possible for her to panel her library and office as well as remodel the kitchen and bathrooms. Her home was her haven, her retreat, her sense of accomplishment. Because it was not far from Mount Vernon, she had jokingly named it Mount Vernon, Jr.

Being here in this hotel, even totally aside from her need to find Lily, had brought back the painful memory of all the years she had lived in Cornwall. It had made her feel once again like the girl whose father and mother were the joke of the town.

It made her remember how it felt to be desperately in love with Reed and then have to hide the grief of his death from everyone. All these years I've wondered if I made a mistake in giving up Lily, she thought. Coming back here, I'm beginning to understand that without my parents helping me, it would have been just about impossible to keep her and care for her properly.

As she dried and brushed her hair, she realized that she believed Sam Deegan's premise that the threat to Lily was all about money. "Jean," he had said, "think about this. Is there one single person who has a reason to want to hurt you? Have you ever gotten a job someone else wanted? Have you ever 'skunked' anyone, as the kids would say?"

"Never" had been her honest reply.

Sam had somehow managed to convince her that whoever was contacting her would soon demand money. But if it *is* about money, I believe that someone from around here learned I was pregnant, Jean thought, and that person was able to find out who adopted my baby. And maybe because there was a lot of talk about the reunion and publicity noting that I was one of the honorees, that person decided it was the right time to contact me.

As she looked in the bathroom mirror, she realized that she was startlingly pale. She ordinarily wore little makeup in the daytime, but now she touched her cheeks with blush and deliberately selected a lip color a little deeper than usual.

The realization that she was probably going to be staying in Cornwall for at least a few days meant that she had brought several changes of clothing. She decided today to wear a favorite cranberry turtleneck sweater over dark gray slacks.

Her determination to take action to find Lily had removed some of her terrible sense of helplessness. She clipped on earrings and gave a final brush to her hair. She put the brush down on the dresser, realizing it was the same size and shape as the one she had received in the mail with the strands of Lily's hair.

At that moment the name of the nurse who had been in Dr. Connors' office passed through her mind: Peggy Kimball.

Jean yanked open the drawer of the night table and pulled out the phone book. A quick look disclosed several Kimballs, but she decided that the one she would try first was the listing "Kimball, Stephen and Margaret." It wasn't too early to call. A woman's voice was on the answering machine: "Hi. Steve and Peggy aren't here now. At the tone please leave a message with your phone number, and we'll get back to you."

Can you remember a voice after twenty years, or am I just hoping I remember that voice? Jean asked herself as she carefully chose her words. "Peggy, I'm Jean Sheridan. If you were a nurse in Dr. Connors' office twenty years ago, it's terribly important that I speak with you. Will you please call me at this number as soon as possible."

While the phone book was open, she turned to the "C" listings. Dr. Edward Connors would have been at least seventy-five by now if he had lived. The odds were his wife was somewhere around that age as well. Sam Deegan was going to ask the pastor of St. Thomas about her, but maybe she was still listed. The doctor had lived on Winding Way; there was a Mrs. Dorothy Connors listed on Winding Way. Feeling hopeful, Jean dialed the number. The silvery voice of an older woman answered. When she hung up the phone a few minutes later, Jean had an appointment to visit Mrs. Dorothy Connors at eleven-thirty that morning.

42

On Monday morning at ten-thirty, Sam Deegan was in the office of Rich Stevens, the district attorney of Orange County, filling him in on the missing Laura Wilcox and the threat to Lily.

"I served the order for the telephone records of the Glen-Ridge House at one this morning," he said. "Both the clerk and that kid from Stonecroft are positive that it was Laura Wilcox who made the call, but they also agree that she sounded distressed. The hotel records showed that it was a 917 number on the ID, so we know she called from a cell phone. The judge was very unhappy at having his sleep interrupted last night.

"I served the subpoena for the subscriber's name and address, but I had to wait until 9:00 A.M. when the telephone business office was open."

"What did you find out from the records?" Stevens asked.

"The kind of information that makes me sure Wilcox is in trouble. The phone was one of those that are bought with one hundred minutes of available calling time and then discarded."

"The kind used by drug dealers and terrorists," Stevens snapped.

"Or, in this case, maybe a kidnapper. The cell site is Beacon in Dutchess County, and you know how wide an area that covers. I've already talked to our tech guys, and they tell me there are two more power stations in Woodbury and New Windsor. If a new call comes in, we can triangulate it and pinpoint the location it's being made from. We could also do that if the power was left on, but unfortunately it's been turned off."

"I never turn off the power on my cell phone," Stevens commented.

"Neither do I. Most people don't. That's another reason to believe that Laura Wilcox was forced to make that phone call. She has her own phone registered to her name. Why wouldn't she use that, and why isn't it on now?"

He then laid out his suggested course of action. "I want to get rap sheets on all the graduates who attended the reunion," he said, "both men and women. A lot of them haven't been back here in twenty years. Maybe we'll come up with something from someone's past, find someone who has a history of violence or has been institutionalized. I want the relatives of the five dead women from the lunch table to be contacted to see if there was anything suspicious about their deaths. We're also trying to contact Laura's parents. They're on a cruise."

"Five from one lunch table and a sixth one missing," Stevens said incredulously. "If there isn't something suspicious, it's because it wasn't noticed. If I were you, I'd start with the last one. It's so recent that if the cops in L.A. know about the other women, they may take a hard look at labeling Alison Kendall's death a drowning accident. We'll send for all of the police reports in all of those cases."

"The office at Stonecroft is sending over a list of the graduates who attended the reunion, as well as a list of the other people who were at the dinner," Sam said. "They have addresses and phone numbers of all the graduates and at least some of the townspeople who attended. Of course, some people bought a table and didn't provide names of guests, so it will take extra time to find out who they are." Exhausted, Sam could not conceal a yawn.

It was an acknowledgment of the sense of urgency he had communicated to the district attorney that Rich Stevens did not suggest his veteran investigator catch some sleep. Instead he said, "Get some of the other guys started on doing the follow-up, Sam. Where are you going now?"

Sam's smile was rueful. "I have an appointment with a priest," he said, "and I'm hoping he'll be the one to do the confessing."

43

The discovery of the body of Helen Whelan became a major story for the media. The disappearance of the popular teacher forty-eight hours earlier had already been given heavy coverage, but now the confirmation of her murder was a prime interest story because it had also triggered alarm throughout the small towns of the Hudson Valley.

The fact that her dog had been savagely attacked and his leash was still wrapped around the victim's wrist when her body was found gave added spice to the possibility that a random or serial killer was on the loose in this area that was normally drenched in history and tradition.

The Owl had dozed intermittently throughout Sunday night. After his first visit to Laura at ten-thirty, he'd managed to catch a few hours of rest. Then his dawn visit had given him the satisfaction of reducing her to trembling pleas for mercy—mercy she had denied him in their school years together, he had reminded her. After that second visit he had showered for a long time, hoping that the hot water would help relieve the terrible throbbing in his arm. The wound from the dog bite was festering. He had stopped at the old drugstore in town, where he used to shop as a kid, but then he'd walked out immediately. He had been about to pick up peroxide and antibiotic salves and bandages. Then it had occurred to him that the cops weren't necessarily stupid. They might have put a notice out to local pharmacies to watch for someone buying those kinds of medical supplies.

Instead he went to one of the big chains and bought shaving supplies, toothpaste, vitamins, crackers and pretzels and sodas, and then, in a moment of inspiration, he'd added cosmetics, cold cream, moisturizing lotion, and deodorant. Only then had he thrown into the mix the supplies he needed, the peroxide, bandages, salves.

He hoped he wasn't getting a fever. His body felt warm, and he knew his face was flushed. With all the useless camouflage items he had tossed into the basket at the drugstore, he had managed to forget to include aspirin. But that he could safely buy anywhere. Most of the time, most of the world has a headache, he thought, smiling to himself at the mental image conjured up by that reasoning.

He turned up the volume on the television. They were showing pictures of the crime scene. He observed intently how muddy it seemed. He hadn't remembered the area as being that swampy. That meant the tires of his rental car were probably embedded with dirt from that area. It would be wise to leave the car in the garage of the house where so far he was allowing Laura to continue to live. He'd rent another mid-priced, mid-sized, unobtrusive black sedan. That way, if for any reason anyone started to nose around and check the cars of the reunion group, his would be passed over.

As The Owl was selecting a jacket from the closet, a breaking story came across the screen: "Young reporter from Stonecroft Academy in Cornwall-on-Hudson reveals the disappearance of actress Laura Wilcox may be linked to a fiend he calls 'The Lunch Table Serial Killer.' "

44

"Monsignor, I cannot emphasize sufficiently the urgency of our request," Sam Deegan told Monsignor Robert Dillon, pastor of the Church of St. Thomas of Canterbury. They were in the rectory office. The monsignor, a thin man with prematurely white hair and rimless glasses that illuminated intelligent gray eyes, was behind his desk. The faxes Jean had received were spread out in front of him. In a chair directly across from the desk, Sam was putting Lily's hairbrush back in a plastic bag.

"As you can see, the latest communication suggests that Dr. Jean Sheridan's daughter is in grave danger. We intend to try to trace her original birth certificate, but we are not even sure if it was registered here or in Chicago where the baby was born," Sam continued.

Even as he spoke, he felt the hopelessness of trying to make a quick breakthrough. Monsignor Dillon couldn't be more than in his early forties. Clearly he had not been around twenty years ago when Lily might have been baptized in this church, and, of course, her adoptive parents would have registered her under their surname and her new first name.

"I do understand the urgency, and I'm sure you understand that I must be cautious," Monsignor Dillon said slowly. "But, Sam, the biggest problem is that people don't necessarily baptize babies within a few weeks or even months anymore. It used to be that an infant was baptized within six weeks of its birth. Now we see them toddling in to receive the sacrament. We don't approve of that trend, but it does exist and *did* exist even twenty years ago. This is a fairly large and busy parish, and not only our own parishioners but frequently the grandchildren of parishioners are baptized here."

"I understand, but perhaps if you could start with the three months after Lily's birth, we could at least try to track those baby girls. Most people aren't secretive about adoptions, are they?"

"No, as a rule, they're proud of the fact they're adoptive parents."

"Then unless the adoptive parents themselves are behind these faxes to Dr. Sheridan, I think they would want to know of a possible threat to their daughter."

"Yes, they would. I'll have my secretary compile the list, but you do understand that before I give it to you, I will have to contact all the people listed personally and explain only that a girl adopted at that time may be in danger."

"Monsignor, that could take time, and that's just what we may not have," Sam protested.

"Father Arella can work with me. I'll have my secretary make the calls, and while I'm speaking with one party, she'll alert the next to stand by to hear from me. It shouldn't take that long."

"And what about the ones you don't reach? Monsignor, this nineteen-year-old girl may be in grave danger."

Monsignor Dillon picked up the fax, his expression deepening with concern as he studied it. "Sam, as you say, this last communication is frightening, but you can understand why we have to be careful. To protect us from possible legal problems, get a subpoena. That way we can release the names to you immediately. But I would suggest that you allow me to talk to as many of these families as possible."

"Thank you, sir. I won't take any more of your time right now."

They both stood up. "It occurred to me that your correspondent is something of a Shakespearean scholar," Monsignor Dillon observed. "Not too many people would have used a fairly obscure quote like this one about the lilies."

"That occurred to me as well, Monsignor." Sam paused. "I should have thought to ask this immediately: Are any of the priests who were assigned here at the time Jean's baby might have been baptized still with the diocese?"

"Father Doyle was the assistant pastor, and he died years ago. Monsignor Sullivan was the pastor at that time. He moved to Florida with his sister and brother-in-law. I can give you the latest address we have for him."

"I'd like to have that."

"It's right here in my file drawer. I'll give it to you now." He opened the drawer, pulled out a folder, glanced in it, and wrote a name, address, and phone number on a slip of paper. He handed it to Sam, saying, "Dr. Connors' widow is a parishioner. If you wish, I can call and ask her to see you. She might remember something about that adoption."

"Thanks, but that won't be necessary. I spoke to Jean Sheridan just before coming here. She found Mrs. Connors' address in the phone book and is probably on her way to see her right now."

As they walked to the door, Monsignor Dillon said, "Sam, I just remembered something. Alice Sommers is our parishioner also. Are you the investigator who has continued to work on her daughter's case?"

"Yes, I am."

"She has told me about you. I hope you know how much comfort it has given her to know that you haven't stopped trying to find Karen's murderer."

"I'm glad that it's helped her. Alice Sommers is a very brave woman."

They stood at the door. "I was shocked to hear on the radio this morning that the body of the woman who was walking her dog has been found," Monsignor Dillon commented. "Is your office involved with that case?"

"Yes, we are."

"I understand that, like Karen Sommers, it appears to be a random killing and that she was also stabbed to death. I know it seems implausible, but do you think there is any chance that there is a connection between those murders?"

"Monsignor, Karen Sommers died twenty years ago," Sam said carefully. He did not want to share the fact that the same possibility had been preying on his mind, particularly since the stab wounds had been in exactly the same area of the chest.

The Monsignor shook his head. "I guess I'd better leave the detecting to you. It was just a thought that occurred to me, and because you're so close to the Sommers case, I felt I should mention it." He opened the front door and shook Sam's hand. "God bless you, Sam. I'll pray for Lily, and I'll get back to you with the names as fast as we can put them together."

"Thank you, sir. Do pray for Lily, and while you're at it, remember Laura Wilcox."

"The actress?"

"Yes. We're afraid she's in trouble, too. No one has seen her since Saturday night."

Monsignor Dillon stared at Sam's retreating back. Laura Wilcox was at the Stonecroft reunion, he thought incredulously. Has something happened to her as well? Dear God, what's going on here?

With a fervent silent prayer for the safety of both Lily and Laura, he returned to his office and dialed his secretary. "Janet, please drop everything else you're doing and get out the baptismal records of nineteen years ago, from March through June. As soon as Father

Arella returns, tell him I have a job for him and to cancel any other plans he may have made for the day."

"Of course, Monsignor." Janet hung up the phone and looked longingly at the grilled cheese and bacon sandwich and container of coffee that had just been delivered to her desk. As she pushed back her chair and begrudgingly got to her feet, she mumbled to herself, "My God, from the tone of his voice you'd think it was a matter of life and death."

45

Dorothy Connors was a frail septuagenarian who Jean could see at first glance suffered from rheumatoid arthritis. She moved slowly, and the joints of her fingers were swollen. Her face showed lines of pain, and she wore her white hair very short, probably, Jean thought, because raising her arms was a distinct effort.

Her home was one of the desirable high-up properties that overlooked the Hudson. She invited Jean to the sunroom off the living room where, as she explained, she spent most of her waking time.

Her vivid brown eyes brightened when she talked about her husband. "Edward was the most wonderful man and husband and doctor who ever walked the face of the earth," she said. "It was that dreadful fire that killed him, the loss of his office and all his records. It brought on his heart attack."

"Mrs. Connors, I explained to you on the phone that I've been getting threats about my daughter. She would be nineteen and a half now. I am frantic to find her adoptive parents and warn them about the possible danger to her. I was a girl from this town. Please help me. Did Dr. Connors talk to you about me? I could see where he would. My mother and father were the town joke, with their public quarrels, and they only stayed together long enough to shove me into college. That was why your husband understood I could never go to them for help. He arranged the cover-up story, establishing my reason for going to Chicago. He even came out and delivered the baby himself in the emergency section of the nursing home."

"Yes, he did that for a number of girls. He wanted to help them maintain their privacy. Jean, fifty years ago it wasn't easy for a girl to have a baby out of wedlock. Do you know that the actress Ingrid Bergman was denounced in Congress when she gave birth to an illegitimate child? Standards of behavior change—for better or worse, you decide. Today most of the world doesn't think a thing about an unmarried woman bearing and raising a child, but my husband was old-fashioned. Twenty years ago he was deeply concerned about protecting his young pregnant mothers' privacy, even with me. Until you told me, I never even knew that you had been his patient."

"But you *did* know about my parents."

Dorothy Conners looked at Jean for a long moment. "I knew they had problems. I also saw them at church and chatted with them a number of times. My guess, my dear, is that you only remember the bad times. They were also attractive, intelligent people who unfortunately were ill-suited to each other."

Jean felt the sting of a rebuke and in an odd way sensed that she had been put on the defensive. "I can guarantee you that they were ill-suited to each other," she said, hoping that the anger she felt was not reflected in her voice. "Mrs. Connors, I *do* appreciate that you let me visit you on such short notice, but now I'll be brief. My daughter may be in very real danger. I know that you fiercely guard Dr. Connors' memory, but if you know anything about where he might have placed her, you owe it to me and to her to be honest with me."

"Before God, Edward never discussed patients in your situation with me, and I never heard your name mentioned by him."

"And he kept no records at home, and all his office records are gone?"

"Yes, they are. The entire building was so totally destroyed that arson has always been suspected but never proved. Certainly no records survived."

Clearly Dorothy Connors could give her no help. Jean rose to go. "I remember that Peggy Kimball was the office nurse when I saw Dr. Connors. I've left a message for her and hope she'll call me. Maybe she'll know something. Thank you, Mrs. Connors. Please don't get up. I'll find my way out."

She offered her hand to Dorothy Connors and then was shocked to see that the expression on the other woman's face could only be construed as extreme alarm.

46

Mark Fleischman checked into the Glen-Ridge House at one o'clock, dropped off his bag, phoned Jean's room but got no answer, and then went down to the dining room. He was surprised and pleased to see Jean sitting alone at a corner table, and with quick strides, he hurried over to her.

"Are you waiting for anyone, or would you like company?" he asked, then watched as the somber expression on her face was replaced by a warm smile.

"Mark, I didn't expect to see you! Of course, sit down. I was just about to order lunch, and nobody's planning to join me."

"Then consider yourself joined." He settled on the chair opposite her. "I put my briefcase with my cell phone in the trunk of the car by mistake," he said, "so I didn't get your message till I unpacked last night. I called the hotel early this morning, and the operator told me that Laura wasn't back and that the police were checking phone records. That's when I decided to rearrange my schedule and come back. I flew down and rented a car."

"That was very nice of you," Jean said sincerely. "We're all terribly worried about Laura." Quickly she gave him a rundown of what had transpired since he had left after the brunch the day before.

"You say you came back to the hotel with Sam Deegan, that man you were having a drink with the other night, and when you knew Laura was missing, he began an investigation?" Mark queried.

"Yes," Jean said, realizing she had awakened Mark's curiosity as to why Sam Deegan had been with her in the first place. "Sam followed me to the hotel because I was giving him something that our friend Alice Sommers is interested in seeing."

Alice *is* interested in seeing the faxes, she told herself, so it's not a complete fabrication. Looking across the table at Mark and seeing the concern in his eyes made her want to tell him about Lily, to ask him as a psychiatrist if he thought the threats were genuine, or whether someone was only setting her up for blackmail.

"Ready for menus?" the waitress chirped.

"Yes, thank you."

They both decided on a club sandwich and tea. "Coffee for breakfast, tea for lunch, and a glass of wine to start dinner," Mark said. "I've noticed that seems to be your routine, too, Jeannie."

"I guess it is."

"I've noticed a lot of things about you this weekend, and they reminded me of the years we were at Stonecroft."

"Such as?"

"Well, you always were very smart in school. You were also very quiet. And I remember that you were very sweet—that hasn't changed. Then I thought about one time during the freshman year when I was really down and you were very kind to me."

"I don't remember that."

"I won't go into it, but you were, and I also admired the way you held your head high when you were upset about your parents."

"Not always." Jean cringed inwardly, remembering the times she had started crying in class from the stress of the arguments at home.

It was as though he could read her mind, Jean realized, as Mark Fleischman continued. "I tried to hand you my handkerchief one day when you were upset, but you just shook your head and dabbed furiously at your eyes with a soggy Kleenex. I wanted to help you then, and I want to help you now. Coming from the airport I heard on the radio that the reporter kid who hounded us at the reunion is talking to the media about what he calls 'The Lunch Table Serial Killer.' Even if you're not worried about that possibility, I am. And with Laura missing, you're the only one of those girls left."

"I wish I was just worried about myself," Jean said.

"Then what are you worried about? Come on, Jean, tell me. I am trained to spot stress in people, and if I've seen anyone under stress, it was you the other night when you were talking to Sam Deegan, who you now tell me is an investigator from the district attorney's office."

The busboy was pouring water into their glasses. It gave Jean a moment to think. I *do* remember when Mark wanted to give me his handkerchief, she thought. I was so angry at myself for crying, and equally angry at him for noticing. He wanted to help me then. He wants to help me now. Should I tell him about Lily?

She saw him studying her and knew he was waiting her out. He wants me to talk to him. Should I? She looked directly back at him. He's one of those men who looks as good with glasses as without them, she thought. He has wonderful brown eyes. Those little specks of yellow in them are like sunlight.

She shrugged and raised her eyebrows. "You remind me of a professor I had in college who, when he asked a question, would just stare at you until he got an answer."

"That's exactly what I'm doing, Jean. One of my patients calls it my wise owl look."

The waitress came to the table with the sandwiches. "Right back with your tea," she said cheerfully.

Jean waited until the tea was poured, then said quietly, "Your wise owl look has convinced me, Mark. I guess I will tell you about Lily."

47

Sam Deegan's first act upon arriving at his office was to call the district attorney in Los Angeles and ask to be put in touch with Carmen Russo, the investigator who had headed the inquiry into the death of Alison Kendall.

"Death by accidental drowning was the determination, and we're sticking by that," Russo told him. "Her friends agree that she went for an early swim every morning. Door was open to the house, but nothing was taken. Pricey jewelry on top of her vanity. Five hundred dollars cash and credit cards in her wallet. She was extremely neat. Nothing out of place anywhere in the house, on the grounds, or in the pool house. Except for being dead, she was in perfect health. Her heart was strong. No sign of alcohol or drugs."

"Any suggestion at all of violence?" Sam asked.

"A slight bruise on her shoulder, but that was it. Without more evidence, it's not enough to suggest that it was a homicide. We took photographs, of course, but then released the body."

"Yes, I know. Her ashes are buried here in the family plot," Sam said. "Thanks, Carmen." He realized he was reluctant to break the connection. "What is going on with her home?"

"Her parents live in Palm Springs. They're up in years. From what I understand, they have Kendall's housekeeper still taking care of the place until they can bring themselves to have an estate sale. They can't be hungry for money. In that location the house has to be worth a couple of million bucks."

Discouraged, Sam hung up the phone. His every instinct told him that Alison Kendall had not died a natural death. By pointing out that the five dead women from the same class at Stonecroft had shared the same lunch table, Jake Perkins had latched onto something. Sam was sure of it. But if Kendall's death hadn't raised suspicion, how much luck would he have in trying to establish a pattern of murder with the four others who had died over a stretch of nearly twenty years?

His phone rang—it was Rich Stevens, the district attorney. "Sam, thanks to that big mouth Perkins, we've had to call a press conference to make some kind of statement. Come on in here, and we'll figure out what to say."

Five minutes later, in Stevens' office, they debated the best way to defuse the media onslaught. "We believe we may have a serial killer. We've got to make this guy feel secure," Sam argued. "We tell it like it is. Alison Kendall's death was the result of accidental drowning. Even knowing that four other women who were once close friends have died, the Los Angeles police find nothing suspicious about her death. Laura Wilcox phoned the hotel to say her plans were indefinite. It is nothing more than a matter of conjecture on the part of a hotel employee that she sounded nervous. She is an adult with the right to privacy and should be treated as such. We are making inquiries into the deaths of the other women who shared the lunch table years ago, but it is obvious the accidents that claimed their lives—or, in the case of Gloria Martin, her suicide—indicate no pattern that suggests a serial killer."

"I think a statement like this makes us look pretty damn naïve," Rich Stevens said flatly.

"I *want* us to look naïve," Sam shot back. "I want whoever is out there to think we're a bunch of dopes. If Laura is still alive, I don't want him to panic before we have a chance to save her."

There was a tap at the door. One of the young new investigators on the staff was obviously excited. "Sir, we're going through the student personnel folders of the Stonecroft graduates who attended the reunion and may have something on one of them, Joel Nieman.

"What about him?" Stevens asked.

"When he was a senior, he was questioned about the fact that Alison Kimball's locker was tampered with. The screws had been removed from the hinges so that when she opened the door, it fell on her and knocked her down. She suffered a mild concussion."

"Why was he questioned?" Sam asked.

"Because he was really upset about something she had written in the school newspaper. The senior year school play was *Romeo and Juliet.* Nieman had the part of Romeo, and Kendall wrote something really nasty about him not being able to remember his lines. He prided himself on memorizing Shakespeare, and went around the school saying what he'd like to do to her. He told everybody the problem had been a couple of seconds of stage fright and was not a case of him forgetting lines. Right after that, she got bowled over by the locker door.

"There's other stuff, too. He has a lousy temper and has been hauled in after a couple of bar fights. He was almost indicted last year for some imaginative accounting practices, and his wife is away most of the time, like right now."

Monsignor Dillon and I both caught the fact that the guy who's contacting Jean about Lily quoted an obscure sonnet from Shakespeare, Sam thought.

He stood up. "Romeo, Romeo, wherefore art thou, Romeo?"

As Rich Stevens and the young investigator stared at him, Sam said, "That's exactly what I'm going to find out right now. Then we'll see what other lines from Shakespeare Joel Nieman might be able to quote for us."

48

At six-thirty The Owl returned to the house and crept up the stairs. This time Laura had obviously sensed his presence or had anticipated that he would be visiting, because when he entered the room and turned the flashlight on her, he could see that she was already trembling.

"Hello, Laura," he whispered. "Are you glad I'm back?"

Her breathing was harsh and shallow. He watched as she tried to shrink back against the mattress.

"Laura, you must answer me. Here, let me loosen the tape. Better than that, I'll take it off. I brought you something to eat. Now, are you glad I'm back?"

"Ye-yes, I'm glad," she whispered.

"Laura, you're stuttering. I'm surprised at you. You ridicule people who stutter. Show me how you ridicule them. No, never mind. I can't stay too long. I brought you a peanut butter and jelly sandwich and a glass of milk. You used to eat that every day in grammar school. Do you remember that?"

"Yes . . . yes."

"I'm glad you remember. It's important that we don't forget the past. Now I'll allow you to use the bathroom. Then you may eat your sandwich and drink the milk."

With a quick gesture he pulled her to a sitting position and cut the cords on her wrists. The movement was so fast that Laura swayed and reached out her hand. Inadvertently she grasped The Owl's arm.

He gasped with pain and clenched his fist, ready to strike her, but then he stopped. "You couldn't have known that my arm is very sore, so I must not hold it against you. But never touch that arm again. Understand?"

Laura nodded.

"Stand up. After you have visited the bathroom, I will permit you to sit in the chair and eat."

With tentative, unsteady steps, Laura obeyed. The night light in the bathroom made it possible for her to see the taps on the sink and turn them on. With a hurried gesture she splashed water on her face and hands and smoothed back her hair. If I can only stay alive, she thought. They've got to be looking for me. Please God, let them be looking for me.

The handle of the bathroom door turned. "Laura, it's time."

Time! Was he going to kill her now? God . . . please . . .

The door opened. The Owl pointed to the chair beside the dresser. Silently, Laura shuffled over to it and sat down.

"Go ahead," he urged. "Start to eat." He picked up the flashlight and directed the light on her neck so that he could watch her expression without blinding her. He was pleased to see that she was crying again.

"Laura, you're so afraid, aren't you? And I bet you're wondering how I knew that you ridiculed me. Let me tell you a story. Twenty years ago this weekend a bunch of us were home from our different colleges and got together one night. There was a party. Now, as you know, I was never part of the crowd, of the inner circle. Far from it, in fact. But for some reason I was invited to that party, and you were there. Lovely Laura. That night you were sitting on the lap of your latest conquest, Dick Gormley, our erstwhile baseball star. I was eating my heart out, Laura, that's how much of a crush I still had on you.

"Alison was at the party, of course. Quite drunk. She came over to me. I never liked her. Frankly, I was afraid of that tongue of hers—razor-sharp when she turned it on you. She reminded me that early in senior year I had had the temerity to ask you to go on a date. 'You . . . ' she said with a sneer and laughed. 'The owl asking Laura out.' And then Alison demonstrated for me how you mimicked me when we were in the second-grade school play. 'I am annnnnn . . . ow . . . owwwlll . . . and . . . and . . I . . . live . . . in . . . a . . . a . . .' "

"Laura, your imitation of me must have been superb. Alison assured me that the girls at your lunch table screamed with laughter every time they thought of it. And then you reminded them that I had been dopey enough to wet my pants onstage before I ran off. You even told them that."

Laura had been taking bites of the sandwich. Now he watched as she dropped it onto her lap. "I'm sorry. . . ."

"Laura, you still don't understand that you have lived twenty years too long. Let me tell you about it. The night of that party, I was drunk, too. I was so drunk that I forgot you had moved. I came here that night to kill you. I knew where your family kept the extra key under that fake rabbit in the backyard. The new people kept it there, too. I came into this house and up to this room. I saw the flow of hair on the pillow and thought it was you. Laura, I made a mistake when I stabbed Karen Sommers. I was killing *you*, Laura. I was killing *you!*

"The next morning I woke up vaguely remembering that I'd been here. Then I found out what had happened and realized that I was famous." The Owl's voice became rushed with excitement at the memory. "I didn't know Karen Sommers. No one even dreamed of connecting me to her, but that mistake liberated me. That morning I understood that I have the power of life and death. And I've been exercising it ever since. Ever since, Laura. Women all over the country."

He stood up. Laura's eyes were wide with fear; her mouth hung open; the sandwich lay in her lap. He leaned toward her. "Now I have to go, but think about me, Laura. Think how lucky you have been to have enjoyed a bonus twenty years of life."

In savagely quick movements, he tied her hands, taped her mouth, pulled her up from the chair, pushed her back on the bed, and fastened the long rope over her body.

"It began in this room, and it will end in this room, Laura," he said. "The final stage of the plan is about to unfold. Try to guess what it might be."

He was gone. Outside the moon was rising, and from the bed Laura could see the faint outline of the cell phone on top of the dresser.

49

At six-thirty Jean was in her hotel room when she finally received the call she'd been hoping would come. It was from Peggy Kimball, the nurse who had been in Dr. Connors' office when she was his patient. "That's a pretty urgent message, you left, Ms. Sheridan," Kimball said briskly. "What's going on?"

"Peggy, we met twenty years ago. I was a patient of Dr. Connors, and he arranged a private adoption for my baby. I need to talk to you about it."

For a long moment Peggy Kimball did not say anything. Jean could hear the voices of children in the background. "I'm sorry, Ms. Sheridan," Kimball said, a note of finality in her voice. "I simply cannot discuss the adoptions Dr. Connors handled. If you want to begin to trace your child, there are legal ways of going about it."

Jean could sense that Kimball was about to break the connection. "I've already been in touch with Sam Deegan, an investigator from the district attorney's office," she said hurriedly. "I have received three communications that can only be construed as threats to my daughter. Her adoptive parents have got to be warned to watch out for her. Please, Peggy. You were so kind to me then. Help me now, I beg you."

She was interrupted by Peggy Kimball's alarmed shout: "Tommy, I warn you. Don't throw that dish!"

Jean heard the sound of glass breaking.

"Oh, my God," Peggy Kimball said with a sigh. "Look, Ms. Sheridan, I'm baby-sitting my grandkids. I can't talk now."

"Peggy, can I meet you tomorrow? I'll show you the faxes I've received threatening my daughter. You can check on me. I'm a dean and professor of history at Georgetown. I'll give you the number of the president of the college. I'll give you Sam Deegan's number."

"Tommy, Betsy, don't go near that glass! Wait a minute. . . . by any chance are you the Jean Sheridan who wrote the book about Abigail Adams?"

"Yes."

"Oh, for heaven's sake! I loved it. I know all about you. I saw you on the *Today* show with Katie Couric. You two could be sisters. Will you still be at the Glen-Ridge tomorrow morning?"

"Yes, I will."

"I work in neonatal at the hospital. The Glen-Ridge is on the way there. I don't think I'll be any help to you, but do you want to have a cup of coffee around ten?"

"I would love to," Jean said. "Peggy, thank you, thank you."

"I'll call you from the lobby," Peggy Kimball said hurriedly, then her voice became alarmed. "Betsy, I warn you. Don't pull Tommy's hair! Oh, my God! Sorry, Jean, it's becoming a free-for-all here. See you tomorrow."

Jean replaced the receiver slowly. That sounds like mayhem, she thought, but in a crazy way, I envy Peggy Kimball. I envy her the normal problems of normal people. People who mind their grandkids and have to clean up messy babies and spilled food and broken dishes. People who can see and touch their daughters and tell them to drive carefully and be home by midnight.

She had been sitting at the desk of her room in the hotel when Kimball phoned. Scattered in front of her were the lists she had been trying to compile, mostly the names of people in the nursing home who had befriended her and also the professors at the University of Chicago where she had spent all her spare time taking extracurricular courses.

Now she massaged her temples, hoping to rub away the beginnings of a headache. In an hour, at seven-thirty, at Sam's request, they would be having dinner together in a private dining room on the hotel's mezzanine floor. The guests included the honorees, Gordon and Carter and Robby and Mark and me, Jean thought, and, of course, Jack, the chairman of the godforsaken reunion. What is Sam hoping to accomplish by getting all of us together again?

She realized that unburdening herself to Mark had been a mixed blessing. There was astonishment in his eyes when he said, "You mean that on graduation day at age eighteen, when you were tripping up to the stage to accept the History medal and a scholarship to Bryn Mawr, you were aware that you were expecting a baby and that the guy you loved was lying in a casket?"

"I don't expect either praise or blame for that," she had told him.

"For God's sake, Jean. I'm neither praising nor blaming you," he'd said. "But what an ordeal. I used to go to West Point to jog and had seen you once or twice with Reed Thornton, but I had no idea it was more than a casual friendship. What did you do after the graduation ceremony?"

"My mother and father and I had lunch. It was a really festive lunch. They had done their Christian duty by me and could now separate with a clear conscience. After we left the restaurant, I drove to West Point. Reed's funeral Mass had been that morning. I put the flowers my parents gave me at the graduation ceremony on Reed's grave."

"And shortly after that you saw Dr. Connors for the first time?"

"The next week."

"Jeannie," Mark had said, "I always felt that, like me, you were a survivor, but I can't imagine what you must have been going through, being alone at a time like that."

"Not alone. I gather somebody must have known about it or found out about it even then."

He had nodded and then said, "I've read up on your professional life, but what about your personal life? Is there someone special, or has there been someone special you might have confided in?"

Jean thought of the answer she had given him. "Mark, remember the words of the Robert Frost poem. 'But I have promises to keep, / And miles to go before I sleep. . . .' In a way I feel like that. Until now, when I've had to talk about her, there's never been a single soul I've ever wanted to tell about Lily. My life is very full. I love my job and love writing. I have plenty of friends, both men and women. But I'll be honest. I've always had a feeling that there is something unresolved in my life that has to be settled, a sense that in a way my life itself has been held in abeyance. Something needs to be finished before I can put this behind me. I think I'm beginning to understand the reason for that. I still wonder if I shouldn't have kept my baby, and now that she may need me I'm so helpless, I want to turn back the clock and have the chance to keep her this time."

Then she had seen the look on Mark's face. *Or are you setting up a manufactured scenario because of your need to find her?* He might as well have shouted the question. Instead he had said, "Jean, of course you must pursue this, and I'm glad Sam Deegan is helping you since you're obviously dealing with an unbalanced individual. However, as a psychiatrist, I warn you that you must be very careful. If because of these implied threats you are able to access confidential records, you may intrude into the life of a young woman who isn't ready or willing to meet *you*."

"You think that I have been sending those faxes to myself, don't you?" Jean winced, remembering how angry she had been when she realized that some people jumped to that conclusion.

"Of course I don't," Mark had said promptly. "But answer me this: If you received a call right now asking you to meet Lily, would you go?"

"Yes, I would."

"Jean, listen to what I'm saying. Someone who somehow found out about Lily may be deliberately getting you into a fever pitch so that you'll be vulnerable to rushing off to meet her. Jean, you've got to be careful. Laura is missing. The other girls at your table are dead."

He had left it at that.

Now Jean stood up. She was due downstairs for dinner in forty minutes. Maybe an aspirin would prevent the oncoming headache she sensed, and a hot bath would revive her, she thought.

The phone rang at seven-ten as she was stepping out of the tub. For a moment she debated about letting it ring, then grabbed a towel and rushed into the bedroom. "Hello."

"Hi, Jeannie," a smiling voice said.

Laura! It was Laura.

"Laura, where are you?"

"Where I'm having a lot of fun. Jeannie, tell those cops to pick up their jacks and go home. I'm having the time of my life. I'll call you soon. Bye, dear."

50

Late Monday afternoon Sam went to interview Joel Nieman at his office in Rye, New York.

After keeping him waiting in the reception area for nearly half an hour, Nieman invited him into his decidedly upscale private suite. His entire manner suggested ill-concealed annoyance at the interruption.

Doesn't look much like Romeo to me, Sam thought as he studied Nieman's pudgy features and dyed reddish brown hair.

Nieman airily dismissed the suggestion that he had made a date with Laura during the reunion. "I heard that nonsense about the lunch table killer on the radio," he volunteered. "That school reporter, Perkins, started it, I gather. They ought to put a net over his head and cart him away until he grows up. Listen, I was in class with those girls. I knew them all. The idea that their deaths are related is nonsense. Just start with Catherine Kane. Her car skidded into the Potomac when we were college freshmen. Cath was always a fast driver. Look up the number of speeding tickets she got in Cornwall during her senior year, and you'll see what I mean."

"That may be," Sam said, "but don't you think it's a remarkable case of lightning striking in the same place, not twice but *five* times?"

"Sure, it's pretty creepy that five girls from the same table died, but

I could introduce you to the guy who services our computers. His mother and his grandmother dropped dead of heart attacks on the same day thirty years apart. Day after Christmas. Maybe they realized how much they spent for presents, and it got to them. Could be, don't you think?"

Sam looked at Joel Nieman with acute distaste but also with the sense that underneath his show of disdain there was a sense of unease. "I understand your wife left the reunion on Saturday morning to go on a business trip."

"That's right."

"Were you alone at your home on Saturday night after the reunion dinner, Mr. Nieman?"

"As a matter of fact, I was. Those long-winded affairs make me sleepy."

This guy isn't the kind who goes home alone when his wife is away, Sam thought. He took a shot in the dark. "Mr. Nieman, you were observed leaving the parking lot with a woman in the car."

Joel Nieman raised his eyebrows. "Well, perhaps I did leave with a woman, but she wasn't pushing forty years old. Mr. Deegan, if you're on a fishing expedition with me because Laura took off with some guy and hasn't resurfaced, I suggest you call my lawyer. And now, if you'll excuse me, I have a number of phone calls to make."

Sam got to his feet and ambled toward the door, obviously in no haste. As he passed the bookcase, he paused and looked at the middle shelf. "You have quite a collection of Shakespeare, Mr. Nieman."

"I have always enjoyed the Bard."

"I understand you were Romeo in your senior play at Stonecroft."

"That's right."

Sam chose his words carefully. "Wasn't Alison Kendall critical of your performance?"

"She said I forgot my lines. I didn't forget them. I had a moment or two of stage fright. Period."

"Alison had an accident in school a few days after the play, didn't she?"

"I remember that. The door of her locker fell on her. All the guys were questioned about it. I always thought that they should have been talking to the girls. A lot of them couldn't stand her. Look, this is going to get you nowhere. As I told you, I would bet my bottom dollar the other four lunch table deaths were accidents. There's absolutely no pattern to them. On the other hand, Alison was a mean kid. She trampled on people. From what I read about her, she never changed. I could see where someone might decide she'd been swimming long enough the day she drowned."

He walked to the door and pointedly opened it. "Speed the parting guest," he said. "That's Shakespeare, too."

Sam hoped he was professional enough not to allow his face to show exactly what he thought of Nieman and his cavalier dismissal of Alison Kendall's death. "There's also a Danish proverb that says fish and guests smell after three days," he observed. Especially dead guests, he thought.

"That was more famously paraphrased by Benjamin Franklin," Joel Nieman said quickly.

"Are you familiar with the Shakespeare quote about dead lilies?" Sam asked. "It's somewhat in the same vein."

Nieman's laugh was an unpleasant, mirthless bark. " 'Lilies that fester smell far worse than weeds.' That's a line from one of his sonnets. Sure, I know it. In fact, it's one I think about a lot. My mother-in-law's name is Lily."

Sam drove from Rye to the Glen-Ridge House faster than he approved, allowing the speedometer to climb. He had asked the honorees and Jack Emerson to meet him for dinner at seven-thirty. His gut instinct had been that one of the five men—Carter Stewart, Robby Brent, Mark Fleischman, Gordon Amory, or Emerson—held the key to Laura's disappearance. Now, after interviewing Joel Nieman, he wasn't as sure.

In effect, Nieman had admitted that he did not go home alone the night of the dinner. At Stonecroft he had been the prime suspect in the locker incident. He'd almost gone to jail for assaulting another man in a bar fight. He made no attempt to conceal his satisfaction that Alison Kendall was dead.

At the very least, Joel Nieman could use a great deal more scrutiny, Sam reasoned.

It was exactly seven-thirty when Sam entered the Glen-Ridge House. On the way into the private room, he passed the omnipresent Jake Perkins, sprawled on a chair in the lobby. Perkins jumped to his feet. "Any new developments, sir?" he asked cheerfully.

If there were, you'd be the last to know, Sam thought, but he managed not to let his annoyance show in his voice. "Nothing to report, Jake. Why don't you go home?"

"Pretty soon I'll be on my way. Oh, here's Dr. Sheridan. I'd like to catch her for a minute."

Jean was coming out of the elevator. Even from a distance Sam could see that there was something about her that suggested distress. It was the way she walked so quickly across the lobby toward the dining room. That sense of urgency made his own step quicken to catch up with her.

They met at the door of the dining room. Jean started to say, "Sam, I heard from—" Then, noticing Jake Perkins, she closed her lips.

Perkins had overheard. "Who did you hear from, Dr. Sheridan? Was it Laura Wilcox?"

"Go away," Sam said firmly. He took Jean's arm, propelled her through the dining room door, and closed it firmly.

Carter Stewart, Gordon Amory, Mark Fleischman, Jack Emerson, and Robby Brent were already there. A small bar had been set up, and all the men stood around with glasses in hand. At the click of the door they all turned, but when they saw the expression on Jean's face, any greetings they were about to offer were forgotten.

"I just heard from Laura," she told them. "I just heard from Laura."

Over dinner the initial relief they all felt began to be replaced by uncertainty. "I was shocked to hear Laura's voice," Jean said. "But then she hung up before I could ask her anything."

"She didn't sound nervous or upset?" Jack Emerson asked.

"No. If anything, she sounded upbeat. But she didn't give me a chance to ask her a single question."

"Are you sure you were speaking to Laura?" Gordon Amory asked the question that Sam knew was on everyone's mind.

"I *think* I was," Jean said slowly. "But if you asked me to swear under oath that it was Laura, I couldn't do it. It *sounded* like her, but . . ." She hesitated. "I have friends in Virginia, a couple, who sound exactly alike on the phone. They've been married fifty years, and the timbre of their voices is the same. I say, 'Hello, Jane,' and David laughs and says, 'Guess again.' Then when we've been chatting a few moments, of course I can pick up their different nuances. It was something like that with Laura's call. The voice is the same, but maybe not exactly the same. We didn't talk long enough to be certain one way or the other."

"The point is, though, that if the phone call *was* from Laura and she's aware that she's considered missing, why wouldn't she be somewhat more specific about her plans?" Gordon Amory asked. "I wouldn't put it past someone like that Perkins kid to try to keep his hot story going by pulling a stunt like this. Laura was on that TV series for a couple of years. She has a distinctive voice. Maybe some drama student Perkins knows is imitating her for him."

"What do you think, Sam?" Mark Fleischman asked.

"If you want a cop's response, it's that whether or not Laura Wilcox made that call, I'm not satisfied by it."

Fleischman nodded. "That's the way I feel."

Carter Stewart was cutting his steak with decisive strokes. "There is another factor that should be considered. Laura is an actress on the skids. I happen to know she's just this side of being homeless."

He glanced around the table and looked smugly at the startled expressions on the faces of the others. "My agent phoned. There was a juicy little item in the business section of the *L.A. Times* today. The IRS is foreclosing on Laura's house to satisfy a tax lien."

He paused to lift the fork to his lips, then continued: "Which means that Laura may well be desperate. Publicity is the name of the game for an actress. Good publicity, bad publicity, it doesn't really matter. Anything to keep your name in the headlines. Maybe this is her way of doing it. Mysterious disappearance. Mysterious phone call. Frankly, I think we're all wasting our time worrying about her."

"It never crossed my mind that you were worried about her, Carter," Robby Brent commented. "I think that other than Jean, the only person who really might be concerned is our chairman, Jack Emerson. Right, Jack?"

"What's this?" Sam wondered aloud.

Robby smiled innocently. "Jack and I had a date this morning to look at some real estate that I might invest in, or at least might have considered investing in were it not so wildly overpriced. Jack was on the phone when I got to his place, and while I waited for him to talk to yet another few potential suckers, I looked over the collection of pictures in his den. There was a pretty sentimental inscription on one of Laura, dated exactly two weeks ago. 'Love and kisses and hugs to my favorite classmate.' It makes me wonder, Jack. How many hugs and kisses did she give you over the weekend, and is she still giving them to you?"

For an instant Jean thought that Jack Emerson would physically attack Robby Brent. Emerson bolted up, slapped both hands on the table, and stared across at Robby. Then, in a visible effort to control himself, he clenched his teeth and slowly lowered himself back into the chair. "There is a lady present," he said quietly. "Otherwise, I'd be using the kind of language you understand best, you miserable little toad. Maybe you've made a good living ridiculing people who managed to accomplish something in their lives, but as far as I'm concerned, you're still the same birdbrained dope who couldn't find his way to the bathroom at Stonecroft."

Dismayed at the exchange of raw hostility, Jean's eyes swept the room to be sure there was no waiter present to overhear Jack Emerson's outburst. When her gaze reached the door, she could see that it was partly open. She had no doubt as to who was on the other side, taking in every word of the conversation.

She exchanged glances with Sam Deegan. Sam stood up. "If you'll excuse me, I think I'd better skip coffee," he said. "I have a phone call to trace."

51

Peggy Kimball was a generously sized woman of about sixty who emanated an air of warmth and intelligence. Her salt-and-pepper hair had a natural wave; her complexion was smooth except for the fine lines around her mouth and eyes. Jean had the immediate impression that Peggy was a no-nonsense person and that it would take a lot to faze her.

They both waved away menus and ordered coffee. "My daughter picked up her kids an hour ago," Peggy said. "I had cornflakes and cocoa with them at seven o'clock, or was it at six-thirty?" She smiled. "You must have thought you were listening to Armageddon on the phone last night."

"I teach a college freshman class," Jean said. "Sometimes I think those students sound younger than toddlers, and they certainly can be noisier."

The waiter poured the coffee. Peggy Kimball looked directly at Jean, her bantering demeanor gone. "I do remember you, Jean," she said. "Dr. Connors handled many adoptions for young girls in your position. I felt sorry for you because you were one of the very few who ever came to the office alone. Most of the girls were accompanied by a parent or some other concerned adult, sometimes even by the baby's father, who was usually just another scared teenage kid."

"Be that as it may," Jean said quietly, "we're here because I am a concerned adult worrying about the nineteen-year-old girl who is my daughter and who may need help."

Sam Deegan had taken the original faxes, but she had made copies of them along with the DNA report, which verified that the strands of hair on the brush were Lily's. She took them out of her bag and showed them to Kimball. "Peggy, suppose it was your daughter," she said. "Wouldn't you be upset? Wouldn't you construe all this as a threat?" She looked Peggy in the eye.

"Yes, I would."

"Peggy, do you know who adopted Lily?"

"No, I do not."

"A lawyer had to have handled the paperwork. Do you know what lawyer or law firm Dr. Connors used?"

Peggy Kimball hesitated, then said slowly, "I doubt there was a lawyer involved in your case, Jean."

There's something she's afraid to tell me, Jean thought. "Peggy, Dr. Connors flew out to Chicago a few days before my due date, induced labor, and took Lily from me hours after she was born. Do you know if he registered her birth in Chicago or back here?"

Kimball stared reflectively at the coffee cup she was holding, then looked back at Jean. "I don't know about you specifically, Jean, but I do know that sometimes Dr. Connors registered a birth directly to the adoptive parents, as though the woman had been the natural mother."

"But that's *illegal*," Jean protested. "He had no right to do that."

"I know he didn't, but Dr. Connors had a friend who knew he was adopted and spent his adult life trying to track his birth family. It became an obsession with him, even though he was deeply loved by the adoptive parents and was treated exactly as they treated their birth children. Dr. Connors said it was a damn shame that he ever was told he was adopted."

"Then you're saying that maybe there was no original birth certificate, and no lawyer involved. Lily may believe that the people who adopted her are her natural parents!"

"It's possible, especially since Dr. Connors flew to Chicago to deliver your baby himself. Over the years he sent several girls to that nursing home in Chicago. It usually meant he was bypassing registering the birth with the natural mother's name on the certificate. Jean, there's something else you must realize. Lily's birth may not necessarily have been registered either here or in Chicago. It might have been treated as an 'at-home birth' in Connecticut or New Jersey, for example. Dr. Connors was well known throughout the area for arranging private adoptions."

She reached across the table and impulsively grasped Jean's hand. "Jean, you talked to me at that time. I remember that you said you wanted your baby to be happy and to be loved, and you hoped that it would grow up with a mother and father who were crazy about each other and who also thought the sun rose and set on their child. I'm sure you told Dr. Connors the same thing. Maybe, in a way, he thought he was carrying out your wishes by sparing Lily the longing to find you."

Jean felt as though huge metal doors had slammed shut right in front of her face. "Except now I *have* to find her," she said slowly, the words catching in her throat. "I *have* to find her. Peggy, you did imply that Dr. Connors didn't treat all his adoptions that way."

"No, he did not."

"Then he used a lawyer for some of them?"

"Yes, he did. That would be Craig Michaelson. He's still practicing, but he moved to Highland Falls years ago. You know where that is, I'm sure."

Highland Falls was the town nearest to West Point. "Yes, I know where it is," Jean said.

Peggy took a final sip of coffee. "I have to leave—I'm due at the hospital in half an hour," she said. "I wish I could have been more help, Jean."

"Maybe you can be," Jean said. "The fact remains that somebody found out about Lily, and maybe that happened at the time I was pregnant. Is there anyone else who was working in Dr. Connors' office who might have had access to the records?"

"No," Peggy said. "Dr. Connors kept those files under lock and key."

The waiter laid the check on the table. Jean signed it, and together the women walked into the lobby. Jack Emerson was sitting in a chair near the front desk, a newspaper on his lap. He nodded to Jean as she stood at the door saying good-bye to Peggy, then he stopped her as she passed him on the way to the elevator.

"Jean, any further word from Laura?"

"No." She was curious why Jack Emerson was in the hotel. Surely after that ugly exchange at the dinner table last night, he wouldn't want to run into Robby Brent. Then when he spoke she wondered if he could read her mind.

"I want to apologize for that exchange with Robby last night," Emerson said. "I hope you realize that was a lousy insinuation he made. I didn't ask Laura for that picture. I had written asking her to be an honoree at the reunion, and she sent it with her note of acceptance. She probably mailed out a thousand of those publicity pictures and inscribed all of them with hugs and kisses and love."

Was Jack Emerson studying her to see if she bought that explanation of the picture in his den? Jean wondered. She couldn't be certain. "You're probably right," she said dismissively. "Well, if you'll excuse me, I've got to run." Then she paused, her curiosity getting the better of her. "You look as though you're waiting for someone."

"Gordie, I mean *Gordon*, did ask me to take him around and look at some property after all. He didn't like anything the hot shots from the country club showed him yesterday. I have exclusives on a couple of sites that would be perfect for corporate headquarters."

"Good luck. Oh, here's the elevator. See you, Jack."

Jean walked rapidly to the elevator and waited as some people exited. Gordon Amory was the last to get out. "Did you hear any more from Laura?" he asked hurriedly.

"No."

"All right. Keep me posted."

Jean stepped into the elevator and pushed the number of her floor. Craig Michaelson, she thought. I'll call him the minute I get to the room.

Outside the hotel, Peggy Kimball got into her car and fastened her seat belt. Frowning in concentration, she tried to place the man who had nodded to Jean Sheridan in the lobby. Of course, she thought. That was Jack Emerson, the real estate guy who bought the property after our building burned down ten years ago.

She put the key in the ignition and turned it. Jack Emerson, she thought contemptuously. There had been a suggestion at the time that he might have had something to do with that fire. He not only wanted that property, but it had come out that he knew the building like the back of his hand. In high school he had made his spending money working a couple of evenings a week on the cleaning crew there. Was he working in the building when Jean was seeing Dr. Connors? Peggy wondered. We always scheduled girls like her in the evening so that they wouldn't run into other patients. Emerson might have spotted her and put two and two together.

She began to back out of the parking space. Jean wanted to know about anyone who might have been working in the office, she thought. It might be worth mentioning Jack Emerson to her, even though she was absolutely certain that neither he nor anyone else could have gotten into those locked files.

52

Sam Deegan's subpoena for the telephone records that would show the area where Laura's phone call to Jean had originated produced exactly the same results as the one he'd gotten a day earlier. The second call from Laura had been made from the same kind of cell phone—the kind that could be purchased with one hundred minutes of available calling time and did not require a subscriber's name.

At eleven-fifteen on Tuesday morning, Sam was in the district attorney's office giving him an update. "It's not the same phone Wilcox used Sunday night," he told Rich Stevens. "This one was purchased in Orange County. It has a 845 exchange. Eddie Zarro is out checking the places in the Cornwall area that sell them. Of course, it's been turned off, just like the one Wilcox used to phone the Glen-Ridge desk clerk Sunday evening."

The district attorney spun a pen in his fingers. "Jean Sheridan can't be one hundred percent certain she was talking to Laura Wilcox."

"No, sir, she can't."

"And the nurse—what's her name, Peggy Kimball?—told Sheridan that Dr. Connors may have arranged an illegal private adoption for her baby?"

"That's what Mrs. Kimball thinks."

"Have you heard anything from the priest at St. Thomas about baptismal records?"

"So far they're drawing a blank. They've been pretty successful reaching people who had baby girls baptized within that three-month period, but they haven't come up with one single instance of anyone admitting that their child had been adopted. The pastor, Monsignor Dillon, is smart. He called in some of the long-timers on the parish council who were around twenty years ago. They knew of families who had adopted children, but not one of them has a girl who's nineteen and a half now."

"Is Monsignor Dillon still working on it?"

Sam rubbed his hand over his head and thought again of how Kate used to tell him that he was weakening the roots of his hair. He decided it was a sign of his fatigue that from thoughts of Kate his mind jumped to Alice Sommers. It seemed more like two weeks than two days since he had seen her. But then, since early Saturday morning when Helen Whelan was reported missing, everything had been spinning out of control.

"Is Monsignor Dillon still searching through the files, Sam?" Rich Stevens asked again.

"Sorry, Rich. I guess I was woolgathering there for a minute. The answer is yes, and he's also called some of the neighboring parishes and asked them to do a discreet check on their own. If they think they have anything, Monsignor Dillon will let us know, and we can subpoena their records."

"And is Jean Sheridan following up on Craig Michaelson, the lawyer who handled some of Dr. Connors' adoptions?"

"She's seeing him at two o'clock."

"What's your next step, Sam?"

They were interrupted by the ringing of Sam's cell phone. He grabbed it from his pocket, glanced at the ID, and the fatigue suddenly dropped from his expression. "It's Eddie Zarro," he said as he pushed the talk button. "What have you got, Eddie?" he snapped.

As the district attorney watched, Sam's mouth dropped. "You've got to be kidding me. God, I feel so dumb. Why didn't I think of that, and what is that little weasel up to? Okay. I'll meet you at the Glen-Ridge. Let's hope he didn't decide to take off today."

Sam closed the phone and looked at his boss. "A cell phone with one hundred minutes on it was bought at the drugstore on Main Street in Cornwall a few minutes after seven last night. The clerk remembers distinctly the man who made the purchase because he's seen him on television. It was Robby Brent."

"The comedian? Do you think he and Laura Wilcox are together?"

"No, sir, I don't. The clerk in the drugstore watched Brent after he left. Brent stood on the sidewalk and made a phone call. According to him, it was at exactly the same time that Jean Sheridan received the call supposedly from Laura Wilcox."

"You mean that you think—

Sam interrupted. "Robby Brent is a comedian by some standards, but by everyone's standard he's a first-class mimic. My guess is the guy was imitating Laura's voice on that call to Jean Sheridan. I'm on my way to the Glen-Ridge. I'm going to find that jerk and make him explain to me what he was up to."

"Do that," Rich Stevens snapped. "He'd better have a damn good story, or else let's slap him with a charge for hindering a police investigation."

53

How long had it been? Laura had the sense that she was lapsing in and out of something that was more than sleep. How long had it been since The Owl was here? She wasn't sure. Last night, around the time she had sensed he would be coming back, something had happened. She'd heard sounds on the stairs, then a voice—a voice she knew.

"Don't!" Then he had shouted the name she had been forbidden to even whisper.

It was Robby Brent who had shouted, and he sounded terrified.

Did The Owl hurt Robby Brent last night?

I think so, Laura decided, as she willed herself to slip once more into a world where she didn't have to remember that The Owl might come back and that one of the times he returned he would pick up the pillow, hold it over her face, press it down, and . . .

What had happened to Robby? Some time after she heard his voice last night, The Owl had come to her and given her something to eat. He had been angry, so angry that his voice had trembled as he told her that Robby Brent had imitated her voice.

"I had to sit through dinner wondering if somehow you had gotten to the phone, but then my common sense told me that, of course, if you had been able to reach the phone, you would have called the police, not Jean, to say that you were fine. I was suspicious of Brent,

Laura, but then that nosey kid reporter was there, and I thought maybe he was up to some trick. Robby was so stupid, Laura, so stupid. He followed me here. I left the door open, and he came in. Oh, Laura, he was so stupid."

Did I dream that? Laura wondered hazily. Did I make that up?

She heard a click. Was it the door? She squeezed her eyes shut as raw panic raced through her body.

"Wake up, Laura. Raise your head to show that you're glad I'm back. I must talk to you, and I want to feel that you care about everything I tell you." The Owl's voice became hurried, high-pitched. "Robby suspected me and tried to set a trap for me. I don't know where I let my guard down, but I took care of him. I told you that. Now Jean is getting too close to the truth, Laura, but I know what I can do to lead her astray and then ensnare her. You do want to help me, don't you?

"Don't you?" he repeated loudly.

"Yes," Laura whispered as she tried to make her voice audible through the gag.

The Owl seemed appeased. "Laura, I know you're hungry. I've brought you something to eat. But first I have to tell you about Jean's daughter, Lily, and explain to you why you have been sending Jean threatening notes about her. You do remember sending those notes, don't you, Laura?"

Jean? A daughter? Laura stared up at him.

The Owl had turned on the small flashlight and laid it on the bedside table facing her. The light was shining across her neck and penetrating the darkness immediately around her. Looking up, she could see that he was staring back down at her, motionless now. Then he raised his arms.

"I remember." She mouthed the words, trying to make them audible to him.

Slowly his arms lowered to his sides. Laura closed her eyes, weak with relief. It had almost been the end. She had not responded quickly enough.

"Laura," he whispered. "You still don't understand. I am a bird of prey. When I have been disturbed, there is only one way I know to make myself whole. Don't tempt me with your obstinacy. Now tell me what we are going to do."

Laura's throat was parched. The gag was pressing against her tongue. Beneath the numbness in her hands and feet, the throbbing was intensifying as every muscle tightened with fear. She closed her eyes, struggling to concentrate. "Jean . . . her daughter. . . . I sent notes."

After she opened her eyes, the flashlight was turned off. He was no longer hovering over her. She heard the click of the door. He was gone.

From somewhere nearby she could catch the faint aroma of the coffee he had forgotten to give her.

54

The office of Craig Michaelson, Attorney at Law, was located on Old State Road, only two blocks past the motel where Jean and Cadet Carroll Reed Thornton had spent their few nights together. As Jean approached the motel, she slowed down and blinked back tears.

Her mental image of Reed was so strong, her memory of their time together so intense. She felt that if she slipped into room 108, he would be there, waiting for her. Reed with his blond hair and blue eyes, his strong arms that wrapped around her, making her feel a kind of happiness that in all her eighteen years of life she had never imagined possible.

"I dream of Jeannie . . ."

For a long time after Reed died, she would wake up with the music of that song drifting through her mind. We were so in love, Jean thought. He was Prince Charming to my Cinderella. He was kind and smart, and he had a maturity far beyond his twenty-two years. He loved the military life. He encouraged me as a writer. He teased me that someday when he was a general, I'd be writing his biography. When I told him I was pregnant, he was worried because he knew what his father's reaction would be to an early marriage. But then he said, "We'll just move up our plans, Jeannie, that's all. Early marriages are not exactly unheard of in my family. My grandfather got married the day he graduated from West Point, and my grandmother was only nineteen."

"But you told me your grandparents knew each other from the time they were babies," she had pointed out. "That's a lot different. They'll see me as a townie who got pregnant so that I could get you to marry me."

Reed had covered her mouth with his hand. "I won't listen to that kind of talk," he'd said firmly. "Once they know you, my parents will love you. But on the same subject, you'd better introduce me to your mother and father pretty soon."

I had wanted to be a student at Bryn Mawr when I met Reed's parents, Jean thought. By then my mother and father would have split. If his parents had met them separately, they probably would have liked them well enough. They wouldn't necessarily have learned about their problems.

If Reed had lived.

Or even if he had to die young, if it had happened after we were married, I still could have kept Lily. Reed was an only child. His parents might have been angry about our marriage, but they surely would have been thrilled to have a grandchild.

We all lost big-time, Jean thought achingly as she put her foot down on the accelerator and sped past the motel.

Craig Michaelson's office occupied an entire floor of a building that Jean knew had not been there when she and Reed were dating. His reception area was attractive with paneled walls and wide chairs that had been upholstered in an antique tapestry pattern. Jean decided that at least on the surface it would seem that the Michaelson firm was prosperous.

She had not been sure what to expect. On the drive to Highland Falls from Cornwall she had decided that if Michaelson had been part of Dr. Connors' system of improperly registering births, he would be something of a charlatan and surely very much on the defensive.

After she had waited ten minutes, Craig Michaelson came out to the reception area himself and personally escorted her into his private office. He was a tall man in his early sixties, with a big frame and slightly sloping shoulders. His full head of hair, more dark gray than silver, looked as though he might have just left the barber. His dark gray suit was well cut, and his tie was a subdued gray-and-blue print. Everything about his appearance as well as the tasteful furnishings and paintings in his office suggested a reserved and conservative man.

Jean realized that she was not sure if that wasn't the worst possible scenario. If Craig Michaelson was *not* involved in Lily's adoption, then this was going to be another dead end in her search to find her.

She looked directly at the lawyer as she told him about Lily and showed him the copies of the faxes and the DNA report. She sketched out her own background, reluctantly emphasizing her academic standing, the honors and awards she had received, and the fact that because of her best-selling book her financial success was a matter of public record.

Michaelson never took his eyes off her face except when he examined the faxes. She knew he was sizing her up, trying to decide if what she was telling him was the truth or just an elaborate hoax.

"Because of Dr. Connors' nurse, Peggy Kimball, I know that some of the adoptions the doctor arranged were illegal," she said. "What I need to know, what I beg you to tell me, is this: Did you handle my child's adoption yourself, or do you know who adopted her?"

"Dr. Sheridan, let me start by telling you that I never had any part in an adoption that was not handled to the strictest letter of the law. If at any time Dr. Connors was bypassing the law, he did so without my knowledge or involvement."

"Then if you did handle my baby's adoption, are you telling me that it was registered with my name as the mother and the name of Carroll Reed Thornton as the father?"

"I am saying that any adoption I handled was legal."

Years of teaching students, a small percentage of whom had been adept at dissembling and half-truths, had made Jean feel capable of spotting that practice whenever she encountered it. She knew she was encountering it now.

"Mr. Michaelson, a nineteen-and-a-half-year-old girl may be in danger. If you handled the adoption, you know who adopted her. You could try to protect her now. In fact, in my opinion, you have a moral obligation to try to protect her."

It was the wrong thing to say. Behind silver-framed glasses, Craig Michaelson's eyes turned frosty. "Dr. Sheridan, you have demanded that I see you today. You have come in with a story for the truth of which I have only your word. You have virtually suggested that I might have broken the law in the past, and now you are *demanding* that I break the law in order to help you. There are legal ways to have birth records released. You should go to the district attorney's office. I believe that they would petition the court to open those records. I can assure you that is the only way you should be going about this inquiry. As you yourself point out, it is possible that at the time you were expecting the baby someone might have seen you in Dr. Connors' office and somehow got into your file. You also pointed out that this may be all about money. Frankly, my guess is that you're right. Someone knows who your daughter is and suspects you will pay for the knowledge."

He stood up.

For a moment Jean remained seated. "Mr. Michaelson, I have pretty good instincts, and my instinct is that you handled my daughter's adoption and that you probably did it legally. My other very strong instinct is that whoever is writing to me and is close enough to Lily to steal her hairbrush is dangerous. I am going to go to court to try to get the records released. The fact remains, though, that in the interval, something might happen to my child because you are stonewalling me now. If it does, and I find out about it, I don't think I'll be responsible for what I'll do to you."

Jean could not control the tears that were spilling from her eyes. She turned and hurried from the room, not caring that the receptionist and several people in the reception area looked up at her in astonishment as she ran past them. When she reached her car, she flung open the door, got in, and buried her face in her hands.

And then she went deadly cold. As clearly as though Laura were in the car with her, she could hear her voice pleading, "Jean, help me! Please, Jean, help me!"

55

From the front window of his office, his face drawn with concern, Craig Michaelson watched Jean Sheridan as she rushed to her car. She's on the level, he thought. This isn't about a woman obsessed to find her child and fabricating a wild story. Should I warn Charles and Gano? If anything happened to Meredith, it would destroy them both.

He would not, could not, reveal Jean Sheridan's identity to them, but he could at least make Charles aware of the threats to his adopted daughter. It should be his decision as to what he might tell Meredith or how he might try to protect her. If the story about the hairbrush was true, maybe Meredith would remember where she was when she mislaid it or lost it. It might be one way to try to trace the sender of the faxes.

Jean Sheridan had said that if anything happened to her daughter, something I could have prevented, she wouldn't be responsible for what she would do to me, he recalled. Charles and Gano would feel exactly the same way.

His decision made, Craig Michaelson went to his desk and picked up the phone. He did not need to look up the number. Crazy coincidence, he thought as he dialed. Jean Sheridan doesn't live far from Charles and Gano. She's in Alexandria. They're in Chevy Chase.

The phone was picked up on the first ring. "General Buckley's office," a crisp voice said.

"This is Craig Michaelson, a close friend of General Buckley. I need to speak to him on a matter of great importance. Is he there?"

"I'm sorry, sir. The General is abroad on official business. Can someone else help you?"

"No, I'm afraid not. Will you be hearing from the General?"

"Yes, sir. The office is in touch with him regularly."

"Then tell him it is most urgent that he call me as soon as possible." Craig spelled his name and gave the number of his cell phone as well as his office number. He hesitated, then decided not to say that it concerned Meredith. Charles would respond to an urgent message as soon as he received it—he was confident of that.

And, anyhow, Craig Michaelson thought as he replaced the receiver, Meredith is safer at West Point than she would be almost anyplace else.

Then the unwelcome thought came to him that even being at West Point had not been enough to prevent the death of Meredith's natural father, Cadet Carroll Reed Thornton, Jr.

56

The first person Carter Stewart saw when he walked into the Glen-Ridge House at three-thirty was Jake Perkins, who was, as usual, sprawled on a chair in the lobby. Doesn't that kid have a home? Stewart wondered, as he walked to the phone at the end of the front desk and dialed Robby Brent's room.

There was no answer. "Robby, I thought we were supposed to get together at three-thirty," Stewart snapped in response to the computerized suggestion to leave a voice message. "I'll be in the lobby for another fifteen minutes or so."

As he hung up, he spotted the investigator Sam Deegan sitting in the office behind the front desk. Their eyes met, and Deegan got up, clearly on his way to talk to him. There was something decisive in the way Deegan moved which made Stewart aware that this would not be an idle conversation.

They stood across the desk from each other.

"Mr. Stewart," Sam said. "I'm glad to see you. I left a message for you at your hotel and was hoping to hear back from you."

"I've been working with my director on the script for my new play," Carter Stewart said, his tone abrupt.

"I see you were on the house phone. Are you meeting someone now?"

Stewart found himself resenting Sam Deegan's question. None of your business, he wanted to say, but something about Deegan's attitude made the remark die on his lips. "I have an appointment with Robby Brent at three-thirty. Before you ask me why I have an appointment, which is clearly your next question, let me satisfy your curiosity. Brent has agreed to star in a new sitcom. He has seen the first few scripts and feels they are off-target—that, in fact, they fall flat—and he asked me to take a look at them and give him my professional opinion as to whether or not they can be salvaged."

"Mr. Stewart, you've been compared to literary playwrights like Tennessee Williams and Edward Albee," Sam said sharply. "I'm just a run-of-the-mill kind of guy, but most of those situation comedies are insults to the intelligence. I'm surprised that you'd be interested in judging one of them."

"It was not my choice." Stewart's tone was icy. "After dinner last night, Robby Brent asked me to look at the scripts. He offered to bring them to my hotel, but as you can understand, that would have involved my having to dislodge him from my suite after I'd glanced at the material. It was much easier to stop by here on the way back from my director's home. And even though I do not *write* sitcoms, I am a very good judge of writing in *any* form. Do you know if Robby is expected soon?"

"I have no idea of his plans," Sam said. "I came here to talk to him also. I didn't get a response when I called him, and then realized that no one had seen him all day, so I had the maid go into his room. His bed had not been slept in. It appears that Mr. Brent is missing."

Sam was not sure that he wanted to give that much information to Carter Stewart, but his instinct told him to divulge it and watch for Stewart's reaction. It turned out to be stronger than he had anticipated.

"*Missing!* Oh, come now, Mr. Deegan. Don't you think this scenario has played itself out long enough? Let me explain: There is a part in this proposed series for a sexy blonde not unlike the vanished Laura Wilcox. The other day at West Point, specifically at the lunch table, Brent was telling Laura that she might be perfect for that part. I am beginning to think that the entire three-ring circus surrounding her disappearance is nothing more than a publicity stunt. And now, if you'll excuse me, I won't waste any more of my time waiting around for Robby."

I don't like that guy, Sam thought as he watched Carter Stewart leave. Stewart was wearing a somewhat tattered dark gray sweatsuit and dirty sneakers, a hobo's outfit that Sam figured had probably cost a fortune.

My feelings for him aside, has he put his finger on everything that's going on? Sam wondered. In the more than three hours that he had been sitting in the office, he had been doing some hard thinking and in the process had become more and more irritated.

We know Brent made the phone call impersonating Laura, he reasoned. He bought a cell phone that appears to be the one that the call to Jean was made on. The clerk who sold it to him saw him dialing at exactly the time Jean thought Laura was talking to her. I'm beginning to think Stewart may be right, that all this is a way of getting publicity. And, in that case, why am I wasting my time here when I have a killer loose in Orange County who dragged an innocent woman into his car and stabbed her to death?

When he had arrived at the Glen-Ridge House, Eddie Zarro was waiting for him, but Sam sent him back to the office, saying there was no need for the two of them to hang out in the lobby waiting for Brent. Sam debated, then decided that now he'd get Zarro to relieve him and go home. I need a decent night's sleep, he decided. I'm so tired I can't think straight.

As he opened his cell phone to call the office, he realized that

Amy Sachs, the desk clerk, was at his elbow. "Mr. Deegan," she began, her voice little more than a whisper, "you've been here since before noon, and I know you haven't had a single thing to eat. May I order coffee and a sandwich for you?"

"That's very kind, but I'll be leaving soon," Sam told her. As he spoke, he wondered how close Amy Sachs had been when he was talking to Stewart. She didn't appear to make any sound when she walked, and she made very little when she opened her mouth. Why do I bet her hearing is acute? Sam wondered sardonically as he watched her exchange a glance with Jake Perkins. And why do I bet that the minute I'm out of sight, she fills Jake in on the fact that Brent isn't around and that Stewart thinks all this hoopla is a publicity stunt?

Sam went back into the office. From there he had a good view of the main entrance. A few minutes later he saw Gordon Amory come in, and he hurried to catch him before he got on the elevator.

Amory was clearly not in the mood to talk about Robby Brent. "I have not spoken to him since that vulgar display last night," he said. "As a matter of fact, since you witnessed it, Mr. Deegan, and also heard Robby's attack on Jack Emerson, I think you should know that I have been out since ten o'clock this morning with Emerson, looking at real estate. He is the exclusive agent on some genuinely fine parcels of land. He also showed me the properties he had offered Robby for consideration. I must tell you, they were fairly priced and, in my opinion, excellent long-range investments—which is to say that anything Robby Brent insinuates, says, or does should be examined for motivation beyond the obvious. Now, if you'll excuse me, I have a number of phone calls to make."

The elevator door was opening. Before Amory could step into it, Sam said, "Another moment, please, Mr. Amory."

With a resigned smile that was almost a sneer, Amory turned back to him.

"Mr. Amory, Robby Brent did not sleep in his room last night. We believe it was he who imitated Laura Wilcox on the phone call to Jean Sheridan. Your colleague, Mr. Stewart, feels that Brent and Wilcox may be carrying on a hoax for publicity for Mr. Brent's new television series. What do you think?"

Gordon Amory raised an eyebrow. For an instant he looked dumbstruck; then a look of amusement came over his face. "A publicity stunt! Of course, that makes sense. In fact, if you look at Page Six of the *New York Post*, they're already suggesting that very thing about Laura's disappearance. Now Robby vanishes, and you tell me that he made the phone call to Jean last night. And the whole time we're all sitting around worrying about them."

"Then you think it's possible we're all wasting our time worrying about Laura?"

"*Au contraire*, it has not been a waste, Mr. Deegan. The one positive thing is that Laura's supposed disappearance has proven to me that I still have the milk of human kindness flowing in my breast. I was so concerned about her that I was planning to offer her a role in my new series. I'll bet you're right. The dear girl has other fish to fry and is doing it most successfully. And now I really must go."

"I assume you'll be checking out soon," Sam suggested.

"No, I'm still looking at property. But I guess I won't be seeing you around, since now you can get back to solving real crimes. Goodbye."

Sam watched Amory get into the elevator. Another one who thinks he's intellectually superior to an investigator, he thought. Well, let's just wait and see. Sam could feel his nerves fraying as he walked back across the lobby. Whether or not Laura's disappearance is a publicity stunt, the fact still remains that five women from the lunch table are dead.

He had been hoping Jean would get back before he left, so he was delighted to see her standing at the front desk. He hurried to her side, anxious to hear about her meeting with the lawyer.

She was asking about messages. Always afraid she'll get another fax about Lily, Sam thought. And who can blame her? He put his hand on her arm. When she turned, he could see that her eyes looked as if she might have been crying. "Buy you a cup of coffee?" he offered.

"A cup of tea would be great."

"Ms. Sachs, when Mr. Zarro returns, please ask him to join us in the coffee shop," Sam said to the room clerk.

In the coffee shop he waited until Jean's tea and his coffee had been served before he spoke again. It seemed to him that Jean was still trying to regain her composure. Finally he said, "I gather it didn't go well with the attorney Craig Michaelson."

"It did and it didn't," Jean said slowly. "Sam, I would stake my life that Michaelson handled the adoption and may know where Lily is now. I was rude to him. I practically threatened him. On the way back here I pulled the car over to the side of the road and called to apologize to him. I also pointed out that if he does know where she is, she might remember where she lost her hairbrush, and that might be a direct link to whoever is threatening her."

"What did Michaelson say to that?"

"It was odd. He said that that had already occurred to him. Sam, I'm telling you he knows where Lily is, or at least how to trace where she is. He did say, using the words 'I urge you most strongly,' that I should have you or at least the district attorney's office petition a judge to open the records immediately and warn her parents of this situation."

"Then I would say that he obviously takes seriously what you told him."

Jean nodded in agreement. "I didn't think he did when I was in his office, but maybe my outburst—I swear I was on the verge of throwing something at him—may have convinced him. His attitude had done a one-hundred-and-eighty-degree turn when I talked to him twenty minutes later on the phone." She glanced up. "Oh, look, here's Mark."

Mark Fleischman was making his way to their table. "I told Mark about Lily," Jean said hurriedly, "so you can talk in front of him."

"You did, Jean? Why?" Sam was dismayed.

"He's a psychiatrist. I thought he might be able to offer some input into whether or not these faxes are real threats."

As Mark Fleischman came nearer, Sam saw that Jean's smile became genuinely pleased. Be careful, Jeannie, he wanted to warn her. In my book this guy is carrying a lot of baggage. There's a tension bubbling under the surface in him that a cop like me can feel.

Sam also did not miss the way Fleischman momentarily covered Jean's hand with his at her invitation for him to join them.

"I'm not interfering?" Mark asked, looking at Sam for reassurance.

"As a matter of fact, I'm glad to catch you," Sam told him. "I was about to ask Jean if she had heard from Robby Brent today. Now I can ask you both."

Jean shook her head. "I haven't."

"Nor, thankfully, have I," Fleischman said. "Is there any reason you thought we might have heard from him?"

"I was about to tell you, Jean. Robby Brent must have left the hotel after dinner last night. So far he has not come back. We've pretty much determined that the call you thought came from Laura was made on a prepaid cellular phone that Brent had just bought, and we're also fairly confident that the voice you heard was actually his. As you know, he's a superb mimic."

Jean looked at Sam, astonishment and distress reflected in her face. "But *why?*"

"At the luncheon at West Point on Saturday, did you hear Brent talk to Laura about possibly being on his new television series?"

"I did," Mark Fleischman said. "But I didn't know whether or not he was joking."

"He did say there was a part Laura might want to play," Jean confirmed.

"Both Carter Stewart and Gordon Amory think Brent and Laura may be pulling a hoax on us. What do you think?" Sam's eyes narrowed as he looked at Mark Fleischman.

Behind his glasses, Mark's eyes became thoughtful. He looked past Sam, then directly at him. "I think it's entirely possible," he said slowly.

"I disagree," Jean said emphatically. "I absolutely disagree. Laura is in trouble—I feel it; I know it." She hesitated, then decided against telling them that she felt as if she had heard Laura's plea for help. "Please, Sam, don't think like that," she begged. "Don't give up trying to find Laura. I don't know what Robby Brent is up to, but maybe he was just trying to throw us off the track by pretending to be her and saying she was fine. She's *not* fine. Really, I know she's not fine."

"Take it easy, Jeannie," Mark said gently.

Sam stood up. "Jean, we'll talk again first thing in the morning. I'll want you to come to my office on that other matter we were discussing."

Ten minutes later, with Eddie Zarro waiting in case Robby Brent returned to the hotel, Sam wearily got into his car. He turned on the engine, hesitated, thought for a moment, then dialed Alice Sommers. When she answered, he was struck once more by the silvery tone of her voice. "Any chance you have a glass of sherry for a tired detective?" he asked.

Half an hour later he was sitting in a deep leather chair, his feet on the ottoman, facing the fire in Alice Sommers' den. Taking the last sip of sherry, he put the glass on the table beside him. It had not taken too much persuasive power to have Alice convince him to catnap while she prepared an early dinner. "You have to eat," she pointed out. "Then you can go straight home and get a decent night's sleep."

As his eyes began to close, Sam gave a sleepy glance at the curio cabinet beside the fireplace. He was asleep before whatever object he saw there had triggered a startled response in his subconscious.

57

Amy Sachs went off duty at four o'clock, shortly after Sam Deegan left the Glen-Ridge House. She and Jake Perkins had arranged to meet at a McDonald's about a mile away. Now, over hamburgers, she was filling him in on Sam Deegan's activities and the conversation she had managed to overhear between him and, as she described him, "that uppity playwright, Carter Stewart."

"Mr. Deegan came to the hotel looking for Mr. Brent," she explained. "Eddie Zarro, the other investigator, was waiting for him. They both looked kind of mad. The minute Mr. Deegan couldn't reach Brent on the phone, he made Pete, the bellman, take them up to Brent's room. When Brent didn't answer the door, Mr. Deegan told Pete to open it. That's when they found out that Mr. Brent hadn't come back last night."

Between bites of hamburger, Jake was jotting in his notebook. "I thought Carter Stewart checked out after the reunion," he said. "What made him come back this afternoon? Who was he meeting?"

"Stewart told Mr. Deegan that he had agreed to go over scripts for Robby Brent's new television show. Then they were talking about a cell phone. I couldn't get all of it because Mr. Deegan doesn't speak loud. Mr. Stewart isn't all that loud, either, but his voice carries, and I've been blessed with good hearing. In fact, Jake, they said my grandmother, even at age ninety, could hear a worm slither through the grass."

"My grandmother is always telling me I mumble," Jake said.

"Actually, you *do* mumble," Amy Sachs whispered. "But, anyhow, Jake, when Mr. Deegan asked Mr. Stewart if he thought all this was a publicity trick by Laura Wilcox and Robby Brent, Mr. Stewart seemed to think it was. And maybe I missed something, but didn't Dr. Sheridan get a call from Laura Wilcox last night?"

Jake was practically salivating with the unexpected torrent of information. All afternoon he felt as if he had been watching a silent movie. He sat in the hotel lobby observing the activity but not daring to hang around the desk or obviously try to overhear the conversations. "Yes, Dr. Sheridan *did* get a call from Laura Wilcox. I happened to be around when they were talking about it in the small dining room."

"Jake, I don't think I've got this all straight. You know how it is—you hear part of one thing, then part of another. You can get only so near to people without seeming to be too near, but I get the impression that Robby Brent may have made that call last night and pretended to be Laura Wilcox."

Jake's hand was in midair, firmly grasping the uneaten portion of the hamburger. Slowly he lowered it to the plate. It was obvious he was mentally computing what Amy had just told him. "Robby Brent made that call and now he's not around, and they think all this is just a publicity stunt for some new television series?"

Amy's oversized glasses bobbled on her nose as she nodded happily. "Sounds like a reality series, doesn't it?" she asked. "Do you think that maybe there are hidden cameras filming in the hotel now?"

"It's something to wonder about," Jake agreed. "You're a sharp lady, Amy. When I open my own newspaper, I'm going to make you a columnist. Anything else you've noticed?"

She pursed her lips. "Just one thing. Mark Fleischman—you know, the really cute honoree who's a psychiatrist—"

"Sure, I know him. What about him?"

"I *swear* he has a crush on Dr. Sheridan. He went out early this morning, and when he came back, the first thing he did was come rushing to the desk and phone Dr. Sheridan. I overheard him."

"Of course," Jake said, grinning.

"I told him she was in the coffee shop. He thanked me, but before he hightailed it into the coffee shop, he asked if Dr. Sheridan had received any more faxes today. He looked almost disappointed when I said no, and he asked me if I was *sure* she hadn't gotten one. Even if he does have a crush on her, I think it's a little nervy of him to ask about her mail, don't you?"

"In a way I do, yes."

"But he is nice, and I asked him just casually if he'd had a pleasant day. He said yes, he'd been looking up some old friends at West Point."

58

After Sam Deegan left, Jean Sheridan and Mark Fleischman sat for nearly an hour at the table in the coffee shop. He reached over and covered her hand with his as she told him about meeting Craig Michaelson, about becoming convinced that Michaelson had handled Lily's adoption, and about verbally attacking him when she felt he was refusing to understand that Lily might be in genuine danger.

"I did call to apologize," she explained. "When I did, I pointed out that it's just possible Lily might remember where she was when her hairbrush disappeared. That could be a direct link to who might have taken it, unless, of course, her adoptive parents are behind all this."

"That's a real possibility," Mark agreed. "Are you taking Michaelson's advice to petition the court to open the file?"

"Absolutely. I'm meeting Sam Deegan in his office tomorrow morning."

"I think that's smart. Jean, what about Laura? You don't believe this is just some publicity stunt, do you?"

"No, I don't." Jean hesitated. It was nearly four-thirty, and the late afternoon sun was sending slanting shadows through the almost deserted coffee shop. She looked across the table at Mark. He was wearing an open sport shirt and dark green sweater. He's one of those men who'll always have a boyish look, she thought—except for his eyes. "Who was that teacher we had who called you an 'old soul'?" she asked.

"That was Mr. Hastings. And what brought that up?"

"He said you were wise beyond your years."

"I'm not sure it was meant as a compliment. You're leading up to something, Jeannie."

"I guess I am. My understanding of old souls is that they have great insight. When I got in the car after I left Craig Michaelson's office, I was upset. I told you that. But then, Mark, if Laura had been in the car with me, I couldn't have heard her speak more clearly. I heard her voice saying, 'Jean, help me. Please, Jean, help me.' "

She scrutinized his expression. "You don't believe me, or you think I'm crazy," she said defensively.

"That's not true, Jeannie. If anyone believes in the power of the mind to communicate, I do. But if Laura is really in trouble, where does Robby Brent fit into the picture?"

"I have no idea." Jean raised her hand in a gesture of helplessness, then lowered it as she looked around. "We'd better get out of here. They're already setting the tables for dinner."

Mark signaled for the check. "I wish I could ask you to have dinner with me, but tonight I have the unique privilege of breaking bread with my father."

Jean looked at him closely, not sure of how to respond. The expression on his face was inscrutable. Finally she said, "I know you've been estranged from him. Did he call you?"

"I walked past the house today. His car was there. Impulsively, quite impulsively, I went up and rang the bell. We had a long talk—not long enough to settle anything, but he did ask me to meet him for dinner. I said I would, on the condition that he would be prepared to answer certain questions I was going to ask him."

"And he agreed?"

"Yes, he did. Let's see if he keeps his word."

"I hope whatever you have to work out can be worked out."

"So do I, Jeannie, but I'm not counting on it."

They got in the elevator together. Mark punched the buttons for the fourth and sixth floors.

"I hope your view is better than mine," Jean said. "I overlook the back parking lot."

"Then it is better," he agreed. "I'm facing the front. If I'm in the room at the right time, I get to see the sunset."

"And if I happen to be awake, I get to see who comes rolling in around daybreak," Jean said as the elevator stopped at the fourth floor. "I'll see you, Mark."

The message signal on the phone in her room was blinking. The call was from Peggy Kimball and had come in only a few minutes earlier. "Jean, I'm on my break at the hospital, so I'll make this fast. After I left you, it occurred to me that Jack Emerson worked for the clean-up crew in our office building around the time you were seeing Dr. Connors. I told you Dr. Connors always kept his file keys in his pocket, but he must have had a spare hidden somewhere because I remember that one day he forgot to bring his key ring to the office but still was able to open the files. So maybe Emerson or someone like him *did* get a look at your records. Anyhow, I thought you should know. Good luck."

Jack Emerson, Jean thought as she replaced the receiver and sank down on the bed. Could he be the one who's doing this to me? He's always lived in this town. If the people who adopted Lily live here, too, he may know them.

She heard a sound and turned in time to see a manila envelope being slid under the door. She hurried across the room and yanked the door open.

An apologetic bellman was trying to straighten up. "Dr. Sheridan, a fax came for you right after a whole stack came for one of the other guests. Your fax got put in with his material. He just came across it and brought it down to the desk."

"It's all right," Jean said softly, fear almost closing her throat. She closed the door and picked up the envelope. Her hand shaking, she ripped it open. It's going to be about Lily, she thought.

It *was* about Lily. The fax read:

> Jean, I am so terribly ashamed. I always knew about Lily, and I know the people who adopted her. She's a wonderful girl. She's smart; a college sophomore and very happy. I didn't mean to make you think I was threatening her. I need money desperately and thought I could get it this way. Don't worry about Lily, please. She is fine. I will be in touch with you soon. Forgive me and please let people know that I'm all right. The publicity stunt was Robby Brent's idea. He's going to try to straighten it out. He wants to talk to his producers before he has to make a statement to the press.
>
> Laura

Her knees weak, Jean sank onto the bed. Then, crying with relief and joy, she dialed Sam's cell phone.

Jean's call jolted Sam from the peaceful nap he had been enjoying while Alice Sommers busied herself in the kitchen. "Another fax, Jean? Take it easy. Read it to me." He listened. "My God," he said. "I can't believe that woman would do this to you."

"You're talking to Jean? Is she all right?" Alice was standing in the doorway.

"Yes. Laura Wilcox has been sending the faxes about Lily. She's apologized, saying she never intended to hurt Lily."

Alice took the phone from him. "Jean, are you too upset to drive?" She listened. "Then come over here . . ."

When Jean arrived, Alice looked into Jean's face and saw the luminous joy she would have experienced herself if somehow years ago Karen had been spared. She put her arms around her, "Oh, Jean, I've been praying and praying."

Jean hugged her fiercely. "I know you have. I cannot believe that Laura has done this to me, but I am sure that Laura would never hurt Lily. And so it *was* all about money, Sam. My God, if Laura was that desperate, why didn't she just ask me straight out to help her? Half an hour ago I was ready to tell you that I thought Jack Emerson must be the one who knew about Lily."

"Jean, come in, sit down, and calm down. Have a glass of sherry and tell me what you mean by that. What does Jack Emerson have to do with this?"

"I just learned something that made me believe he was behind it." Obediently, Jean slipped off her coat, went into the den, sat on the chair nearest the fire, and, trying to keep her voice steady, told them about the call from Peggy Kimball. "Jack worked in that office at the time I was Dr. Connors' patient. He planned this reunion to get us all here. In his den he has that picture of Laura that Robby Brent talked about. It all seemed to fit—until the fax was delivered. Oh, I didn't tell you. The fax came in around noon but got mixed in with someone else's stuff."

"You should have received it at *noon?*" Sam asked quickly.

"Yes, and if I had, I wouldn't have gone to see Craig Michaelson.

As soon as I got it, I tried to phone him so that in case he was planning to contact Lily's adoptive parents, I could tell him to hold off until I heard from Laura again. There's no need now to alarm them or her."

"Have you told anyone else about this fax from Laura?" Sam asked quietly.

"No. I got it right after I went upstairs to my room. Mark and I sat and talked for at least an hour after you left us. Oh, I should call Mark now before he goes out to dinner. He'll be so glad to hear about this. He understands just as much as you two do how desperately worried I've been."

Dollars to doughnuts, Jean told Fleischman about the possibility that the hairbrush might be traced to the place where Lily lost it, or who she was with when she lost it, Sam thought grimly as he watched Jean reach for her cell phone.

He exchanged glances with Alice and saw they were sharing the same concern. Was this fax really from Laura, or was it one more bizarre twist in an ongoing nightmare?

Then there is another scenario, Sam thought. If Jean is right, and Craig Michaelson *did* handle the adoption, it's possible that Michaelson might already have contacted Lily's adoptive parents and discussed the missing brush.

Unless this communication from Laura was on the level, Lily had become a danger to whoever was sending the faxes. And whoever was doing it might have thought about the hairbrush being traced to him.

I'm not ready to accept that these faxes were from Laura, Sam thought. Not yet anyway. Jack Emerson worked in Dr. Connors' office, has always lived in town, and could easily be friends with a couple from Cornwall who might have adopted Lily.

Mark Fleischman may have won Jean's confidence, but I'm not convinced. There's something going on inside that guy that has nothing to do with going on television and giving advice to dysfunctional families, he decided.

Jean was leaving a message for Fleischman. "He's not in," she said, then sniffed and turned to Alice, a smile on her face. "Something smells wonderful. If you don't invite me to dinner, I'm going to invite myself. Oh, dear God, I'm so happy. *I'm so happy!*"

59

Night-time is my time, The Owl thought as he frantically waited for darkness. He had been a fool to risk going back to the house during the daytime—he might have been seen. But then he had gotten the unsettling feeling that maybe Robby Brent was not dead after all, that, actor that he was, he had pretended to be unconscious. He could just picture him crawling out of his car and making his way to the street—or maybe even going up the stairs to find Laura and call 911.

The image of Robby alive and able to get help had become so powerful that The Owl had no choice but to go back to confirm for himself that he was indeed dead, that he was exactly where he had left him, in the trunk of his car.

It was almost like the first time he had taken a life, that night in Laura's house, The Owl thought. Through the haze of memory he recalled tiptoeing up the back stairs, heading to the room where he had expected to find Laura. That was twenty years ago.

Last night, knowing that Robby Brent was following him, it hadn't been hard to outsmart him. But then he'd had to dig in Robby's pocket for his keys so he could drive his car into the garage. His first rental car, the one with the muddy tires, was occupying one space in the garage. He'd driven Robby Brent's car into the other space and then dragged Brent's body to it from the staircase where he had killed him.

Somehow he had revealed himself to Robby Brent. Somehow Robby had figured it out. What about the others? Was a circle closing so that soon he would no longer be able to escape into the night? He didn't like uncertainty. He needed reassurance—the reassurance that came only when he carried out the deed that reaffirmed his mastery over life and death.

At eleven o'clock he began to drive through Orange County. Not too near Cornwall, he thought. Not too near Washingtonville, where Helen Whelan's body was found. Maybe Highland Falls would be a good choice. Maybe somewhere in the vicinity of the motel where Jean Sheridan had stayed with the cadet would be the place to look.

Maybe one of the sidestreets near that motel would be the place where he was destined to find his victim.

At eleven-thirty, as he cruised down a tree-lined street, he observed two women standing on a porch beneath an overhead light. As he watched, one turned, went back inside, and closed the door. The other began to go down the porch stairs. The Owl pulled over to the curb, turned off the lights of the car, and waited for her as she cut across the lawn to the sidewalk.

She was looking down, walking swiftly, and did not hear him when he got out of the car and moved to the shadow of the tree. He stepped out as she passed him. He could feel The Owl spring from its cage as his hand covered her mouth, and he swiftly slid the rope around her neck.

"I'm sorry for you," he whispered, "but you have been chosen."

60

The body of Yvonne Tepper was discovered at 6:00 A.M. by Bessie Koch, a seventy-year-old widow who supplemented her Social Security check by delivering *The New York Times* to her customers in the Highland Falls area of Orange County.

She had been about to turn her car into Tepper's driveway, one of her sales pitches being her "no bare feet" policy. "People don't have to come down the driveway to get my papers," she explained in her flyers. "The paper is there when you open your door." The campaign was a loving tribute to her now deceased husband who typically went out in his bare feet to retrieve the morning newspaper from wherever their own delivery man had thrown it, usually nearer the curb than the front steps.

At first Bessie's mind did not accept the evidence of her eyes. There had been an overnight frost, and Yvonne Tepper was lying between two bushes, on grass that still glittered with shiny patches of icy moisture. Her legs were bent, and her hands were in the pockets of her navy blue parka. Her appearance was so neat and orderly that Bessie's first impression was that she must have just fallen.

When the reality hit, Bessie stopped the car with an abrupt slam of the brakes. Flinging open the door, she raced the few feet to Tepper's body. For a few moments she stood over it, numb with shock as she took in the woman's opened eyes, her slack mouth, and the cord that was twisted around her neck.

Bessie tried to call for help but was unable to force a sound past her throat and lips. Then she turned and stumbled back to the car and into the driver's seat. She leaned on the horn. In the nearby houses, lights flashed on, and annoyed residents rushed to their windows. Several men ran outside to see the cause of the commotion—ironically, all of them barefooted.

The husband of the neighbor Yvonne Tepper had been visiting when she was waylaid by The Owl jumped into the passenger seat of Bessie's car and firmly pulled her hands off the blaring horn.

That was when Bessie was finally able to scream.

61

Sam Deegan was weary enough to sleep the sleep of the just, even though the instinct that made him a good cop was not satisfied that the latest fax Jean had received was on the level.

The alarm woke him at 6:00 A.M., and he lay in bed briefly with his eyes closed. The fax was the first conscious thought in his mind. Too glib, he thought again. Covers everything. But it's doubtful that a judge would grant a rush order to open Lily's file now, he decided.

Maybe that had been the point of the fax. Maybe someone had panicked, fearing that if a judge allowed the file to be opened and Lily had been questioned about her missing hairbrush, it might have implicated him.

It was that scenario that worried Sam. He opened his eyes, sat up, and threw back the covers. On the other hand, he thought, mentally playing devil's advocate, it does make sense that Laura somehow learned years ago that Jean was pregnant. At dinner Jean had told Alice and him that, before she disappeared, Laura had made a reference to Reed Thornton. "I'm not sure if she used his name," Jean said. "But I was surprised that she even had known I was dating a cadet."

I don't trust that fax, and I still think it's too much of a coincidence that five women died in the order that they were sitting at a lunch table, Sam thought as he plodded into the kitchen, plugged in the coffee maker, and went into the bathroom and turned on the shower.

The coffee was ready when he got back to the kitchen, dressed for the office in a jacket and slacks. He poured orange juice into a glass and dropped an English muffin into the toaster. When Kate was alive, he always had oatmeal for breakfast. Even though he had tried to convince himself that it wasn't difficult—putting a third of a cup of oatmeal in a bowl, adding a cup of low-fat milk and sticking the bowl in the microwave for two minutes—it just never came out right. Kate's was so much better. After a while he'd given up trying to make it for himself.

It had been nearly three years since Kate lost her long battle with cancer. Fortunately, the house wasn't so big that, with the boys raised and out, he felt the need to sell it. You don't get to live in a big house on an investigator's salary, Sam thought. A lot of other women might have complained about that, but not Kate. She loved this house, he thought. She had made it a home, and no matter how rough his day had been, he'd been happy and grateful to return to it at night.

It's still the same house, Sam thought as he picked up the newspaper from outside the kitchen door and settled down at the breakfast table. But it feels a lot different without Kate. Last night, dozing in Alice's den, he'd had the same kind of feeling there that he used to have about this place. Comfortable. Warm. The sound of Alice preparing dinner. The mouthwatering smell of roast beef drifting into the den.

He then remembered that, as he had been dozing off, something had caught his attention. What was it? Did it have something to do with Alice's curio cabinet? Next time he dropped in, he'd take a look. Maybe it was the demitasse cups she collected. His mother had loved them, too. He still had some of hers in the china closet.

Should he put butter on the English muffin, or eat it dry? he wondered.

Reluctantly, Sam decided not to use butter. I sure went off my diet last night, he recalled. That Yorkshire pudding Alice made was terrific. Jean enjoyed it as much as I did. She had been about ready to break under the tension of worrying about Lily. It was good to see her really relax. She's been looking as if she was carrying the weight of the world on her shoulders.

Let's hope that fax was on the level and that we hear from Laura again soon.

The phone rang just as he opened the newspaper. It was Eddie Zarro. "Sam, we just heard from the police chief in Highland Falls. A woman was found strangled on her front lawn there. The D.A. wants all of us in his office ASAP."

There was something Eddie was holding back. "What else?" Sam snapped.

"There was one of those little pewter owls in her pocket. Sam, we've got a full-blown nut case out there. I've got to warn you also that it was on the radio this morning that the Laura Wilcox disappearance is a publicity stunt she dreamed up with that comedian, Robby Brent. Rich Stevens is a very unhappy guy about all the time we've wasted over Wilcox when he has a homicidal maniac in Orange County on his hands. So do yourself a favor and don't bring up her name."

62

When Jean awoke, she was astonished to see that it was nine o'clock. She shivered as she got out of bed. The window was open a few inches from the bottom, and a cold breeze was blowing through the room. She hurried over and closed the window, then opened the blinds. Outside the sun was breaking through the overhead clouds, reflecting, she decided, the way she was feeling. The sun was breaking through the clouds in her life, and she was filled with a sense of euphoria. Laura is the one who has been contacting me about Lily, she reasoned, and if there is anything I can stake my life on, it is that Laura would never harm her. This is all about her need for money.

Still, I hope she gets in touch with me again soon, Jean thought. I should despise her for what she has put me through, but I realize now how desperate she was. There was something frenetic about her behavior on Saturday evening. I remember how she acted when I tried to talk to her before the honoree dinner. I asked her if she had seen anyone carrying a rose at the cemetery. She kept trying to brush me off, and finally she practically threw me out of her room. Was it because she could see how upset I was and felt guilty about what she was doing to me? Jean wondered. I'll bet anything she put the rose on the tombstone. She would have guessed that I'd visit Reed's grave.

Jean's last conscious thought before she fell asleep last night had been that she must let Craig Michaelson know about the fax from Laura. If on his own he had chosen to contact Lily's adoptive parents it simply wasn't fair to continue to worry them.

She slipped on her robe, went over to the desk, fished in her pocketbook for Michaelson's card, and phoned his office. He took her call immediately, and her heart sank at his reaction to what she told him.

"Dr. Sheridan," Craig Michaelson said, "have you verified that this latest communication is actually from Laura Wilcox?"

"No, and I can't. But do I believe she sent it? Absolutely. I confess that I was shocked to learn Laura knew about Lily and must have known I had been dating Reed. She certainly never let on at the time. Anyway, we also know, because of the cell phone Robby Brent bought and the time element of when I supposedly heard from Laura, that Robby must have made the phone call to me, imitating her voice. So I think we have two situations going here. Laura knows who Lily is, and she is broke and desperate for money. Then Robby concocted Laura's disappearance because he intends to use her on his new sitcom and was just trying to generate publicity. If you knew Robby Brent, you would understand it's the kind of performance—and sneaky trick—that he is utterly capable of carrying out."

Again she waited for reassurance from Craig Michaelson.

"Dr. Sheridan," he said finally, "I can understand your relief. As you very correctly surmised, when you came to my office yesterday, I was not at all convinced that you might not be concocting a story because you were obsessed with your need to locate your daughter. Frankly, your outburst was what convinced me that you were absolutely on the level. So I'm going to level with you now."

He did handle the adoption, Jean thought. He knows who Lily is and *where* she is.

"I considered the potential danger to your daughter serious enough to contact her adoptive father. He happens to be out of the country right now, but I'm sure I will hear from him shortly. I am going to tell him everything you have told me including who you are. As you know, you and I do not have an attorney-client privilege, and I feel I owe it to him and to his wife to make them aware that you are both believable and responsible."

"That is absolutely fine with me," Jean said. "But I don't want those people to go through the hell I've been going through these last few days. I don't want them to get the impression that Lily is in danger now, because I don't think she is anymore."

"I hope she is not, Dr. Sheridan, but I think until Ms. Wilcox comes forward, we should not be too sanguine about the fact that a serious problem may not still exist. Did you show this fax to the investigator you told me about?"

"Sam Deegan? Yes, I did. As a matter of fact, I gave it to him."

"May I have his phone number?"

"Of course." Jean had memorized Sam's number, but the continuing concern in Craig Michaelson's voice upset her enough that she could not be sure she remembered it. She looked it up, gave it to him, then said, "Mr. Michaelson, we seem to have reversed positions. Why are you so worried when I'm so relieved?"

"It's that hairbrush, Dr. Sheridan. If Lily remembers anything about the details of losing it—where she was, who she was with—it is a direct link to the person who sent it. If she recalls having been in the company of Laura Wilcox, then we can believe the contents of the recent fax are on the level. But knowing the adoptive parents and knowing Ms. Wilcox's rather well documented lifestyle, I find it a big stretch to think that your daughter was likely to be around her."

"I see," Jean said slowly, suddenly chilled by the logic of his reasoning. She ended the call with Michaelson, after agreeing to keep in touch. She then immediately dialed Sam's cell phone, but got no answer.

Her next call was to Alice Sommers. "Alice," she said, taking a deep breath. "Please be frank with me. Do you think there's any chance that the fax from Laura, or supposedly from Laura, was a ploy to slow us down, to keep me from contacting Lily's adoptive parents and asking about the hairbrush?"

The answer was the one she feared yet instinctively knew she was going to receive. "I didn't trust it at all, Jeannie," Alice said reluctantly. "Don't ask me why, but it didn't ring true to me, and I could tell Sam felt exactly the same way."

63

As Eddie Zarro had warned, District Attorney Rich Stevens was upset and angry. "These broken-down performers come into this county doing publicity stunts and waste our time when we have a maniac on our hands," he barked. "I'm going to issue a statement to the press to the effect that both Robby Brent and Laura Wilcox may face criminal charges for creating a hoax. Laura Wilcox has admitted that she's been sending those faxes threatening Dr. Sheridan's daughter. I don't care whether Dr. Sheridan is in a forgiving mood or not. I'm not. It's a crime to send threatening letters, and Laura Wilcox is going to answer for it."

Alarmed, Sam hastened to calm Stevens. "Wait, Rich," he said. "The press does not know about Dr. Sheridan's daughter or the threats to her. We can't let that out now."

"I'm aware of that, Sam," Rich Stevens snapped. "We're only going to refer to the publicity stunt that Wilcox confessed to in that last fax." He handed Sam the file on his desk. "Photos of the crime scene," he explained. "Take a look at them. Joy was the first one of our people to get there after the call came in. I know the rest of you have heard this already, but, Joy, fill Sam in on the victim and what the neighbor told you."

There were four other investigators in addition to Sam and Eddie

Zarro in the district attorney's office. Joy Lacko, the only woman in the group, had been an investigator for less than a year, but Sam had enormous respect for her intelligence and ability to extract information from shocked or grief-stricken witnesses.

"The victim, Yvonne Tepper, was sixty-three years old, divorced, with two grown sons, both of whom are married and live in California." Joy had her notebook in her hand but did not consult it as she looked directly at Sam. "She owned her own hairdressing salon, was very well liked, and apparently had no enemies. Her former husband has remarried and lives in Illinois." She paused. "Sam, all of this is probably irrelevant, given the pewter owl we found in Tepper's pocket."

"No fingerprints on it, I assume?" Sam queried.

"No fingerprints. We know it has to be the same guy who grabbed Helen Whelan Friday night."

"What neighbor did you talk to?"

"Actually, everyone on the block, but the one who knows anything is the one Tepper had been visiting and had probably just left when she was waylaid. Her name is Rita Hall. Tepper and she were close friends. Tepper had brought some cosmetics from her salon for Mrs. Hall and ran over with them when she got home last night, sometime after ten o'clock. The two women visited for a while and watched the eleven o'clock news together. Hall's husband, Matthew, had already gone to bed. Incidentally, this morning he was the first person to reach Bessie Koch, the woman who found the body and was blowing the horn of her car to get help. He was smart enough to tell the other neighbors to keep away from the body and to call 911."

"Did Yvonne Tepper leave Mrs. Hall's house directly after the news was over?" Sam asked.

"Yes. Mrs. Hall walked her to the door and stepped out onto the porch with her. She remembered that she wanted to tell Tepper something she'd heard about a former neighbor. She said they didn't stand there longer than a minute and that the overhead light was on, so they could have been seen. She said she noticed a car slow down and pull over to the curb, but she didn't think anything of it. Apparently the people across the street have teenagers who are always coming and going."

"Does Mrs. Hall remember anything about the car?" Sam asked.

"Only that it was a medium-sized sedan, either dark blue or black. Mrs. Hall went back into her house and closed the door, and Mrs. Tepper cut across the lawn to the sidewalk."

"My guess is that she was dead less than a minute later," Rich Stevens said. "The motive wasn't robbery. Her handbag was on the sidewalk. She had two hundred bucks in her wallet and was wearing a diamond ring and diamond earrings. The only thing that guy wanted to do was kill her. He grabbed her, pulled her onto her own lawn, strangled her, left her body behind a bush, and drove away."

"He stayed long enough to drop the owl in her pocket," Sam observed.

Rich Stevens looked from one to the other of his investigators. "I've been turning over in my head whether or not to release the information about the owl to the papers. Maybe someone would know something about a guy who's obsessed with owls or possibly keeps them as a hobby."

"You can imagine what a field day the media would have if they knew about the owl being left in the victims' pockets," Sam said quickly. "If this nut is on an ego trip, and I think he is, we'll be feeding him what he wants, to say nothing about the possibility of setting a copycat killer loose."

"And it's not as though we'd be warning women by releasing that bit of information," Joy Lacko pointed out. "He leaves the owl *after* he kills his victim, not before."

At the end of the meeting it was agreed that the best course of action was to warn women against being alone on the street after dark and to acknowledge that evidence pointed to the fact that both Helen Whelan and Yvonne Tepper had been murdered by the same unknown person or persons.

As they got up to go, Joy Lacko said quietly, "What scares me is that right now some perfectly innocent woman is going about her business, not realizing that in the next few days, just because she happens to be in the wrong place at the wrong time when that guy comes cruising by, her life will be over."

"I am not conceding that yet," Rich Stevens said sharply.

I am, Sam thought. I am.

64

On Wednesday morning, Jake Perkins attended his scheduled classes, with the exception of the creative writing seminar, which he felt he was more equipped to teach than the current instructor. Just before the lunch break, in his capacity as a reporter for the *Stonecroft Gazette*, he went into the office of President Downes for his scheduled interview, in which Downes was supposed to give his comments on the glorious success of the reunion.

Alfred Downes, however, was clearly not in good temper. "Jake, I realize I had promised you this time, but actually it's quite inconvenient now."

"I can understand, sir," Jake responded soothingly. "I guess you've seen on the news that the district attorney may press criminal charges against two of our Stonecroft honorees because of this publicity hoax."

"I am aware of that," Downes said, his voice icy.

If Jake noticed the frosty tone, he did not show it. "Do you think that all this adverse publicity reflects badly on Stonecroft Academy?" he asked.

"I would think that's obvious, Jake," Downes snapped. "If you're going to waste my time asking stupid questions, then get out of here now."

"I don't mean to ask stupid questions," Jake said quickly, his tone apologetic. "What I was leading up to is that at the dinner, Robby Brent gave a check for ten thousand dollars to our school. In light of his actions of the last few days, are you inclined to return that donation to him?"

It was a question that he was sure would make President Downes squirm. He knew how much Downes wanted a new addition to the school to be built during his term as president. It was common knowledge that, while Jack Emerson had dreamed up this reunion, along with the idea of the honorees, Alfred Downes had been delighted by the concept of it. It meant publicity for the school, a chance to show off the successful graduates—the message being, of course, that they learned everything they needed to know at good old Stonecroft—and it would also be a chance to wring donations from them and other alumni at the reunion.

Now the media were speculating about the eerie coincidence of five women from the same lunch table who had died since they graduated from Stonecroft, and Jake knew that wouldn't make anyone want to send their kids there. And now the Laura Wilcox and Robby Brent publicity scheme was another blow to the prestige of the school. His face set in earnest lines, his red hair sticking up even more than usual, Jake said, "Dr. Downes, as you know, my deadline for the *Gazette* is coming up. I just need a quote from you about the reunion."

Alfred Downes looked at his student with near loathing. "I am preparing a statement, and you will have a copy of it by tomorrow morning, Jake."

"Oh, thank you, sir." Jake felt a measure of sympathy for the man sitting across the desk from him. He's worried about his job, he thought. The board of trustees might give him the gate. They know Jack Emerson started the reunion fiasco because he owns the land they'll have to buy for a new addition, and that Downes went along with it. "Sir, I was thinking—"

"Don't think, Jake. Just be on your way."

"In a moment, sir, but please listen to this suggestion. I happen to know that Dr. Sheridan, Dr. Fleischman, and Gordon Amory are still at the Glen-Ridge and that Carter Stewart is staying across town at the Hudson Valley. Perhaps if you invited them to dinner and had some photos taken with them, it would be a way of putting Stonecroft back in a good light. Nobody could question any of *their* achievements, and pointing them out would offset the negative effect of the misconduct of the other two honorees."

Alfred Downes stared at Jake Perkins, thinking that in his thirty-five years of teaching he had never come across a student as nervy or as street-smart as he was. He leaned back in his chair and waited a long minute before responding. "When do you graduate, Jake?"

"I'll have enough credits by the end of this year, sir. As you know, every semester I've loaded up with extra classes. But my folks don't think I'll be ready to go off to college next year, so I'm happy to stay here and graduate with my class."

Jake looked at Dr. Downes and noted that he did not seem to share his happiness. "I have another idea for an article that you might like," he said. "I've done a lot of research on Laura Wilcox. I mean, I've gone over back issues of the *Gazette* and the *Cornwall Times* for the years she was here, and, as the *Times* reported, she was always the belle of the ball. Her family had money; her parents doted on her. I'm going to do a feature article for the *Gazette* to show how, with all the advantages Laura Wilcox enjoyed, she's the one who's having a hard time now."

Jake sensed that he was about to be interrupted, so he rushed on. "I think an article like that will serve two purposes, sir. It will show the kids at Stonecroft that having all the advantages doesn't guarantee success, and it will also show how the other honorees who had to struggle were better off for it. I mean, Stonecroft has both scholarship students and kids who work after school to help pay their tuition. That might motivate them, and besides, it looks good in print. The big-time media is looking for follow-up stories; it's the kind of thing they might pick up."

Gazing at the picture of himself on the wall behind Jake's head, Alfred Downes considered Jake's reasoning. "It's possible," he admitted reluctantly.

"I'm going to take pictures of the houses where Laura lived while she was growing up in Cornwall. The first one is empty now, but it was renovated recently and looks really good. The second house her family moved to on Concord Avenue is what I would call a tract mansion."

"A tract mansion?" Downes asked, bewildered.

"You know, it's one of a bunch of houses on one block that are too big or too ostentatious for the neighborhood. They're sometimes called McMansions."

"I never heard either expression," Downes said, more to himself than to Jake.

Jake jumped to his feet. "Not important, sir. But I have to tell you, the more I think about it, the more I like the idea of doing a story on Laura with her homes in the background and pictures of her when she was here at Stonecroft and later ones when she became famous. Now I'll get out of your way, Dr. Downes. But maybe I should give you another piece of advice. If you can put that dinner together, I suggest you skip inviting Mr. Emerson. My impression is that none of the honorees can stand him."

65

At ten o'clock Craig Michaelson received the call he had been expecting. "General Buckley is on the line," his secretary announced.

Craig picked up the phone. "Charles, how are you?"

"I'm fine, Craig," a concerned voice answered. "But what about this matter of extreme urgency? What's wrong?"

Craig Michaelson drew in his breath. I should have known there was no way of beating around the bush with Charles, he thought. He didn't get to be a three-star general for no reason. "First of all, it may not be as worrisome as I thought," he said, "but I consider it a matter of genuine concern. As you probably suspected, it's about Meredith. Yesterday, Dr. Jean Sheridan came to see me. Have you ever heard of her?"

"The historian? Yes. Her first book was about West Point. I enjoyed it very much, and I believe I've read all her subsequent books. She's a good writer."

"She's more than that," Craig Michaelson said bluntly. "She's Meredith's natural mother, and I have called you because of something that she has brought to my attention."

"Jean Sheridan is Meredith's mother!"

General Charles Buckley listened intently as Michaelson told him what he knew of Jean Sheridan's history and of the Stonecroft reunion and the perceived threat to Meredith. He interrupted only occasionally, to clarify what he was hearing. Then he said, "Craig, as you know, Meredith is aware that she is adopted. Since she was a teenager, she has expressed interest in finding her natural mother. At the time you and Dr. Connors arranged the adoption, you told us that her father had been killed in an accident prior to his college graduation and her mother was an eighteen-year-old about to go to college on a scholarship. Meredith knows that much."

"Jean Sheridan is aware that I am revealing her identity to you. What I did not tell you twenty years ago is that Meredith's natural father was a cadet who died in a hit-and-run accident on the grounds of West Point. It would have made it too easy for you to determine who he was."

"A cadet! No, you didn't tell me that."

"His name was Carroll Reed Thornton, Jr."

"I know his father," Charles Buckley said quietly. "Carroll never got over his son's death. I can't believe that he is Meredith's grandfather."

"Trust me, he is, Charles. Now, Jean Sheridan is so relieved to believe that Laura Wilcox was the one contacting her about Lily, as she had called Meredith, that she's willing to accept this last fax with Laura's supposed apology as gospel. I don't."

"I can't imagine where Meredith would have met Laura Wilcox," Charles Buckley said slowly.

"Exactly my reaction. And there's something else. If Laura Wilcox is on the level about being behind these threats, I can tell you right now that the district attorney in this county is going to prosecute her."

"Is Jean Sheridan still in Cornwall?"

"Yes, she is. She's going to wait in the Glen-Ridge House until she hears from Laura again."

"I'm going to phone Meredith and ask her if she ever met Laura

Wilcox and if she remembers where she left that hairbrush. There are meetings here at the Pentagon that I can't get out of today, but Gano and I will fly up to Cornwall tomorrow morning. Will you contact Jean Sheridan and say that her daughter's adoptive parents would like to meet her for dinner tomorrow evening?"

"Of course."

"I don't want to alarm Meredith, but I can ask her to promise me that she won't go outside the West Point grounds until we see her on Friday."

"Can you count on her keeping that promise?"

For the first time since they had begun speaking, Craig Michaelson heard his good friend General Charles Buckley sound relaxed. "Of course I can. I may be her father, but I'm also way up there in the chain of command. Now we know that Meredith is an army brat in both her natural and adoptive families, but remember, she's also a West Point cadet. When she gives her word to a senior officer, she doesn't break it."

I hope you're right, Craig Michaelson thought. "Let me know what she tells you, Charles."

"Of course."

An hour later General Charles Buckley called back. "Craig," he said, his voice troubled, "I'm afraid you're right to be skeptical about that fax. Meredith is absolutely certain that she never met Laura Wilcox, and she doesn't have the vaguest idea where she lost that hairbrush. I would have pressed her more, but she has a big exam in the morning and is terribly worried about it, so it absolutely wasn't the time to upset her. She's delighted that her mother and I"—he hesitated, then continued firmly—"that her mother and I are coming up to see her.

Over the weekend, if all works out, we'll tell her about Jean Sheridan and give them a chance to meet each other. I asked Meredith to promise me to stay at the Academy until we saw her, and she laughed at me. She said she has another test on Friday and so much studying to do that she won't see the light of day until Saturday morning. But she did make the promise."

It sounds okay, Craig Michaelson thought as he replaced the receiver, but the cold hard fact is that Laura Wilcox did *not* send that fax, and Jean Sheridan has got to be made aware of that.

For easy access, he had placed Jean's card directly under the phone on his desk. He reached for it, picked up the phone, and started to dial Jean's number. Then he broke the connection. She wasn't the one to call, he decided. She had given him the number of that investigator from the district attorney's office. Where was it? What was his name? he wondered.

After a moment of rummaging around on the top of his desk, he saw the notation he had made: Sam Deegan, followed by a phone number. That's what I want, Michaelson thought, and he began to dial.

66

Last night—or was it this morning? she wondered—he had thrown a blanket over her. "You're cold, Laura," he said. "There's no need for that. I've been thoughtless."

He's being kind, Laura thought dully. He even brought jam with the roll and remembered that she liked skim milk in her coffee. He was so calm, she almost relaxed.

That was what she wanted to remember, not what he had told her as she sat in the chair, sipping the coffee, her legs still bound but her hands free.

"Laura, I wish you could understand the feeling I get when I'm driving along the quiet streets, watching for my prey. There is an art to it, Laura. Never drive too slowly. A patrol car watching for speeders is just as likely to pounce on the car that is not moving at an appropriate pace as one that's going too fast. You see people who know they've had too much to drink make the mistake of inching along the road, a sure sign that they don't trust their own judgment, and a sure sign to the police, too.

"Last night, Laura, I searched for prey. As a tribute to Jean, I decided to go to Highland Falls. That's where she had her little trysts with the cadet. Did you know about that, Laura?"

Laura shook her head in response. He became angry.

"Laura, speak up! Did you know that Jean was having an affair with that cadet?"

"I saw them together once when I went to a concert at West Point but didn't think much of it," Laura had told him. "Jeannie never said a word about him to any of us," she had explained. "We all knew she went up to the Point a lot because even then she was planning to write a book about it."

The Owl had nodded, satisfied with her answer. "I knew Jean often went up on Sundays with her notebook and sat on one of the benches overlooking the river," he had said. "I went looking for her one Sunday and saw him join her. I followed them when they went for a walk. When they thought they were alone, he kissed her. I kept track of them after that, Laura. Oh, they went to great pains not to be viewed as a couple. She didn't even go to the dances with him. That spring, I observed Jean carefully. I wish you could have seen the expression on her face when they were together and away from other people. It was *luminous!* Jean, quiet, kind Jean, whom I felt was my fellow sufferer, given her tumultuous home life, my soul mate—she was living a life from which she had *excluded* me."

I thought he had a crush on me, Laura reasoned, and that he hated me for making fun of him. But he really loved Jeannie. The horror of what he had told her was still seeping into her consciousness.

"Reed Thornton's death wasn't an accident, Laura," he said. "I was driving through the grounds that last Sunday in May, twenty years ago, just on the chance that I might see them. Handsome, golden-haired Reed was walking alone on the road that leads to the picnic grounds. Maybe they were meeting there. Did I mean to kill him? Of course I did. He had everything I didn't have—looks and background and a promising future. And he had Jeannie's love. It wasn't fair. Agree with me, Laura! *It wasn't fair!*"

She stammered a reply, anxious to agree with him and avoid his anger. Then he told her in detail about the woman he had killed the night before. He said he had apologized to her, but when it was Laura's time to die, and Jean's, there wouldn't be any apologies.

He said that Meredith would be the last of his prey. He said that she would complete his need—or at least it was his hope that she would complete his need.

I wonder who Meredith is, Laura thought drowsily. She slipped into a sleep that was filled with visions of owls gliding toward her from branches, rushing at her, hooting eerily, wings fluttering softly, as she tried to run from them on legs that would not, could not, move.

67

Jean, help me! Please, Jean, help me! Laura's pleading voice, which had sounded so vivid in her head as she sat in the car outside Craig Michaelson's office the day before, began playing over and over again in Jean's mind, as though it was an echo of the doubts Alice had expressed about the authenticity of the fax.

For long minutes after she said good-bye to Alice, Jean sat at the desk, Laura's voice haunting her, as she tried to decide rationally whether Sam and Alice were right. Perhaps she had rushed to accept the fax as real because she needed to believe that Lily was safe.

Finally she got up, went into the bathroom, and for long minutes stayed under the shower, letting the water splash over her hair and face. She shampooed her hair, kneading her scalp as though the pressure of her fingers might unscramble the confusion in her mind.

I need to go for a long walk, she thought, as she wrapped her terry cloth robe around her body and turned on the hair dryer. That's the only way I can possibly clear my head. When she was packing for the weekend, she had impulsively thrown her favorite red jogging suit into her suitcase. Now she was grateful to be able to reach for it, but remembering how cold it had felt with the window open, she took the precaution of wearing a sweater underneath the jacket.

She noted the time as she put on her watch. It was ten-fifteen, and she realized she had not had a cup of coffee. No wonder my brain is muddled, she thought ruefully. I'll get a container to go from the coffee shop and drink it while I'm walking. I'm not hungry, and I feel as if the walls of this place are closing in on me.

As she zipped up the jacket, an uneasy thought crossed her mind. Every time I leave this room, I'm taking the chance of missing a call from Laura. I can't stay here day and night. But wait a minute! I think I can leave my own message on the room phone.

She read the instructions on the phone, picked up the receiver, and pushed the message record button. Taking care to speak clearly, and with the volume of her voice slightly raised, she said, "This is Jean Sheridan. If it's important that you reach me, please call me on my cell phone, 202-555-5314. I'll repeat. That is 202-555-5314." She hesitated, then added in a rush, "Laura, I want to help you. Please call me!"

Jean replaced the receiver with one hand and dabbed her eyes with the other. All the earlier euphoria of thinking that Lily was completely safe had evaporated, but something inside her stubbornly refused to believe that the fax had not come from Laura. The room clerk who took the first phone call from Laura had said she sounded nervous, Jean reminded herself. Sam told me that Jake Perkins, who managed to listen in on that call, had agreed. Robby Brent's call to me imitating Laura and saying that everything was fine was another one of his tricks. He probably talked Laura into this publicity scheme, and now she's afraid of the fallout. And I believe that if she didn't threaten me about Lily herself, then she knows who *did*. That's why I've got to make her realize I want to help her.

Jean got up, reached for her shoulder bag, but decided she didn't want to be bothered carrying it. Instead she put a handkerchief, her cell phone, and her room key in her pocket. Then, as an afterthought, she plucked a twenty-dollar bill from her wallet. This way, if

I want to stop somewhere and get a croissant when I'm out, I can do it, she thought.

She started to leave the room, then realized she was forgetting something. Of course, her sunglasses. Annoyed at her inability to concentrate, she went back to the dresser, pulled the glasses out of her bag, walked quickly to the door, opened it, and with a decisive snap, pulled it closed behind her.

The elevator was empty when it stopped at her floor—not like the weekend, she thought, when every time I stepped into it, I bumped into someone I hadn't seen in twenty years.

In the lobby, banners welcoming the Top 100 Sales Representatives of the Starbright Electrical Fixtures Company were being tacked over the front desk and dining room doors. From Stonecroft to Starbright, Jean thought. I wonder how many honorees *they* have, or are all one hundred of them honorees?

The clerk with the large glasses and soft voice was behind the front desk, reading a book. I'm sure she's the one who got the call from Laura, Jean thought. I want to talk to her myself. She walked over to the desk and glanced at the name tag on the clerk's uniform. It read "Amy Sachs."

"Amy," Jean said with a friendly smile, "I'm a good friend of Laura Wilcox, and like everyone else, I've been terribly concerned about her. I understand that you and Jake Perkins were the ones who spoke to her on Sunday night."

"Jake grabbed the phone when he heard me say Ms. Wilcox's name." Amy's defensive tone raised the level of her voice to near normal range.

"I understand," Jean said soothingly. "I've met Jake and know how he operates. Amy, I'm glad that he heard Laura's voice. He's smart, and I trust his impression. I know you hardly met Ms. Wilcox, but do you absolutely believe you were speaking to her?"

"Oh, I *do*, Dr. Sheridan," Amy Sachs said solemnly. "Don't forget, I was very familiar with her voice from watching her on *Henderson County*. For three years I never missed that program. Like clockwork, Tuesday nights at eight o'clock, my mother and I were in front of the television to see it." She paused, then added, "Unless I was working, of course, which I tried not to do on Tuesday nights. But sometimes they'd have to ask me to come in because someone was sick, and then my mother would tape the program for me."

"Well then, I'm sure you would know Laura's voice. Amy, will you tell me yourself how Laura sounded to you on that call?"

"Dr. Sheridan, I have to tell you she sounded *funny*. I mean funny *different*. Just between us, my first impression was that maybe she was hungover, because I know she had a drinking problem a couple of years ago. I read about it in *People*. But now I really think Jake was right. Ms. Wilcox didn't sound like she'd had too much to drink; she sounded nervous—very, very nervous."

Amy's voice lowered to its usual near-whisper. "In fact, Sunday night, after I talked to Ms. Wilcox, when I went home I told my mother that she reminded me of the way I used to sound when our elocution teacher in high school was trying to make me talk louder. I was so scared of her that my voice would start to quiver because I'd be trying not to cry. That's the best way I can describe how Ms. Wilcox sounded to me!"

"I see." *Jean, help me! Please, Jean, help me!* I was right, Jean thought. This is *not* about a publicity stunt.

Amy's triumphant smile at being able to describe her reaction to Laura's voice vanished almost before it appeared. "And, Dr. Sheridan, I do want to apologize that your fax yesterday got caught in Mr. Cullen's mail. We pride ourselves on our prompt and careful delivery of faxes that come in for our guests. I have to be sure to explain that to Dr. Fleischman when I see him."

"Dr. Fleischman?" Jean asked, her curiosity aroused. "Is there any reason why you would explain that to him?"

"Well, yes. Yesterday afternoon, when he came in from his walk, he stopped at the desk and phoned your room. I knew you were in the coffee shop and told him that he could find you there. Then he asked if you had received any new faxes, and he seemed surprised when I said you hadn't. I could tell he knew you were expecting one."

"I see. Thank you, Amy." Jean tried not to show how shocked she was at what the desk clerk had told her. Why would Mark ask a question like that? she wondered. Forgetting that she had intended to get a container of coffee, she walked numbly through the lobby and out the front door.

It was even colder outside than she had expected, but the sun was strong and there was no wind, so she decided she would be okay. She slipped on her sunglasses and began to walk away from the hotel grounds, headed no place in particular. Her mind was suddenly filled with a possibility she did not want to accept. Was Mark the person who had been sending the faxes about Lily? Had he sent Lily's hairbrush to her? Mark, who had been so comforting when she had confided her anguish to him, who had covered her hand with his and made her feel that he wanted to share her pain?

Mark knew I was dating Reed, Jean thought. He told me himself that he saw us when he was jogging at West Point. Did he somehow find out about Lily? Unless he's been sending the faxes, why would he be concerned that I hadn't received one by mid-afternoon yesterday? Is he behind all this, and if he is, would he hurt my child?

I don't want to believe that, she thought, agonized by the prospect. I *can't* believe that! But why would he ask the clerk if I'd received a fax? Why didn't he ask me?

Not thinking about where she was going, Jean walked through streets that she had known intimately as a child. She passed Town

Hall without seeing it, went as far along Angola Road as the turn-off from the highway, retraced her steps, and finally, an hour later, went into a combination delicatessen–coffee shop at the end of Mountain Road. She sat at the counter and ordered coffee. Dejected and once again deeply worried, she realized that neither the cold air nor the long walk had succeeded in helping to clarify her thinking. I'm worse off than when I started, she thought. I don't know who to trust or what to believe.

According to the large red stitching on his jacket, Duke Mackenzie was the name of the scrawny gray-haired man behind the counter. He obviously was in the mood to chat. "You new around here, Miss?" he asked as he poured the coffee.

"No. I grew up here."

"By any chance, were you with that twenty-year reunion group from Stonecroft?"

There was no way of not answering the man. "Yes, I was."

"Where in town did you live?"

Jean gestured toward the back of the store. "Right up there on Mountain Road."

"No kidding? We weren't here then. Used to be a dry cleaner on this spot."

"I remember." Even though the coffee was almost too hot to drink, Jean began sipping it.

"My wife and I liked the town and bought this place about ten years ago. Had to do a complete renovation. Sue and I work hard, but we enjoy it. Open at 6:00 A.M. and don't close till 9:00 P.M. Sue's back there in the kitchen right now, making all the salads and doing the baking. We just do short-order stuff at the counter, but you'd be surprised how many people stop in for a quick cup of coffee or a sandwich."

Only half-listening to the torrent of words, Jean nodded.

"Over the weekend some of the Stonecroft alumni dropped in here when they were walking around town," Duke continued. "They couldn't believe how property values have gone up. What numbe did you say you were on Mountain Road?"

Reluctantly, Jean told him the address of her childhood home Then, anxious to get away, she gulped most of the rest of the coffee even though it was burning her mouth. She stood up, put the twenty dollar bill on the counter, and asked for a check.

"Second cup's free." Duke was clearly anxious not to lose her ear

"No, that's fine. I'm running late."

While Duke was at the cash register making change, Jean's cel phone rang. It was Craig Michaelson. "I'm glad you left a forwarding number, Dr. Sheridan," he said. "Can you talk without being over heard?"

"Yes." Jean stepped away from the counter.

"I have just spoken to your daughter's adoptive father. He and hi wife are coming into this area tomorrow and would like to have din ner with you. Lily, as you called your daughter, knows she is adopte and has always expressed an interest in knowing her natural mothe Her parents want that to happen. I don't want to go into too much de tail over the phone, but I will tell you this much: it is virtually impos sible that your daughter ever met Laura Wilcox, so I think you have to assume the last fax is a hoax. But because of her present location, you can be assured that she is safe."

For a moment, Jean was so stunned that she could not say a single word.

"Dr. Sheridan?"

"Yes, Mr. Michaelson," she whispered.

"Are you free for dinner tomorrow night?"

"Yes, of course."

"I will pick you up at seven o'clock. I suggested that having dinne at my home would give the three of you privacy. Then, very soon, perhaps as early as this weekend, you will meet Meredith."

"Meredith? Is that her name? Is that my daughter's name?" Jean realized her voice was suddenly high-pitched, but she could not control it. I'm going to see her soon, she thought. I'll be able to look into her eyes. I can put my arms around her. She did not care that tears were streaming down her cheeks or that Duke was staring at her and absorbing every word she said.

"Yes, it is. I didn't mean to tell it to you now, but it doesn't matter." Craig Michaelson's voice was kind. "I understand how you feel. I'll pick you up at the hotel tomorrow evening at seven."

"Tomorrow evening at seven," Jean repeated. She clicked off the phone and for a moment stood perfectly still. Then, with the back of her hand, she brushed away the tears that were streaming down her cheeks. *Meredith, Meredith, Meredith,* she thought.

"Looks like you got good news," Duke volunteered.

"Yes, I did. Oh, dear God, yes I did." Jean picked up her change, left a dollar on the counter and, in a joyful trance, walked out of the delicatessen.

Duke Mackenzie watched intently as Jean Sheridan left his shop. She looked pretty glum when she came in, he thought, but from the way she looked after she got that phone call, you'd think she won the lottery. What the heck did she mean when she asked what her daughter's name is?

He watched from the window as Jean began to walk up Mountain Road. If she hadn't left so fast, he'd have asked her about that fellow with the dark glasses and cap who had been coming in the last couple of mornings, right after they opened at six o'clock. He always ordered the same thing—juice, a buttered roll, and coffee to go. When he got back in his car, he drove up Mountain Road. Last night he came in again, just before closing time, and ordered a sandwich and coffee.

That guy's a funny duck, Duke thought as he wiped the already spotless counter. I asked him if he was part of the Stonecroft reunion, and he gave me a wiseguy answer. He said, "I *am* the reunion."

Duke ran the sponge under hot water and squeezed it. Maybe, tomorrow, if he comes in, I'll tell Sue to wait on him, and I'll sit in the car and follow to see who he's visiting on Mountain Road, he thought. I wonder if it's Margaret Mills. She's been divorced for a couple of years, and everyone knows she's looking for a boyfriend. Won't hurt to check it out.

Duke poured a cup of coffee for himself. Lots going on around here since those reunion people showed up last week, he thought. If that quiet guy stops in tonight for a sandwich and coffee, I'll ask him about the gal who was just here. I mean she's from the reunion and she's really attractive so he must at least know who she is. It's crazy that she had to be told her own daughter's name. Maybe he knows what's up with her.

Duke chuckled as he downed another swig of coffee. Sue was always telling him that curiosity killed the cat. I'm not curious, Duke reassured himself. I just like to know what's going on.

68

At twelve o'clock Sam Deegan tapped on the door of the district attorney's office and walked in without waiting for a response.

Rich Stevens was poring over notes on his desk and looked up, his expression showing irritation at the abrupt interruption.

"Rich, sorry to barge in, but this is important," Sam told him. "We're making a big mistake if we don't take the threat to Jean Sheridan's daughter seriously. I had a message to call Craig Michaelson, the lawyer who handled the adoption. We just connected. Michaelson has been in touch with the adoptive parents. The father is a three-star general at the Pentagon. The girl is a second-year cadet at West Point. The General called her and asked if she had ever met Laura Wilcox. The answer is absolutely not. And she doesn't remember where she lost the hairbrush."

There wasn't a trace of annoyance left in Rich Stevens' expression as he leaned back in his chair and entwined his fingers, always a sign to those who knew him that he was deeply concerned.

"That's all we need," he said, "to have the daughter of a three-star general being threatened by some nut. Are they putting a bodyguard on the girl at the Point?"

"From what Michaelson tells me, she has two big exams, one tomorrow, one Friday. She laughed at the suggestion that she'd leave the grounds. The father didn't want to upset her by telling her about these threats. He and the mother are flying up tomorrow to meet Jean Sheridan. The General wants to come in here and talk to you Friday morning."

"Who is he?"

"Michaelson didn't want to give that information over the phone. The girl knows she's adopted, but until this morning the General and his wife had no idea of the identity of the natural parents. Jean Sheridan swears she never told anybody about the baby until she started getting thc faxes. I say whoever found out about the baby and knew who had adopted her, learned it at the time she was born. Michaelson is sure his records were never seen by anyone. Jean Sheridan suspects the leak occurred in the doctor's office where she was a maternity patient, which at least gives us a starting point in trying to figure out who might have had access to the records."

"Then if Laura Wilcox isn't involved in the threats and didn't send that last fax apologizing for them, I've stuck my neck out by calling her disappearance a publicity stunt," Rich Stevens said bitterly.

"We can't be sure about that part of it yet, Rich, but we can be pretty damn sure that she's not the one threatening the girl. Which raises the question, if Laura *didn't* send that fax, was it sent to make us drop the investigation?"

"Which is what I told you to do. All right, Sam. I'll pull you off the homicides. I wish we knew the name of the cadet. I'll ask you again: Is the General *positive* that she's safe?"

"According to Michaelson, she is because of the tests. He says that if she's not in class, she's studying in her room. She assured her father she wouldn't leave the West Point campus."

"Then with all the security at West Point, she should be all right, at least for the present. That's a relief."

"I'm not so sure about that. Being on the grounds of West Point didn't save her natural father's life," Sam said grimly. "He was a cadet. Two weeks before graduation he was the victim of a hit-and-run driver. They never found the person who killed him."

"Any question that it wasn't an accident?" Stevens asked sharply.

"From what Jean Sheridan tells me, it never occurred to anyone that Reed Thornton—that was his name—was deliberately run down. They believed the driver panicked and then was afraid to turn himself in. But in light of all that's been happening, it wouldn't be a bad idea to look at the file on that case."

"Run with it, Sam. God Almighty, can you just see what the media will do if they ever get their hands on this? Three-star general's daughter, a West Point cadet, threatened. Her natural father, a cadet, died in a mysterious accident at the Point. Her natural mother is an acclaimed historian and a best-selling author."

"There's more," Sam said. "Reed Thornton's father is a retired brigadier general. He still doesn't know he has a granddaughter."

"Sam, I'll ask you one more time: Are you sure, are you positive that the girl is safe?"

"I have to accept the fact that her adopted father is satisfied that she's safe."

As Sam got up, he noticed a pile of notes on Rich Stevens' desk. "More tips about the homicides?"

"Sam, in the couple of hours you've been out, I've lost count of how many calls have poured in about suspicious-looking men. One of them came from a woman who swore she'd been followed out of the supermarket. She got the guy's license plate number. The suspect turned out to be an FBI agent who's visiting his mother. We've had two calls about strange cars in schoolyards. Both of them turned out to be fathers waiting for their kids. We have a nut who confessed to the murders. The only problem is he's been in jail for the last month."

"Any psychics call yet?"

"Oh, sure. Three of them."

The phone on Stevens' desk rang. He picked it up, listened, then put his hand over the speaker. "I'm holding for the governor," he said, raising his eyebrows.

As Sam left the room, he heard the district attorney saying, "Good morning, Governor. Yes, it is a very serious problem, but we're working round the clock to . . ."

To find the perpetrator and bring him to justice, Sam thought. Let's hope that happens before any more pewter owls get planted on dead women.

Including a nineteen-year-old West Point cadet—that chilling possibility darted through his mind as he walked down the corridor to his own office.

69

"Lily . . . Meredith. Lily . . . Meredith," Jean whispered over and over as she walked up Mountain Road, her hands in her pockets, her sunglasses hiding the tears of happiness she could not stop shedding.

She wasn't sure why she had wandered up that street except that when she rushed out of the coffee shop, she knew she wasn't ready to go back to the hotel. She passed houses that had belonged to neighbors years ago. How many of them still live here? she wondered. I just hope I don't run into anyone I know.

She slowed her step as she came near the house she had lived in. When she had driven by on Sunday morning, she hadn't had the chance to really study what the present owners had done with it. She glanced around. There was no one on the street to observe her. For a moment she stopped and put her hand on the split rail fence that now enclosed the property.

They must have added at least two more bedrooms when they renovated, she decided as she studied the house. When we lived here, there were only three bedrooms, one for each of us—Mother, Dad, and me. When we were kids, Laura used to ask me about that: "Don't your mother and father sleep together? Don't they *like* each other?"

I had read in an advice column in one of those women's magazines that no woman should have to sleep in the same room with her husband if he snored a lot. I told Laura my father snored a lot. She said, "So does mine, but they still sleep together."

I said, "Well, mine do, too, sometimes." But they didn't.

Now she looked up at the second floor at the two center windows. Those are the windows of my room, Jean thought. God, how I hated the flowered wallpaper. It was so busy. When I was fifteen, I begged Dad to cover the walls with bookshelves. He really was handy with projects like that. Mother objected, but he did it anyhow. After that, I called my room the library.

I remember the first day I was sure that my period was late and the days that followed when I prayed it would come. I promised God I'd do anything He wanted if I could just not be pregnant.

Well, now I'm glad I was, Jean thought fiercely. Lily . . . Meredith. I may meet her as soon as this weekend. At some point I'll probably slip and call her Lily, then have to explain, although maybe by then she'll understand. I wonder how tall she is. Reed was over six feet, and he told me that his father and grandfather were taller than he was.

Lily is safe—that is absolutely the most important thing in the world. But Craig Michaelson is sure that she never met Laura. So how would Laura know about the faxes?

Jean had intended to turn and start back to the Glen-Ridge but instead impulsively walked past her old house, up to Laura's former home. She stopped and stood in front of it.

As she had observed from the car on Sunday morning, the house and grounds were being maintained regularly. The house looked freshly painted, the flagstone walk was bordered with autumn flowers, and the lawn was swept free of leaves. Even so, with the shades drawn in every window, the house had a closed, unwelcoming look. Why would anyone buy a house, renovate it, keep it up, and not enjoy living in it? Jean wondered. She had heard a rumor that Jack

Emerson owned it. He's supposed to be quite the ladies' man. I wonder if he's kept it as a love nest for his girlfriends. If he does own it, now that his wife has moved to Connecticut, it would be interesting to see if he still needs it.

Not that I care, God knows, Jean thought as she turned and started back to the hotel. With a conscious effort she tried to put her anticipation about meeting Lily aside and concentrate on Laura and the new scenario that had been evolving in her mind.

Robby Brent.

Had Robby Brent been behind the faxes about Lily? she asked herself, trying to reason through that scenario. Maybe he's the one who found out I was pregnant. Maybe now he realizes that he could be prosecuted for sending those threats and wants Laura to take the blame because he suspects I would feel sorry for her.

It's possible, Jean decided as she passed the delicatessen and reluctantly waved to Duke, who was tapping on the window and waving at her. Robby Brent is just nasty enough to have somehow found out about Lily, and then, when the reunion came up, have sent those faxes as a cruel joke. I understand that he does a couple of benefits a year. It's possible he met Lily's family that way. Look how rotten he was, the way he ridiculed Dr. Downes and Miss Bender at the dinner. Even the way he presented his check to Stonecroft was an insult.

It was a scenario that made sense to her. If Robby sent those faxes and the hairbrush, he had to be worried about criminal prosecution, she reasoned. If he planned the publicity stunt with Laura, then that has backfired. In that case, he probably will be in touch with his producers to figure out a story. The media are going to hound them for an explanation.

On the other hand, Jack Emerson worked evenings in Dr. Connors' office and might have gotten into his files. Besides that, I need to know why Mark asked the clerk about my receiving a fax and then was disappointed to learn I didn't get one. Well, at least I can find that out fast enough, Jean thought as she turned onto the walkway that led to the Glen-Ridge.

When she stepped into the lobby, the warmth inside enveloped her, and she realized that she had been shivering. I ought to go up and soak in the tub, she reflected. Instead, she went to the front desk where a now busy Amy Sachs was checking in the early arrivals of the Starbright Electrical Fixtures Company event. She picked up the in-house phone, but when the customer Amy was waiting on was searching in his bag for his wallet, Jean managed to catch the clerk's eye and ask, "Any mail?"

"Not a bit," Amy whispered. "You can count on me, Dr. Sheridan. No more mistakes with your faxes."

Jean nodded as she gave the operator Mark's name. He answered on the first ring. "Jean, I was worried about you," he said.

"You've been worrying me, too," she said in an even tone. "It's nearly one o'clock, and I haven't had anything but half a cup of coffee all day. I'm going to the coffee shop. I'd be glad if you'd join me, but don't bother to stop at the desk and check to see if I've had any new faxes. I haven't."

70

True to his word, when he left President Downes' office, Jake Perkins went directly to the classroom that had become headquarters for the newspaper. There he dug through the files of *Gazette* pictures that had been taken during the four years that Laura Wilcox had been a student at Stonecroft. In preparation for the reunion, he had looked through the yearbooks and found pictures of her. But now he wanted to get others, maybe some that were a little more candid than the yearbook shots.

In the next hour he found some photos that were right on target. Laura had been in a number of school plays. One of them was a musical, and he found a great picture of her performing in a chorus line, a standout in a Rockette-like group, with her high kick and dazzling smile. No question, she was a knockout, Jake thought. If she were in school now, there isn't a guy I know who wouldn't be trying to get her attention.

He snickered to himself as he thought of the way in which a boy would have tried to win favor with a girl back then, probably by offering to carry her books. Today he'd offer to drive her home in his Corvette, he thought.

It was when he came across the graduation picture of Laura's class that Jake's eyes widened. He used a magnifying glass to examine the faces of the graduates. Laura, of course, looked beautiful, with her long hair spilling over her shoulders. She even managed to be attractive while wearing that stupid mortarboard. It was Jean Sheridan's picture that shocked him. Her hands were clasped together. There were tears welling in her eyes. She looks sad, Jake thought, really sad. You'd never guess she'd just walked off with the History medal and a full scholarship to Bryn Mawr. From the expression on her face, you'd swear she'd just been told she had two days to live. Maybe she was sorry to leave this place. Go figure.

He moved the magnifying glass from one to the other of the graduates, looking for the honorees. One by one he picked them out. They've all changed a lot, he thought. A couple of them looked like real losers back then. Gordon Amory, for example, was almost unrecognizable. Boy, was be ugly, he thought. Jack Emerson was Fat Boy even then. Carter Stewart needed a haircut—no, make that a total makeover. No-neck Robby Brent was already going bald. Mark Fleischman looks like a beanpole with a head on it. Joel Nieman was standing next to Fleischman. Some Romeo, Jake thought. If I were Juliet, I'd have killed myself at the thought of being stuck with him.

Then he noticed something. Most of the graduates had inane grins on their faces, the kind people save for group pictures. The biggest smile, however, was on the face of one guy who wasn't looking directly at the camera but instead was staring at Jean Sheridan. Talk about contrasts, Jake thought. She looks as if she's lost her last friend, and he's wearing an ear-to-ear grin.

Jake shook his head as he looked at the pile of pictures on the table in front of him. I have enough now, he thought. Next he would talk to Jill Ferris, the teacher in charge of the *Gazette*. She's a good sport, Jake thought. I'll convince her to let me use the picture of Laura dancing on the front page of the next issue, and the graduation picture on the back page. Between them, they bring out the theme of the story—the had-it-all girl who's now on the skids and the nerds who made it big-time.

His next stop was the studio where the camera equipment was kept. There he ran into Ms. Ferris, who let him sign out the heavy old-fashioned camera that he delighted in using when he was on a photo shoot. In his opinion it had a sharpness that no digital camera could possibly match. The fact that it was a backbreaker did not faze him when he was on an important assignment, especially since this assignment was one he had dreamed up himself.

He did admit to himself that his newly acquired driver's license and the ten-year-old Subaru his parents had bought for him made his jaunts around town considerably easier than when he used to play roving reporter on his bicycle.

Camera over his shoulder, notebook and pen in one pocket, recorder in the other in case he happened to run into someone worth interviewing, Jake was on his way.

Can't wait to do the house where Laura Wilcox grew up. I'll shoot from both the front and the back. After all, it was the house where that medical student, Karen Sommers, was murdered, and the police were sure then that the killer went in the back door. That will add another human interest touch to the story, he decided.

71

Carter Stewart spent the better part of Wednesday morning in his suite at the Hudson Valley Hotel. He had arranged to meet that afternoon with Pierce Ellison, the director of his new play, and would be going to Ellison's home. They were scheduled to discuss fixes the director wanted, but first Stewart wanted to make some script changes on his own.

Thank you, Laura, he thought, smiling maliciously as he made subtle alterations to the character of the scatterbrained blonde who is murdered in the second act. Desperation, he thought—that's what I was missing. On the surface she's twinkling, but we've got to feel how frantic and frightened she really is, that she'll do anything to save herself.

Carter despised interruptions when he was writing, a fact his agent, Tim Davis, knew very well. But at eleven o'clock the jarring ring of the phone shattered his concentration. It was Tim.

He began with a profuse apology: "Carter, I know you're working, and I promised I wouldn't bother you unless it was absolutely necessary, but—"

"It had *better* be absolutely necessary, Tim," Carter snapped.

"The thing is, I just got a call from Angus Schell. He's Robby

Brent's agent, and he's going nuts. Robby promised to send in his edits on the scripts for his new TV show by yesterday at the very latest, and they still haven't arrived. Angus has left a dozen messages for Robby but hasn't heard from him. The sponsor is already furious about the publicity stunt the media say Robby is pulling with Laura Wilcox. They're threatening to bail out on the series."

"Which is of no importance to me whatsoever," Carter Stewart said, his tone frigid.

"Carter, you told me the other day that Robby was going to show you the edits he made. Did you see them?"

"No, I did not. As a matter of fact, when I took the trouble to go over to his hotel for the purpose of reviewing those edits, he was not there, nor have I heard from him since. Now, if you'll excuse me, I was working very well until you interrupted me."

"Carter, please. Let me get this straight. You think that Robby *did* make the edits he promised the sponsor?"

"Tim, try to get *this* straight. Yes, I assume Robby made the edits. He told me he had. He asked me to look at them. I told him I would look at them. Then he wasn't there when I went to his hotel. In other words, to repeat in order to make myself perfectly clear, he made the edits and he wasted my time."

"Carter, I'm sorry. Look, I'm really sorry," Tim Davis said, anxious to placate his client. "Joe Dean and Barbara Monroe have already been cast for running parts and it means the world to them to get that series on the air. From what we read in the papers, both Wilcox and Robby left just about everything in their rooms at that hotel. Could you, would you, I beg you, could you see if by any chance he left the scripts there? The last time I spoke to Robby, he bragged that his rewrites were going to make the scripts hilarious. He hardly ever used that word, and when he did, he meant it. If we can get our hands on them by overnight mail, we might be able to salvage the show. The sponsor wants a surefire comedy, and we all know Robby is capable of delivering it."

Carter Stewart said nothing.

"Carter, I don't like to overplay my hand, but twelve years ago when you were still knocking on doors, I took you on and got your first play produced. Don't misunderstand me. It's been great for me ever since, but right now I'm calling in that chip, not for myself but for Joe and Barbara. I gave you your break. Today I want you to give them the chance to have theirs."

"Tim, you are so eloquent, you almost bring tears to my eyes," Carter Stewart said, his tone now reflecting amusement. "Surely there's something in all of this for you besides friendship for your old buddy Angus and paternal feelings for young talent. Someday you must tell me what it is. However, since you have totally ruined my creative concentration, I will go over to Robby's hotel now and see if I can bludgeon my way into his room. You might prepare the way by phoning ahead, claiming you're his agent, and explaining that Robby has instructed you to send me to pick up the scripts."

"Carter, I don't know how—"

"To thank me? I'm sure you don't. Good-bye, Tim."

Carter Stewart was wearing jeans and a sweater. His jacket and cap were on the chair where he had thrown them earlier. With an irritated sigh he got up, put on the jacket, and reached for the cap. Before he could leave the room, the phone rang. It was President Downes, inviting him to cocktails and dinner at his residence at Stonecroft.

The last thing on God's earth I need, Carter thought. "Oh, I'm sorry," he said, "but I do have dinner plans"—with myself, he added silently.

"Then perhaps just for cocktails," President Downes suggested nervously. "I would consider it a great favor, Carter. You see, I will have a photographer here to take pictures of you and the other honorees who are still in town."

The other honorees who are still in town—that's a good way to put it, Carter thought sarcastically. "I'm afraid—" he began.

"Please, Carter. I won't keep you long, but in light of the events of the past few days, I do need to have photos of the four truly distinguished recipients of our plaques of honor. I need them to replace the group pictures we took at the dinner. You can understand how very important that will be as we launch our building drive."

There was no hint of mirth in Carter Stewart's barklike laugh. "It seems to be my day to atone for the many sins of my life," he said. "What time do you want me to be there?"

"Seven o'clock would be ideal." President Downes' voice was bubbling with gratitude.

"Very well."

An hour later Carter Stewart was in Robby Brent's room at the Glen-Ridge House. Both Justin Lewis, the manager, and Jerome Warren, the assistant manager, were in the room with him, and both were visibly distressed at what they considered to be the potential liability to the hotel for allowing Stewart to take anything from the room.

Stewart went over to the desk. A thick pile of scripts was stacked on top of it. Stewart flipped through some of the pages. "There," he said. "As I explained to you, and as you can see, these are the scripts Mr. Brent edited, the ones that the production company needs immediately. I won't take possession of them for even an instant." He pointed to Justin Lewis. "You pick them up." He pointed to Jerome Warren. "You hold the express envelope to drop them in. Then you can decide between you who addresses it. Now, are you satisfied?"

"Of course, sir," Lewis said nervously. "I hope you understand our position and why we have to be so careful."

Carter Stewart did not answer. He was staring at the notation Robby Brent had propped on the desk phone: "Made appointment to show scripts to Howie Tuesday, 3:00 P.M."

The manager had seen it, too. "Mr. Stewart," he said, "I understood that you were the one who had the appointment to go over these scripts with Mr. Brent."

"That's right."

"Then may I ask who is Howie?"

"Mr. Brent was referring to me. It's a joke."

"Oh, I see."

"Yes, I'm sure you do. Mr. Lewis, have you ever heard the saying that he who laughs last laughs best?"

"Yes, I have," Justin Lewis said, bobbing his head in confirmation.

"Good." Carter Stewart began to chuckle. "It applies in this situation. Now let me give you that address."

72

After Sam left Rich Stevens' office, he went down to the coffee shop in the courthouse and ordered coffee and a ham-and-Swiss on rye to go.

"You mean 'with shoes,' " the new counterman said cheerfully. Noting Sam's bewildered expression, he explained, "You don't say 'to go' anymore. You say 'with shoes.' "

I could have lived the rest of my life without knowing that, Sam thought when he got back to his office and was taking the sandwich out of the bag.

He placed his lunch on his desk and turned on his computer. An hour later, the sandwich eaten, the last sip of coffee forgotten in the container, he was putting together all the information he had gathered on Laura Wilcox.

I have to acknowledge that you can find a lot on the Internet, Sam thought, but you can also waste a lot of time in the process. He was looking for the kind of background that would not be found in Laura's official biography, but so far he hadn't uncovered anything that was helpful.

Because there was a depressingly long list of Laura Wilcox references, he began to open the ones that he thought might prove revealing. Laura's first marriage, when she was twenty-four, had been to

Dominic Rubirosa, a Hollywood plastic surgeon. "Laura is so beautiful that in our home my talent will be wasted," Rubirosa was quoted as saying after the ceremony.

Sam grimaced. Isn't that touching, especially since the marriage lasted exactly eleven months. I wonder what happened to Rubirosa? Maybe he's still in touch with Laura. He decided to look him up and found an article showing a picture of him and his second wife at their wedding. "Monica is so beautiful that she will never have need of my professional services" was the quote attributed to Rubirosa that day.

"A little variation but not enough. What a jerk," Sam said aloud as he clicked back to the spread on Laura's first wedding.

There was a picture of her parents at the ceremony—William and Evelyn Wilcox of Palm Beach. On Monday, when Laura hadn't shown up, Eddie Zarro had left a message on her parents' phone, asking them to contact Sam. When there was no response, he'd had a Palm Beach policeman go to the house. A gossipy neighbor told the cop that they were on a cruise, but she wasn't sure which one. She volunteered that they kept to themselves, "were kind of cranky old people," and that she got the impression they were angry at some of the stuff that came out in Laura's messy second divorce.

Cruise ships get the news, Sam thought. With all the media coverage about Laura these past few days, you'd think they'd make some inquiries. It's odd that we still haven't heard from them. I'll see if the Palm Beach cops can't dig deeper and find out what cruise they're on. Of course, it's just possible that Laura tipped them off not to worry about her.

He glanced up as Joy Lacko came into his office. "The boss just pulled me off the homicides," she said. "He wants me to work with you. He said you'd explain." From her expression it was clear to Sam that Joy was not happy about being reassigned.

Her annoyance faded as Sam filled her in on what he had learned about Jean Sheridan and Lily, her daughter. The fact that Lily's adoptive father was a three-star general aroused her interest, as did the realization that it seemed impossible Laura Wilcox had sent the last fax to Jean Sheridan, the one that claimed that she had been behind all the threats. "And I still cannot believe that five women from the same lunch table at Stonecroft Academy died in the order in which they sat at the table," he concluded. "If it isn't one of those incredible strokes of fate, it would mean that Laura is destined to be the next one to die."

"You mean you have two celebrities missing, which may or may not be a publicity stunt; you have a West Point cadet, the adopted daughter of a general, being threatened, and you have five women dead in the order they sat at the table at school. No wonder Rich thinks you need help," Joy said matter-of-factly.

"I *do* need help," Sam admitted. "Finding Laura Wilcox is top priority, both because she's obviously in danger if those five deaths can be proven to be homicides, and because she may have known about Lily and told someone else about her."

"What about Laura's family? How about her close friends? Have you talked to her agent?" Lacko had her notebook out. Pen in hand, she waited for Sam's answers.

"You're asking the right questions," Sam said. "On Monday I put in a call to her agency. It turns out Alison Kendall had handled Laura herself. It's been a month since Kendall died, but no one at the agency has been assigned to take her over."

"That's unusual," Joy said. "I'd think that would be one of the first things they'd do."

"Apparently the reason is that she's in debt to them; they'd been giving her advances. Alison had been willing to carry her, but the new chief executive isn't. They promised to get back to us if they hear from her, but don't hold your breath. I get the distinct feeling that the agency is not really very interested in Laura."

"She hasn't appeared in anything significant since *Henderson County*, and that's been off the air for a couple of years. With all the twenty-year-old pop-tarts in the news, I guess she's considered a senior citizen by Hollywood standards," Joy observed dryly.

"I think you're right," Sam agreed. "We're also trying to locate her parents to see if she's talked to them. I've already spoken to the guy in California who investigated Alison Kendall's death, and he says there's no indication of foul play there. But I'm not satisfied. When I told Rich Stevens about the lunch table girls, he put in an order to get the files on all the deaths from the police who handled the investigations on each of them. The oldest goes back twenty years, so it may take the rest of the week to get everything. Then we'll go through the files with a fine-tooth comb and see if anything jumps out at us."

He waited while Joy jotted some notes in her book. "I want to go to the Website of the local papers where the so-called three accidents occurred and see if there were any questions raised in them at the time about the deaths. The first was in the car that went off the road into the Potomac; the second was the one who disappeared in the avalanche at Snowbird; the third was killed when the plane she was piloting crashed. Alison was the fourth. Finally, I want to see what was written about the supposed suicide of the girl from that lunch table."

He anticipated Joy's next question. "I have their names, the dates, and where they died listed here." He pointed to a typewritten sheet on his desk. "You can copy it. Then I want to find what the Internet will spit out about Robby Brent that might be helpful. I warn you, Joy. Even with two of us working on this, it will take a lot of time to get it done."

He got up and stretched. "When we're finished with all that, I'm going to call the widow of a certain Dr. Connors and tell her that I need to pay her a visit. He was the doctor who delivered Jean Sheridan's baby. Jean met Mrs. Connors the other day and had the distinct feeling that she was holding back some information, something that made her very nervous. Maybe I can get it out of her."

"Sam, I'm good at getting stuff from the Internet, and I'm probably one hundred times faster than you at it. Let me take over doing the research, and you visit the doctor's wife."

"The doctor's widow," Sam said, and then he wondered why he had found it necessary to correct Joy. Maybe it was because Kate had been on his mind all day. I'm not Kate's husband, he thought. I'm her widower. There's a difference of day and night.

If Joy was annoyed at the correction, she did not show it as she picked up the list on the table. "I'll see what I can find. Talk to you later."

Dorothy Connors had been reluctant to meet with Jean, and when Sam phoned, she adamantly insisted that she had no information that would be helpful to him. Realizing that he had to be tough with her, he finally said, "Mrs. Connors, I have to be the judge of whether or not you can assist our investigation. I want no more than fifteen minutes of your time."

Reluctantly, she agreed to let him come to see her that afternoon at three.

His phone rang as he was straightening the top of his desk. It was Tony Gomez, the police chief of Cornwall. They were old friends. "Sam, do you know this kid Jake Perkins?" Tony asked.

Do I? Sam thought as he rolled his eyes in the general direction of heaven. "I know him, Tony. What about it?"

"He's been going around town taking pictures of homes, and I have a complaint from a couple of people who thought he might be setting them up for a robbery."

“Forget it,” Sam said. “He’s harmless. He has delusions of being an investigative reporter.”

“It’s more than a delusion. He says he’s working on the Laura Wilcox disappearance as your special assistant. Can you verify that?”

“My special assistant? For God’s sake!” Sam began to laugh. “Throw him in jail,” he suggested. “And when you do, try to lose the key. I’ll talk to you, Tony.”

73

"Jean, I had a very good reason for inquiring at the desk about whether or not you had received a fax," Mark said quietly as he joined her in the coffee shop.

"Then explain it to me, please," she said, her tone equally subdued.

The waiter had placed her at the same table where they had sat for several hours the day before. But today the warmth and sense of developing intimacy that had characterized their earlier meeting was missing. Mark's expression was troubled, and Jean knew that she was conveying to him the doubt and mistrust of him that had been building in her mind.

Lily—Meredith—is safe, and I am going to meet her soon, she thought. That was the essential, the alpha and omega of what mattered right now. But receiving the hairbrush in the mail last month, then the threatening faxes, and finding the rose on Reed's grave—each and every incident had torn her apart with worry.

I should have had that last fax by mid-afternoon yesterday, Jean remembered as she looked across the table at Mark. She felt as if they were taking each other's measure, seeing each other today in a different light. I thought I could trust you, Mark, she thought. Yesterday you were so sympathetic, so understanding when I told you about Lily. Were you only mocking me?

Like her, he was wearing a jogging suit. His was dark green and seemed to make his eyes seem more hazel than brown. The expression in them was troubled. "Jean, I'm a psychiatrist," he said. "My job is to try to understand the workings of the mind. God knows you've been going through enough hell without my adding to it. Frankly, I was hoping you would continue to hear from whoever is sending those messages to you."

"Why?"

"Because it would be a sign that he or she wants to stay in touch. Now you've heard from Laura, and you're satisfied that she wouldn't hurt Lily. But the point is that she communicated with you. That's what I was looking for yesterday. Yes, I was troubled when the desk clerk said that nothing had come in. I was worried about Lily's safety."

He looked at her, and his expression of concern changed to astonishment. "Jean, were you thinking that I'd been sending those faxes to you, that I *knew* the one you got late yesterday should have arrived earlier? Were you *really* entertaining that thought?"

Her silence was his answer.

Do I believe him? Jean wondered. I don't know.

The waiter was standing at the table. "Just coffee," Jean said.

"I seem to recall that on the phone you told me you haven't eaten all day," Mark said. "Back at Stonecroft you liked grilled cheese and tomato. You still like that?"

Jean nodded.

"Two grilled cheese and tomato sandwiches and two cups of coffee," Mark ordered for both of them. He waited until the waiter was out of earshot before he spoke again. "You still haven't said anything, Jeannie. I don't know whether that means you believe me or you don't believe me or you're not sure. I admit I find that pretty damn disappointing but certainly understandable. Just answer me this: Are you still satisfied that Laura has been sending those faxes and that Lily is safe?"

I am not going to tell him about the call from Craig Michaelson, Jean thought. I can't afford to trust anyone. "I am satisfied that Lily is safe," she said cautiously.

Mark obviously realized that she was being evasive. "Poor Jean," he said. "You don't know who to trust, do you? I can't say I blame you. But what are you going to do now? Just wait here indefinitely until Laura surfaces?"

"At least for the next few days," Jean said, intent on being as vague as possible. "What about you?"

"I'll stay till Friday morning, then I must get back. I have patients I need to see. Fortunately I had shows already taped, but now I can't delay work on the new ones. Anyhow, as of Friday my room has been reserved by someone attending the lightbulb convention, or whatever it is."

"One hundred top sales reps are being honored," Jean told him.

"More honorees," Mark said. "I hope all one hundred make it home safely. I assume you're going to respond to President Downes' plea to be at his place for cocktails and a photo shoot tonight."

"I don't know a thing about it," Jean protested.

"He's probably left a message on your phone. It shouldn't take too long. From what Downes said, he wanted to make it a dinner, but Carter and Gordon already have dinner plans. Actually, I do, too. My father wants me to have dinner with him again."

"Then I guess your father answered the questions you said you were going to ask him," Jean suggested.

"Yes, he did. Jeannie, you know half the story. You deserve to hear the rest of it. My brother, Dennis, died a month after he graduated from Stonecroft. He was supposed to start Yale in the fall."

"I know about the accident," Jean said.

"You know *something* about the accident," Mark corrected. "I had just finished the eighth grade at St. Thomas and was starting at Stonecroft in September. My parents gave Dennis a convertible for his graduation. You probably didn't know him, but he excelled in everything. He was number one in his class, the captain of the baseball team, the president of the student council, great-looking and funny, and a genuinely nice guy. After four miscarriages my mother had managed to produce the golden child."

"Which was hard for you to compete with, I would think," Jean observed.

"I know people believe that, but actually, Dennis was great to me. He was my big brother. Talk about hero worship."

It seemed to Jean that Mark was talking more to himself than to her. "He played tennis with me. He taught me how to play golf. He took me for rides in that convertible, and then, because I bugged him so much, he taught me how to drive it."

"But you couldn't have been more than thirteen or fourteen," Jean said.

"I was thirteen. Oh, I never drove on the street, of course, and he was always in the car with me. Our house has quite a bit of property. The afternoon of the accident, I had been pestering Dennis all day for a ride. Finally, around four o'clock, he tossed me the keys and said, 'Okay, okay, get in the car. I'll be right there.'

"I was sitting, waiting for him, counting the minutes till he got in so I could be the hotshot driving the convertible. Then a couple of his friends showed up, and Dennis told me he was going to shoot some baskets with them. 'I promise you'll have your chance in an hour or so,' he said. Then he called out, 'Turn off the engine and be sure to put on the parking brake.'

"I was disappointed, and I was mad. I slammed into the house. My mother was in the kitchen. I told her that I'd be glad if Dennis' car slid down the hill and crashed into the fence. Forty minutes later it did slide down the hill. The basketball net was at the base of the driveway. The other guys got out of the way. Dennis didn't."

"Mark, you're the psychiatrist. You *have* to know that it wasn't your fault."

The waiter was back with the sandwiches and coffee. Mark took a bite of his sandwich and sipped the coffee. It was obvious to Jean that he was struggling to keep his emotions in check. "Intellectually, yes, but neither of my parents was ever the same toward me after that. Dennis was the Christ child in my mother's eyes. I can understand that. He had everything. He was so gifted. I heard her tell my father that she was sure I had deliberately left the brake off, not to deliberately hurt Dennis but hoping to pay him back for disappointing me."

"What did your father say?"

"It's what he *didn't* say. I expected him to defend me, but he didn't. Then some kid told me that my mother had said that if God wanted one of her boys, why did it have to be Dennis?"

"I heard that story," Jean admitted.

"You grew up wanting to get away from your parents, Jean, and so did I. I always felt we were kindred spirits. We both threw ourselves into academics and kept our mouths shut. Do you see your parents much?"

"My father lives in Hawaii. I visited him there last year. He has a lady friend who's quite nice, but he proclaims from the rooftops that one marriage cured him of ever walking down the aisle again. I spent a few days around Christmas with my mother, who seems genuinely happy now. She and her husband have visited me a few times. I admit that it does make me gag a bit to see the two of them holding hands and nuzzling each other, when I think of how she behaved with my father. I guess I'm over resenting them, except for the fact that at age eighteen I didn't think I could turn to them for help."

"My mother died when I was in medical school," Mark said. "I wasn't told that she'd had a heart attack and was dying. I would have jumped on a plane and come back to say good-bye to her. But she didn't ask for me. In fact, she said she didn't want to see me. It felt like the final rejection. I didn't attend the funeral. After that I never came home again, and my father and I have been on the outs for fourteen years." He shrugged. "Maybe that's why I decided to be a psychiatrist. 'Physician, heal thyself.' I'm still trying."

"What were the questions you asked your father? You told me he answered them."

"The first one was why he didn't send for me when my mother was dying."

Jean wrapped both hands around the coffee cup and picked it up. "What was his answer?"

"He told me that my mother had become delusional. Shortly before she had the heart attack, she had gone to a psychic who told her that her younger son had deliberately released the brake because he was jealous of his brother and wanted to hurt him. Mother had always believed in the possibility that I had wanted to damage Dennis' car, but the psychic put her over the edge. That may even have brought on the heart attack. Want to hear the other question that I asked my father?"

Jean nodded.

"My mother couldn't stand any kind of drinking, and my father liked to have a drink in the late afternoon. He'd sneak into the garage where he kept some booze hidden on the shelf behind the paint cans, or he'd pretend to be cleaning the inside of his car and have a little cocktail party of his own. Sometimes he'd sit in Dennis' car and have his nip. I know I left that brake on. I know Dennis didn't go near the car. He was playing basketball with his friends. Certainly my mother wouldn't get into the convertible. I asked my father if he had sat in Dennis' car that afternoon, having his couple of scotches, and if so, didn't he think it was possible he might have released that brake accidentally?"

"What did he say?"

"He admitted that he was in the car and got out of it only a minute or so before it rolled down the hill. He never had the courage to tell my mother, not even when that psychic poisoned her mind about me."

"Why do you think he admitted it now?"

"I was walking around town the other night, thinking of how people go through life with unresolved conflicts. My appointment book is filled with patients who are living examples of that. When I saw my father's car in the driveway—that same driveway, incidentally—I decided to go in and, after fourteen years of silence, have it out with him."

"You saw him last night, and you're seeing him again tonight. Does that mean a reconciliation?"

"He's going to be eighty years old soon, Jean, and he's not well. He's been living a lie for twenty-five years. He's almost pathetic, talking about how he wants to make it up to me. Of course he can't, but maybe seeing him will help me understand and put it behind me. He's right about the fact that if my mother knew he had been drinking in the car and had caused the accident, she would have gotten rid of him that same day."

"Instead, on an emotional level she withdrew from *you*."

"Which, in turn, contributed to the total sense of inadequacy and failure that I remember feeling at Stonecroft. I tried to be like Dennis, but I certainly wasn't as good-looking. I wasn't an athlete, and I wasn't a leader. The only time I felt any sense of camaraderie was when some of us worked a job together in the evenings our senior year. We'd go out afterward and have a pizza. Perhaps the good part is that I learned compassion for kids who have it tough, and as an adult I have tried to make their paths a little smoother."

"According to what I hear, you're doing a good job of it."

"I hope so. The producers want to move the show to New York, and I've been asked to join the staff of New York Hospital. I think I'm ready to make the change."

"A new beginning?" Jean asked.

"Exactly—where what can't be forgiven or forgotten may at least be relegated to the past." He raised his coffee cup. "Shall we drink to that, Jeannie?"

"Yes, of course." As badly as I was hurt, it was worse for you, Mark, she thought. My parents were too busy hating each other to understand what they were doing to me. Your parents let you know they preferred your brother, and then your father deliberately let your mother believe the one thing that she could never forgive you for. What did *that* do to your soul?

Her instinct was to reach across the table and lay her hand on his, the same gesture with which he had comforted her yesterday. But something held her back. She simply could not trust him. Then she realized she wanted to pick up on something he had just said. "Mark, what was the evening job you worked at during senior year?"

"I was with the office clean-up crew in a building that has burned down since then. Jack Emerson's father got a bunch of us jobs there. I guess you weren't around when we were joking about it the other night. Every one of the guys who is an honoree pushed a broom or emptied wastebaskets over there."

"*All* of you?" Jean asked. "Carter and Gordon and Robby and you?"

"That's right. Oh, and one more. Joel Nieman, a.k.a. Romeo. We all worked with Jack. Don't forget, we were the ones who didn't have to practice for games or travel with teams. We were perfect for that job." He paused. "Wait a minute. You should know that building, Jean. You were Dr. Connors' patient."

Jean felt her body turn icy. "I didn't tell you that, Mark."

"You must have. How else would I have known it?"

How else, indeed? Jean wondered as she pushed her chair back. "Mark, I have a few phone calls to return. Do you mind if I don't wait while you get the check?"

74

Ms. Ferris was in the studio when Jake returned to school. "How'd you make out, Jake?" she asked as she watched him struggle to close the door while he carefully juggled the heavy camera, moving it off his shoulder and onto the desk.

"It was an adventure, Jill," Jake admitted. "I mean Ms. Ferris," he quickly amended. "I decided to do a chronological womb-to-the-present account of Laura Wilcox. I got a great long shot of St. Thomas of Canterbury Church, and as luck would have it, there was a baby carriage outside. I mean a *real* baby carriage, not one of those strollers or rollers or whatever they stick kids in these days."

He was taking his recorder out of his pocket as he took off his coat. "Freezing out there," he complained, "but at least the police station was warm."

"The police station, Jake?" Jill Ferris asked cautiously.

"Uh-huh. But let me explain in chronological order. After the church, I got some background pictures, to give people who don't live here a sense of the community. I realize I'm doing this story for the *Gazette*, but I fully expect it to be picked up by larger publications and to find a wider audience."

"I see. Jake, I don't want to rush you, but I was just leaving."

"This will only take a minute. Then I photographed Laura's second house, the McMansion. It's quite impressive if you like that sort of tacky grandeur. It has a big front yard, and whoever lives there now has stuck a few Grecian statues on the lawn. In my opinion they look pretentious, but it will make readers understand that Laura did *not* have a 'surprise lunch' childhood."

" 'Surprise lunch' childhood?" Jill Ferris asked, bewildered.

"Let me explain. My grandfather told me about a comedian named Sam Levenson who said his family was so poor that his mother bought cans off a pushcart for two cents each. They were that cheap because the labels had fallen off, and nobody knew what was inside them. She'd tell her kids that they were having a 'surprise lunch.' They never knew what they were going to eat. Anyhow, the pictures of Laura's second house reflect a solid middle-class, even slightly upper-middle-class upbringing."

Jake's expression darkened. "After I took some long shots of the houses surrounding Laura's former home, I drove across town to Mountain Road where she had lived for the first sixteen years of her life. It's a very pleasant street, and, frankly, the house is more to my taste than the one with the Grecian statues. Anyhow, I'd barely begun to shoot when a squad car pulled up and a most aggressive policeman wanted to know what I thought I was doing. When I explained that I was exercising my right as a private citizen to take photographs in the street, he invited me to get in his squad car, and he drove me to the station house."

"He *arrested* you, Jake?" Jill Ferris exclaimed.

"No, ma'am. Not exactly. The captain questioned me, and since I felt I had been of valuable service to Investigator Deegan when I alerted him that Laura Wilcox sounded extremely nervous when she called to ask the hotel to hold her room, I felt I had the right to explain to the captain that I was a special assistant to Mr. Deegan in the investigation of Laura's disappearance."

I'm going to miss this kid when he graduates, Jill Ferris thought. She decided that it wouldn't hurt to be a few minutes late for her appointment at the dentist. "Did the captain believe you, Jake?" she asked.

"He called Mr. Deegan, who not only did not back me up but suggested that the captain should toss me in jail and then lose the key." Jake looked hard at his teacher. "It's not funny, Ms. Ferris. I feel Mr. Deegan broke a trust. The captain, as it turns out, was much more sympathetic. He was even kind enough to say that I could finish my photos tomorrow, since I got to take only a few pictures of the house on Mountain Road. He *did* warn me that I'd better not trespass on anyone's property. I'm going to develop today's film now, and with your permission, I'll sign the camera out again tomorrow and finish my shoot."

"That'll be fine, Jake, but remember, those older cameras aren't being made anymore. Don't let anything happen to it, or I'll be the one in trouble, not you. Now, I've got to run."

"I'll guard it with my life," Jake called after her. I mean it, he thought as he rewound the roll of film and removed it from the camera. But even though the captain warned me not to set foot on anyone's property, for the sake of getting proper coverage for my story, I have to commit an act of civil disobedience, he told himself. I intend to get pictures of the back of Laura's house on Mountain Road. Since no one is living there, I'm sure I won't be noticed.

He went into the darkroom and began developing the pictures, one of his favorite tasks. He found it thrilling and creative to watch people and objects begin to emerge from the negatives. One by one he clipped the prints on a clothesline to dry, then got out his magnifying glass and studied them carefully. They were all good—and he didn't mind saying so himself—but the single shot he'd been able to take of Laura's house on Mountain Road before the cop showed up was the most interesting of the lot.

There's something about that house, Jake thought. It makes me want to put my head under the covers and hide. What *is* it? Everything is in shipshape condition. Maybe that's it. It's too neat. Then he peered closer. It's the shades, he thought triumphantly. The ones in the bedroom at the end of the house aren't the same as the others. In the picture they come through a lot darker. I didn't notice that when I was shooting, but the sun was pretty bright then. He whistled. Wait a minute. When I looked up the Karen Sommers story on the Internet, I think I remember that she was murdered in the corner bedroom, on the right-hand side of the house. I remember a picture of the crime scene with those windows circled.

Why not show a separate picture of just those two windows in my story? he asked himself. I could point out that there is a dark aura surrounding the fatal room where one young woman was murdered and where Laura slept for sixteen years. It would give it a nice, eerie little touch.

To his disappointment the enlargement of the photograph revealed that the difference in color was probably caused by interior dark shades that had been drawn behind the decorative ones visible from the street.

Or *should* I be disappointed? Jake asked himself. Suppose someone is staying there who doesn't want a light to show? It would be a great place to hide. The house has been renovated. There's furniture on the porch, so I assume it's furnished. No one lives there. Who bought it anyhow? Wouldn't it be a scream if Laura Wilcox owns her old house and is holed up there now with Robby Brent?

It's not the dumbest hunch I've ever had, he decided. Should I bounce it off Mr. Deegan? he asked himself.

The heck I will, he decided. It's probably a crazy idea, but if there's anything to it, it's my story. Deegan told the captain to toss me in jail. Now he can just go fly a kite. He gets no more help from me.

75

Sam's visit to Dorothy Connors' home lasted exactly the fifteen minutes he had promised her. When he saw how infirm she was, he proceeded gently, and he quickly surmised that the concern she had shown was for her late husband's reputation. Knowing that made it easier for him to get to the point.

"Mrs. Connors, Dr. Sheridan spoke to Peggy Kimball, who at one time worked for your husband. To assist Dr. Sheridan in finding her daughter, Ms. Kimball stated that Dr. Connors on occasion may have circumvented the rules governing adoptions. If that is your concern, I can tell you right now that Dr. Sheridan's daughter has been located and the adoption was absolutely legal. In fact, Dr. Sheridan is going to have dinner with the adoptive parents this evening and will meet her daughter very soon. That part of the investigation is over."

The naked relief reflected in the woman's expression was confirmation that he had dispelled her concerns. "My husband was such a wonderful man," she said. "It would have been awful if ten years after his death, people began to think he had done something wrong or illegal."

He did, Sam thought, but that's not why I'm here. "Mrs. Connors, I promise you that nothing you tell me will ever be used in a way that could sully your husband's reputation. But please answer this question: Do you have any knowledge whatsoever of how someone might have had access to Jean Sheridan's maternity file in your husband's office?"

There was no trace of nervousness left in Dorothy Connors' voice or manner when she looked Sam straight in the eye. "You have my word of honor that I have no knowledge of any such person, but if I did, I would share it with you."

They had been sitting in the sunroom that Sam suspected was where Mrs. Connors spent most of her time. She insisted on walking him to the door, but as she opened it, she hesitated. "My husband handled dozens of adoptions during the forty years he practiced medicine," she said. "He always took a picture of the baby after it was born. He put the date of birth on the back of each picture, and if the mother had named the baby before she signed it away, he wrote that down, too."

She closed the door. "Come with me into the library," she said. Sam followed her through the living room, continuing through French doors that led to an alcove filled with bookshelves. "The photo albums are in here," she said. "After Dr. Sheridan left, I found the picture of her baby with the name Lily inscribed on the back. I confess, I was terribly afraid that hers might have been one of the adoptions that couldn't be traced. But now that Dr. Sheridan has located her daughter and is going to meet her, I'm sure she would like to have a picture of Lily when she was three hours old."

Stacks of photo albums took up one entire section of the shelves. The section had been labeled with dates going back forty years. The album Mrs. Connors pulled out had a page marker in it. She opened it, slid a picture from its plastic covering, and handed it to Sam. "Please tell Dr. Sheridan how happy I am for her," she said.

When Sam got back to the car, he carefully tucked away in his inside breast pocket the picture of a wide-eyed infant with long lashes and wisps of hair framing her face. What a beauty, he thought. I can only imagine how rough it must have been for Jean to give her up. I'm not that far from the Glen-Ridge. If she's there, I'll drop it off for her. Michaelson was going to call Jean after he spoke to me, so she's probably all squared away about meeting the adoptive parents.

When Sam called up, Jean was in her room and readily agreed to meet him in the lobby. "Give me ten minutes," she said. "I just got out of the tub." Then she added, "Nothing is wrong, is it, Sam?"

"Nothing wrong at all, Jean." Not at the moment, at least, he thought, even though a pervasive sense of unease would not leave him.

He had expected Jean to be radiantly happy at the prospect of meeting Lily, but he could see that something was troubling her. "Why don't we go over there?" he asked, nodding his head toward a far corner of the lobby where a sofa and chair were unoccupied.

It did not take long for Jean to tell him her concern. "Sam, I am beginning to believe that Mark is the one sending the faxes," she said.

He saw the pain in her eyes. "Why do you think that?" he asked quietly.

"Because he let slip that he knew I was a patient of Dr. Connors. *I* never told him that. There's more. He was inquiring at the desk yesterday to see if I had received a fax and apparently was disappointed that it hadn't come in. That was the one mistakenly included with someone else's mail. Mark told me he worked at Dr. Connors' office in the evening during the time I was seeing the doctor. Finally, he admitted he saw me at West Point with Reed. He even knew Reed's name."

"Jean, I promise you, we'll take a very close look at Mark Fleischman. I'll be honest. I haven't been happy that you've been confiding in him. I hope you didn't pass on to him anything that Michaelson told you this morning."

"No, I didn't."

"I don't want to alarm you, but I think you need to be careful. I bet we're going to find that the person sending the faxes is someone from your graduating class. Whoever it turns out to be—Mark or one of the others who attended the reunion—I don't believe anymore that it's about money. I think we're dealing with a psychotic and a potentially dangerous personality."

He studied her for a long minute. "You were beginning to like Fleischman, weren't you?"

"Yes, I was," Jean admitted. "That's why it's hard for me to believe that he may be a totally different person from how he appears on the surface."

"You don't know that yet. Now I have something that may perk you up." He took Lily's picture out of his pocket, explaining what it was before he handed it to her. Then from the corner of his eye, he saw Gordon Amory and Jack Emerson coming through the front entrance of the hotel. "You may want to take it upstairs before you look at it, Jean," he suggested. "Amory and Emerson just showed up, and if they see you, they'll probably come over."

Jean quickly whispered, "Thanks, Sam," took the picture from him, and hurried to the elevator.

Sam saw that Gordon Amory had spotted her and was going to try to catch her. He hurried to intercept him. "Mr. Amory," he said, "have you decided how long you'll be staying here?"

"I'll be leaving by the weekend, at the latest. Why do you ask?"

"Because if we don't hear from Ms. Wilcox soon, we are going to treat her as a missing person. In that case we'll need to speak at greater length to the people who were around her just before she disappeared."

Gordon Amory shrugged. "You'll hear from her," he said dismissively. "However, for the record, if you wish to contact me, I expect to be in the general area even after I check out here. Through Jack Emerson, as our agent, we are making an offer on a large tract of land where I plan to build my corporate headquarters. So when I leave the hotel I plan to stay in my Manhattan apartment for several weeks."

Jack Emerson had been speaking to someone near the desk. Now he joined them. "Any news of the toad?" he asked Sam.

"The toad?" Sam raised his eyebrows. He was perfectly aware that Emerson meant Robby Brent, but he wasn't about to let on.

"Our resident comedian, Robby Brent. Isn't he smart enough to know that all guests, missing or otherwise, like fish, smell after three days? I mean, enough already with the publicity stunt."

Emerson's had a couple of shots of whiskey for lunch, Sam thought, noting the man's flushed complexion.

Ignoring the reference to Brent, he said, "Since you live in Cornwall, I assume you'll be available if I need to talk with you about Laura Wilcox, Mr. Emerson. As I just explained to Mr. Amory, we will be listing her as a missing person if we don't hear from her soon."

"Not so fast, Mr. Deegan," Emerson said. "The minute Gordie—I mean, Gordon—and I have finished putting this deal together, I'm out of here. I have a place in St. Bart's that it's time for me to visit. Putting this reunion together was a lot of work. Tonight we take some more pictures at President Downes' house, have a drink with him, and then this reunion is *really* over. Who gives a damn whether or not Laura Wilcox and Robby Brent ever show up? The Stonecroft Academy building committee doesn't need their kind of publicity."

Gordon Amory had been listening with an amused smile on his face. "I must tell you, Mr. Deegan, that I think Jack has put it very well. I tried to catch Jean, but she was in the elevator and I missed her. Do you know her plans?"

"I don't," he said. "Now if you'll excuse me, I have to get back to my office." I wouldn't tell any of those guys what Jean is doing, he thought as he crossed the hotel lobby, and I hope she heeds my warning not to trust any of them.

His cell phone rang as he was getting into his car. It was Joy Lacko. "Sam, I've got a hit," she told him. "On a hunch I checked out the report on Gloria Martin, the suicide, before I started researching the accidental deaths. At the time of her death there was a big article about Martin in her local newspaper in Bethlehem."

Sam waited.

"Gloria Martin killed herself by putting a plastic bag over her head. And, Sam, get this: When they found her, she had a small pewter owl clutched in her hand."

76

To Duke Mackenzie's delight, at five minutes of nine that evening the taciturn participant in the Stonecroft reunion stopped in again. He ordered a grilled cheese and bacon sandwich, and coffee with skim milk. While the sandwich was grilling, Duke hastened to start a conversation. "A lady from your reunion was in this morning," he said. "Said she used to live on Mountain Road."

He could not see past the man's dark glasses, but something in the way his body stiffened made Duke sure he had gotten his attention.

"Do you know her name?" the visitor asked casually.

"Nope, sir, I don't. I can describe her to you though. Really pretty, with brown hair and blue eyes. Her daughter's name is Meredith."

"She told you that!"

"No, sir. Don't ask how it happened, but someone she was talking to on the phone told her that. I could tell she was all shook up about it. I can't figure out why she wouldn't know her own daughter's name."

"I wonder if she was talking to someone else from our reunion," the visitor mused. "By any chance did she mention the name of the person she was talking to?"

"No. She did say that she'd see them—I mean him or her—tomorrow night at seven o'clock."

Duke turned his back to the counter, picked up a spatula, and removed the sandwich from the grill. He did not see the cold smile on his customer's face, nor did he hear him whisper to himself, "No, she won't, Duke. No, she won't."

"Here you go, sir," Duke said cheerfully. "I see you're taking your coffee with skim milk. They say that's healthier, but for me, I like good old-fashioned cream in my coffee. Figure I don't have to worry. My father was still bowling a great game at eighty-seven."

The Owl tossed money on the counter and left with a mumbled good night. He felt Duke's eyes following him as he walked to the car. I wouldn't put it past him to follow me, he thought. He's just nosy enough. He doesn't miss anything. I can't stop there anymore, but it really doesn't matter. By this time tomorrow it will be finished.

He drove slowly up Mountain Road but decided not to turn into the driveway at Laura's house. Funny, I still call it that, he thought. Instead, he drove well past it and watched in the rearview mirror until he was sure he was not being followed. Then he made a U-turn and started making his way back, always watching for the headlights of other cars. When he was at his destination, he switched off his headlights, made a sharp turn into the driveway, and drove to the comparative safety of the enclosed backyard.

Only then did he allow himself to concentrate on what he had just heard. *Jean knew Meredith's name!* It had to be the Buckleys that Jean was going to be meeting tomorrow night. Meredith couldn't have remembered where she lost the hairbrush, or by now that detective, Sam Deegan, would have been knocking at his door. It meant he had to move more swiftly than he had anticipated. He would have to enter and leave this house several times tomorrow in broad daylight. But he simply could not leave this car parked outside. That was out of the question. Even though the backyard was enclosed, a neighbor might spot it from a second-story window and phone the police. Laura's house was supposed to be uninhabited.

Robby's car, with his body in the trunk, took up half of the garage. The first rental car that might have left telltale tire tracks at the place where he had taken Helen Whelan's body was in the other parking space. He had to get rid of one of those cars so he could have access to the garage. The rental car would be traced back to him, he reasoned. I have to keep that until it's safe to return it.

I've come so far, The Owl thought. The journey has been so long. I can't stop now. It must be completed. He looked at the sandwich and coffee he had bought for Laura. I didn't have any dinner, he thought. What difference does it make if Laura eats or doesn't eat tonight? She won't have that long to be hungry tomorrow.

He opened the bag and ate the sandwich slowly. He sipped the coffee, reflecting that he preferred it black. When he was finished, he got out, unlocked the door to the kitchen, and went inside. Instead of going up the stairs to Laura's bedroom, he opened the door from the kitchen to the garage and deliberately slammed it behind him as he pulled on the plastic gloves he always kept in the pocket of his jacket.

Laura would hear the sound and begin to tremble with the agony of uncertainty that this might be the time he had come to kill her. But she also would be hungry by now and would be anticipating what he had brought her to eat. Then, when he didn't come up the stairs, both the fear and anticipation would build and build until she was broken, ready to do what he wanted, ready to obey.

In a way he wished he could reassure her that soon it would be over, because to reassure her was to reassure himself. He understood that the pain in his arm was distracting him. The dog bites had seemed to be healing, but now the worst one had become inflamed again.

He had left Robby's keys in the ignition of the car. Repelled at the thought of Robby's lifeless body, covered by blankets and sprawled in the trunk, he clicked the garage door open, got in Robby's car, and backed it out. In a few minutes, which seemed like an eternity, he had his second rental car safely hidden in the garage.

With the headlights off until he was halfway down the block, The Owl began driving Robby Brent's car the few miles to its final destination in the Hudson River.

Forty minutes later, his task accomplished and having walked from the spot where he had sunk the car, he was safely back in his room. His mission tomorrow would be treacherous, he reflected, but he would do his best to minimize the danger. Before daybreak he would walk back to Laura's house. Maybe he would have Laura call Meredith and say she was her birth mother. She would ask to meet her outside West Point for just a few minutes after breakfast. Meredith knows she's adopted, The Owl thought. She talked about it freely enough to me. There's no nineteen-year-old who wouldn't jump at the chance to meet her birth mother, he was confident of that.

And then when he had Meredith, Laura would phone Jean for him.

Sam Deegan wasn't stupid. Even now he might be delving into the deaths of the other girls from the lunch table, investigating the accidents that hadn't been accidents. It wasn't until Gloria that I began to leave my signature, The Owl thought, and the irony is that the first one had been a trinket the stupid woman bought herself.

"You've really made it big, and to think we used to call you 'The Owl,'" she'd said with a laugh, a little drunk, still totally insensitive. Then she showed him the pewter owl, still wrapped in plastic. "I happened to see it at one of those places in the mall that sell this kind of junk," she explained, "and when you phoned to say you were in town, I went back and bought one. I thought we'd have a good laugh about it."

He had a lot of reasons to be grateful to Gloria. After she died he'd bought a dozen of those five-dollar, inch-long pewter owls. Now there were three left. He could get more, of course, but when he had used the three he still had, it might be the end of his need for them. Laura and Jean and Meredith. One owl for each.

The Owl set his alarm for 5:00 A.M. and went to sleep.

77

To sleep, perchance to dream, Jean thought as she restlessly turned on her side and then onto her back. Finally she turned on the light and got out of bed. The room felt too warm. She walked across the room and opened the window wider. Maybe I'll get to sleep now, she thought.

The baby picture of Lily was on the night table. She sat on the edge of the bed and picked up the photograph. How could I have let her go? she agonized. *Why* did I let her go? She felt as if she was on an emotional roller coaster. Tonight I'm going to meet the man and woman who were given Lily right after she was born. What do I say to them? Jean wondered. That I am grateful to them? I am, but I'm ashamed to admit that I'm also jealous of them. I wanted to experience everything that they experienced with her. Suppose they change their minds and decide that I shouldn't meet her yet?

I need to meet her, and then I need to go home. I want to get away from all the Stonecroft people. Last night the atmosphere at President Downes' cocktail party was dreadful, she thought as she turned off the light and lay down again. Everyone seemed to be uptight, but each in a different way. Mark—what is going on inside him? she wondered. He was so quiet and went out of his way to avoid me. Carter Stewart was in a foul mood, growling that he'd lost an entire day's work chasing after Robby's scripts. Jack Emerson had an edge on him and was gulping double scotches. Gordon seemed okay until President Downes kept trying to show him blueprints of the proposed new building. Then he practically exploded. He pointed out that at the dinner he had presented a check for $100,000 for the building fund. I can't believe the way he raised his voice and asked if anyone had noticed that the more you give, the more people try to drag out of you.

Carter was just as rude. He said that since he never made donations to anything, he didn't have that problem. Then Jack Emerson followed those two by bragging that he was donating half a million dollars to Stonecroft for the new communications center.

Only Mark and I said nothing, Jean thought. I will make a donation, but it's going to be for scholarships, not buildings.

She didn't want to think anymore about Mark.

She looked at the clock. It was a quarter of five. What should I wear tonight? I didn't bring all that many changes. I don't know what kind of people Lily's adoptive parents are. Do they dress casually, or do they tend to be more formal? The brown tweed jacket and slacks I wore on the drive might be the best choice. It's a sort of in-between outfit.

I know those pictures the photographer took at President Downes' house are going to be awful. I don't think one of the men even attempted a smile, and I felt as if I were grinning like the Cheshire cat. Then, when that nervy kid Jake Perkins showed up and asked to take a picture of all of us for the *Gazette*, I thought President Downes would have a heart attack. But I felt sorry for the poor kid because of the way Downes practically threw him out.

I hope Jake doesn't have Georgetown on his list of colleges he wants to attend, although he certainly does make life interesting.

Thinking about Jake brought a smile to Jean's lips, relieving for the moment the tension that had been building up since she had heard she was going to meet Lily's adoptive parents.

The smile disappeared as quickly as it came. Where *was* Laura? she thought. This is the beginning of the fifth day since she disappeared. I can't stay here indefinitely. I have classes next week. Why do I persist in believing that I'll hear from her?

I am not going to be able to go back to sleep, she finally decided. It's much too early to get up, but at least I can read. I hardly opened yesterday's newspaper and don't know what's going on in the world.

She went back across the room to the desk, picked up the newspaper, and brought it back to the bed. She propped up the pillow and began to read, but then her eyes started to close. She did not feel the newspaper slip from her grasp, as she finally fell into a heavy sleep.

At a quarter of seven her phone rang. When Jean saw the time on the clock next to the phone, her throat closed. It has to be bad news, she thought. Something has happened to Laura—or to Lily! She grabbed the receiver. "Hello," she said anxiously.

"Jeannie, . . . it's me."

"Laura!" Jean cried. "Where are you? How are you?"

Laura was sobbing so violently that it was hard to understand what she was saying. "Jean, . . . help me. I'm so scared. I've done such a . . . crazy . . . thing. . . . Sorry. . . . Faxes . . . about . . . about Lily."

Jean stiffened. "You never met Lily. I know that."

"Robby, . . . he . . . he . . . took . . . her . . . brush. It . . . was . . . his . . . idea."

"Where is Robby?"

"On . . . way . . . California. He's . . . blam-blaming . . . me. Jeannie, meet me . . . please. By yourself, just by yourself."

"Laura, where are you?"

"In . . . motel. . . . Someone . . . recognized me. I have to . . . go."

"Laura, where can I meet you?"

"Jeannie . . . the Lookout."

"You mean Storm King Lookout?"

"Yes . . . yes."

Laura's sobs became louder. "Kill . . . myself . . ."

"Laura, listen to me," Jean said frantically. "I'll be there in twenty minutes. It's going to be all right. I promise you, it's going to be all right."

At the other end of the line, The Owl swiftly disconnected the phone. "My, my, Laura," he said approvingly. "You are a good actress after all. That was an Academy Award–winning performance."

Laura had slumped back against the pillow, her head turned from him, her sobs subsiding into quivering sighs. "I only did it because you promised that now you wouldn't hurt Jean's daughter."

"So I did," The Owl said. "Laura, you must be hungry. You haven't had a thing since yesterday morning. I can't guarantee the coffee. The counterman in the delicatessen down the hill was getting too inquisitive about me, so I went to another place. But see what else I brought."

She did not respond.

"Turn your head, Laura! Look at me!"

Wearily she obeyed. Through swollen eyes she could see that he was holding up three plastic bags.

The Owl began to laugh. "They're presents," he explained. "One is for you, one is for Jean, and one is for Meredith. Laura, can you guess what I'm going to do with them? *Answer me, Laura! Can you guess what I'm going to do with them?"*

78

"Sorry, Rich. No one will ever tell me that it's only a bizarre coincidence that Gloria Martin, one of the Stonecroft lunch table girls, had a pewter owl in her hand when she died," Sam said flatly.

It had been another sleepless night. After the call from Joy Lacko, he had gone straight back to the office. The file on Gloria Martin's suicide had come in from the Bethlehem police department, and together they had analyzed every word of it, as well as the newspaper accounts of her death.

When Rich Stevens got to the office at 8:00 A.M., he called them in for a conference. After listening to Sam, he turned to Joy. "What do you think?"

"At first I thought it was a slam dunk, that The Owl nut case had been killing girls from Stonecroft for the past twenty years and is back in this area," Joy said. "Now I'm not so sure. I talked to Rudy Haverman, the cop who handled Gloria Martin's suicide eight years ago. He did a very credible investigation. He told me that Martin was into that kind of junk. She apparently was big for picking up cheap tchotchkes of animals and birds and such. The one she was holding when she died was still in its plastic wrap. Haverman found the vendor who sold it to her in the local mall; she distinctly remembered Martin telling her that she was buying it as a joke."

"You say the blood-alcohol level shows that she was smashed when she died?" Stevens asked.

"She was. It registered at .20. According to Haverman, she started drinking after she was divorced, and she went so far as to tell her friends that she didn't have anything to live for."

"Joy, have you found anything in the files of the other women from the lunch table indicating that one of those pewter owls was found in their hands or in their clothing when their bodies were examined?"

"Not so far, sir," Joy admitted.

"I don't care whether or not Gloria Martin bought that owl herself," Sam said stubbornly. "The fact she had it in her hand says to me that she was murdered. So what if she told her friends she was depressed? Most people feel depressed after a divorce even if they're the ones who wanted it. But Martin was very close to her family and knew how devastated they'd be if she killed herself. She didn't leave a suicide note, and from the amount of alcohol she'd imbibed, it's a miracle to me that she managed to get the bag over her head and still hang on to the owl."

"Do you agree with that assessment, Joy?" Rich Stevens snapped.

"I do, sir. Rudy Haverman is convinced it's a suicide, but he hasn't dealt with two other bodies with pewter owls in their pockets."

Rich Stevens leaned back and folded his hands. "For the sake of argument, let's say that whoever killed Helen Whelan and Yvonne Tepper *may*—and I repeat *may*—be involved in the death of at least one of the deceased Stonecroft lunch table girls."

"The sixth, Laura Wilcox, is missing," Sam said. "Which leaves only Jean Sheridan. I warned her yesterday to trust no one, but I'm not sure if that's going far enough. She may need actual protection."

"Where is she now?" Stevens asked.

"At her hotel. She called me around nine o'clock last night from her hotel room to thank me for something I gave her yesterday. She'd been at a cocktail party given by the president of Stonecroft Academy, and was having dinner sent up to her room. She's meeting her daughter's adoptive parents tonight and said she hoped she'd be able to calm down and get a good night's sleep."

Sam hesitated, then continued. "Rich, sometimes you've got to trust your instincts. Joy is doing a great job digging through the files on the Stonecroft deaths. Jean Sheridan would turn me down flat if I suggested she get a bodyguard, and she'd feel the same way if you offered her protection. But she likes me, and if I tell her I want to hang around with her whenever she leaves the hotel, I think she'd go along with it."

"I think that's a good idea, Sam," Stevens agreed. "All we need is to have something happen to Dr. Sheridan."

"One more thing," Sam added. "I'd like to put surveillance on one of the reunion guys who's still in town. His name is Mark Fleischman, Dr. Mark Fleischman. He's a psychiatrist."

Joy looked at Sam, her eyebrows raised in astonishment. "Dr. Fleischman! Sam, he gives the most sensible advice I've ever heard from anybody on television. A couple of weeks ago he did a program warning parents about kids who feel rejected at home or at school, and how some of them grow up damaged and emotionally warped. We see enough of that, don't we?"

"Yes, we do. But from what I understand, Mark Fleischman got badly hurt both at home and in school," Sam said grimly, "so maybe he was talking about himself."

"See who's available for surveillance," Rich Stevens said. "One more thing—we'd better list Laura Wilcox as a missing person. This is the fifth day she's been gone."

"I think that if we were being totally honest, we'd be listing her as 'missing, presumed dead,'" Sam said flatly.

79

After she hung up from Laura, Jean splashed water on her face, ran a comb through her hair, threw on her jogging suit, dropped her cell phone in her pocket, grabbed her pocketbook, and rushed out of the hotel to her car. Storm King Lookout on Route 218 was fifteen minutes from the hotel. It was still early, and traffic would be light. Normally a careful driver, she pressed her foot on the accelerator and watched the speedometer climb to seventy miles an hour. The clock showed that it was two minutes past seven.

Laura is desperate, she thought. Why does she want to meet me there? Is she planning to hurt herself? The mental image of Laura getting there first and maybe being desperate enough to climb over the railing and throw herself off haunted Jean. The Lookout was hundreds of feet above the Hudson.

The car skidded on the final turn, and for a frightening moment Jean was not sure if she could straighten it, but then the wheels righted and she could see that a car was parked near the telescope at the observation site. Let it be Laura, she prayed. Let her be there. Let her be all right.

Her tires screeched as she pulled into the parking area, turned off her engine, got out, and rushed to fling open the passenger door of the other car. "Laura—" Her greeting died on her lips. The man behind the wheel was wearing a mask, a plastic mask that was the face of an owl. The eyes of the owl, with black pupils set in pools of yellow iris, were surrounded by tufts of white down that gradually changed in color, deepening to brown around the beak and lips.

He was holding a gun.

Terrified, Jean turned to run, but a familiar voice ordered, "Get in the car, Jean, unless you want to die here. And do not speak my name. It is forbidden."

Her car was only a few feet away. Did she dare try to run for it? Would he shoot her? He was raising the gun.

Numb with fear, she stood uncertainly; then, playing for time, she slowly started to put her foot into the car. I'll jump back, she thought. I'll duck. He'll have to get out to shoot me. I may be able to get back in my car. But in a lightning-quick gesture, he grabbed her arm, and pulled her the rest of the way into the car, then reached past her and slammed the door.

In an instant he was backing up, turning onto Route 218, heading toward Cornwall. He ripped off the mask and grinned at her. "I am The Owl," he said. "I am The Owl. You must never call me by any other name. Do you understand?"

He's insane, Jean thought as she nodded. There were no other cars on the road. If one came along, could she lean over and blow the horn? Better to take her chances here on the road than let him get her alone someplace where she couldn't get help. "I am . . . an . . . ow–owl . . . and . . . and . . . I . . . lllive . . . in . . . a . . ." he chanted. "Remember, Jeannie? Remember?"

"I remember." Her lips began to form his name and then froze before any sound came. He's going to kill me, she thought. I'll grab the wheel and try to cause an accident.

He turned and smiled at her, an openmouthed smirk. The pupils of his eyes were black.

My cell phone, she thought. It's in my pocket. She shrank back against the seat and fumbled for it. She managed to slide it out and edge it to her side where he couldn't see it, but before she could attempt to open the cover and dial 911, The Owl's right hand shot over.

"We're getting into traffic," he said. His strong fingers, crooked like talons, flew to her neck.

She jerked back away from him and, with her last conscious thought, pushed the cell phone between the seatback and the cushion.

When she woke up, she was tied to a chair; there was a gag on her mouth. The room was dark, but she could make out the figure of a woman lying on the bed across the room, a woman in a dress that sparkled and caught the tiny glimmers of light that broke through the sides of the thick shades.

What happened? Jean thought. My head hurts. Why can't I move? Is this a dream? No, I was going to meet Laura. I got in the car and—

"You're awake, Jeannie, aren't you?"

It was an effort to turn her head. He was standing in the doorway. "I surprised you, didn't I, Jean? Do you remember the school play in the second grade? Everybody laughed at me. You laughed at me. Remember?"

No, I didn't, Jean thought. I felt sorry for you.

"Jean, answer me."

The gag was so tight that she wasn't sure if he could hear her response: "I remember." To be sure he understood, she nodded her head vigorously.

"You're smarter than Laura," he said. "Now I must go. I'll leave you two together. But I'll be back soon. And I'll have someone with me you've been *dying* to see. Guess who?"

Then he was gone. From the bed Jean heard a whimpering sound. Then, her voice muffled by the gag but still audible, Laura began moaning: "Jeannie, . . . promised . . . wouldn't hurt Lily . . . but he's going . . . going to kill her, too."

80

At a quarter of nine, on his way to the Glen-Ridge House, Sam decided that it was not too early to call Jean. When she didn't answer her room telephone, he was disappointed but not worried. If she had dinner in her room last night, she has probably gone to the coffee shop for breakfast. He debated about calling her on her cell phone but decided against it. By the time I place the call, I'll be there, he thought.

The first sense that something might be wrong came when he could not find her in the coffee shop, and again when she did not answer her room phone. The desk clerk could not be sure if she had gone out for a walk. He was the man with the funny colored hair. "That's not to say she *didn't* go out," he explained. "Early morning is a busy time for us, with people checking out."

Sam saw Gordon Amory coming out of the elevator. He was dressed in a shirt and tie and an obviously expensive dark gray business suit. When he saw Sam, he went over to him. "By any chance have you spoken to Jean this morning?" he asked. "We were supposed to have breakfast together, but she didn't show up. I thought she might have overslept, but she doesn't answer in her room."

"I don't know where she is," Sam said, trying to hide his growing anxiety.

"Well, she was tired when we all got back here last night, so maybe it slipped her mind," Amory said. "I'll catch her later. She said she'll be around until tomorrow anyhow." With a brief smile and a wave of his hand he was on his way to the front door of the hotel.

Sam took out his wallet and looked for Jean's cell phone number but couldn't find it. Exasperated, he decided that he must have left it in the pocket of the jacket he'd been wearing the day before. There was one person he knew, however, who might have it—Alice Sommers.

As he dialed Alice's number, he realized again how much he anticipated hearing the sound of her voice. I had dinner with her the night before last, he thought. I wish we had plans for tonight.

Alice did have Jean's number and gave it to him. "Sam, Jean called me yesterday to say how excited she is about meeting Lily's adoptive parents. She also said there was a chance that over the weekend she'll actually meet Lily. Isn't that wonderful?"

A reunion with the daughter you haven't seen in nearly twenty years. Alice is thrilled for Jean, but it has to be one more kick-in-the-teeth reminder to her that Karen's been gone practically the same amount of time, Sam thought. He was disappointed to realize that whenever he was emotionally touched, he covered himself by sounding somewhat abrupt. "It's great for her. Alice, I've got to run. If you happen to hear from Jean, and I haven't spoken to her, ask her to give me a call, okay? It's important."

"You're worried about her, Sam, I can tell. Why?"

"I'm a *little* concerned. There's a lot going on. Listen, she's probably just out for a walk."

"Let me know the minute you hear from her."

"I will, Alice."

Sam snapped the phone closed and walked over to the hotel desk. "I'd like to know whether Dr. Sheridan ordered room service this morning."

The answer came quickly: "No, she did not."

Mark Fleischman was walking through the front door into the lobby. He spotted Sam at the desk and went over to him. "Mr. Deegan, I want to talk to you. I'm worried about Jean Sheridan."

Sam looked at him coldly. "Why do you say that, Dr. Fleischman?"

"Because in my opinion, whoever is communicating with her about her daughter is dangerous. With Laura missing, Jean is the only woman of the so-called lunch table girls who is both alive and unharmed."

"I've thought about that, Dr. Fleischman."

"Jean is angry with me and doesn't trust me. She misread my reason for speaking to the clerk about a fax. She won't listen to anything I say to her now."

"How did you know that she was Dr. Connors' patient?" Sam asked bluntly.

"Jean asked me that, and I told her initially that I'd heard it from her. I've been thinking, however, and I know now where it came up. When the other honorees—I mean Carter and Gordon and Robby and I—were joking with Jack Emerson about working on the office clean-up crew for his father, one of them mentioned it. I just don't remember which one."

Was Fleischman telling the truth? Sam wondered. If so, I've been barking up the wrong tree. "Go over that conversation, Dr. Fleischman," he urged. "It's very, very important."

"I will. Yesterday Jeannie went for a long walk. I suspect she has done the same thing again this morning. I checked her room—she's not there—and I don't see her in the dining room. I'm going to drive around town and see if I can find her."

Sam knew it was too soon for the investigator assigned to surveillance on Fleischman to have arrived. "Why don't you wait a little while and see if she shows up," he suggested. "The odds are that driving around, you'll miss her."

"I don't intend to sit around and do nothing when I'm worried about her," Fleischman said abruptly. He handed Sam his card. "I'd very much appreciate it if you'd let me know when you hear from her."

He walked swiftly through the lobby toward the entrance of the hotel. Sam watched him go, conflicted in his reaction to the man. I wonder if you took any drama medals at Stonecroft, he thought. Either you're on the level, or you're one hell of a good actor, because outwardly you appear just as worried about Jean Sheridan as I am.

Sam's eyes narrowed as he watched Fleischman swiftly depart through the front door. I'll give it a little while longer, he thought. She may just be out for a walk.

81

The chair he had tied her to was against the wall, next to the window, and facing the bed. There was something about the room that was familiar. With growing horror and the sense of being in the midst of a nightmare, Jean strained to hear Laura's muffled outpourings. She mumbled almost constantly and seemed to be slipping in and out of consciousness as she tried to talk through the gag that gave her voice an eerie, throaty tone. The result was a sound that was almost a growl.

She never used his name. "The Owl" was how she referred to him. Sometimes she would recite his line from that second-grade play: "I am an owl, and I live in a tree." Then she would suddenly lapse into a disquieting silence, and only an occasional shuddering sigh told Jean that Laura was still breathing.

Lily. Laura had said that he was going to kill Lily. But she was safe. Surely she was. Craig Michaelson had promised her that Lily was safe. Was Laura delusional? She must have been here since at least Saturday night. She keeps saying that she's hungry. Hasn't he fed her? She must have had something to eat.

Oh, my God, Jean thought as she remembered Duke, the counterman at the deli–coffee shop at the bottom of the hill. He had told her about a man from the reunion who stopped in regularly to pick up food—Duke was talking about *him!*

She twisted her hands in an effort to see if she could pull the cords apart, but they were too tight. Was it possible that he had killed Karen Sommers in this same room? Was it possible that he had deliberately run over Reed at West Point? Had he killed Catherine and Cindy and Debra and Gloria and Alison, as well as those two women in this area who were murdered this week? I saw him drive into the hotel parking lot early Saturday morning, Jean thought, with his headlights turned off. Maybe if I had told Sam about that, he would have investigated him, *stopped* him.

My cell phone is in his car, Jean thought. If he finds it, he'll throw it away. But if he *doesn't* find it, and if Sam tries to locate it the same way he did the phone Laura used to call me, maybe we have a chance. Please, God, before he hurts Lily, let Sam try to trace my phone.

Laura's breathing became gasping gulps, then formed into barely coherent words: "Cleaner's bags . . . cleaner's bags . . . no . . . no . . . no."

Even with the dark shades over the windows, a little light managed to seep into the room. Jean could see the outline of plastic bags suspended by hangers that had been hooked over the arm of the lamp by the bed. She could see writing across the front of the one directly facing her. What was it? Was it a name? Was it . . . ? She couldn't quite make it out.

Her shoulder was touching the edge of the heavy shade. She threw her weight to one side, then to the other, until the chair moved a few inches, and the shade caught on her shoulder and was tilted away from the window frame.

The added light made the thick black marker pen writing on the plastic bag clear enough to be read: LILY/MEREDITH.

82

Jake could not skip his first class at 8:00 A.M., but as soon as it was over, he rushed to the studio. In his opinion the prints of the pictures he had taken yesterday looked even better in daylight than they had under the overhead light in the late afternoon. He congratulated himself as he studied them.

The McMansion on Concord Avenue really looks so "see me, I'm rich," he thought. The house on Mountain Road is such a great contrast to it—middle-class, comfortable suburban, but now with a mystique about it. At home that evening he had checked the Internet and confirmed that Karen Sommers had been murdered in the corner bedroom on the right side of the second floor. I know Dr. Sheridan used to live next door when she was growing up, Jake thought. I'll stop at the hotel and see if she can confirm that was Laura's room. It probably was. According to the floor plan of the Sommers murder on the Internet, it's the other large bedroom on that floor. It makes sense that precious only-child Laura got it. Dr. Sheridan will probably tell me. She's been nice—not like old "Throw-Him-in-Jail" Deegan.

Jake put the prints of yesterday's pictures in the bag with his extra film. He wanted to have them available while he was shooting, in case he needed them for comparison.

At 9:00 A.M. he was approaching Mountain Road. He had decided that it wouldn't be smart to park in the street. People noticed strange cars, and that cop might recognize his pride and joy. At times like this he wished he hadn't painted it with zebra stripes.

I'll have a soda and a Danish, leave my car at the deli, and walk up to Laura's house, he decided. He had borrowed one of his mother's oversized shopping bags from Bloomingdale's. There'd be no car and no camera in sight. I can sneak down Laura's driveway and get my pictures of the back of the house. I hope the garage doors have windows. That way I can tell if there are any cars parked inside.

At 9:10 he was sitting at the counter of the delicatessen at the foot of Mountain Road, chatting with Duke, who had already explained that he and Sue, his wife, had owned the place for ten years, that it used to be a dry cleaner, that they were open from 6:00 A.M. to 9:00 P.M. and that they both enjoyed being here. "Cornwall is a quiet town," Duke said as he whisked an imaginary crumb from the counter, "but a nice town. You say you go to Stonecroft Academy? That's pretty tony. Some of the reunion people were in here. Oh, there he goes."

Duke's eyes had darted to the window that faced Mountain Road.

"There who goes?" Jake asked.

"The fellow who's been coming in early mornings and some late evenings to pick up coffee and toast or coffee and a sandwich."

"Know who he is?" Jake asked, not really caring.

"Nope, but he's another one of your reunion people, and he's been coming and going all morning. I saw him go out in his car, come back a little while later, and now he's on his way again."

"Uh-huh," Jake said as he got up and pulled some squashed dollar bills out of his pocket. "I feel like stretching my legs. Is it okay if I leave my car outside for about fifteen minutes?"

"Sure, but not more than that. As it is, we don't have enough parking spots."

"Don't worry. I'm in a hurry, too."

Eight minutes later Jake was in the backyard of Laura's former home, taking pictures. He photographed the back of the house and even took a couple of shots of the kitchen through the door. A grill covered the glass pane over the door, but looking in, he could see a fair amount of the room. It could be a display kitchen in Home Depot, he thought. The counters that he could see were bare—no toaster, no coffee pot, no canisters, no cutsie-pie plates or trays or radio or clock. Absolutely no sign of occupancy. I guess for once in my life I was wrong, he decided reluctantly.

He studied the tire tracks on the driveway. There have been a couple of cars here, he thought. But that could be from the guy who rakes the leaves. The garage doors were closed and didn't have windows, so he couldn't check for cars.

He went back up the driveway, crossed the street, and took several more pictures of the front of the house. I guess that'll do it, he thought. I'll go and develop them right away. Then I'll phone Dr. Sheridan and ask her if she remembers which bedroom was Laura's when they were kids.

It would have been more fun to have found Laura Wilcox and Robby Brent holed up here, he thought as he put the camera back in the shopping bag and started down the hill. But what can you do? You can cover a story, but you can't invent one.

83

After her first class, West Point yearling Meredith Buckley rushed to her room for a final review of her notes for the exam in linear algebra, the course that was proving to be the toughest of her second year at West Point.

For twenty minutes she focused intensely on the notes. As she was putting them back in the folder, the phone rang. She was tempted not to answer it, but thinking that it might be her father calling to wish her luck on the exam, she picked it up and then smiled. Before she could speak, a cheerful voice was saying, "May I have the pleasure of inviting Cadet Buckley, daughter of the distinguished General Charles Buckley, to share another weekend with her parents and myself at my home in Palm Beach?"

"You don't know how wonderful that sounds," Meredith said fervently as she thought of the glamorous weekend she had enjoyed with her parents' friend. "I'll come anytime except, of course, when West Point has other plans for me, which is just about always. I hate to seem rude, but I'm heading into an exam."

"I need five, make that three, minutes of your time. Meredith, I was at a class reunion at Stonecroft Academy in Cornwall. I think I mentioned to you I was going to it."

"Yes, you did. I'm so sorry, but I simply can't talk now."

"I'll be fast. Meredith, a classmate of mine who attended the reunion is an intimate friend of Jean, your birth mother, and has written a note to you about her. I promised to deliver the note to you personally. Tell me when to be in the museum parking lot, and I'll be waiting for you with it in hand."

"My *birth* mother? Someone who was at your reunion *knows* her?" Meredith could feel her heart pounding as she gripped the phone. She looked at the clock. She absolutely *had* to get to class. "I'll be finished with my exam at eleven-forty," she said hurriedly. "I could be in the parking lot at ten of twelve."

"That works out for me. Ace your exam, General."

It took all of Cadet Meredith Buckley's training to force herself to put out of her mind the realization that in a little more than an hour she would know something tangible about the girl who at age eighteen had given birth to her. The only information she had so far was that her mother had been about to graduate from high school when she learned she was pregnant and that her father had been a college senior who was killed in a hit-and-run accident before she was born.

Her parents had talked to her about her birth mother. They had promised Meredith that after she was graduated from West Point, they would try to learn her identity and then arrange a meeting between them. "We have no idea who she is, Meri," her father had told her. "We do know, because the doctor who delivered you and arranged the adoption told us, that your birth mother loved you deeply and that giving you up was probably the most unselfish and difficult decision she would ever have to make in her whole life."

All this ran through Meredith's mind as she tried to concentrate on the linear algebra exam. But she could not block out the awareness that every tick of the clock brought her closer to greater knowledge of the mother she now knew as Jean.

As she handed in her exam and rushed toward Thayer Gate and the military academy museum, she realized that the reference to Palm Beach had solved the question her father had asked her yesterday on the phone. *That's* where I lost my hairbrush, she remembered suddenly.

84

A stony-faced Carter Stewart came into the hotel at ten o'clock, while Sam was sitting in the lobby. Sam made a beeline for him, catching him at the desk. "Mr. Stewart, I'd like to have a word with you if I may."

"In a minute, Mr. Deegan." The clerk with the wood-chip-colored hair was behind the desk. "I need to see the manager, and I need to get into Mr. Brent's room again," Stewart snapped at him. "The production company has received yesterday's package. Apparently there is one more script that is vitally needed, and I have been asked to do the proverbial good deed once more. Since the script was not on top of the desk, it will involve going *through* the desk."

"I'll summon Mr. Lewis immediately, sir," the clerk said nervously.

Stewart turned to Sam. "If they do refuse to let me go rummaging through Robby's desk, I don't care. I will have paid the debt of gratitude that my agent insists I owe him. He has now agreed that it has been paid in full. He doesn't know it yet, but that gives me the moral right to fire him, which I intend to do this afternoon."

Stewart turned back to the clerk. "Is the manager here, or is he out in the field picking flowers?"

What a nasty human being, Sam thought. "Mr. Stewart," he said, his tone icy, "I have a question, and I need to know the answer to it. A few nights ago, I understand you, Mr. Amory, Mr. Brent, Mr. Emerson, Dr. Fleischman, and Mr. Nieman were joking about working together on the evening cleaning crew of an office building managed by Mr. Emerson's father."

"Yes, yes, something about that came up. That was the spring of our senior year. Another tender memory of my glorious time at Stonecroft."

"Mr. Stewart, this is very important. Did you hear anyone mention that Dr. Sheridan had been a patient of a Dr. Connors who had an office in that building?"

"No, I did not. And, besides, why would Jean have been a patient of Dr. Connors? He was an obstetrician." Stewart's eyes widened. "Oh, my. Have we a little secret about to come out, Mr. Deegan? Was Jeannie a patient of Dr. Connors?"

Sam looked at Stewart with loathing. He wanted to kick himself for the way he had framed the question, and he wanted to punch Stewart for his leering response to it. "I asked you if someone had made that statement," he said. "I did not for one instant suggest that it was true."

Justin Lewis, the manager, had come up behind them. "Mr. Stewart, I understand you wish to go into Mr. Brent's room and go through his desk. I am afraid that I really can't allow that. I spoke to our law firm yesterday after I let you take those scripts, and they were quite upset about it."

"There we are," Stewart said. He turned his back on the manager. "My business here is pretty well wrapped up, Mr. Deegan," he said. "My director and I have completed going over his suggested changes for my play, and I have had quite enough of hotel life. I'm going back to Manhattan this afternoon, and I wish you good luck waiting for Laura and Robby to bob to the surface."

Sam and the hotel manager watched him exit the lobby. "That is one nasty guy," Justin Lewis told Sam. "It's obvious that he hates Mr. Brent."

"Why do you say that?" Sam asked quickly.

"Because a note Mr. Brent left on his desk referring to Mr. Stewart as 'Howie' obviously got under his skin. From what Mr. Stewart said, it was Mr. Brent's idea of a joke, but then Mr. Stewart asked me if I knew that saying about 'he who laughs last laughs best.' "

Before Sam could comment, his cell phone rang; the caller was Rich Stevens. "Sam, we have a call in from the Cornwall cops. A car was spotted in the Hudson. It was partially submerged, but caught on rocks, which is why it didn't go all the way down. There's a body in the trunk. It's Robby Brent, and it appears he's been dead for a couple of days. You'd better get over there."

"Right away, Rich." Sam snapped his phone closed. *"He who laughs last laughs best."* When *Laura and Robby "bob to the surface."* Bobbing, as in water? he wondered. Was Carter Stewart, once known as Howie, not only a celebrated playwright but a psychopathic killer as well?

85

At ten o'clock Jake was back in the darkroom at the school, developing his latest set of pictures. The ones he had taken of the back of the Mountain Road house really didn't contribute anything to his story, he decided. Even the door with its decorative grill had a Norman Rockwell, down-home feeling. The shot into the kitchen wasn't bad, but who wanted to look at bare countertops?

This morning was basically a waste, Jake decided. I shouldn't have bothered cutting my second class. As the quick shot he had taken of the house from the front began to develop, he could see that it was a little out of focus. He might as well deep-six it. He'd never use it in the article.

He heard his name being called from outside the darkroom. It was Jill Ferris, and she sounded upset. She couldn't be mad at me, he thought—it wasn't her class I cut. "I'll be right out, Ms. Ferris," he called.

As soon as he opened the door he could tell by the look on her face that something had really shaken her up. She didn't bother to say hello to him. "Jake, I took a chance you might be in there," she said. "You interviewed Robby Brent, didn't you?"

"Yes, I did. A good interview if I do say so myself." She's not going to kill it, is she? Jake thought with dismay. Old Downes probably wants to forget that Brent and Laura Wilcox ever set foot in Stonecroft.

"Jake, it just came over the news. Robby Brent's body was found in the trunk of a car submerged near Cornwall Landing."

Robby Brent dead! Jake grabbed his camera. I still have a lot of film left, he thought. "Thanks, Jill," he yelled, as he raced out the door.

86

The car with Robby Brent's body had gone into the Hudson at Cornwall Landing. The normally tranquil park, with its benches and weeping willows, was now the center of police activity. The area had been hastily taped-off to hold back the curious bystanders who, like the media, were gathering in ever-increasing numbers.

When Sam arrived at ten-thirty, the body of the late Robby Brent had already been placed in a body bag and in the morgue wagon. Cal Grey, the medical examiner, filled Sam in. "He's been dead at least a couple of days. Stab wound in the chest. Went right through his heart. I have to wait till I can take measurements, but I've got to tell you, Sam, that it appears to be the same kind of jagged-edge knife that killed Helen Whelan. From what I can see, whoever murdered Brent was either a lot taller or was standing on something like a staircase where he was above the victim. That knife went in at a distinct angle."

Mark Fleischman is tall, Sam thought. Talking to Fleischman, he could understand why Jean had been drawn to him. He had a plausible explanation for the reason he had inquired about the fax and for his knowledge that Jean had been a patient of Dr. Connors. Was he being honest, or was he a little too glib? Sam wasn't sure.

Before coming to the crime scene, Sam had called Jean on her cell phone, but she had not answered. He left her an urgent message to call him and then dialed Alice Sommers again.

Alice had partially reassured him. "Sam, when Jean was talking about meeting Lily's adoptive parents tonight, she mentioned that she wished she had brought more clothes with her. Woodbury Mall is less than half an hour away. I wouldn't be surprised if she simply decided to ride over there and do some shopping."

It was a reasonable supposition, and it had helped to partially allay Sam's concern for Jean. But now the concern was building, and he knew it was his instinct warning him not to wait any longer to begin an active search for her.

"Robbery wasn't the motive," Cal Grey was saying. "Brent was wearing an expensive watch and has six hundred bucks in his wallet and a half-dozen credit cards. How long has he been missing?"

"He hasn't been seen since after dinner on Monday night," Sam said.

"My bet is that he didn't last long after that," Grey commented. "Of course the autopsy will pin down the time of death much more accurately than I can now."

"I was at that dinner," Sam said. "What was he wearing when you got him out of the trunk?"

"Beige jacket, dark brown slacks, and a brown turtleneck sweater."

"Then unless he slept in his clothes wherever he went, he died on Monday night."

Cameras were flashing as photographers behind the tape took pictures of the car that had been Robby Brent's coffin. A salvage truck had hoisted it out of the river, and now, still attached to the cable, it was standing on the bank, dripping water as technicians continued to photograph it from every angle.

A local policeman filled Sam in on the details, sketchy as they were. "We think the car may have been dumped around ten o'clock last night. A couple who live in New Windsor were jogging past here at about a quarter of ten. They say they saw a car parked near the railroad tracks and that someone was in it. They turned and started back about half a mile down the road. When they reached this point again, the car was gone, but a man was walking fast along Shore Road."

"Did they get a good look at him?"

"No."

"Did they mention if he was tall? I mean *really* tall?" Sam asked.

"They can't agree. The husband said the guy was average size; the wife thought he was pretty tall. Both of them wear distance glasses and admit they barely got an impression of the guy, but they are sure that a car was parked here, that ten minutes later it was gone, and that someone was leaving this area on foot and in a big hurry."

God deliver me from eyewitnesses, Sam thought. As he turned back, he spotted Jake Perkins pushing his way to the front of the group behind the tape. He was carrying a camera that reminded Sam of the kind he had seen in a book about the great World War II photographer Robert Capa.

I wonder if that kid has the gift of bilocation, Sam thought. It's not only that he *seems* to be everywhere; he *is* everywhere. His eyes met Jake's, but Jake looked away immediately. He's sore at me for telling Tony to throw him in jail after he claimed to be my special assistant investigating Laura's disappearance, Sam thought. I could have given him a break and at least said that he's trying to be helpful, because he was. After all, he was the one who tipped me off that Laura sounded nervous on that phone call.

He was debating whether to go over and speak to Jake when his cell phone rang. He snapped it out of his pocket, hoping the call would be from Jean. Instead it was from Joy Lacko. "Sam, a call came into 911 a few minutes ago. A BMW convertible registered to Dr. Jean Sheridan has been parked at Storm King Lookout on 218 for a couple of hours. The call was made by a salesman who drove past it around seven-forty-five and then again twenty minutes ago. He thought it seemed odd that the car was there so long and decided to check to see if there was a problem. The keys are in the ignition, and her pocketbook is on the passenger seat. It doesn't look good."

"That's why she hasn't been answering her phone," Sam said heavily. "My God, Joy. Why didn't I insist that she have a bodyguard? Is the car still at the Lookout?"

"Yes. Rich knew you'd want to look over the location before we moved it." Joy's voice was sympathetic. "I'll keep in touch, Sam."

The vehicle with Robby Brent's body was starting to back up. Three bodies in less than a week in that meat wagon, Sam thought. Don't let the next one be Jean Sheridan, he prayed. Please don't let the next one be Jean.

87

Jake Perkins had immediately regretted not acknowledging Sam Deegan when their eyes met. It was one thing not to give the detective any information he might come across, but it was another thing to cut off all contact with him. No good reporter, no matter how insulted he'd been, would ever do that.

He would have loved to ask Deegan for a statement about Robby Brent's murder, but he knew better than to do that. He knew what the official line would be—that Brent was the victim of a homicide by person or persons unknown. They hadn't released the cause of death, but it was a cinch it wasn't suicide. Nobody climbs into the trunk of a car while it's rolling into the river.

Maybe Deegan knows where Dr. Sheridan is, Jake thought. He had tried to phone Jean, but there was no answer in her room. He did want to get confirmation from her that Laura Wilcox had slept in the murder bedroom on Mountain Road.

Struggling with the heavy camera, Jake worked his way through the crowd of photographers and reporters and caught up with Sam at his car. "Mr. Deegan, I've been trying to get in touch with Dr. Sheridan. Do you by any chance know where I could reach her? She doesn't answer her phone."

Sam was about to get into his car. "What time did you try her?" he asked sharply.

"About nine-thirty."

That was the same time I tried her, Sam thought. "I don't know where she is," he snapped as he got in his car. He slammed the door closed and turned on the siren.

Something's up, Jake thought. He's worried about Dr. Sheridan, but he's not making the turn back to the hotel. He's going too fast for me to follow him. I might as well go back to school and clean up the darkroom. Then I'll head over to the Glen-Ridge and see what's going on.

88

On the way to the observation point, Sam phoned the Glen-Ridge House and asked to be put through to the manager immediately. When Justin Lewis got on, Sam said, "Look, I can get a subpoena for your phone records, but I can't waste the time. Dr. Sheridan's car has just been found, and she is missing. I want you to give me right now a list of the phone numbers of all calls received by Dr. Sheridan between ten o'clock last night and nine o'clock this morning."

He had been prepared for an argument but did not get one. "Give me your number. I'll call you right back," the manager said crisply.

Sam put his cell phone on the passenger seat as he raced toward Storm King Lookout. He rounded the bend and saw Jean's blue convertible with a policeman standing beside it. He pulled up behind it and had his notebook and pencil out when Lewis called back. The man obviously had understood the need for urgency. "Dr. Sheridan received seven phone calls this morning," he said crisply. "The first came at quarter of seven!"

"At quarter of seven?" Sam interrupted.

"Yes, sir. It was made on a cell phone from this area. The name of the subscriber was not given. The number is . . ."

Stunned and disbelieving, Sam wrote down the number that he

recognized as the same one Robby Brent had called from on Monday night when he had imitated Laura's voice on the call to Jean.

"The other calls have been identified as coming from a Mrs. Alice Sommers and a Mr. Jake Perkins. They both tried to reach Dr. Sheridan several times. There are two from your own number."

"Thank you. You've been very helpful," Sam said abruptly, and he clicked off. Robby Brent has been dead for a couple of days, he thought, but someone used the phone he bought in the drugstore to entice Jean Sheridan to leave the hotel. She must have rushed out right after that call came in. Her car was spotted here at 7:45 this morning. Who was she expecting to meet here? She had promised to be careful, and there were only two people she would have met without question. Sam was sure of it.

He was aware that the cop standing by Jean's car was giving him a curious stare, but he ignored him. Jean expected to meet either her daughter, Lily, or Laura, Sam thought as he looked blankly at the mountains on the other side of the river.

Had she been forced from her car at gunpoint, or had she walked over to another vehicle on her own?

Whoever this psychopath is, he has Jean. Is Jean's daughter *really* safe? Sam wondered suddenly. He opened his wallet, raced through the cards inside, found the one he wanted, tossed the others on the passenger seat, and dialed Craig Michaelson's cell phone. After five rings a computer voice advised him to leave a message. Swearing under his breath, he dialed Michaelson's office.

"I am so sorry," his secretary apologized. "Mr. Michaelson is in a conference at another attorney's office and cannot be interrupted."

"He's got to be interrupted," Sam snapped. "This is a police matter—a matter of life and death."

"Oh, sir," the manicured voice chided, "I'm sorry, but—"

"Listen to me, young lady, and listen hard. You get Michaelson, and you tell him that Sam Deegan phoned. Tell your boss that Jean Sheridan has disappeared and that it is *imperative* he contact West Point immediately and warn them to put a bodyguard on her daughter. Do you understand me?"

"Of course I do. I will try to reach him, but—"

"No buts. *Reach him!*" Sam shouted, then snapped his phone closed. He got out of the car. I have to put a track on Robby Brent's phone, he thought, but it probably won't do any good. There's only one hope.

He brushed past the policeman, who started to explain that he knew the salesman who had alerted them to the car being there and that nobody could be more reliable. Jean's shoulder bag was on the seat.

"Nothing has been taken out of it?" he snapped.

"Of course not, sir." The young policeman was clearly offended at the suggestion.

Sam didn't bother to assure him that he meant nothing personal by the question. He dumped the contents of Jean's bag on the passenger seat, then searched the glove compartment and all the storage areas inside the car. "If it's not too late, we may have gotten the break we need," he said. "She was probably carrying her cell phone. It's not here."

It was 11:30 A.M.

89

It was 11:45 A.M. before Craig Michaelson phoned Sam, who by then was back in the Glen-Ridge House. "My secretary tried to get me, but I had left the meeting and forgot to turn on my cell phone," he explained hurriedly. "I just got to the office. What's going on?"

"What's going on is that Jean Sheridan has been abducted," Sam said tersely. "I don't give a damn if her daughter is in West Point and surrounded by an army. I want you to be sure that a special guard is put on her. We have a psychopath running loose around here. The body of one of the other Stonecroft honorees was pulled out of the Hudson a couple of hours ago. He'd been stabbed to death."

"Jean Sheridan is missing! The General and his wife are on the eleven o'clock shuttle from Washington right now, on their way to have dinner with her tonight. I can't get in touch with them while they're on a flight."

Sam's pent-up worry and frustration exploded. "Yes, you can," he shouted. "You could get a message through the airline to the pilot, but it's too late for that now anyway. Give me the name of Jean Sheridan's daughter, and I'll call West Point myself. I want it now."

"She is Cadet Meredith Buckley. She's a second-year student, a yearling. But the General assured me that Meredith would not leave the West Point campus either Thursday or Friday because of the tests she has scheduled."

"Let's pray the General is right," Sam snapped. "Mr. Michaelson, in the unlikely event I meet any resistance when I call the superintendent at the academy, please be available for an immediate phone call."

"I'll be in my office."

"And if you're not, make sure your cell phone is on."

Sam was in the office behind the hotel's front desk, the place where he had started the investigation into the disappearance of Laura Wilcox. Eddie Zarro had joined him there. "You want to keep your cell phone line open, don't you?" Eddie asked.

Sam nodded, then watched as Eddie dialed the West Point number. While waiting for the call to go through, he frantically searched his memory for anything that might suggest another path of action. The technical guys were triangulating on Jean's cell phone, something they expected to complete within minutes. When they did, they'd be able to pinpoint the exact location of the phone. That should help—assuming it isn't in a garbage heap somewhere, Sam thought.

"Sam, they're ringing the superintendent's office," Eddie said. Sam's tone when he picked up the phone was only slightly less forceful than the one he'd used with Craig Michaelson. When he spoke to the superintendent's secretary, he did not mince words. "I am Detective Deegan from the Office of the District Attorney of Orange County. Cadet Meredith Buckley may be in serious danger from a homicidal maniac. I need to speak to the superintendent immediately."

He did not have to wait more than ten seconds before the superintendent was on the phone. He listened to Sam's brief explanation, then said, "She's probably in an exam right now. I'll have her brought to my office immediately."

"Just let me be sure that you have her," Sam asked. "I'll hold on."

He held the phone for five minutes. When the superintendent came back on, his voice was charged with emotion. "Less than five minutes ago, Cadet Buckley was seen leaving Thayer Gate and going over to the parking lot of the Military Academy Museum. She has not returned, and she is neither in the parking lot nor in the museum."

Sam didn't want to believe what he was hearing. Not her as well, he thought, not a nineteen-year-old kid! "I understood that she promised her father she wouldn't leave West Point," he said. "Are you *sure* she went outside?"

"The cadet didn't break her word," the superintendent said. "Although it's open to the public, the museum is considered part of the West Point campus."

90

Jill Ferris was in the studio when Jake got back to Stonecroft. "Robby Brent's body was in the meat wagon by the time I got there," he said, "but they'd pulled the car out of the water. He was found in the trunk. I bet President Downes is having a heart attack or at least a bleeding ulcer. Can't you see the publicity we'll be getting now?"

"The president is very upset," Jill Ferris admitted. "Jake, are you through with the camera?"

"I think so. You know, Jill—I mean Ms. Ferris—it wouldn't have surprised me if Laura Wilcox was found in the trunk of that car with Brent. I mean, what's happened to her? I'd bet the ranch that she's dead, too. And if she is, the only one at that lunch table still alive is Dr. Sheridan. If I were her, I'd hire a bodyguard. I mean, when you think how many so-called celebrities won't stir unless they're surrounded by a couple of muscle men, why wouldn't someone like Dr. Sheridan, with a *real* reason to worry, not get some protection?"

It was a rhetorical question, and Jake was already on his way into the darkroom, so he got no answer.

He wasn't sure what he would do with his shots of the crime scene. It was unlikely that they'd ever see the light of day in the *Stonecroft Academy Gazette*. Still, he was certain that he'd eventually find a place for them, even though he hadn't yet received an offer to be a roving reporter for the *New York Post.*

When the pictures were developed, he viewed them with intense pleasure. From different angles he had caught the starkness of the car with its sides dented from hitting a rock pile in the river and its open trunk, dripping water. He also had gotten a good shot of the meat wagon, its lights flashing as it backed away.

The pictures he had taken in the morning of the Mountain Road house were still clipped and hanging on the line. His gaze fell on the last one, the out-of-focus picture of the front of the house. As he looked closely at it, his eyes widened.

He grabbed the magnifying glass, studied the picture, then unclipped it and rushed out of the darkroom. Jill Ferris was still there, grading papers. He dropped the picture in front of her and handed her the magnifying glass.

"Jake," she protested.

"This is important, really important. Look at this picture and tell me if something looks out of place or different. Please, Ms. Ferris, really look."

"Jake, you'd drive anyone crazy," she said with a sigh, taking the magnifying glass from him to study the print. "I guess you mean that the shade on that window on the second floor in the corner is kind of lopsided. Is that it?"

"That's *exactly* it," Jake exulted. "It wasn't lopsided yesterday. I don't care how empty that kitchen looks—somebody's living in that house!"

91

Sam had returned to the Glen-Ridge House rather than go back to the office in Goshen because he was beginning to feel certain that one of the honorees, or perhaps Jack Emerson or Joel Nieman, was responsible for the threats to Lily. All of them had worked in the building where Dr. Connors' office was located. At some point over the weekend, one of them had referred to Jean as having been his patient. But which one he hadn't yet determined.

Fleischman had insisted he heard one of those other men mention that Jean was Connors' patient. Of course, he could be lying, Sam thought. Stewart denied ever hearing the remark. And he could be lying, too. But at least at the Glen-Ridge he could keep an eye on Fleischman and Gordon Amory, who were still checked in there. The fact that Jean was missing would be picked up by reporters and be broadcast, and he'd bet anything that the news would bring Jack Emerson rushing there as well.

He'd already asked Rich Stevens to put surveillance on all of them. That would kick in soon.

At ten after twelve he got the call he was hoping to receive from the technical guys. "Sam, we have a fix on Jean Sheridan's phone."

"Where is it?"

"In a moving car."

"Can you tell where the car is?"

"Near Storm King, heading toward the Cornwall area."

"He's coming from West Point," Sam said. "He has the cadet. Don't lose him. Don't lose him."

"We don't intend to."

92

"Please turn the car around," Meredith said. "I am not permitted to leave the grounds. When you asked me to sit in the car, I thought you meant just to talk for a minute. I'm sorry you left the letter about my mother in your other pocket, but I'll have to wait to get it. Please, I must go back, Mr.—"

"You were about to use my name, Meredith. I don't want you to do that. You must refer to me as Owl or The Owl."

She stared at him, fear suddenly gripping her. "I don't understand. Please take me back." Meredith grasped the handle of the passenger door. If he stops for a light, I'll jump out, she thought. He's different. He even looks different. No, not just different—crazy! Questions of doubt, unanswerable questions, flitted through her mind. Why did Dad ask me to promise I wouldn't leave the grounds? Why did he ask me about the hairbrush that I lost? What does this have to do with my birth mother?

The car was speeding north along Route 218. He's going way over the speed limit, Meredith thought. Please, God, let us pass a cop. Let a cop see us. She considered grabbing the steering wheel, but there were cars coming in the other direction; somebody in one of them might get killed. "Where are you taking me?" she demanded. Something was pressing into her back. She moved forward in the seat, but it was still there. What was it?

"Meredith, I lied when I said I met your mother's friend at the reunion. I met your *mother* there. I'm taking you to see her."

"My mother! Jean! You're taking me to see her?"

"Yes, I am. And then the two of you are going to join your birth father in heaven. You'll have a wonderful reunion, I'm sure. You look a lot like him, you know. At least you look as he did before I smashed into him on the road. You know where that happened, Meredith? On the road near the picnic grounds at West Point. That's where your real daddy died. I wish you'd had a chance to visit his grave. His name is on the tombstone: Carroll Reed Thornton, Jr. He would have graduated one week later. I wonder if they'll bury you and Jeannie beside him. Wouldn't that be nice?"

"My father went to West Point, and *you* killed him?"

"Of course I did. Do you think it was fair for him and Jean to be so happy and leave me out in the cold? *Do you think that was fair, Meredith?*"

He turned his head and glared at her. His eyes were flashing. His lips were pressed together so tightly that his mouth seemed to have disappeared beneath flaring nostrils.

He's crazy, she thought. "No, sir. It doesn't seem fair," she replied, trying to keep her voice steady. I can't show him how scared I am.

He seemed mollified. "Your West Point training. 'Yes, ma'am.' 'No, sir.' I didn't ask you to call me sir. I told you to call me 'Owl.' "

They had passed the cutoff for Storm King Mountain and were on the outskirts of Cornwall. Where are we going? Meredith wondered. Is he really taking me to my mother? Did he really kill my father and is he planning to kill us now? What can I do to stop him? Don't panic, she warned herself. Look around. See if there's anything you can use to defend yourself. Maybe there's a bottle of water somewhere. I could hit him in the face with it. It might give me enough time to reach the ignition key and stop the car. We're passing enough cars now that somebody might notice a struggle. But as she glanced around, she saw absolutely nothing she could use to defend herself.

"Meredith, I can read your thoughts. Don't even think about trying to attract attention to yourself, because if you do, you will not live to get out of this car. I have a gun, and I will use it. At least I am offering you a chance to meet your mother. Don't be foolish and throw it away."

Meredith's hands were gripped together. What was pressing against her back? Maybe, maybe it was something that would give her a chance to save herself and save her mother. With infinite care she unclasped her hands and moved her right hand slowly to her side. She sat up straighter in the seat as she slid her hand behind her back. Her fingers touched the edge of a narrow object that felt familiar.

It was a cell phone. She had to tug to get it loose, but The Owl didn't seem to notice. They were driving through Cornwall now, and he was looking from side to side as though afraid he'd be stopped.

Meredith moved her hand slowly back, the phone cupped in it. She flipped it open, glanced down, and her finger pressed 91—

She did not see his hand shoot across the car seat, but she felt it as he grabbed her neck. She slumped forward, unconscious, as The Owl grabbed the phone, lowered his window, and threw it onto the road.

Less than ten seconds later, a mail truck rumbled over it, breaking it into bits of plastic.

"Sam, we've lost him," Eddie Zarro said. "He's in Cornwall, but we're not getting any more signals."

"How did you lose him?" Sam shouted. It was a stupid, useless question. He knew the answer—the phone had been discovered and destroyed.

"What do we do now?" Zarro asked.

"Pray," Sam said. "We pray."

93

Jake again asked permission to leave his car outside the delicatessen, and once more it was granted, but Duke's curiosity was now at a fever pitch. "Who are you taking pictures of, sonny?" he asked.

"Just of the neighborhood. As I told you, I'm doing a little story for the *Stonecroft Academy Gazette*. I'll give you a copy when I finish." Jake had an inspiration. "Better yet, I'll mention you in it."

"That'd be nice. Duke and Sue Mackenzie. No capital *k* in Mackenzie."

"Gotcha."

Jake's cell phone rang as, camera over his arm, he was starting out the door. The call was from Amy Sachs, on duty at the hotel. "Jake," she whispered, "you should be over here. All hell is breaking loose. Dr. Sheridan is missing. They found her car abandoned at Storm King Lookout. Mr. Deegan is in the office here. I just heard him shouting about something being lost."

"Thanks, Amy. I'll be right over," Jake said. He turned to Duke. "Guess I won't need that space after all, but thanks anyhow."

"There goes that fellow from the reunion I was telling you about," Duke said, pointing to the street outside. "He's going kind of fast. He'll get a ticket if he's not careful."

Jake looked out quickly enough to see and recognize the driver. "He's been buying stuff here?" he asked.

"Yup. Didn't come in *this* morning, but most days he'd buy coffee and toast, and sometimes stop by for coffee and a sandwich at night."

Could he have been buying it for Laura? Jake wondered. And now Dr. Sheridan is missing. I've got to call Sam Deegan. I'm sure he'll want to check Laura's old house. Then I'll go up there and wait for him, he decided.

He dialed the hotel. "Amy, put Mr. Deegan on. It's important."

Amy didn't take long to come back. "Mr. Deegan told me to tell you to get lost."

"Amy, tell Mr. Deegan that I think I know where he can find Laura Wilcox."

94

Jean looked up as the door to the bedroom was pushed open. The Owl was standing in the doorway. In his arms he was carrying a slender figure, dressed in the dark gray uniform of a West Point cadet. With a satisfied smile he walked across the room and lay Meredith at Jean's feet. "Behold, your daughter!" he said triumphantly. "Look into her face. See the features that must be familiar to you. Isn't she beautiful? Aren't you proud?"

Reed, Jean thought, it's Reed! Lily is Reed incarnate! The narrow aquiline nose, the wide-set eyes, the high cheekbones, the pale golden hair. Oh, my God, has he killed her? No, no—she's breathing!

"Don't hurt her! Don't you *dare* hurt her!" she cried. When she tried to shout, her voice became muffled. From the bed she could hear Laura's frightened sobs.

"I'm not going to hurt her, Jeannie. But I am going to *kill* her, and *you* are going to watch. Then it will be Laura's turn. Then yours. By then I think I'll be doing you a favor. I can't imagine you would want to live after watching your daughter die, will you?"

At a deliberately slow pace, The Owl walked across the room, removed the hanger with the plastic bag on which he had written "Lily/Meredith," and carried it back. He knelt beside Meredith's unconscious form and slid the hanger out of the bag. "Do you want to pray, Jean?" he asked. "I think the Twenty-third Psalm is appropriate for you to recite at this time. Go ahead—'The Lord is my shepherd . . .' "

Stunned and horrified, Jean watched as The Owl began to slide the plastic over Lily's head.

"No, no, no . . ." Before the plastic reached Lily's nostrils, she tipped the chair, falling forward, protecting her child with her body. The chair hit The Owl on his arm and pinned it. He screeched with pain. As he struggled to pull it loose, he could hear from downstairs the sound of the front door being smashed open.

95

When Sam Deegan got on the phone with Jake after Amy Sachs had explained to him that Jake thought he knew where Laura was being kept, he did not give Jake the chance to deliver the speech he had hastily prepared.

Jake wanted to say, "Mr. Deegan, notwithstanding the fact that you publicly disclaimed my assistance and made me the subject of ridicule, I am being generous enough to help you in your investigation, particularly since I am very concerned about Dr. Sheridan."

He got only as far as "Notwithstanding the fact" when Sam interrupted. "Listen, Jake. Jean Sheridan and Laura are in the hands of a homicidal maniac. Don't waste my time. Do you know where Laura is, or don't you?"

At that, Jake almost tripped over his own tongue as he rushed to tell what he knew.

"Somebody is staying in Laura's old house on Mountain Road, Mr. Deegan, even though it's supposed to be unoccupied. One of the honorees from the reunion has been buying food at the delicatessen down the street from the house almost every day. He just drove by. I think he was on his way to the house." Jake had barely spit out the name of the man before he heard the click of Sam's phone.

That sure got Deegan's attention, Jake thought as he waited on the street near Laura's old house. It wasn't more than six minutes later that Deegan and that other detective, Zarro, were screeching to a stop at the curb, followed by two patrol cars. They hadn't used the sirens to announce their arrival, which Jake had found disappointing, but he supposed they wanted to surprise the guy.

He had told Sam he was sure that whoever was in the house was in the corner front bedroom. Immediately after that, they broke down the front door and rushed in. Sam had yelled to him to stay outside.

Fat chance, Jake thought. He'd given them time to get to the bedroom, then followed, the camera slung over his shoulder. As he got to the top of the stairs, he heard a door slam. The other front bedroom, he thought. Somebody's in there.

Sam Deegan came out of the back corner bedroom, his gun drawn. "Get downstairs, Jake!" he ordered. "There's a killer hiding up here."

Jake pointed down the hall. "He's in there."

Sam and Zarro and a couple of the cops ran past him. Jake rushed to the door of the front bedroom, looked inside, and, after an instant of total shock at what he was seeing, focused his camera and began snapping pictures.

He took a photograph of Laura Wilcox. She was lying on the bed, her gown crumpled, her hair matted. A cop was supporting her head and holding a glass of water to her lips.

Jean Sheridan was sitting on the floor, holding in her arms a young woman dressed in the uniform of a West Point cadet. Jean was crying and whispering, "Lily, Lily, Lily," over and over again. At first Jake thought the girl was dead, but then he saw that she was beginning to stir.

Jake aimed his camera and was able to record for posterity the moment Lily opened her eyes and, for the first time since the day she was born, looked into the eyes of her birth mother.

96

It will be only a matter of seconds before they force open the door, The Owl thought. I came so close to completing the mission. He looked at the pewter owls he had clasped in his hand, the ones he had intended to place with the bodies of Laura and Jean and Meredith.

Now he would never have the chance.

"Give yourself up," Sam Deegan shouted. "It's over. You know you can't escape."

"Oh, but I can," The Owl thought. He sighed and took his mask out of his pocket. He slipped it on and looked into the mirror over the bureau to be sure it was properly in place. He put the pewter owls on the dresser.

"I am an owl, and I live in a tree," he said aloud.

The pistol was in his other pocket. He took it out and held it against his temple. "Night-time is my time," he whispered. Then he closed his eyes and pulled the trigger.

At the sound of the shot, Sam kicked the door and it flew open. With Eddie Zarro and the cops behind him, he rushed inside.

The body was sprawled on the floor, the gun beside it. He had fallen backward, and the mask was still in place, blood seeping through it.

Sam bent down, pulled off the mask, and looked into the face of the man who had taken the lives of so many innocent people. In death the scars from the plastic surgery were clearly visible, and the features that some surgeon had managed to make so attractive now seemed twisted and repulsive.

"Funny," Sam said. "Gordon Amory was the last one I would have figured to be The Owl."

97

That night Jean had dinner with Charles and Gano Buckley at Craig Michaelson's home. Meredith was already back at West Point. "After the doctor checked her over, she insisted on going back today," General Buckley said. "She was still worried about her physics exam tomorrow morning. She is such a disciplined kid. She'll make a great soldier." He was trying not to show how shaken he had been when he learned how near to death his only child had come.

"Like the goddess, Minerva, she sprang full-fledged from her father's brow," Jean said. "It's exactly what Reed would have done." She lapsed into silence. She could still feel the unspeakable joy of the moment when the cop had cut her loose from the chair and she had been able to put her arms around Lily. She could feel the poignant beauty of the sound of Lily whispering, "Jean—Mother."

They had been taken to the hospital to be checked. There, she and Lily had sat side by side talking, beginning to catch up on nearly twenty years. "I always imagined what you looked like," Lily had said. "I think I pictured you just as you are."

"And I you. I'll have to learn to call you Meredith. It's a beautiful name."

When the doctor cleared them for release, he said, "Most women after your ordeal would be on tranquilizers. You two are troupers."

They had stopped in to see Laura. Seriously dehydrated, she was on an IV and sedated into a healing sleep.

Sam had returned to the hospital to drive them back to the hotel. But as they met in the lobby, the Buckleys arrived. "Mom, Dad," Meredith had called, and with sad understanding, Jean had watched her fly into their arms.

"Jean, you gave her life, and you saved her life," Gano Buckley said quietly. "From now on you will always be a part of her life."

Jean looked across the table at the handsome couple. They both appeared to be about sixty years old. Charles Buckley had steel gray hair, piercing eyes, strong features, and an air of authority that was balanced by the charm of his manner and the warmth of his smile. Gano Buckley was a delicately pretty, small-boned woman who had enjoyed a brief career as a concert pianist before she became a military wife. "Meredith plays beautifully," she told Jean. "I can't wait for you to hear her."

The three were going together to visit Meredith at the academy on Saturday afternoon. They're her mother and father, Jean thought. They're the ones who brought her up, cared for her and loved her and made her the marvelous young woman she is today. But at least now I'll have a place in her life. Saturday, I'll go with her to Reed's grave, and I'll tell her about him. She must know what a remarkable person he was.

It was a profoundly bittersweet evening for her, and she knew the Buckleys understood when, pleading exhaustion, she left soon after coffee was served.

When Craig Michaelson dropped her off at the hotel at ten o'clock, she found Sam Deegan and Alice Sommers waiting in the lobby.

"We figured you might want to have a nightcap with us," Sam said. "Even with all the lightbulb people here, they managed to save a table for us in the bar."

With tears of gratitude in her eyes, Jean looked from one to the other. They understand how hard tonight has been for me, she thought. Then she spotted Jake Perkins standing near the front desk. She beckoned to him, and he rushed over to her.

"Jake," she said, "I was so out of it this afternoon that I don't know whether or not I really thanked you. If it weren't for you, neither Meredith nor Laura nor I would be alive today." She put her arms around his neck and kissed his cheek.

Jake was visibly moved. "Dr. Sheridan," he said. "I just wish I had been a little smarter. When I saw those pewter owls on the dresser next to Mr. Amory's body, I told Mr. Deegan that I had found one on Alison Kendall's grave. Maybe if I had told him when I found it, they might have decided to get you a bodyguard right away."

"Never mind that," Sam said. "You couldn't know at that time that the owl meant anything. Dr. Sheridan is right. If you hadn't figured out that Laura might be in that house, they'd all be dead. Now, let's go inside before we lose that table." He considered for a moment and sighed. "You come too, Jake."

Alice was standing next to him. Sam could see that what Jake had just said had startled her.

"Sam, last week on her anniversary, I found a pewter owl at Karen's grave," she said quietly. "I have it at home in the curio cabinet in the den."

"That's it," Sam said. "I've been trying to remember what I noticed in your cabinet that bothered me, Alice. Now I know what it was."

"Gordon Amory must have been the one who put it there," Alice said sadly.

Sam put his arm around her as they walked into the bar. It's been a hell of a day for her, too, he thought. He had told Alice that The Owl had admitted to Laura that he had murdered Karen by mistake. Alice was devastated to learn that Karen had been killed only because she happened to come home that night. But she said that at least it took the cloud of suspicion off Karen's boyfriend, Cyrus Lindstrom, and at least now she could hope for some degree of closure.

"I'll take that owl out of the cabinet when I drive you home tonight," he said. "I don't want you to look at it again."

They were at the table. "It's closure for you as well, isn't it, Sam?" Alice asked. "For twenty years you never gave up trying to solve Karen's death."

"In that sense it's closure, but I hope it's still all right with you if I continue to drop in for a visit occasionally."

"You'd better, Sam, you'd just better. You've gotten me through the last twenty years. You can't quit on me now."

At the table Jake was about to sit next to Jean when he felt a tap on his shoulder. "Do you mind?"

Mark Fleischman slipped into the chair. "I stopped at the hospital to see Laura," he told Jean. "She's feeling better, although, of course, she's rocky emotionally. But she'll be okay." He grinned. "She said she'd be glad to go into therapy with me."

Jake took the seat on the other side of Jean. "I believe that if anything, this harrowing experience will prove to be a turning point in her career," he said earnestly. "With all this publicity she's bound to get a lot of offers. That's show business."

Sam looked at him. My God, he's probably right, he thought. And with that realization, he decided to order a double scotch instead of a glass of wine.

Jean had learned from Sam that Mark had driven all over town trying to find her, and then when Sam called him, he had rushed to the hospital where she, Meredith, and Laura had been taken. He had left without seeing her when he was assured that she was going to be released shortly. She had neither seen nor spoken to him all day. Now she looked directly at him. The tenderness with which he was looking at her made her deeply ashamed of the way she had mistrusted him. And at the same time it touched her deeply.

"I'm sorry, Mark," she said. "I'm so terribly, terribly sorry."

He covered her hand with his, the same gesture that a few days earlier had comforted and warmed her and made her feel a spark that had long been missing in her life.

"Jeannie," Mark said, smiling, "don't be sorry. I'm going to give you lots of chances to make it up to me. That I promise you."

"Did you ever suspect that it was Gordon?" she asked.

"Jean, the fact is that under the surface there was a lot going on with all our fellow honorees, not to mention the reunion chairman. Jack Emerson may be a shrewd businessman, but I wouldn't trust him as far as I could throw him. My father told me that Jack is known locally as a womanizer and a mean drunk, although he's never been known to be physically aggressive. They all believe that he burned down that building ten years ago. One of the reasons is that on the night of the fire, a security guard who probably was paid off by him did an unusual walk-through to be sure no one was still in the building. It was a suspicious thing to do, but it does suggest that Emerson has never wanted to kill anybody.

"I really believed for a while that Robby Brent could have been the one who killed the girls at your lunch table. Remember what a surly kid he was? And he was nasty enough at the reunion dinner to make me think he was capable of doing physical as well as emotional harm. I looked up references to him on the Internet. He'd talked to an interviewer about his fear of poverty and claimed that he had money buried all over the country on land that he owned but had registered in fictitious names. He was quoted as saying that he was the dumb kid in his smart family and was considered a nerd at school. He said that he had learned the art of ridicule because he was constantly the butt of jokes himself. He ended up hating just about everyone in town."

Mark shrugged. "But then, just when I was sure he was The Owl, as we now know him, Robby disappeared."

"We think he suspected Gordon and followed him to that house," Sam said. "There were bloodstains on the staircase."

"Carter has so much anger in him that I thought he might be capable of murder," Jean said.

Mark shook his head. "Somehow I never did. Carter continually vents his anger by his nasty attitude and also through his plays. I've read the scripts of all of them. You should read them sometime. You'll recognize some of the characters as people you've known. That's the way he gets his revenge against those whom he regarded as his tormentors. He didn't need to go beyond that."

Jean realized that Sam, Alice, and Jake were listening intently to Mark. "That left only Gordon Amory and you," she said.

Mark smiled. "Notwithstanding your doubts, Jeannie, I knew *I* wasn't guilty. The more I studied Gordon, the more suspicious I became of him. It's one thing to fix a nose that's been broken or to get baggy eyes tightened, but to totally alter your external appearance has always seemed somewhat bizarre to me. I didn't believe him when he said that he'd give Laura a job on one of his TV series. It was obvious to me that he resented her playing up to him at the reunion when he well knew that she was only trying to use him. But then this morning, when Gordon was in the hotel after you disappeared, I thought I had been wrong about him. Quite frankly, when I was driving around looking for you, I was frantic. I was sure that something terrible had happened to you."

Jean turned to Sam. "I know you talked to Laura at the hospital. Did she tell you whether Gordon revealed to her how he had managed to make four of the other deaths look like accidents, and Gloria's death look like a suicide?"

"Gordon bragged about that to Laura. He told her that he had stalked all the girls before he killed them. Catherine Kane's car skidded into the Potomac after he had tampered with her brakes. Cindy Lang wasn't caught in the avalanche—he accosted her on that slope and dropped her body in a crevice. There was an avalanche that afternoon, and everyone assumed that she had been caught in it. Her body was never recovered."

Sam took a slow sip of his scotch, then continued. "He called Gloria Martin and asked her if he could stop by for a drink. By then she knew how successful he was and how handsome he had become, so she agreed. But she still couldn't resist getting in a dig at him and ran out to buy the owl figure. Gordon got her drunk, and when she fell asleep, smothered her with a plastic bag and left the owl in her hand."

Alice gasped. "My God, he was so evil."

"Yes, he was," Sam agreed. "Debra Parker was taking flying lessons at a small airfield. The security there was lax. Gordon had a pilot's license himself, so he knew just how to sabotage her plane before she took off on her first solo flight. And Alison's death was simple—he just held her under the water in her pool."

Sam looked sympathetically at Jean. "And I know, Jean, that he told both you and Meredith that he ran over Reed Thornton with his car."

Mark had not taken his eyes off Jean. "When I saw Laura a little while ago at the hospital, she told me that he had three plastic bags with each of your names on them and that he was going to use them to smother you, Laura, and Meredith. My God, Jeannie, when I think of that, I go crazy. I couldn't bear to have anything happen to you."

Slowly, deliberately, he took her face in his hands and kissed her, a long, tender kiss that said everything he had not yet put into words.

There was a sudden flash, and they looked up, startled. Jake was now standing, his camera still trained on them. "It's only a digital," he explained, beaming, "but I know a good photo op when I see it."

Epilogue

West Point, Graduation Day

"I can't believe it's been over two and a half years since Meredith came back into my life," Jean told Mark. Her eyes shining with pride, she watched as the graduates marched onto the field, splendid in their formal dress uniforms: gray cutaway jackets with bright gold buttons, starched white pants, white gloves, and hats.

"An awful lot has happened in that time," he agreed.

It was a magnificent morning in June. Michie stadium was filled with the proud families of the cadets. Charles and Gano Buckley were sitting directly in front of them. On Jean's other side, retired General and Mrs. Carroll Reed Thornton watched as the granddaughter they had come to adore passed by.

So much good has come after so much pain, Jean thought. She and Mark had just celebrated their second wedding anniversary and the first birthday of their baby son, Mark Dennis. Mothering her baby, sharing with him all the wonderful moments unfolding in his life, was softening the pain of not having been able to take care of Meredith. Meredith was crazy about her little brother, even though, as she had laughingly pointed out, she wouldn't be available for much baby-sitting. When the ceremony was over, she would be a second lieutenant in the United States Army.

She and Jake were little Mark's godparents. Jake's pleasure in the honor was expressed in the barrage of articles on baby care that he was constantly sending them from Columbia University, where he was now a student.

Sam and Alice were seated a few rows away. I'm so glad they ended up together, Jean thought. It's been wonderful for both of them.

Sometimes Jean had nightmares about the horror of that reunion week. But she often reflected that those circumstances had brought her and Mark together. And if she had never gotten those faxes, she might never have known Meredith.

It all began here at West Point, she thought, as the first notes of "The Star Spangled Banner" were sounded by the band.

Throughout the ceremony, her mind kept going back to the spring afternoon when Reed first sat down beside her on the bench and began to talk to her. He was my first love, she thought tenderly. He'll always be in my heart. Then, as Cadet Meredith Buckley's name was called to receive the West Point diploma that Reed had not lived long enough to accept, Jean was certain that somehow he was here with them today.

A Wee Nip at the 19th Hole

A History of the St. Andrews Caddie

by

RICHARD MACKENZIE

CollinsWillow

An Imprint of HarperCollins*Publishers*

First published in the United States in 1997 by
Sleeping Bear Press
121 South Main Street
PO Box 20
Chelsea, MI 48118

This edition published in 1998 by
CollinsWillow
an imprint of HarperCollins*Publishers*

3 5 7 9 8 6 4 2

A CIP catalogue record for this book is
available from the British Library

ISBN 0 00 218847 3

Cover photo: A group of caddies standing outside the R&A, circa 1890. Dan Ferguson, caddie and golf professional, is on the far left. Professionals like Dan were now being recognised by the Club with increased caddie tariffs and the added bonus of tuition fees to supplement their income. The professional was now becoming distinct from the ordinary caddie.

Typeset in Great Britain by Kirklane Ltd.
Edinburgh and St. Andrews

Printed in Great Britain

DEDICATED TO

Amy, Nicki and Matthew

ACKNOWLEDGEMENTS

I am grateful to the many people who have given freely of their time to help make this book happen.

Michael Bonallack, Secretary of the Royal & Ancient Golf Club, and Lachlan McIntosh, Administration Secretary for the R&A, both facilitated my acquisition of Club records, photographs and documents, and encouraged me in my endeavour. The Royal & Ancient Golf Club kindly gave me permission to use these valuable materials in the book.

Peter Lewis, Director of the British Golf Museum, also gave me access to materials and invaluable encouragement. Fiona Grieve, Curator, and Elinor Clark, Assistant Curator, helped greatly by patiently searching for materials, and Hilary Webster, Visitor Services Manager, provided both tea and good cheer.

The St. Andrews Links Trust, with their continued development of the Caddie Department, have provided a good basis for my interaction with so many members of the international golfing community, and this has also become part of the formative planning of the book.

Jim Moore and especially John Di Falco and Bob McCrum offered their friendship and early support, and Bob in particular was an unfailing motivator. And more than anything, I want to thank all of the St. Andrews caddies, both past and present, who inspired me to give them their place in the history of this royal and ancient game.

Finally, I wish to thank my editor Marcia Julius, without whose skill and hard work this book would not have taken the form it has.

Foreword

Anyone who plays the Old Course for the first time without having a St. Andrews Caddie is as unprepared as one who sets out to climb Mount Everest without a guide.

Not only will the round be made easier, and safer on the nerves, but also it will be an enjoyable and educational experience.

For over two hundred years, caddies have been walking the most famous piece of golfing land in the world, advising players of vastly different abilities, not only on the club to take, but also on the type of shot required and, most importantly on the Old Course, exactly the line on which to play.

In this highly readable and enjoyable book, Rick Mackenzie reminds us how caddies first came to St. Andrews, the way in which they have added so much to the folklore of the links and the great contribution which they have made and continue to make to the game of golf for the benefit of those who visit "The Home of Golf".

Long may they continue their work for generations to come.

M. F. BONALLACK
Secretary, Royal and Ancient Golf Club

Golfer holing out on the first green of the Old Course, circa 1880. Notice how the golfer's line to the hole is blocked by his opponent's ball. This was called a 'stymie'. Abolished in 1952 as being an "unfair advantage" and an "embarrassment," the stymie introduced the element of luck or good fortune, unforeseen factors of which the golfer had no control. It had to be accepted in the spirit of the game, maybe with gratitude if yours was the ball obstructing an opponent's line to the hole!

Contents

Caddie Profile: Trap Door

Some caddies had ingenious ways of earning extra money. One such caddie was Willie Johnson, known as 'Trap-Door,' who made a fair amount from 'lost' golf balls. Willie pretended that one leg was shorter than the other and had a special boot made which had a hollow sole, large enough to fit the diameter of a golf ball. During a search in the *whins* or anywhere else, he would work the ball into his hollow boot and declare it lost. The cavity in his boot could hold up to half a dozen golf balls!

Introduction

The game of golf has traditionally been surrounded by a certain mystique, a distinctive quality which has elevated much of the written material from the strictly prosaic into a more philosophical realm. The caddie has always had a place in that body of lore, usually in apocryphal tales or stories interlaced with fun and humour. I found a typical example some years ago, when I read an article in an old local newspaper dating from the late nineteenth century in which the St. Andrews caddies were described standing sentry-like by the corner of the Old Union Parlour, the forerunner of today's Royal & Ancient Golf Club. Over the years this corner had effectively become their property, and the scene was described thus:

> Consecrated by the fumes of their three-penny cut tobacco wafting in the air, they stand, *blue wi' the cauld* of bleak midwinter or bronze-like with the *gey strang* heat o' midsummer, their fortunes would vary but ever optimistic, and if business was slow, a wee nip at the 19th hole would always warm the inner man.

In truth, until recently the caddie's lot has not been a particularly fortunate one. Although satisfied with their role, in the late nineteenth and early part of the twentieth century they were effectively social outcasts, as caddying was viewed by society in general as 'not a fit and proper job.' In a time of strong class and social distinctions, even local trades people saw themselves as superior to the caddie, who was considered on a par with a street cleaner or a marker in a billiards saloon. Because of the seasonal nature of the work, most lived in a state of poverty. During this period, some members of the R&A took an active interest in their own caddies' welfare by gifting them food and clothing during the hard times when there was no work on the links. With the introduction of the Caddies Benefit Fund in 1891, the Club went to even greater lengths to assure that basic needs were met during the winter months. In spite of this genuine need, the caddies remained a proud and free-spirited band of men, who never lost the hope encompassed in the very motto of St. Andrews itself: *dum spiro spero* (while I breathe, I hope).

My own interest in the history of the St. Andrews caddie developed from some two decades of involvement as a professional caddie both abroad and here at home. The many hours I've spent in libraries, newspaper archives, and in conversation with old-time traditional caddies have given me a glimpse into the lives of some of the characters who spent their days *grasshoppin'* over the links of St. Andrews. One such character, 'Auld Daw' Anderson, was a senior caddie whose *pawky* sense of humour was as legendary as his philosophical wit. He said, "Although devoid of material things, we were rich in courtesy *tae oor* golfers, which in turn made us rich in life."

Over the years, golf has changed from a predominately amateur to a high-profile professional sport. During this time, there has been a corresponding rise in the fortunes of the caddies, who are no longer merely beasts of burden, underpaid and always at the beck and call of the golfer. Today's caddie is a professional whose knowledge and judgement can make an important difference to the golfer with whom he works, and both his remuneration and his status on the links reflect this. During the writing of this book, I have come to appreciate more than ever before the value of the time-honoured tradition of the St. Andrews caddie, a tradition now embodied in the men and women who today *work the land*, still serving the golfer just as colourful characters like Lang Willie, Hole in His Pocket and Stumpie Eye did all those years ago.

Richard Mackenzie
St. Andrews, Scotland

Engraving of golfers on the links of St. Andrews, circa 1880. Notice that the ball is being played two club lengths away from the hole—there is still no defined green. The young caddie, having taken sand from the hole, has prepared a tee for his golfer.

Andrew Greig at the Old Course starter's box, circa 1910. Andrew Greig was the official starter for the Old Course from 1894 until his death in 1915. His starter's box on wheels was a converted Victorian bathing hut, at one time used by lady bathers who swam in the 'gey cauld' waters that surrounded St. Andrews. At a time when the links were rich in personalities, Andrew was one of the most colourful characters. He also had a keen sense of humour. One day he was approached by a Frenchman who asked if he could play the Old Course and gave his name as "Fouquier." "Weel," replied Andrew, "When I cry oot Tamson, jist you step on tae the tee!"

His niece was the first female bag carrier to work on the links. When she carried in the 1913 Amateur Championship, her golfer had no more than five clubs in his kit, a far cry from some of the heavy golf bags which became fashionable in the mid-thirties.

The Cawdys

For hundreds of years the business of carrying clubs has been a way of life for a breed of hardy St. Andreans. Golfers have found that local knowledge of the links goes a long way, and perhaps at no other place is it more true than on the Old Course. Deception is the Old's secret weapon. What can seem like a good drive might finish up amongst the prickly gorse bushes, or land in one of the many hidden pot bunkers. With names like the Coffins, Hell and the infamous Beardies, they lurk out of sight, waiting to trap the unwary. It was said many years ago that when you land in any of those bunkers, "there is only enough room for an angry man and his *niblick*!" *

With acres of gorse bushes, those dreaded bunkers and fairways which flatter to deceive, the caddie is an essential companion and guide. At no other course in the world is the continuity of caddie knowledge handed down from one generation to the next, taking you back in time to the early *pawky* caddie personalities such as Lang Willie, Hole in His Pocket and Stumpie Eye, names that conjure up images of another age. They may be long gone, but the spirit of these men lives on in today's professional caddie. Gone is the complex individual, the perennial thorn in the side of golfers and society alike, who saw himself as a free spirit with a *braw* conceit, for whom no amount of regulation could improve his language or dress sense! Paradoxically, these very men who often lived hand-to-mouth, sometimes sleeping rough in bunkers or wherever they could find shelter, at the same time formed such a fundamental part of the game that the Rules of Golf decree

* All italicized Scottish words will be found in the Scottish Glossary at the back of the book.

the caddie to be the only person a player can consult in singles play for advice, and that any infringement of this rule committed by the caddie incurs the same penalty as if committed by the golfer himself.

Sketch of golfers on the St. Andrews links, circa 1700. The Old Union Parlour, precursor to today's Royal & Ancient Golf Club, is the leftmost building in the distance. The Swilcan Burn ran almost the length of the present first and eighteenth fairways. In 1847, Hugh Lyon Playfair, Captain of the R&A and Town Provost, carried out land reclamation and widened this area by building a breakwater to stop the sea encroaching onto the grassy areas during high tide. The reclamation in effect widened the links at this point, and when Tom Morris took over as Keeper of the Green in 1864, he returfed the whole area.

When does the first mention of a caddie appear? The reputed source of the name is given as Mary Queen of Scots. A keen golf enthusiast, she played the game in France where her clubs were carried by young students called "Les Cadets." Such was her passion for the game, she found time to play in the grounds of Seton Palace in East Lothian only a few days after her husband Lord Darnley was murdered in 1567. The earliest mention of the word *caddie* appears in the accounts records of one Andrew Dixon, a ballmaker (1655-1729), who lived near Leith in Edinburgh. He was employed as a fore-caddie by the future King James II, then Duke of York. The name was taken up in the eighteenth century by the male and female water carriers in and around Edinburgh, who were called "Cawdys." This sense of the word indicated a messenger or porter, and early references to the Edinburgh Cawdys described them as "useful blackguards, who attend coffee houses and public places to run errands" and "wretches who lie in streets at night, but were always trusted and never unfaithful." In spite of this, the group was cohesive enough to elect one of their senior members as the Constable of Cawdys, who had virtually complete control over this unique fraternity, with the ability to fine a member or mete out corporal punishment. In those days, as now, caddies had to be registered and issued with a badge before they could ply their trade.

Gentlemen golfers were quick to apply the word to mean 'the man who carries the sticks,' and the boy who ran ahead of the players had become the fore-caddie. The first written evidence of the St. Andrews caddies was recorded on 27 June 1771 in the Minutes of the Society of St. Andrews Golfers, the precursor to today's Royal & Ancient Golf Club. This passage, which expresses the first interest in their welfare, reads:

> The Captains and Company agree and appoint that in time coming, the caddies who carry the clubs, or run before the players, or are otherwise employed by the Gentlemen Golfers, are to get four pence sterling for going the length of the hole called the "Hole O' Cross," and if they go further than that hole they are to get sixpence and no more. Any Gentlemen transgressing this rule are to pay, two pint bottles of Claret, at the first meeting they shall attend.

The course then was not what we know today. It was about half the width and today's seventeenth hole was then the first. The links were originally covered with rough grass, thick gorse and wild heather, and the course was marked out with march stones, with *whin* bushes all the way up the right-hand side of what is the outward part of today's course. Given the undulating land, thick grass and rough ground, it is easy to see why the fore-caddie came into his own at St. Andrews. But the hand of man was already at work. Tom Morris was appointed Keeper of the Green in 1864, after which time he developed a new first and eighteenth green on the Old Course and was involved in widening the fairways. The famous double greens were already in place by the time Tom came from Prestwick. The then-Captain of the R&A, Provost Hugh Lyon Playfair, was instrumental in having the seven double greens cut that St. Andrews is famous for today. These enabled golfers to play either the original left-hand course or the new right-hand one. The right-hand course in time became the accepted one and was used for the first ever Open, played at St. Andrews in 1873.

Thus for over four centuries, the business of carrying golf clubs has been a way of life for this unique and at times perplexing breed, who in all kinds of weather can still be seen lugging their *man's* clubs around the rolling windswept links of St. Andrews. And if the carrying of the clubs is their trade, then knowledge of the courses is their craft, a craft barely understood by the millions of spectators who today follow the sport, either by foot or glued to their television sets.

Over the years the caddie has added richness and colour to this Royal & Ancient game, either in humorous anecdote or in the role played by the early ball- and clubmakers. They cajoled, counselled, inspired and occasionally bullied their *man* around the golf course. David Corstorphine, one of the senior caddies, always offered the same advice before each round: "*Dinna* risk *awthing*, we'll play *wi' oor heids*." With this wisdom, it seems such a short step to the caddies giving instruction on how to play, and in time becoming the first professional golfers. Even the caddies who never actually played the game themselves knew the links intimately and were well aware of their *man's* strengths and failings. They saw themselves as a kind of senior partner, who could judge the wind strength, choose the club, and dictate the target area, leaving the simple business of hitting the ball to the player.

Today, the ball- and clubmaking skills may have disappeared, but the good local caddie still has to wait his turn on the daily list and is still in great demand. With over a quarter century of experience in his craft, the St. Andrews caddie can be in his own way a hard and inexorable taskmaster who, from the moment he takes charge of your clubs, assumes the role of the brains of the outfit!

Nineteenth-century engraving of golfers on the Old Course. The R&A Clubhouse, built in 1854, is now prominent on the skyline, and the homes/workshops of Tom Morris and Allan Robertson line the right-hand side of the fairway. Since the links were public land, the townsfolk apparently felt free to stroll around—even within range of the golfers! The caddies are wearing the traditional 'Tam O'Shanter bunnets,' and their golfers are wearing the accepted uniform jackets of the Club.

David Corstorphine

Circa 1910. Standing outside the Caddie Superintendent's box under the watchful eye of Caddie Superintendent James Jolly, caddie David Corstorphine has cleaned up his *man's* clubs and awaits the golfer, ready to do battle.

In 1910, new regulations called for caddies to be "tidy in dress, sober when on duty and civil to his man." The caddie was now no longer "free as the fowls o' the air to ply his trade." According to the Town's Greens Committee, they had to come under the influence of the modern demand for regulation.

Caddies and the R&A

After the mid-nineteenth century, local caddies began to be employed on a regular basis by members of the Royal & Ancient Golf Club. There were several good reasons for this, one being the local rule that matches having a caddie in them could play through those which did not. P. G. Tait, a university professor and fanatical golfer, took advantage of this rule. The Professor would play up to six rounds a day, wearing out quite a few caddies in the process. His son, golfing legend Freddie Tait, was a supreme player who in 1895 broke the record for the Old Course with a round of 72. Freddie was seldom seen on the links without his pet dog Nails.

The regular members of the R&A had their own special caddies, and both groups of men added to the character of the links. Club member "Old Sutherland" would have been lost without his trusty caddie Andra' Strath, and both have bunkers on the Old Course named after them. Old Sutherland actually filled in one of the more troublesome of these bunkers late one night with the help of some rebels in the shape of Club members and caddies. The following day the Greens Committee duly reopened it and it is still there today.

Two other R&A members were never seen on the links without their ponies. John Whyte Melville, known as 'Mounty' to the caddies, not only used his pony to ride from his house down to the links but also set off on his round astride his trusty steed, with his breathless caddie trotting fast behind! Mr. Wolfe Murray, one of the older Club members who played golf almost to the end of his days, also used a pony for his rounds. He employed two caddies, one to carry the clubs and one to hold the pony while he got off to play his shot, a practice which led to intense arguments between the caddies about who should have the easier job of holding the pony!

Around this time, local professionals began taking their favourite caddies with them as they moved between courses for tournament play. Allan Robertson always had 'Daw' Anderson, Tom Morris had 'Kirky' and Willie Dun preferred James Wilson, each caddie in his own right an excellent golfer or clubmaker. After play, caddies and players would gather in the local bars and exchange stories, the losers sharing in the entertainment by the generosity of the winners, with the innkeepers getting most of the prize money! This custom still exists amongst the local caddies from the earning of a good week's caddying.

Not all caddies had two legs: painting of R&A member General Sir John Low of Clatto, riding the links at St. Andrews on his faithful cream pony, circa 1870.

Captain in 1865, Sir John played golf well into his 90s, and took to his pony when walking became difficult during the latter part of a round, dismounting between shots. Perhaps droppings left by his trusty steed led to some of the many revisions of Rule 23 (Loose Impediments) which were made by the R&A during the nineteenth century!

Freddie Tait seen in a studio photograph with his pet dog Nails, circa 1895. Freddie broke the Old Course record in that year with a round of 72, and that new record was steadily whittled down until Curtis Strange reduced it to 62 in 1987. Freddie was also the amateur champion in 1896 and 1898. He was admired by all who knew him because of his ready smile and adventurous spirit, but unfortunately golf was to lose a wonderful ambassador at an early age, for Freddie was killed in South Africa while leading his men into action in 1900, age 30. Three lines from Wordsworth's poem The Excursion were chosen for his epitaph:

> *The good die first,*
> *And they whose hearts are dry as summer dust*
> *Burn to the socket.**

* Burn to the base of the candlestick.

KEEPER OF THE GREEN

Early R&A records show that the Club attempted to improve the lot of the caddies and at the same time have someone attached to the Club who would both look after its needs and attend to the course. This resulted in the appointment by the R&A of Club Inspectors of the Links, who were authorised to employ one of the senior caddies to take on the duties of what was to become known as the 'Keeper of the Green.' The term 'green' meant all of the golf links, not what we now call the putting surface. These men were instructed to replace any caddie whom they found "inactive or not doing his duty." The first senior caddie to be employed was Geordie Robertson, who some time later, after repeated *wiggings*, was dismissed as incompetent and incorrigible. David Pirie, another caddie, took over from Geordie in 1823. After David came 'Auld Daw' Anderson, one-time ballmaker and caddie who tended the Old Course for many years and then, upon his retirement, set up a ginger beer stall at the ninth hole. Daw was Keeper of the Green until 1855, and he is credited with having cut two holes on the fifth green of the Old Course. Today, it's the fourth hole on the Old Course which is named 'Ginger Beer,' because that's the location where for many years an old woman sold her brew. In very hot weather, thirsty caddies were apt to bypass the stall and drink from a nearby water pump. Discovering this, the woman took away the pump handle, an act which sparked an ongoing battle between herself and the caddies for the next several years. Sadly, there are no records to show the outcome.

In 1856, after the retirement of 'Auld Daw,' the R&A promoted two caddies, Watty Alexander and Alex Herd, as Keepers of the Green at a joint wage of £6 per year. When extra help was required, local pensioners, who affectionately came to be known as "rabbits," were taken on to cut the holes and sweep rabbit droppings from the greens. These men had no special knowledge of course management, and had only barrows, a couple of shovels, and brushes to work with, a far cry from today's professional greenkeepers. Tom Morris took over as Keeper of the Green in 1863, at a considerably increased salary of £50 per year, plus the help of one additional man during medal weeks.

Greens staff up to their knees in silt doing running repairs on the Old Course prior to the Walker Cup, 1934.

Eddie Adams, Head Greenkeeper for the Old Course since 1990. Just as Tom Morris redesigned the layout of the Old Course prior to the first Open in 1873, so Eddie is supervising the preparation of the course prior to the Millennium Open. Although his job is technically more advanced than in years gone by, the basic principles have remained the same since the days of Old Tom. Beach sand is still used on the course as a top dressing, and bunker sand, fertilizer and water are used in minimal amounts.

The administrative and communication skills required for today's greenkeeper have elevated him/her to the status of a professional manager, as well as promoting the art of greenkeeping as a possible career choice. It's a far cry from Geordie Robertson's 'repeated wiggings'!

Above: Early twentieth century tournament. Crowd control was not a major consideration here—the golfers seem to be lost in a maze of Victorian headwear. The canopies on both sides of the R&A Club windows are no longer there, and the old Victorian 'bathing hut' has now been replaced by today's modern starter's box.

Facing page: By 1865, a set of rules including pay and discipline were proposed, printed and posted in the Clubhouse. By then, Tom Morris had become Keeper of the Green at a salary of £50 per year. Apparently, there was cause for the Club to address the issue of intemperance even in the Boy Caddies.

The ground appears to have been prepared for either Morris, Forgan or Wilson to eventually take over the duties of Caddie Superintendent. Since both Forgan and Wilson preferred the work bench to the golf course, the field was left open to Tom Morris.

Rules and Discipline of Caddies - 1864

1. No Boy under Eleven years of age shall be admitted as a Caddie.

2. Boys admitted as Caddies shall be required to continue their Education and also to attend a Sunday School.

3. Swearing, intemperance, dishonesty and the use of improper or uncivil language shall be strictly prohibited at all times on pain of dismissal.

4. All Boys admitted as Caddies shall be provided with a Cap, bearing the Club Badge which he must wear on the Links, so long as he is to be employed, and return to the Club, when he retires or is dismissed.

5. No Boy who engages himself to a Gentleman in the morning shall be allowed to break that engagement till the day's play is over, or if he does, shall forfeit half his forenoon's pay.

6. All Caddie Boys shall consider themselves as Boys till they reach the age of Eighteen years.

7. Messrs. Morris, Forgan, Wilson, and the Club Steward shall be appointed to fix upon the proper Boys to select as Caddies, to take a supervision of them, and to receive any complaints that have to be made and these to be remitted to the Green Committee for adjudication, and they having full power in this matter their sentence shall be final.

8. All Boys admitted as Caddies in the service shall have a copy of these Rules given them, and in the event of any contravention of them, the guilty party will be liable to suspension if not expulsion from the service.

Below: R&A *member James Balfour is about to tee off with young Jamie Anderson (later a three-time winner of the Open Championship) amongst a group of caddies and golfers, circa 1855. The cottage in the background is the present-day Jigger Inn, then part of the old railway station which was shortly afterwards moved into the town. The relocation made the station more convenient to shops and also solved the problem of passengers disembarking onto the golf course and interrupting play!*

Facing page: rules poster, 1875.

First Class caddies were valued not only for their experience, but their sobriety and conduct on the golf course. Good caddies were expected to make sand tees to the golfer's requirements, and the clever caddie, after completing the tee, would moisten the ball with a well-licked thumb before placing it on top, thereby insuring that some grains of sand stuck to it and created some helpful back spin for his golfer! The caddie would offer advice tailored to his golfer's strengths and weaknesses, club him, and give him lines off the tee and on the green. At the end of the round, he would clean and oil the clubs, lightly rubbing the heads with a fine piece of emery paper, and return them to the Clubhouse where he would be paid his fee.

Second Class caddies were altogether a different breed. Even though some were just as experienced as the more senior caddies, they were less dependable, often drunk, and would at times show no consideration for their golfer. So much was the image of a typical caddie linked with drink that a level of drunkenness was often tolerated which would have seen the 'rogue' out of work in any other job.

RULES

REGARDING

PAY AND DISCIPLINE OF CADDIES,

ADOPTED BY

THE ROYAL AND ANCIENT GOLF CLUB OF ST. ANDREWS,

At a Special General Meeting of the Club, held on 3rd February, 1875.

I.—All Caddies shall be Enrolled,—none being admitted under 13 years of age.

II.—Members of the Club shall employ only Enrolled Caddies.

III.—A List of Enrolled Caddies shall be placed in the Club Hall, and also in the Clubmakers' Shops.

IV.—Caddies shall be divided into Two Classes, according to skill or age, and their services shall be rated as follows:—

First Class Caddies,—Eighteenpence for First Round, and One Shilling for each following Round, or part of Round.

Second Class Caddies,—One Shilling for First Round, and Sixpence for each following Round, or part of Round.

V.—No Caddy, unless previously engaged, can refuse to carry for a Member, under penalty of suspension for a stated time.

VI.—Names of suspended or disqualified Caddies shall be posted.

VII.—Complaints regarding Caddies shall be made through the Keeper of the Green to the Green Committee, who shall award an adequate penalty.

VIII.—The penalty shall be awarded by not less than two of the Green Committee.

IX.—The Keeper of the Green shall have charge of the Caddies, and Members shall apply to him when in want of a Caddy.

X.—Members are particularly urged to report all cases of misconduct on the part of the Caddies, whether during their time of service or otherwise,—such as incivility, bad language, abusing the Green, or any other form of misdemeanour,—which may merit censure or penalty.

XI.—Tom Morris shall be Keeper of the Green, and Superintendent of the Caddies.

THE FLEESING SHEDS

For those mid-nineteenth-century caddies not fortunate enough to be tied to a professional golfer, there arose the need for a set of standard regulations to guard both the caddies and the public. Beginning in 1860, several attempts were made by the R&A to grapple with the regulations governing the employment of caddies, but it was four years before R&A member Major Boothby submitted to the Club a list of caddies to be employed and a set of regulations for their employment. Up to the age of eighteen, 'Boy Caddies' had to continue their education, attend Sunday School and refrain from using bad language picked up from the older caddies. Now all caddies were to be supplied with a cap sporting the Club badge which they had to wear while on the links, and no caddie was allowed on the links who was not on the list.

By 1870, the R&A introduced a further set of rules and regulations, an "interference" to which the caddies reacted by staging a strike for higher wages. A local newspaper stated that "broken down artisans interfered with the rights of the hereditary caddie. Now times have changed and communism has leavened the noble mind." Strong words indeed, but in reality, the caddie's only concern was for the change in his pocket, not a change of times!

Although many of the Club members were sympathetic to the caddies' cause, their action was unsuccessful, because they did not win an increase in the rate. Caddie rates for first class caddies were set at 1/6d* for the first round and 6d for the second or part thereof.

* The British monetary system was changed to decimal currency in 1971. In the old system, one shilling, written as 1/-, would equal 5 new pence in today's

Second class caddies were paid 1/- and 6d for the second round. The recognised tip was 1/-, which most R&A members paid after all the golf clubs had been cleaned. These rates remained the same for many years to come. However, a positive result for both parties was the appointment by the R&A of the Keeper of the Green Tom Morris as the first Caddie Superintendent, with full authority over the striking caddies. It was expected that Tom would be sympathetic with the caddies while also understanding the needs of Club members.

The problem of regulating caddies was not peculiar to St. Andrews. During the next thirty years, nearly thirty of the leading golf clubs throughout Britain requested guidance in this matter from the R&A, seeking standardised rules for caddies. For example, in both Musselburgh and St. Andrews, visitors were being charged exorbitant rates by the caddies, and the caddie shacks were described as "Fleesing Sheds." Both links were public land, so no tariff control could guard against the caddie hell-bent on fleecing the unsuspecting golfer. As the local press observed,

> many remember the manner in which the guileless golfer was pounced upon by hordes of Raggamuffins at St. Andrews Railway station, their battle cry being, 'Carry for you sir, carry for you, sir.' The golfer would surrender, as it were, body and soul, being *deaved* out of all his wits by the incessant clamour, how ultimately in too many cases, he was unconsciously parted from his money.

As a result of these ongoing problems, the R&A Greens Committee established a Register of Authorised Caddies in 1891, along with new stricter provisions for the control of caddies. New regulations, which

---

currency. An old penny, written as 1d, would equal about 1/2 new pence. The rate of one shilling and six pennies (1/6d), which the caddie would pronounce "one and six," would amount to 7 new pence.

included both local Club rules dealing with dress and behaviour and bye-laws covering the employment of caddies, stipulated that "no person should act as a caddie for hire until licensed by the Town Magistrates" and also determined the tariff payable to the caddies, with each caddie agreeing "that the conditions and regulations shall be observed." A licensed caddie could not refuse any engagement with a Club member, and while on the links he had to wear an officially numbered badge, now a rather cumbersome brass plate mounted on a leather armband. To ensure the impartial meting-out of justice, the responsibility for enforcement was now handed to the Town Council, and those who tried to work the links without being registered were brought before the local court. Those arrested and charged with breaking the bye-laws would appear before the magistrate and be given a severe *wigging* with no right of appeal. Justice being summary, if they persisted in 'bootlegging' they would receive "a penalty not exceeding 10/- or seven days imprisonment, and suspension or revocation of his caddie licence." Caddies who broke the Club rules were also faced with the threat of suspension.

Caddie arm badge which all registered caddies were required to wear from 1891 until replaced by the cap and badge.

To enforce these new regulations and to take the first step in formally distancing the Club committees from the day-to-day handling of the caddies, the R&A looked for a man who could take over caddie-related record-keeping and who could employ the needed diplomacy with greater authority than Tom Morris, who after all had started as a caddie himself in St. Andrews and personally knew most of those under his wing. Tom Morris was truly legendary, and one of the great architects of golf history, but this good man took the caddies' interest too much to heart, and thus was unable to enforce the level of authority now required by the R&A. That same year, the Club found the desired combination of administrator, diplomat and disciplinarian in Royal Navy retiree Nicholas Robb, whom they appointed to the position of R&A Club Officer, with the combined duties of Hall Porter, Caddie Superintendent, and Secretary of the newly-established Caddies Benefit Fund, at an annual salary of £60 paid out of Club funds.

Robb's role as Hall Porter made it essential that he be stationed within the Clubhouse. Business of the day was done at a small desk in the hall, where payment to caddies was made after each round. This was also where each caddie would pay a deposit of 2/6d* to Robb at the beginning of the season. He would then issue the caddie with a badge and put his name on the caddie list for that year, which would be displayed in the Clubhouse and in the local clubmakers' shops. By 1912, Nicholas Robb's title had become Caddie Master at St. Andrews.

Nicholas Robb's appointment was initially seen by the caddies as a threat to a comfortable status quo. According to the Greens Committee minutes, the caddies resisted vehemently but were eventually won over by Mr. Robb, who convinced them that the Club was acting on their behalf by "insuring regularity and impartiality of employment to all of the registered caddies." In spite of the caddies' early reaction and the resultant negative publicity in the local press, the caddies still had the interest of the golfer at heart, and it was also

* Two shillings and 6 pennies (2/6d) would have been pronounced by the caddies as "*twa* and six," and would equal about 12 new pence.

reported that it was "unfair to think of them as reckless, couldn't-care-less types, with nothing but money and ale in their heads." At the end of the day, the winning of the match was as important to the caddie as it was to the golfer.

Group of caddies, circa 1910. In spite of so much negative publicity, it was still said of the caddies that it was "unfair to think of them as reckless, couldn't-care-less types, with nothing but money and ale in their heads." The golfer and caddie had a mutual respect for each other, and they shared a common goal: the winning of the match.

Caddie Profile: Tom Morris

Tom Morris' early years were spent as a caddie working the links at St. Andrews. The son of a hand-loom weaver, his skills as a golfer and clubmaker led to him being appointed the Professional at Prestwick. Tom is considered one of the greatest St. Andrews golfers, winning the Championship Belt (the precursor to the Open Championship) in 1861 and 1862 while still at Prestwick, and in 1864 and 1867 after returning to his native St. Andrews.

In 1864, the Royal & Ancient Golf Club decided to appoint someone who would not only take charge of the course management, but would serve as the Honorary Professional to the Club as well. Since Allan Robertson had died in 1859, the only suitable candidate was Tom Morris. Although Old Tom was currently at Prestwick, the St. Andrews native was persuaded to return to his home town and take over the Club duties. He set up business in what had been a 'Sweetie' shop near the Rusacks Hotel, then later moved up the road to the shop opposite the eighteenth green which still bears his name. Here he combined the duties of clubmaker, greenkeeper and Caddie Superintendent. Caddies were now expected to appear for work clean and moderately sober, and Tom inspected them daily—sometimes a singularly unrewarding experience!

With Tom Morris' appointment came the laying down of a new last green on the Old Course. The original finishing hole was in front of the depression known as the 'Valley of Sin.' The area in those days was a much larger hole which was filled in to its present level to constitute the now famous eighteenth at St. Andrews, a compliment to Tom's greenkeeping skills.

Nicholas Robb

Nicholas Robb, who had served 23 years in the Royal Navy, acted as the R&A Hall Porter, and assisted the Greens Committee and the Secretary on medal days. He also assisted members with their clubs and boxes, and issued members with their clubs, ready to be cleaned by the caddies.

Fifteen pounds of Nicholas Robb's annual salary was taken from the Caddie Benefit Fund in the form of a grant, but by 1895, there were insufficient funds to cover this levy, and it was agreed to discontinue payment to Mr. Robb in this form.

CADDIES BENEFIT FUND

Upon his appointment as Officer of the Club in 1891, one of Nicholas Robb's duties was acting as Secretary of the newly-formed Caddies Benefit Fund. This Fund was established by the R&A for the relief of caddies and professional golfers who from old age, illness, accident or other unavoidable cause were incapable of regular work. It also gave temporary assistance to the widows and children of caddies or professional golfers who had been left destitute. Caddies were asked to subscribe to the Fund at the rate of two pence per week from 1st October to 30th June, and 4d per week during July, August and September. This amount was paid to Nicholas Robb each Saturday, but in the event that a caddie could not pay regularly for lack of work on the links or for any other satisfactory reason, his contributions could be deferred with the agreement of the committee. A caddie could also pay his contribution in advance. Mr. Robb was responsible for the weekly dues collection, while Tom Morris and two other professionals were appointed to represent the 'paid ranks' on the R&A Management Committee which controlled the Fund and administered benefits.

In addition to the caddies' contributions, the Fund was supplemented by an annual grant that was set by the R&A, donations and subscriptions from members and other locals, and a percentage of monies taken from Club sweepstakes. This was an important step in the R&A's concern for the caddies' welfare, and reflected the philanthropic attitudes of the Victorian period. Caddies (and their families) received such things as coal and groceries upon presenting a written certificate that they were unable to work on the links. In 1892, twenty-one caddies received assistance from the Fund and three men had their contributions returned when their registrations were withdrawn. In some cases, the caddie's hospital bills were paid from the Fund, and funeral expenses were paid to the families of those caddies who died.

In spite of these good works, by 1895 the Caddies Benefit Fund had virtually petered out because most caddies became increasingly unwilling to part with their hard-earned money. In those difficult times, the penny in the pocket had far more weight than the pound in the ledger for these men used to a hand-to-mouth existence.

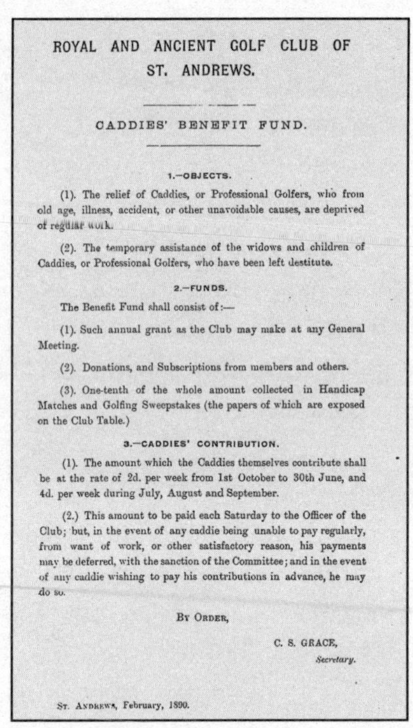

ROYAL AND ANCIENT GOLF CLUB OF ST. ANDREWS.

CADDIES' BENEFIT FUND.

1.—OBJECTS.

(1). The relief of Caddies, or Professional Golfers, who from old age, illness, accident, or other unavoidable causes, are deprived of regular work.

(2). The temporary assistance of the widows and children of Caddies, or Professional Golfers, who have been left destitute.

2.—FUNDS.

The Benefit Fund shall consist of:—

(1). Such annual grant as the Club may make at any General Meeting.

(2). Donations, and Subscriptions from members and others.

(3). One-tenth of the whole amount collected in Handicap Matches and Golfing Sweepstakes (the papers of which are exposed on the Club Table.)

3.—CADDIES' CONTRIBUTION.

(1). The amount which the Caddies themselves contribute shall be at the rate of 2d. per week from 1st October to 30th June, and 4d. per week during July, August and September.

(2.) This amount to be paid each Saturday to the Officer of the Club; but, in the event of any caddie being unable to pay regularly, from want of work, or other satisfactory reason, his payments may be deferred, with the sanction of the Committee; and in the event of any caddie wishing to pay his contributions in advance, he may do so.

By Order,

C. S. GRACE,
Secretary.

St. Andrews, February, 1890.

Poster of the Caddies Benefit Fund, circa 1890.

List of Caddies for 1894

No of Caddies on the Register - 34

Nam of Caddies who have died during the Year 3

Thomas Gordon
Arthur Fenton
Edward Campbell

Names of Caddies who have withdrawn their Name from the Register of Caddies

Henry Brown
John Ferguson
Andrew Kirkaldy
David Herd

Names of Men who have been removed from the Register of Caddies for Non Payment

John Lee
David Cuthbert

Amount of Money paid for Deaths of the above Caddies

Thomas Gordon Amount in Caddie Fund .. 18 .. 4
By to Grant from Caddie Fund to Mrs Gordon £2
By .. Arthur Fenton his Contribution 10 ..
By .. Edward Campbell his Contribution £2 .. 2 .. 8
Total £5 .. 11 ..

Nicholas Bott

Caddie Register, 1894. Andra' Kirkaldy decided to withdraw his registration as a caddie this year, feeling that he could not both caddie and work as a professional golfer. Some other caddies' registrations were withdrawn for non-payment to the Caddies Benefit Fund, but the benefits to caddies and their families can clearly be seen, with assistance given to cover funeral expenses.

List of Caddies Names who has received Assistance from the Fund during Sickness For the past Year

1892		Names		£	S	D
Feb	12th	Arthur Fenton for 3 weeks at 5/ per week			15	
"	24	John Lee Not on the Fund then			2	
March	9	William Wilson	" "		5	
"	16	William Wilson	" "		5	
"	28	William Wilson	" "		5	
April	7th	William Wilson	" "		5	
June	13	James Eddie	" "		5	
July	20	By to Cottage Hospital per T. McGregor for 2 weeks			10	
August	9	James Lister	" "		5	
Oct	19	Arthur Fenton	" "		5	
"	24	Arthur Fenton	" "		5	
"	31	Arthur Fenton	" "		5	
Nov	7th	Arthur Fenton	" "		5	
"	14	William Thomson	" "		5	
"	14	Arthur Fenton	" "		2	6
"	19	William Thomson	" "		5	
"	19	Arthur Fenton	" "		2	6
"	29	David Cuthbert	" "		5	
Dec	27	John Head	" "		5	
"	27	James Lister	" "		5	
1893 Jan	10	By to Mr Kermath for Medicine Supplied to D. Cuthbert and T. McGregor	"		5	11 ½
"	14	William Wilson	" "		5	
"	21	John Lee	" "		2	6
Feb.	22	By to Cottage Hospital for J. Lee for 4 ½ weeks in Hospital at 5/ per week	"	1	2	6
				£4	2	11 ½
"		By to Arthur Fenton from His Contribution for the Funeral expenses of His daughter			10	
				£4	12	11 ½

Nicholas Roth

List of caddies who received assistance, 1892.

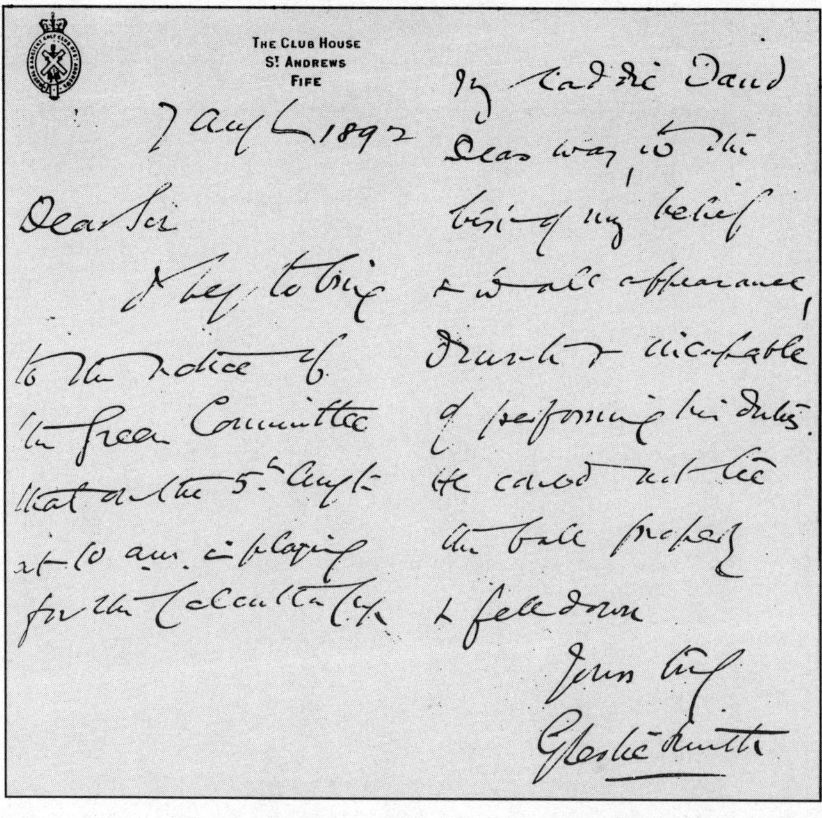
THE CLUB HOUSE
ST ANDREWS
FIFE

7 Augt 1892

Dear Sir

I beg to bring to the notice of the Green Committee that on the 5th Augt at 10 am. in playing for the Calcutta Cup my caddie David Deas was, to the best of my belief & to all appearance, drunk & incapable of performing his duties. He could not tee the ball properly & fell down.

Yours truly
G Leslie Smith

Letter of complaint from R&A member G. Leslie Smith, 1892. The text reads:

> *Dear Sir,*
> *I beg to bring to the notice of the Green Committee that on the 5th of August at 10 am, in playing for the Calcutta Cup, my caddie, David Deas, was, to the best of my belief and to all appearance, drunk and incapable of performing his duties. He could not tee the ball properly and fell down.*
>
> *Yours truly,*
> *G. Leslie Smith*

Mention is also made in the 1893 Caddie Committee minutes of caddie David Gourlay, who in his latter years used his bicycle to carry clubs around the Old Course. He was fined in the local magistrate's court, not for using his bicycle, but for being drunk and cycling without a rear light!

Offences REGISTER

Date ~~No.~~	Offence & NAME.	How disposed of by the Committee ~~Date of Registry.~~	
1891 March 6th	John Kirkcaldy. Being under the influence of drink and refusing to go out with Mr. Sheeson a Member of the Club.	Suspended from duty for the day.	
May 8th	John Ferguson. Drunk and unfit to go out with Mr. Cathcart.	Suspended from duty for one week.	
July 6th (" 3rd)	William Thompson. Drunk while out with Mr. Duff on 3rd July.	Reprimanded	
October 26th	David Cuthbert – Lagging behind and at the 2nd Hole declining to carry longer for Mr. C. McBoyd. (Reported by Mr. J. Cook)	Cautioned	
December 1st	Geo. Wilson Suspended 1 Month for using violent Language to Club Officer And Leaving 2 Young Gentlemen to Carry Clubs for another Gentleman Not A Member of the Club	Suspended from Duty for One Month by order Committee	

Caddie Offences, 1891. Even with all the assistance and consideration given to the caddies by the Club, some individuals still felt the need to express themselves either through drink or disrespect. Unfortunately, in most cases this was practised on the golf course, and as a result, some of the caddies mentioned in the Register were severely reprimanded, and for those caddies who could not adjust to the required standards, had their licences withdrawn.

REGISTER

No.	NAME.	Offences DATE OF REGISTRY. Hole Keeper by Committee	
1892 February 11th	John Kirk was under the influence Of Drink on the above date and did use threatening Language to Mr- Lee A- Member of the Club- John Kirk-	Suspended for 14- days By Order 15-2-92	(1)
April 18th	Reported by Mr J. Smart for being drunk- And refusing to Carry his Clubs After being Engaged by him to do so	21st April - Suspended from duty for 1 Week- By Order-	(2)
June 24.	John Kirk. Drunk at the door of the Club House and making use of foul Language towards Dr Blackwell.	27th June. ~~Name removed from List of Registered Caddies By Order~~ Committee.	(3). Suspended for 10 days from date of Offence N.B.M. R.A.H-
May 8	John Ferguson reported by Mr Blackwell for being Drunk And unfit to go out with Mr Cathcart	" Suspended for one week	

Caddie Offences, 1892.

THE DOG LICENCE

By 1920, the original Caddies Benefit Fund had long since been stopped and patronage of the R&A was diminishing in the wake of the First World War. But some members of the Club were still sensitive to the financial hardship posed for some of the men during the months of December and January when there was little or no work on the links. Some of the older, traditional caddies whose livelihood depended on their seasonal earnings on the links were employed during the winter months as *ghillies* during shoots on nearby estates, and a discretionary, non-contributory fund was introduced for them.

Under the provisions of this new Caddies Benefit Fund, these men were given a voucher for 7/6d which could be exchanged for groceries at most local shops. The caddies referred to the voucher as the 'Dog Licence' since 7/6d was the cost of a licence to own a dog. Some of the better caddies, regardless of age, were also placed on the voucher list. When exchanging the voucher, the caddie badge had to be shown before any goods could be purchased. Some caddies would exchange their badges for the 2/6d deposit after the voucher was gone, but would have to find the money again to ensure their place on the caddie list for the new season. Several of the local pubs were quick to offer the caddies inducements to have the vouchers cashed with them. On one occasion, five pints of beer were offered in exchange for the caddie voucher, a temptation some probably found hard to ignore!

Caddie Profile: Stuart Rodger

As of this writing, there is only one recipient of this new Caddies Benefit Fund alive, Stuart Rodger, now 85. Stuart began caddying when a schoolboy of 13 and worked on the links on and off until he retired in 1975. He was caddie to many fine golfers, but is remembered for his reply when he worked for the former Prime Minister Harold Macmillan. After the round, he was asked by reporters what he thought of Mr Macmillan's golf. He replied, "He's a fine gentleman, but he's nothing but a part-time golfer." Those nearby criticised Stuart for his impoliteness but he defended himself by declaring, "I should know, I'm *wan* myself."

Valid for the the period 15th Dec. 1994 to 15th Jan. 1995, only

St. Andrews, 9/1/95

Please supply STEWART RODGER with groceries to the value of FIFTY POUNDS and charge same to the Caddies Benefit Fund.

Merchants' accounts must be submitted by the 31st January.

Treasurer,
Caddies Benefit Fund.
Royal & Ancient Golf Club of St. Andrews.

Fund voucher for Stuart Roger, *1995. Stuart's retirement is made easier by this annual gift from* R&A *Club funds.*

Application to be enrolled

St. Andrews,

I John Lee 8 January 1894.

being desirous of being placed on the list of caddies registered by the Royal and Ancient Golf Club, promise faithfully to observe all the Laws and Bye-laws laid down by the Committee of Management of that Club, to confirm strictly to the Tariff Rules, and subscribe to the Benefit Fund, on condition of receiving the promised annual bonus.

I Alex. Hay? [illegible]

consider that the above applicant deserves to be enrolled as a registered caddie, and recommend him to the Committee of Management.

ROYAL AND ANCIENT GOLF CLUB.

CADDIES BENEFIT FUND.

To W. Brown

Supply David Corstorphine

with 1 Bag of Coals — 1/2

which charge to the Royal and Ancient Golf Club Caddies Benefit Fund.

William Wright Member of Committee of Management.

Date Feb. 2nd 1891

N.B.—No Account will be paid without this voucher being produced.

Top: Caddie Application, 1894. Subscription to the Caddies Benefit Fund was included in the benefits, but only on condition of receiving the "promised annual bonus."

Bottom: Caddies Benefit Fund voucher, on behalf of caddie David Corstorphine, to a local merchant for bag of coal, 1891.

EDUCATION

Nineteenth-century R&A patronage of the caddies extended into the realm of education. In the early 1870s, R&A member General Moncrieffe decided on a plan to encourage the younger caddies, who would rather earn ninepence or a shilling by carrying a 'bag of sticks' for the golfer than attend school, to learn to read. A rhyme of the period told the story:

Caddying a' the day
Daein' nae wark at a'
Runnin' aboot wi' a wee bag o' sticks
Efter a wee bit ba'! *

A wooden board was put up around the base of the Club flagpole and the ladies of the town gave the caddies 'coffee and instruction.' Unfortunately, large quantities of coffee led to the outdoor "reading room" being used for an "ignoble purpose," and the instruction became useless when the coffee was stopped! Then in 1873 a Greens Committee was introduced. Apart from keeping discipline, its duty was to liaise with the School Board on the matter of evening classes for the caddies.

Consecrated by the fumes of his threepenny cut tobacco, caddie John Lorrie prepares to oil his 'man's' clubs prior to a round.

In the background can be seen the base of the flagpole where the "reading room" was sited.

* Caddying all the day, doing no work at all, running about with a small bag of sticks, after a tiny ball!

In 1875, General Moncrieffe, now Town Provost, introduced formal evening classes for all the registered 'Boy Caddies.' They were held in the Fishers School opposite the Cathedral. Around 30 caddies enrolled for the first lessons, and the best reader and best writer at the end of term were each given 12/-, while the best attendee received 10/-. Even good comportment paid, as the best behaved caddie got an additional 8/-. The catch was that no money was ever handed over to the caddie. Instead, each winner's amount was credited to his 'clothing fund,' controlled by Mr. Forgan the clubmaker.

Older caddies were also encouraged to learn to read. By 1883, the R&A had given a yearly subscription of £50 and sent their day-old newspapers to a workingmen's coffee house near the harbour. The caddies were encouraged to use the Fisherman's Coffee House, and for a time there were some who took advantage of the R&A's kindness. 'College' was the nickname given to one caddie who boasted that after many months in the 'reading room' he was college taught. The coffee house was eventually sold, and it was decided that a proper Caddie Shelter should be erected behind the eighteenth green on the Old Course.

The caddie shelter, for use during wet or snowy weather, was built in 1891. It was sited opposite the main door of the R&A Clubhouse at the location of the present car park, was partially furnished, and had a stove installed. The caddies were supplied with newspapers and a small library. Rules were drawn up for the use of the shelter and the library, and a Vigilance Committee, headed by Tom Morris, was appointed by the caddies themselves to maintain order and discipline within the caddie ranks. On a particularly wet and windy day, one of the older caddies was in the library while waiting for work. He had a book on his knee and was ostensibly reading it, but a lad who knew he couldn't read told him, "The book's the wrong way up!" To this, the senior caddie replied, "Any fool can read a book the *richt* way up. It takes a good man *tae* read it upside *doon*!!"

Additionally, the Greens Committee introduced a revised system of payment as a form of security. The registered caddies who were on the list had to pay a 2/6d deposit at the start of the season. At the end of the year, after any damage done to the Caddie Shelter had been paid for, the Club doubled the money left over and the whole sum was divided amongst those caddies who had gone through the year with a 'clean sheet.' Clothing was provided for needy caddies out of a special fund, especially during the winter months when little or no work was to be found on the links. Golfers would also pass on any surplus clothes to their caddies. Both parties accepted this as normal, with no hint of embarrassment on either side. Indeed, one caddie boasted to his *man* about his close friendship with Mr. Balfour, a former Prime Minister. When this was received with some incredulity, the caddie indignantly snorted, "I should *ken* him *wel* and I *dae*, I'm wearin' a pair o' his *breeks*."

21 april 1892

John Kirk suspended for one week from this date

D. S. L.

Mr. Robb

For drunkenness & disobedience

Suspension of caddie for "drunkenness and disobedience," 1892.

THE BETTER HOLE

Although officially-sanctioned assistance to the caddies from the R&A had stopped by the 1920s, the members' personal interest in their caddies did not diminish. In 1938, Mr. Blackwell, past Captain of the R&A, treated the caddies to a New Year's dinner in the 19th Hole Hotel opposite the eighteenth green of the Old Course, more commonly known by the caddies as the 'Better Hole.' At the dinner, every caddie was given a 12/- voucher for groceries, and the happy caddies, once *fu' o' ale*, often broke into song. Among the most vociferous were Jock Hutchison and Jimmy Ferguson, whose famous *Doo-Dah verses* were enjoyed by everyone. Mrs. Blackwell continued this traditional 'do' for some years after her husband's death, but was forced to temporarily suspend it during the war years.

January 1947 saw the return of the caddies' dinner, this time hosted by Mr. Blackwell's son. Even with the post-war rationing, a hearty meal was enjoyed by all, and the caddies were again recorded as being in fine voice. The Caddie Master 'Wingy' Radley thanked Blackwell's son on behalf of all the caddies.

Sign outside Caddie Shelter, circa 1950. Tips had now become discretionary, since caddies no longer had to 'rub up' their 'man's' clubs. Gratuities were now earned on the golf course.

Caddie Fees

The caddie fee is entirely in the discretion of the player.
It is recommended that it should not exceed 30/- per round plus tip if warranted.

Joint Links Committee St. Andrews

1 A. Trail
2 William Fernie
3 Thomas Kidd Senior
4 Thomas Kidd Junior
5 Robert Martin
6 John Thompson
7 Charles Auchterlonie
8 [illegible] Kirkcaldy
9 James Fenton "Skipper"
10 David Corstorphine
11 John Fairfull
12 Walter Alexander
13 David Wallace
Walker
15 David Ayton
16 William Milne
17 David Gourlay
18 Robert Kinsman
19 Robert Morris
20 John Lees
21 James Lorimer

Caddie register for St. Andrews, circa 1870. Three Open Championship winners are included in this list, Willie Fernie (1893), Thomas Kidd, Jr. (1873), and Robert Martin (1876, 1885).

Also on the list were some local characters and some very fine golfers who never won an Open Championship but figured in tournaments and big-money matches. John Thompson was known as the 'weather man'. James 'Skipper' Fenton gave up his fishing trawler for the links. David 'Wiggy' Ayton was never seen on the links without his wig and bunnet securely fixed on his head! Walter 'Watty' Alexander took over as Caddie Superintendent when Tom Morris was off playing in tournaments or the money matches often arranged between players and R&A Club members.

Royal and Ancient Golf Club,

ST ANDREWS.

Caddies Library 1894

1. Any registered caddie may read the books in the "Caddies Library," while he is in the Shelter; receiving the book he wishes from the Club Officer and returning it to him, when he is done with it.

2. Any registered caddie may receive one volume at a time from the Club Officer and take it home for a period of not longer than one week, returning it thereafter to the Club Officer.

3. Any caddie who injures a book belonging to the library or fails to return it, shall have his name removed from the List of Registered Caddies.

By order of the Committee

William Knight

N.B. *Any registered Caddie convicted of begging from members of the Club or others, is liable to have his name removed from the Registered List.*

By order of the Committee

CADDIES. REGISTER

No.	NAME.	DATE OF REGISTRY.
No. 1	David . Corstorphine	Feb. 2nd 1891
" 2	James . Fenton jun.	"
" 3	Robert . Greig	"
" 4	John . Healy	"
" 5	James . Lawson	"
" 6	William . Wilson	"
" 7	Alexander . Taylor	Feb. 3rd 1891
" 8	Robert . Kinsman	"
" 9	John . Riddle	"
" 10	Arthur . Fenton . Sen.	"
" 11	John , Herd	"
" 12	James , Kinsman	"
" 13	Charles , Auchterlonie	"
" 14	John , Ferguson	"
" 15	George Wilson	"
" 16	John Kirk	"
" 17	James Arbuthnot	Feb. 4th 1891
" 18	David Kirkcaldy	"
" 19	James Palmer	"
" 20	Andrew Kirkcaldy	"
" 21	David Cuthbert	"
" 22	Robert Wilson	"
" 23	William Russel	"
" 24	John Kirkcaldy	"
" 25	Andrew Traill	Feb. 4th 91
" 26	John Lees	Feb. 5th 91
" 27	William Ayton	"
" 28	David Ayton	"
" 29	James Robertson	"
" 30	William Mathers	"

Caddies Register, 1891. Many men who later went on to make a name for themselves as professional golfers or in the administration of the links got their start as caddies. Andra' Kirkaldy came off the register in 1891 when he became a professional golfer. Alexander 'Wingy' Taylor and David Corstorphine graduated from the ranks of the caddies to become Caddie Masters. John Kirk, known as 'Kirky,' became a ballmaker of repute, and was famous for his guttie remakes called 'Kirky's remakes.'

Caddie Profile: ‘Poot’ Chisholm

“Wi guid porritch and a wee nip, yer a’ richt for life.”

When asked about the secret of his long life, ‘Poot’ was heard to say, “*Wi guid porritch and a wee nip, yer a’ richt for life.*”* He was a somewhat disreputably-dressed caddie, and when shown this photograph of himself, he looked at it carefully and then proceeded to ask repeatedly whether it was really of him. After being reassured that it was, ‘Poot’ gravely said, “*Och* man, it’s such a *humblin’ sicht.*”

* With good porridge and a wee nip, you’re all right for life.

The Captain's Dilemma

One of the most famous rituals of the R&A Golf Club is the annual driving-in ceremony by the incoming captain. It takes place at 8am (known as the hangman's hour!) on the last morning of the Club's Autumn Meeting. With one stroke, accompanied by the ceremonial firing of the cannon (the first cannon used was bought for £2 in 1837 from a Prussian Captain, but replaced in 1892 by the one still in use today), the Captain Elect will drive himself into office. On that morning, 20-30 caddies will be standing about in the cold morning air, all waiting expectantly at varying distances down the first fairway. Ever alert and cynical, the caddies by now know the Captain's game, and the unfortunate Captain-Elect who has a habitual slice will feel less confident about his tee shot when he sees a line of caddies all standing by the out-of-bounds fence on the right! As the clock strikes the hour, the caddies all jostle for position, the cannon and drive go off simultaneously and the 'scramble for the ba" is now on, each caddie anxious to retrieve the ball and receive the traditional gold sovereign as a reward.

Right: The first post-war playing-in ceremony was for R&A Captain Roger Wethered in 1946. Since the traditional sovereign was unavailable, the successful caddie, David Herd, proudly displays the £1 note he received.

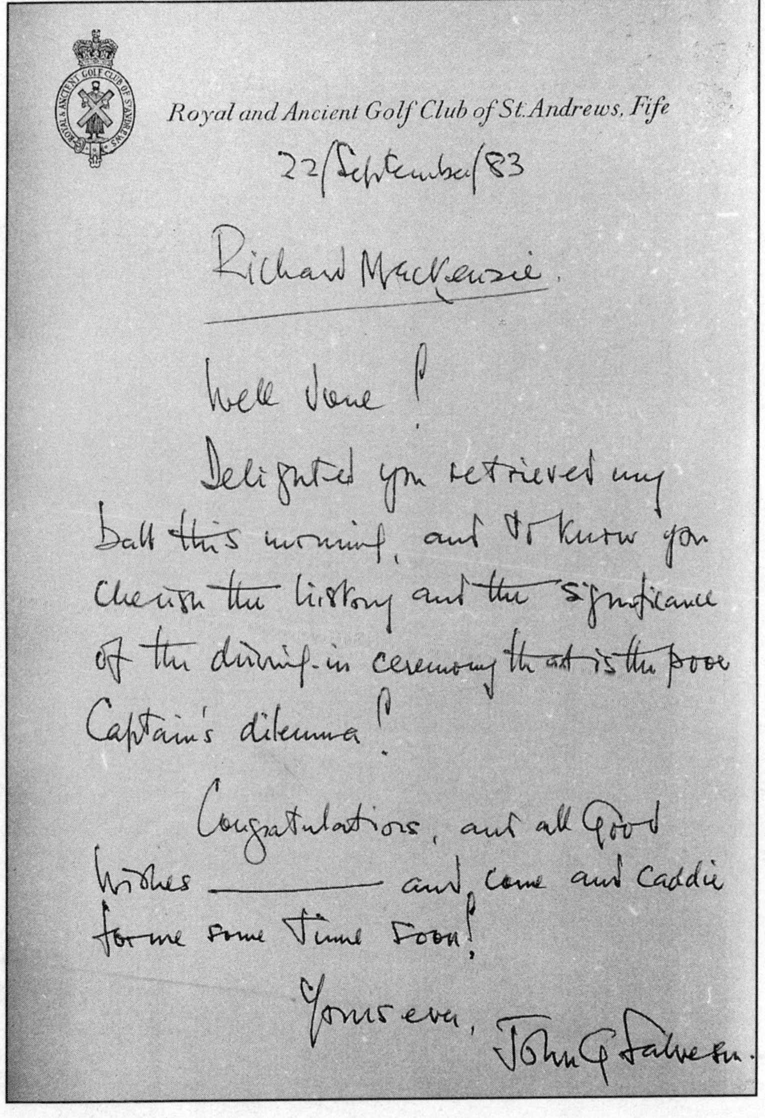

Royal and Ancient Golf Club of St. Andrews, Fife

22/September/83

Richard Mackenzie.

Well done!

Delighted you retrieved my ball this morning, and to know you cherish the history and the significance of the driving-in ceremony that is the poor Captain's dilemma!

Congratulations, and all good wishes ——— and, come and caddie for me some time soon!

Yours ever, John G Salvesen.

The author has joined the long list of successful caddies in retrieving the Captain's ball. The year caddies became part of the ceremony, and the name of the first caddie to return the captain's ball, are not recorded, though the first playing-in of the Captain-Elect, Sir John Whyte Melville, was in 1823. Previously, the winner of the Silver Club automatically became Captain. It may be assumed that the caddies' role in the ceremony began sometime after 1824.

The Caddies' Craft

AULD DAVIE

The earliest recorded St. Andrews caddie was David Robertson. Davie, father of the immortal Allan Robertson, is mentioned in a verse of George Carnegie's famous poem *Golfiana*, published in 1833. It reads:

> Davie, oldest of the Cads
> Who gives half-one to unsuspicious lads
> When he might give them two or even more
> and win, perhaps, three matches out of four!!

A reference in the same poem makes it quite clear that Davie, being a senior caddie, was in great demand as a player and teacher.

In Auld Davie's time, the status of professional had not yet been invented. Although there were some Clubs which offered a special position to senior caddies called Officer to the Club, the men employed were still no more than uniformed caddies, whose duty was to carry the clubs of the Captain and run before him to announce where his ball fell. Auld Davie performed the duty of what was then called the Fore-caddie, a title which is the origin of today's cry 'Fore!', still used to inform those ahead to take care.

David Robertson died in 1836, and Carnegie eulogised him in verse:

Great Davie Robertson the eldest Cad
in whom the good was stronger than the bad
he sleeps in death, and with him sleeps his skill
Which Davie, Statesman-like could wield at will.

'Skipper' Stewart Fenton, circa 1890. Stewart typifies the late nineteenth-century fisherman/caddie. The fishermen, or 'foreigners' as they were known to the traditional caddies, initially may have seemed like 'fish out of water,' but they took to the links with such enthusiasm that eventually their caddying skills and golfing abilities won them acceptance, and in time, their fisherman's garb became the standard form of attire. Some of them, like Skipper, not only knew the game intimately but played a good game as well.

REGULATIONS FOR THE EMPLOYMENT OF CADDIES.

A Register of Caddies, in alphabetical order, approved of by the Committee, will be found in the Club-House, and Members, in accordance with the Resolution of the Club at the General Meeting in September 1890, are required to select their Caddies from it.

(If no particular selection be made the Caddies are to be employed in the order of the Register.)

If at any time it be found necessary to have an additional temporary Register of Caddies, the permanent one must be exhausted before the supplementary is resorted to.

TARIFF FOR CADDIES :—

(1.) During the months of July, August, and September,	1s 6d for each round or part of a round.
(2.) During the rest of year,	1s 6d for 1st round or part of a round, 1s for each subsequent round or part of a round.

N.B.—The Spring and Autumn meeting weeks are excepted from the above.

(3.) During the Spring and Autumn Meeting weeks, exclusive of the Medal Round,	2s for each round or part of a round.
(4.) For the Medal Round, - -	5s.
(5.) For whole Medal Week, inclusive of the Medal Round,	25s.

TARIFF for PROFESSIONALS : — Playing with a Member, 2s 6d for each round or part of a round, and his Caddie's fee. Teaching a Member, 2s 6d for each round or part of a round.

Members may make special arrangements for lengthened periods with Registered Caddies, provided the Club Tariff be not exceeded.

The Committee reserve power to suspend a Registered Caddie for misconduct for a period to be determined by them, and in grave cases to remove a Caddie's name from the Register.

Note.—In all probability there will be a fund of from £50 to £75 per annum at the disposal of the Committee for the assistance of Registered Caddies, in case of need. Caddies registered before the 14th February 1891 will have a prior claim to the benefits of this fund, which will be administered by Rules hereafter to be framed.

Caddies who wish to have their names placed on the Register must apply to Tom Morris.

Caddie Regulations, 1890. Summer and winter rates for caddies are now set at different tariffs, and the professional or teaching caddie is now distinguished by a separate (and higher) rate structure. The 1875 Regulations were still in effect.

Consideration was now given to a fund for registered caddies whereby the Club contributed £50-£75 per annum for assistance in times of need. This was the start of the Caddies Benefit Fund.

Alex Brown, known as 'Pint Size,' circa 1890. Pint Size's tidy dress shows early influence from the fishermen/caddies' smart attire.

Caddie Profile: Sandy Pirie

"instruments of war"

Sandy operated with the idea that no one could ever beat his *man*, and always referred to the clubs as "instruments of war." He would always carry the clubs in his left hand, rather than the time-honoured method of carrying them under arm.

No one had ever seen Sandy try a shot himself, yet he knew every foot of the Old Course. Unlike most caddies, he had the 'grand merit' of silence during any matches in which he was involved, and it was always expected that he would put the correct club into his *man's* hand without being asked.

FEATHERIES AND INTERLOPERS

As the number of golf players increased, there arose a demand for the services of a golf professional who could coach others. In time, the good caddie became a golfer as well.

The transition from the status of senior caddie to golf professional is clearly defined in the Robertson family. David was the last of the senior caddies, while his son Allan, born on 11 September 1815, was the first professional. Allan, said to be the greatest golfer who never won an Open, succeeded in combining the duties of caddie and coach. His skill earned him many honours and recognition as the first of the truly great players, but sadly he died from an attack of jaundice at the age of 44 in 1859, the year before the first ever Open Championship. Just before Allan died, he went around the Old Course in 79, becoming the first man to break 80 on that course. His record stood for 10 years until Tom Morris bettered it.

Besides carrying clubs, mid-nineteenth-century caddies were also employed as ballmakers. Between 1840 and 1848, Allan Robertson employed two other local caddies, Tom Morris and Lang Willie, in making the feather balls known as featheries. Their workshop was Robertson's kitchen, and the balls were sold for 1/8d a ball or £1 a dozen from a window at the back of the house which overlooked the Old Course.

The featherie was the first ball made specifically for golf. Tom Morris said of it, "you were just like a shoemaker, after you filled the *lum hat* with feathers, you stuffed them into a little pocket of tough leather and began to sew." The design had definite drawbacks: a ball was seldom round, and it was prone to sogginess which led to its rapid disintegration. In spite of that, the featherie remained virtually unchanged until the gutta percha ball, or guttie, was introduced to Scotland in 1849 and found to be both cheaper and more durable.

Caddie John Fenton, circa 1890. John was said to have a grand face for funerals, and was always known as 'Treacle', indicating that there was a kind of pathos about him which lasted all the time, much like treacle (molasses) taking forever to run!

THE GUTTIE

There is some speculation as to the inventor of the first guttie ball, but the strongest claim comes from the Reverend Dr. R. Paterson of St. Andrews, who claimed that in 1845, a Hindu statue was shipped to St. Andrews from India packed with "chunks and chips" of gutta percha to prevent damage. As a young boy he discovered it was malleable and fashioned a piece into a ball. His attempts to strike it with a club showed great promise and with perseverance he discovered it flew better and was more durable than the featherie. He later emigrated to America to become a clergyman, but before going he wrote,

> I quit St. Andrews for a louder call,
> and left to golfers all I had, a ball.

As the new ball was inclined to break up in mid-flight, a rule was devised which read, "If a ball splits into separate pieces, another ball may be laid down where the largest portion lies." The guttie's introduction united the caddies in a campaign against it because they thought that part of their living was gone. Headed by Allan Robertson, who in 1844 had sold the considerable number of 2,556 featheries, they boycotted the 'new stuff,' which they said was *nae gowf*. Robertson himself actually attempted to buy up all the gutties found amongst the *whins* by the caddies and even tried to destroy the "interlopers" by fire!

All these efforts were in vain, however, and by 1848 the guttie became widely accepted. In fact, this improvement, along with the opening in 1852 of a new railway linking St. Andrews with Edinburgh and Glasgow, resulted in an enormous increase in the number of people taking up golf and requiring a caddie's service. Thus, contrary to their original fears, things could not have been better for the caddies.

Robertson finally realised he had been mistaken about the guttie, and along with Bob Kirk, another senior caddie and a fine golfer, took to the "new stuff" with such enthusiasm that caddying now took second place to their ballmaking.

There were other changes which resulted from the increased use and popularity of the Old Course. One was the widening of the links with new holes being made, one for the outward and one for the inward players, rather than the single hole on each green. The Old Course originally had 22 holes, 11 out and 11 in. The course started on the hill just behind the R&A Clubhouse with only one flag on each green, and homeward players had the right-of-way to play onto the putting surface. This layout was changed to 18 holes in 1764. At a meeting of the Society of St. Andrews Golfers, a Minute reads:

> The Captains and Gentlemen golfers are of the opinion that it would be for the improvement of the links that the first four holes should be converted into two.

Today, there are seven double greens on the Old Course, and homeward players still have the right-of-way, with the exception of hole number one, where those playing the eighteenth must give priority to the players on the first fairway setting out on their round.

The other important change had to do with the teeing up of the ball. When the guttie with its truer roll made the featherie obsolete, the rules of golf, especially those relating to the green, had to be modified. In 1777, the teeing ground was described as "not nearer than one club length, not further than four club lengths from the hole." By 1822 this had been changed to read "not nearer than two club lengths," and much later it became six club lengths from the hole. Then in 1882, the R&A rules stipulated that the diameter of the hole was to be four inches, increased in 1891 to 4-1/4 inches. The greens were now becoming a recognised well-mown surface used only for putting. The guttie had in essence brought the tee off the green, and the teeing ground as we know it came into being.

Learning from Your Elders

A young caddie watches intently as the champions of the day pose for a photographer on the St. Andrews links, circa 1855.

Auld Kirky, on the far right, has left his box for a round of carrying—the young caddie may have already been a customer of his for a 'Kirky remake'. Caddie/clubmaker James Wilson stands on the left, and bending down in the foreground is Allan Robertson. Auld Daw stands to Kirky's right. The caddie in the central background is Bob Andrew ('The Rook').

KIRKY'S REMAKES

Robertson and his crew were not the only guttie entrepreneurs in St. Andrews. Auld Kirky was a ballmaker who had also been a caddie for many years. He had a box which was situated just opposite George Leslie's Inn in Golf Place. Every day he sat there, cutting up new gutta and boiling the pieces in a little stew-pan. He would then take a piece in each hand and squeeze the material until it was ready for the mould. Once shaped, the balls were taken out, dried, and allowed to firm.

Although on the green the guttie was more consistent than the featherie, the ball was inclined to drop in flight because it was uniformly round and smooth. Eventually, players realised that after the ball became cut and hacked with usage, it flew better. After this, Auld Kirky began hammering each ball in an egg-shaped cup, using a hammer with a broad blade until the ball was more or less symmetrically nicked, then finally giving it a coat of paint. He was also known for his remakes, and the 'box' was very popular with the younger lads who had saved a sixpence for a Kirky remake.

Caddie Profile: Lang Willie

"*pit yer* right foot in the fifth position,
an' pay *attenshin tae* the fiddle!"

Willie Robertson, or 'Lang Willie' as he was known, was much taller than most of his contemporaries. Measuring 6'2", with bent knees and a slouching gate, he was unmistakable in his white moleskin *breeks*, said to be *mither-made*, and a *lum hat* which made him look like a veritable giant. Willie always swore by milk, saying that it was all he would drink, much to the amusement of Allan Robertson, who knew his true drinking habits.

Apart from his reputation as an outstanding caddie, Lang Willie enjoyed playing the fiddle, and was indispensable at weddings. He also taught the *fisher lasses* dancing, and when his services were sought out as a golf coach, he sometimes bewildered his pupils when giving advice on the proper stance: "pit yer right foot in the fifth position, an' pay attenshin *tae* the fiddle!"

Willie suffered several strokes whilst on the golf course. After one, a fellow caddie asked him how he had felt at the time, and Willie answered, "I felt *naething*." Later, his sister said his face looked pale and twisted in the morning. "Nonsense!" cried Willie, but later added, "When I sat *doon tae ma porritch, ma* jaw *widnae* work." He later died of a heart attack while carrying on the Old Course.

RUBBING UP

Although his knowledge of both the links and the game itself was important when a caddie was given a job, his first duty was the rubbing-up of his golfer's clubs. Indeed, during the nineteenth and early twentieth centuries, caddies were paid a tip not for carrying their golfer's clubs but for cleaning them before and at the end of the round.

The task was not taken lightly. Before a round began, the caddie would remove his *man's* clubs from the wooden box in which they had been transported and stored in the clubhouse, undoing the strap which tied the clubs together. He would then pick up the clubs in a tight bundle and carry them under his arm to the bench, where the "rubbing-up" began.

A piece of old emery paper was an essential part of the caddie's equipment because it burnished the metal but did not scratch. He first rubbed along the blade of the iron, front and back, then across at the point and heel. According to Tom Morris, this was done "so as to leave the centre with a different shade from the rest of the club that the eye might be more easily caught when aiming the ball."

The caddie also took pride in having all the woods nicely oiled, and he would put a polish on them like that "on the back of an otter," using a hare's foot lightly dipped in linseed oil from an old tin can. In this way, the shafts developed a skin which made them weather any rain. Hugh Philp's workshop was used for this duty and an old bench was given over to the caddies to 'clean up' their golfer's clubs.

EARLY CLUBMAKERS

The earliest clubmaker in St. Andrews was Hugh Philp, now recognised as the finest clubmaker ever. He had a small workshop which stood a little below the steps of the Marine Hotel (now the Rusacks) alongside the eighteenth fairway of the Old Course. Most of his employees came from the younger caddies, and those showing most interest in the game were made apprentice clubmakers.

James Wilson, who eventually became a recognised clubmaker himself, was the first caddie to work for Old Philp. He eventually took over Philp's workshop in 1852, also employing caddies, such as the legendary Andra' Strath, as apprentice clubmakers. After Hugh Philp's death in 1854, Robert Forgan took over the entire business from James Wilson. Out of the Forgan stable of caddie-cum-apprentices came the famous Jamie Anderson, who became a three-time winner of the Open Championship, winning in 1877, 1878 and 1879. Jamie was the eldest son of 'Auld Daw' Anderson, who was said to have put two of his family through university with not only the proceeds of his ginger beer sales near the ninth hole of the Old Course, but by selling a wee nip or two to the golfers who, on cold and windy days, took advantage of the 'secret stash' under his "wicker basket on wheels"! Jamie later went on to become a very fine clubmaker himself, continuing the tradition of employing caddies in his workshop. Indeed, no less than two future Open winners were to be apprenticed to him. The most colourful of these was Bob Martin, who won the Open twice but described his rather flat swing as that of "an old wife cutting hay."

Bob Martin, St. Andrews caddie and professional golfer, went on to win the Open Championship in 1876 and 1885. He was noted for his long drives and was especially gifted in his use of the cleek. Though a fine golfer, he described his swing like an "old wife cutting hay."

Caddie Profile: Auld Daw

"A wee nip just to warm the inner man!"

Caddie David Anderson, a fine golfer and later Keeper of the Green for the R&A, whose son Jamie won the Open Championship three times in succession, was one of the most respected of the senior caddies. 'Auld Daw' started carrying when still a schoolboy, was once employed by Allan Robertson as a ballmaker, and caddied for Allan throughout most of his professional life. He is better known for his ginger beer stall, which he set up at the ninth hole of the Old Course upon his retirement. He used to offer ginger beer to the thirsty golfer or better yet, a *wee nip (just to warm the inner man!!)* from the flask which he had discreetly hidden in his hip pocket.

This ginger beer bottle was found by the author during a maintenance excavation at the site of Auld Daw's original ginger beer stall near the ninth hole of the Old Course. Bottles like this were common in the late nineteenth century.

BAGPIPES AND CANVAS CONTAINERS

The number of clubs carried in those early days rarely exceeded six, so the caddie was able to carry them loosely underarm like a set of bagpipes. This practice lasted until the ever-increasing number of clubs used in the game led to the introduction of the first golf bag in 1890, the year that the 'Dr. Trails Canvas Container' made its first appearance on the Old Course.

This canvas container, or golf bag as it became known, was referred to as a *poke* by the local caddies. 'Auld Daw,' on being asked for whom he was caddying, replied, "I *dinna ken,* but he's got a *poke o' baffies* like a stag's *heid.*" Most of the professional golfers who travelled any great distances carried their clubs in wooden boxes, like mobile lockers. Although the canvas container made the job of carrying clubs easier, some senior caddies still continued to carry the clubs loose underarm, with the heads pointing downward for easy recognition. They were able to hand the club to their *man* much quicker than the 'bag toter.'

After handing the club to his *man*, an additional task of the caddie was to run forward and spot where the ball had landed. Without this type of precaution, the ball could quite easily have been lost in the heavy gorse and sandy wastes on the links. A local paper reported in 1920 that a caddie who was careless in his duties was given a *wee skelp* (light tap) *on the heid* to make him pay attention. Although painful, the writer added, it was also quite profitable, as the tap was worth sixpence to the injured caddie. Perhaps this explains the reported rise in caddie offences during this period!

Above: caddies James Miles and Alex Elder outside the caddie box, conforming to the new regulation dress code. Their caddie badges can be seen on their jacket lapels.

Right: caddie badge, circa 1899. Because of the need for regulation, caddies were required to register to work on the links, and work was only given to those who could produce their caddie badge or armband.

Caddie Profile: 'Sodger' Mcintyre

John Smith Mcintyre was a quiet man but made himself one of the personalities of the links at a time when the Caddy Shelter was already rich in characters. Sodger, as he was known, started carrying clubs when just a boy, learning all the finer points of the game. He was a good golfer, but preferred to caddie. During the latter part of his career, Sodger caddied for Prime Minister A. J. Balfour, who after a bad shot would always say to him, "If I always got what I wanted, I would never play golf."

Sodger Mcintyre was one of the last of the Old Brigade of caddies. In 1936 he was 71 years old, and he decided to retire after 60 years on the links. Reminiscing about his younger days, he could remember back to Young Tom Morris and the time when the Old Course was much narrower than it is today. "Bunkers in his day were bunkers," enthused Sodger. "Ye used *tae* climb 15 feet *doon intae* the bowels o' Hell, but Hell Bunker's *no'* like hell *ata' noo.* Today, it's a kind o' paradise in hell, with *mair* sand than brimstone, and we only had up *tae* eight clubs *tae* carry, a wooden driver, a *spoon* for second shots, a *mid-spoon*, a *baffy*, a *niblick* and yer putter. With up to twenty-five clubs in a golfer's bag today, caddies are weighed under *wi' a'* that tackle!"

Sadly, Sodger died a year after retiring, but many tributes were paid to him. Roger Wethered, for whom Sodger caddied when he won the Amateur Championship, and former Prime Minister Balfour, returned to St. Andrews to pay tribute to a "fine gentleman."

DOG CADDIES

From the turn of the century, another type of creature became popular on the Old Course amongst golfers and caddies alike. Newcomers would have been surprised to see dogs and men moving in and out of the gorse, no doubt thinking them to be poachers after rabbits. They were, in fact, the dog-caddies and dog-men of St. Andrews.

The dog-caddie, or ball finder, was a dog which was carefully trained to find golf balls. It had long been a recognised custom (continued by some merchants in the present day) that anyone finding balls could sell them to the local clubmakers or shopkeepers, and some of the men at that time could earn upwards of £1 a day with a well-trained dog. If a player lost his ball amongst the *whins* and any of the dog-men were about, they would come across to him and strike a deal. After it had been concluded, the dogs were sent into the *whins* and the player was almost certain to have his ball retrieved.

Since 1921, caddies and golfers have been restricted to looking for balls on the links during the hours from 8pm to 8am only. Some caddies have found to their cost that ignoring this regulation is a sure way of losing rather than making money. One caddie, taken to the old Burgh Police Court under the bye-law, was accused of using his dog to search for balls amongst the *whins* outside the allowed hours. When charged with this offence, the caddie maintained that he was only taking his dog for a walk on the lead. What he failed to explain was that the lead was forty yards long and didn't hinder the dog from making a wide search of the *whins!* When he was fined £1 or ten days in the local jail, he offered to pay the £1, saying that his dog would miss the exercise on the links if he weren't around!

There was also talk of a 'ball-finders' badge being given to those caddies too old to carry clubs, which would allow them to supplement their pensions and at the same time keep them out in 'God's fresh air.' More importantly, it would keep them away from the pubs and their own houses, where they were "nothing but a nuisance" to their already overworked wives!

'Wiggy' Ayton carries his golfer's clubs loose under arm.

Local Lore

The time spent between jobs was a good chance for a caddie to practice his game. Because there was nowhere to practise, the caddies themselves converted a spare piece of ground near the old railway station into a caddies' course, to encourage the younger lads to learn the *game o' gowf.* The location chosen was a piece of rough ground just opposite the seventeenth hole on the Old Course, and the caddies laid out four holes known as the 'Scholars.' Part of this land is now occupied by the Old Course Hotel.

Around the same time, caddies laid out a short putting area on the site of the present Rusacks Hotel. There they would while away the hours until their services were needed or the local pubs opened, whichever came first! But some 'outsiders' disputed the caddies' exclusive rights to the green. While waiting for their husbands to finish their rounds on the Old Course, wives of R&A members would venture onto the 'Caddies Course'. While the caddies were annoyed by this intrusion, it was not in their interest to formally complain, because it was not unusual for members' wives to assist the caddies and their families in lean times by providing them with food and clothing.

The caddies tolerated this situation for many years, until the R&A decided it was in everyone's best interest to look for an exclusive site for the ladies, well away from the critical eyes of the caddies! Today, this putting green is known worldwide as the Himalayas, and has been the home of the Ladies Putting Club since 1867.

The gallery looks on intently as members of the Ladies Putting Club play an early match over the famous Himalayas putting green, before the turn of the century. Most ladies employed young caddies, since the tight corsets popular during this period did not allow the ladies to bend over to retrieve the ball from the hole!

The Ladies Putting Club remained a private club, used by R&A members and their wives, until after the Second World War, when due to financial constraints it was opened to the public. Today, presidents, professionals and the general public all enjoy their round on what is arguably the oldest and most unique putting course in the world.

THE SWILCAN BURN

Prior to the first Open Championship at St. Andrews, the Swilcan Burn was a natural sandy-edged water hazard which swept almost into the centre of the first fairway, not the well-defined narrow channel it is today. To make things even worse, the burn was used by the women of the town to wash and bleach their clothes and sheets, and the washing was then laid out on the fairway and on the surrounding *whin* bushes to dry. The R&A introduced several local rules to handle this unique domestic infringement on the game. In 1851 a new rule was introduced to the effect that, "When a ball lies on clothes, or within one club length of a washing tub, the clothes may be drawn from under the ball and the tub removed." In 1888 the rule was changed to read: "When a ball lies on clothes, the ball may be lifted and dropped behind, without penalty." Golfers must have breathed a sigh of relief when the new local public laundry was built near the East Sands, just opposite the harbour!

Major Boothby is playing to the original first green on the Old Course. To his right is Jamie Anderson, caddie and Open champion in 1877, 1878 and 1879, while standing on the Swilcan Bridge behind him are 'Auld Daw' Anderson and Allan Robertson. Tom Morris Senior, at the far left, looks on intently.

Even without the washing, playing the first hole was a far different experience in those days. The Swilcan Burn would have been reachable from the first tee and the fairway was less than a third of its present width, with the rest a sandy natural hazard. Granny Clark's Wynd was a dirt path leading to the beach, and was used to transport the town's lifeboat across the Old Course and onto the West Sands for launching. When Halkets bunker* was filled in and the sandy area reclaimed, the first and eighteenth fairways were left the wide bunker-less area we know today.

There were many ways of using the Swilcan Burn to earn extra money. A favourite trick was to go further up the burn and stir up the water, making it cloudy at the point where the water today crosses the first and eighteenth fairways. After this, golfers who put their balls in the burn had no chance of finding them. Later that day, the young caddies would fish out the balls from the now clear water and sell them back to the golfers for 1d, or 2d for extra good ones! It was said that when your ball fell into the Swilcan Burn, the young caddie would stamp it into the mud, and then be good enough to try and find it for you. The older caddies would studiously *howk* for stray balls amongst the *whins*. It was believed the employment in both cases was very lucrative!

In fact, the caddies' ingenuity in such matters was nearly boundless. Prior to the lining of the holes on the Old Course with tin in 1890, there were no sand boxes beside the tees. The usual ploy was for the caddie to scoop some sand from the bottom of the hole on each green and use it to tee his golfer's ball at the next hole. More enterprising caddies would carry a small bag of sand around their necks. But many of the younger caddies carried this even further: a common prank was

* Halkets bunker, which was filled in prior to 1873, used to lie on the town side of the first fairway of the Old Course just opposite Granny Clark's Wynd.

to deepen the hole to about 12 inches so that the golfer could not retrieve his ball!

An Important Putt

The gentleman in the black 'lum hat' is Sir Hugh Lyon Playfair, circa 1858. Sir Hugh was an inveterate golfer and was in the habit of monogramming his personal items (clubs, umbrella, etc.) with the slogan, "This was stolen from Sir Hugh Lyon Playfair" in an attempt to prevent his possessions from 'innocently going astray!'

SILLYBODKINS AND SCHOLARS

A stranger passing Allan Robertson's house on the corner of Golf Place would wonder at a dozen or so men and boys, some leaning against the wall of Allan's house gazing over the nearby Lucklaw Hill, anxious that the wind should be "*aff the nairth*" as a sign of good weather. Others, hands in pockets, would be walking up and down contemplating their chances of work that day.

If it was a doubtful morning, Allan would always send senior caddie Charlie Thomson, a self-professed authority on the weather, across to the Old Union Parlour to read what the glass said on the barometer. On his return, Charlie would always say, "I'm o' the *opeenion* that she's further *doon* the day than she was yesterday." Asked what he meant he would reply, "Well Sir, *ah'm jist dootin'* that it'll be very wet, or we'll get *mair* rain. Either way, the rain is God's way o' cleanin' the *coos*!" But even Charlie's ambiguous remark would not daunt the player bent on his round of golf.

If there was not much to do, young boys bent on self-improvement could be seen copying the swings of the senior caddies. Golf balls were too expensive for the caddies to buy, so they would improvise by using *chuckie stanes* (pebbles) or better yet corks, in endless supply due to an apparently free flow of champagne and claret, possibly increased by fines paid by the Gentlemen Golfers after transgressing the rule on payment to caddies!

Sandy Herd, a local caddie and golfer, tells of the ingenuity of the caddie. To make these claret-sodden corks carry against the wind of which St. Andrews gets its fair share, they hit on the idea of inserting screw nails into them to give the corks weight. For some reason not explained by Sandy, they were given the name of *sillybodkins* by the caddies. Sandy went on to become the Open winner in 1902, which was the first time in a major British tournament that the new Haskell ball was used, an innovation which was to change the game much more than the introduction of the guttie.

Sandy Herd and his caddie 'Pauchy' Aitken, circa 1903. Leading up to the 1902 Open in Hoylake, England, Sandy Herd's game was in poor shape (described by Harold Hilton as 'in decadence') but his last minute switch from his favourite guttie to the new Haskell ball was to put 20-30 yards on his game. Before teeing off on his first round for the Open, he gave the new ball scant praise. By the time he had won the Open, however, he enthused to anyone and everyone who would listen! Sandy was always recognisable from the distance by the number of waggles he took before striking the ball!

RIBBED AT ST. ANDREWS

The year 1873 saw the Open Championship leave Prestwick for the first time since its inception in 1860 and come to St. Andrews. A directive was sent out to all Clubs stating that competitors must be known, honest and respectable caddies. The tournament was won by 'Young' Tom Kidd, a local caddie whose father also caddied on the links. Tom was well-known as the longest driver among the professional golfers at that time, and he also introduced the 'ribbed' club, an innovation which considerably aided his Open win. Tom had confided to his friends that he had found a way to play the slippery greens at St. Andrews and boasted, "Ye'll see me *dae* it!" He went on to justify his boast. As the other balls slithered over the greens, Tom's stood stock-still beside the hole. He had carved the face of the clubs with a file which made them as rough as a *peerie* (spinning top). The following year, 26-year-old Tom Kidd set out to defend his title and came in a close second to Tom Morris.

Photo insert of Tom Kidd from a golfing diploma produced in 1910 to commemorate the golden jubilee of the Open Championship. Note that Tom is wearing his Open Winner medal on his jacket lapel. Tom, like many professional golfers, earned a reputation as an expert teacher to many novices, instilling the importance of the 'grip and stance.'

Unfortunately, prize money for those early tournaments was very little—the big money matches were still played between professionals and club members. This was of no benefit to Tom Kidd, though, because he was a local lad who preferred working the links of St. Andrews as a caddie to travelling further afield for the higher stakes, like Tom Morris and his peers. For Tom Kidd, the Open winnings amounted to only £11 plus the medal itself, and a year to the day of winning the championship, Tom actually had to sell that medal to raise money for his forthcoming marriage. Ten years later, on the 16th of January 1884, Tom Kidd died of a heart attack at his home in Rose Lane.

PARISH OF ST. ANDREWS, FIFE.

At St. Andrews, the 23rd *day of* November 1874

It is hereby certified that Christopher Thomas Kidd Golf Caddie with Eliza Ann Lumsden of this Parish

have been three times proclaimed in order to Marriage, and that no objections have been offered.

John Sorley *Session Clerk.*

Thomas Kidd's marriage certificate, 1874.

The Links Act of 1894 meant that patronage of the R&A was reduced and responsibility for the caddies now came under the control of the Burgh Court. Special bye-laws were introduced, including the first set of rules for the licensing of caddies. These bye-laws were implemented by the Town Council in 1896.

The Twentieth Century

FISHERMEN AND FOREIGNERS FEES

At the start of the twentieth century, caddying as a primary occupation was considered a dead-end job, and the traditional caddie—the "old worthy"—came from the poorer people of the town. But now a different type of man began to join the ranks: the local fisherman, who turned to caddying to supplement his ever-decreasing earnings from the declining St. Andrews fishing industry. Along with this change came a change in the public's attitudes towards caddies, who were no longer considered 'ragamuffins' and were becoming more respectable, if not altogether respectful of the golfers!

The regular caddies were not against the 'foreigners,' as they were called, but tradition stated that when a new fisherman had his first caddie fee, he used it to buy drink for the regular caddies. Occasionally this was the prelude to a celebration, and some of the caddies would take to the course the worse for drink. On one occasion, one of the senior caddies called 'Old Grant' was told by his *man*, "You're drunk, I won't have a drunk caddie." Scathingly came Grant's reply: "Maybe I'm drunk, but I'll get sober, you *cannae gowf* and ye'll no' get better!" Off he staggered, scattering his *man's* clubs over the ground!

When they began caddying regularly, the fishermen added a sartorial touch to the links by wearing their fisherman's garb of blue woollen jerseys and peak caps. This sort of 'uniform' became a regular sight on the links for many years. Apart from the fishermen, men from other trades began to rely on golf to supplement their incomes, and many were provided with employment through the continued popularity of the game. Clubmaking and *cleekmaking* gave many blacksmiths work, and joiners combined clubmaking with housebuilding. Many ex-servicemen coming home from the wars took up caddying on their return to civilian life.

Caddies David Melville and John Chisholm, circa 1900. These two retired fishermen took to caddying as the local fishing trade became less lucrative. Their mode of dress brought a sartorial note to the Caddie Shelter.

Caddie Profile: Donal' Blue

Donal' caddied on the links for 'donkey's years,' as he put it. A fisherman by trade, he combined his nets and clubs when the fishing industry in St. Andrews began to decline.

Donal' and his sidekick 'Stumpie Eye' were the heroes of an annual golf match played over the Old Course with a purse of £5 for the winner, put up by the members of the R&A and visitors to the links. This was no ordinary match, for as the players made their way around the course, young lads would gather the men's divots and throw them at their heads as they attempted a shot, or use them to cover their balls. All this led to quite a bit of abuse from Donal' and Stumpie, and the end of the match usually took the form of a *dookin* with both players being thrown into the Swilcan Burn! The two friends were always followed by several hundred spectators who roared continuously at the pantomime. But despite Donal's antics, he was a very good golfer and a respected caddie.

Donal' Blue in one of his many guises, circa 1890. Donal' was the first caddie to go commercial by having postcard photographs of himself printed, which he sold to visiting golfers! He is seen here performing for tourists outside the St. Andrews Castle grounds, where, when not caddying or posing, he worked as a part-time Keeper of the Castle.

A NEW ERA

Many changes took place in the game of golf from about 1900 onwards. The introduction of wood for iron flagpoles on the links at St. Andrews was brought about by the new rubber-cored Haskell balls which were introduced in 1902. It was said that

> the ball would dance and glance so far off the 'iron-sticks,' and poles would not damage the edge of the hole as much as the old heavy wands.

With the change in flagpoles came a ruling involving the caddie. It was suggested that a new and better way to preserve the immediate area around the hole would be for the caddie to stand away from the hole and hold the pole at arms-length so that the caddie

> shall not make the ground uneven about the hole and perhaps raise the lip by standing close up with his tackety boots marking it. Also the caddie does not affect the wind as in the old way, with deliberate nursing being ruled out.

Stainless steel clubs were introduced and the old golfing jacket was replaced by the sleeveless jersey. Tackets in the boots were replaced with shoes which had steel spikes on the soles. Peg tees began to replace sand tees, although it was many years before sand tees were totally dispensed with at St. Andrews.

Caddie Profile: Henry J. Clarke

Sodger Mcintyre's *auld buddy* Henry J. Clarke, another of the senior caddies, died about two weeks after Sodger. Always known by his full name, Clarke lived about three miles outside St. Andrews and he would walk to the links every day, caddie, then walk the three miles home again.

Clarke joined the Royal Navy in 1880 and then joined the Highland Light Infantry, doing service in the Boer War. Later, he served with his regiment at the relief of Khartoum. After the Army, he returned to his first love, the links, but never forgot his military ways, sporting the widest 'military moustache' ever seen on the course! His pall bearers were all R&A Club members, such was the esteem in which the *auld yins,* the traditional caddies, were held.

CODES AND CLOOTS

In 1920, the R&A decided that during medal weeks, the caddie fees were to be reduced by 1/- per round, and any other matches played by members were reduced by 6d a round. The caddies, although very unhappy about the changes, had no alternative but to accept, as there was then no recourse that they could employ. The local magistrates, along with the R&A, had absolute control of the caddies, who were told that they must "accept the new charges, or no licence would be issued."

By 1928, the Town Links Committee had again revised the bye-laws relating to caddies, and had introduced a new voucher system which gave the Caddie Superintendent even more control over the caddies. Later that year, the Committee hired a new Caddie Superintendent, Mr. Fyfe, who increased the fee from the rate of 1/6d per round, which had been in effect for several decades, to 3/- for men and 1/6d for the younger boys. Using this increase as leverage, Fyfe introduced a much-needed new code of discipline.

Since the cleaning of the golfer's clubs was still considered the caddie's primary duty, Fyfe would only give work to those caddies who produced the requisite piece of emery cloth for the job, and any caddie turning up for work without his *cloot* was sent home for the day. An initial cleaning of the golfer's clubs was required before going out on the course, because Fyfe believed it made them "easier to clean after each round." Fyfe was also noted for his unique way of settling disputes between caddies. He would send them to the nearby town bandstand, out of sight of the Club and golfers, with instructions to "go to the bandstand and fight as long as you can stand, then come back and then I'll find you work!"

About this time, an article in the local newspaper mentions a fisherman/caddie named Buff Wilson who, having completed his round, received no tip from the golfer. When the golfer asked Buff if he would turn up at 8am the next morning, Buff, looking first at his voucher and then at his golfer (who was also a fisherman), said in his most *pawky* tone, "Yer no feared to ask me to come *aff* ma boat at that time in the mornin', for *nae mair* than a voucher, three shillin', eighteen clubs, o'er seven miles o' ground, as yer in a habit o' playin'. I think I'd be better at the nets, or under the blankets sleepin'!"

During the 1930s the local Town Council instigated a campaign to rid the courses of unregistered caddies. Two caddies were arrested and brought before the Court along with the golfer who was charged with employing them. As appearances at the Court increased, so did the fines.

St. Andrews Links.

CADDIE'S LICENCE.

BY VIRTUE of the Bye-laws by the Town Council of the Burgh of St. Andrews made and adopted 2nd July, 1923, the Magistrates of the Burgh of St. Andrews hereby authorise Robert Chisholm *to act as a Caddie for the period to* 30th December *subject always to the conditions set forth in the said Bye-laws.*

Dated at St. Andrews this Twelfth *day of* February *19*24

Kingsley Cantley
Town Clerk.

NOTE.—*The Licence Badge issued herewith must be returned to the Town Clerk's Office within one month after the expiry thereof, whereupon the sum of Two Shillings and Sixpence paid therefor will be refunded, if the Licence be not renewed; but in case of failure so to return the Badge, the said sum will be forfeited.*

Caddie licence, 1924.

Tackety Boots and Cloth Bunnets

Caddies, 1924. These caddies are sitting on the bench used for 'rubbing up' the golfers' clubs. Tips were paid for the quality of this work, not necessarily the caddies' performance on the course.

In the background is the old Caddie Shelter which was built in 1891 on the site of what is now the car park by the R&A Clubhouse. The Caddie Superintendent's office is on the left of the building, and the canopy on the right was used by both caddies and the public, since the site of the shelter was "public land."

UNDER ONE ROOF

In 1891, the R&A petitioned the Town Council against the "general behaviour" of the caddies. It was claimed that caddies booked by members were not turning up on time, nor were they prepared to work for the set caddie fee. The Town Council sympathised with the caddies, especially Provost George Murray, who said, "The Club are at fault, they do not engage caddies through the Caddie Master." It was found that the Club expected caddies to be booked and then wait indefinitely for certain members who seldom turned up on time, with no 'waiting time' payable to the caddies. Since visitors were offering more money, the caddies gradually moved to these more lucrative customers. The situation led to some bad feeling between caddies and the Club, and the R&A were reminded that they must book their caddies through the Caddie Master, who was paid to look after the caddies' interest.

This incident was one of many which led the caddies that same year to petition the Town Council to have a Caddie Shelter erected near the flagpole opposite the R&A Clubhouse. The flagpole came from the sailing ship Cutty Sark, and was now the property of the R&A, which used it to fly the Club's standard. This had become a popular area for golfers and caddies to meet up prior to their rounds. The request was agreed to the following year, but as this ground was public land, the Town Council decided that the shelter could not be for the exclusive use of caddies alone, and that the public would have the right to shelter under the building's veranda.

In the early 1930s, a proposal went before the Town Council for the building of a new Caddie Shelter, since the old one was now considered too close to the R&A clubhouse. The new shelter would incorporate "a Caddie Master's office, a urinal and washing facilities, at a cost of £316," but the ablutions were apparently more than the budget allowed for and it was not until the present Caddie Pavilion was built that any consideration was given to the caddies' personal needs. The shelter was extended in 1932, but much to the caddies' disappointment still did not include either a lavatory or any means of lighting. This extension was partitioned off in the late 1970s and converted to a golf shop, run by a local golf teacher, Mr. McAndrew. From that time until the caddies were housed in their present pavilion, the caddies and shop owner merely tolerated each other's existence.

The present Caddie Pavilion was built in 1992 and opened in February 1993. It includes toilets, drying room, washing facilities, colour TV, food and drinks machines—how times have changed! Thankfully, the role of the caddie, and the caddies' welfare, is as much a consideration as any of the other improvements made by the Links Trust.

In the Bleak Midwinter

Caddie Pavilion under snow, 1995. Most caddies must look for alternative work during the winter months.

Caddie Profile: Sid Rutherford

"Chicken, sir!"

Sid Rutherford was one of two brothers, both in their late 70s, who were always vying to be first on the daily list. If his brother Willie was down at the Caddie Shelter by 5am one morning, Sid would make sure he got down the next day at 4:30am. One day during an R&A medal round, Sid and his man were on the first green with the flag just a few yards from the Swilcan Burn. Sid was motioned to stand away from the flag, and he forgot that the burn was just behind him. He took a few backward steps and in he tumbled, clubs and all, followed very quickly by his golfer, not to retrieve Sid but to save his clubs!! After draining out his golf bag, in went the golfer again, this time to collect Sid!

Sid Rutherford could always be heard on the greens with his constant plea to golfers: "Hit the ball, sir, the hole will no come to you, so it won't." If a ball came up short of the hole, Sid would exclaim that the golfer was "Kentucky fried." When asked what he meant, he would respond with a wry smile, "Chicken, sir!"

THE CADDIE'S LOT

Prior to 1938, when the R&A and USPGA jointly agreed to limit the number of clubs carried by any one player to fourteen, there was no limit on the amount of clubs a golfer could carry, and many players would take as many clubs as their bags would hold. The hapless caddie might find himself lugging anything up to 22 clubs in a bag, and indeed there were now so many clubs that their identities were reduced to numbers, not names.

For the old-time golfers such excess seemed to reduce the player's need to develop his shot-making skills, and the R&A stated that "players were virtually buying shots," with the belief that good play depended on having an absurd number of clubs in their bags. For the professional, there was a waning of the traditional feeling that each club had its own identity, hand-picked, each a valued and trusted friend. Allan Robertson, for example, had his own names for all his clubs: 'The Doctor,' 'The Frying Pan,' 'Sir Robert Peel,' etc., each with a specific task. When the 1938 rule became widely known, some of the more well-known professional golfers, including Henry Cotton, declared the new rule "entirely unnecessary... golfers should be allowed to carry as many clubs as they want." They pointed out that caddies "are well remunerated for their efforts."

One caddie not entirely in agreement was Jock Hutchinson, who had his stamina well and truly tested by one enthusiastic golfer. His *man's* leather golf bag contained twenty clubs, two dozen golf balls, a pair of golf shoes, a waterproof suit, and an umbrella. After the game, wiping the sweat from his brow and pointing to his load, he said, "Eighteen holes, six miles and *aw* this for a *twa* and six tip, it's no a caddie he wants, but a *cuddy [donkey]*!"

Another story which serves to underline the importance of paying the caddie a decent tip is the one when at the end of a round the golfer gave his caddie three pennies as a tip. The caddie laid them in his palm, saying to the player, "Sir, are ye aware that I can tell yer fortune from these three coins?" The caddie went on to volunteer that the first one told him, "Yer no' a Scotsman," to which the golfer nodded assent. "An' the second that yer no married," continued the caddie, to which the golfer nodded as well, asking about the third. "*Weel*, the third *wan* tells me that yer father *wisnae* married either!!!"

Beasts of Burden

Caddies and clubs, circa 1920. These two St. Andrews caddies are shown with a typical pre-1938 array of golf bags, most of which contain up to 20 clubs. On the right is Willie Fowls, and on the left is John 'Plum' Melville, a local clubmaker/caddie who carried for Jock Hutchison when he won the 1920 Open Championship.

Caddie Profile: Andra' Kirkaldy

"Caddying in early life, professional golf later, bring a man into good company."

One of the last of the traditional caddies, Andra' Kirkaldy turned professional golfer and later became Honorary Professional to the R&A. Said to be the greatest golfer who never won an Open, he was notorious for his profanity on the course. When being interviewed by a local reporter on the proposal that swearing should be penalised on the golf course, Andra' said, "Quite right, the damned thing should be stamped *oot*!"

Andra' used to reminisce about his early years as a caddie, and maintained that no school board could prevent the younger lads from skipping class and wandering down to the links in the hope of getting a bag. "In those days," said Andra', "young lads born into poverty, with no way of escaping, may have thought of the old caddie adage: 'caddying in early life, professional golf later, bring a man into good company.'" Below are the last six lines of a poem by Andrew Bennet in Andra's honour:

If ye happen tae speak
Tae a lad wi' a cleek,
Or a lass wi' a club, or a caddie,
They'll be donnart and raw,
And nae golfers ata',
If they've no' heard o' Andra' Kirkaldy.*

* If you happen to speak to a lad with a cleek, or a lass with a club, or a caddie, they'll be stupid and raw and no golfers at all if they've not heard of Andrew Kirkaldy!

Andra' Kirkaldy as Honorary Professional to the Royal & Ancient Golf Club, tending a pin during an Autumn Medal meeting, 1920.

THE WAR YEARS

With the war in Europe, all major competitions were suspended, and there was little or no golf played until the end of the conflict in 1945. The links had a strange quiet feel about them. For those caddies not involved in the war, a caddie tournament was introduced, but never became popular, with only five caddies taking part in 1943. The links were 'no-go' areas, and the beach at St. Andrews had tank traps and gun emplacements all the way along the dunes.

During this period the Town Council gave permission to some local farmers to graze up to 150 sheep on the links from the first of April to the first of December. This number must have been exceeded at some stage, as an angry writer in the Letters column of the local newspaper wanted to know why there were "more sheep on the Old Course than blades o' grass!"

During the war years, clothing was rationed and only obtainable with coupons. One elderly R&A member who had exhumed some old clothes from his deepest wardrobe wore them for his walks by the links. One day, in the vicinity of the Caddie Shelter, he was approached by some golfers and asked if he was available to caddie and if he had any golf balls for sale. Apparently his pride was hurt at being mistaken for a caddie, and this prompted him to write a letter to the local newspaper which indignantly ended "and to cap it all to be mistaken for a St. Andrews caddie" and was signed "Ballfinder"!

Sunday golf was introduced to the Eden Course in 1941, but caddies were not allowed to work on that day until it became obvious that with the increased number of golfers playing, caddies were very much needed. Only those registered were allowed to work, with the Eden starter acting as Caddie Manager. It was also decided that caddies working on Sundays were to be paid a double fee, and any caddie not working on that day could play cheap golf on the Eden instead. A Sunday round would only cost 2/-, but not many caddies took up this offer, as they would rather be on the golf course earning "double money."

In the latter half of 1945, the Town Council agreed to increase the caddie fees, which had been decreased in 1938 and were considered to be inadequate for the work. Additional bye-laws were introduced to enable the local magistrates to adjust, when necessary, the fee paid to caddies. The present fees were 3/- for men, and 2/- for younger boys. The fees were now set at 4/- for men and 2/6d for the lads, with an annual review to be written into the bye-laws.

Before the war, 60 caddies had been licensed to work on the links, but during 1946, only 28 men applied for registration. This was one reason for reviewing the caddie fee; another was to consider lowering the age for the younger lads to 13.

When peace returned to the links, the old tradition of "playing in" the Captain of the R&A Golf Club was reintroduced. Not since 1938 had the Captain Elect played himself into office. The R&A decided not to give the traditional sovereign to the caddie who returned the Captain's ball, but there was such an uproar from the caddies and others, it was decided that the ceremony would retain all its "dignified" tradition.

Caddie Profile: 'Guy' Gillespie

"To have Guy on my side is worth a few strokes to me every time."

Wallace Boyd Gillespie, known as 'Guy,' was trained in the hotel industry, but although he was a skilled waiter he preferred the links to the kitchen, and it was as a caddie that he gained fame. Guy spent every spare moment on the links, and although he was a fair golfer, it was his keen perception of the game, and especially his knowledge of the Old Course, that built up his reputation as a caddie.

After Peter Thomson won the 1955 Open Championship at St. Andrews with Guy Gillespie as his caddie, he said of him, "I'm not sure if he belongs to me, or I to him, but he would carry for no other player when I was around, and for my part, to have Guy on my side is worth a few strokes to me every time."

Gary Player and Guy Gillespie on the Swilcan Bridge, circa 1960.

THE CADDIE TOURNAMENTS

The first tournament for caddies was held in 1819, and included in the list of competitors were the ball- and clubmakers who were caddies when not at their workbenches. It was not until 1842, however, that the first winner of the "Caddies Competition," as it had by that time become known, was officially recognised. R&A Minutes show that the Club contributed £50 in prize money, playfully referred to as "in-putts". Tom Morris, then only 21, was the first winner, with a round of 92; his father came a close second. In the same Minutes, mention is made of Allan Robertson, age 27, who was prohibited from competing since his game was considered "far superior to all others." It was believed that no-one else would have a chance if Allan played!

Throughout the years since then, there have been many caddie competitions, most organised by the caddies themselves, but none of them lasting for any significant length of time. Each event typically ended in uproar or severe bouts of drinking, considered par for the course!

For those caddies not overseas during the war years, a Caddie Tournament was organised by the Town Council and the R&A in 1939. Unfortunately, it was raining hard on the opening day and some parts of the links were flooded. As a consequence, only five caddies completed their round, with 'Bunny' Hutchinson the eventual winner, returning a score of 87. In the first year, the first prize was monetary, equal to that offered to the winner of the Open.

In the second year, the prizes were in the form of goods donated by local shopkeepers. Andra' Kirkaldy and his brother Hugh made the final, and Hugh needed a five at the last hole to win. He deliberately took seven, saying as he left the green, "Andra' can *hae* the turkey, the bottle o' whisky is *mair* in my line!" Money prizes were again introduced in the third year but the caddies were becoming greedy, and the amount of prize money on offer led to a considerable amount of cheating. The tournament was cancelled after that, to be reintroduced in 1943 with a non-monetary prize.

It was not until 1990 that an actual caddie-organised annual tournament was begun. For the first time, the tournament was played 'away from home' with a different course chosen each year. Prizes for the competition are donated by local St. Andrews merchants and hoteliers, and the more liquid ones are those most keenly played for!

Inaugural Caddies vs. Links Trust Staff Annual Golf Match, 1993. In the same year that the caddies' own tournament was begun, this Caddies vs. Staff Match started, representing a successful attempt at caddie/management liaison. The match is played over the newest of the five 18-hole courses at St. Andrews, the Strathtyrum Course, and played in October, when the players have the local 'haar' and frost to contend with. The first match was halved by a very benevolent caddie intentionally missing an easy 18" putt on the last hole for what would have been a caddie win! The caddies themselves put into practice a significant link in promoting an easier working relationship all around.

The Lure of the Links

Caddies Jim Moore, John Bradley and Alex Bain, 1996. Jim is a keen golf historian and collector of golf memorabilia. John is a former Caddie Manager, and Alex is employed by the St. Andrews University Information Technology Department during the winter months. In spite of their diverse interests, the lure of the links brings these men back each season.

MECHANICAL CADDIES

By the spring of 1950, the demand for the services of the caddie was decidedly less than before the war. One very obvious reason for this decline was the introduction of the first caddy cart to the Old Course. Late in 1949 at the R&A Autumn Medal, Lord Brabazon had introduced his "mechanical caddie" or golf trolley, a "cheap, reliable and uncomplaining substitute for a caddie." This caused great consternation amongst the caddies, who quite rightly saw it as a threat to their livelihood.

R&A Captain Lord Brabazon of Tara playing in 1952.

Lord Brabazon rewards local caddie David Deas with the traditional sovereign for retrieving his ball. Lord Brabazon's cart was instrumental in reducing the number of caddies able to work on the links.

These *barras*, as they were known by the caddies, were hired from local golf shops, but most of these local contraptions were homemade, using old pram wheels which were very narrow and inclined to spoil the greens. One R&A member, Mr. Sandy Rutherford, patented a broad-wheeled cart and introduced it to St. Andrews, and by 1956, the narrow-wheeled *barras* were banned from the Old Course.

The introduction of the trolley did for some time reduce the demand for caddies, and in 1955 the Town Council paid off the Caddie Master as unnecessary, handing over this responsibility to the Old Course starter. It was not until the early 1970s, when even the broad-wheeled caddy carts were blamed for damaging the turf on the Old Course and were withdrawn as well, that demand for caddies increased sufficiently for the position of Caddie Manager to be reinstated. Caddy carts were not reintroduced on the Old Course until 1989, and then only for a limited part of the day. In 1974, with the abolition of the Town Council after a reorganisation of local government, the St. Andrews Links Trust was established by an Act of Parliament to maintain the links and ensure continuity in the operation of the golf courses.

Caddie Manager Rick Caffrey (leftmost) and some of the caddies, 1983. They are standing outside of the old Caddie Shelter which was located behind the eighteenth green of the Old Course. The building now houses a shop selling St. Andrews Links Trust merchandise.

The increasing popularity and earnings potential of the game in general led to an improved status for the St. Andrews caddies. In 1984 they felt strong enough as a group to support each other by staging a series of one-day strikes, the first major incident since 1870. The first change the caddies demanded of the Links Trust was the introduction of a grading system which would recognise the more senior caddies. This was agreed to, with either Gold or Silver grading for caddies and Bronze for the younger junior caddies or bag carriers. On the strength of this initial success, the caddies now asked for an increase in their rates. This also was agreed upon, with new rates set at £17, £13, and £9 respectively.

But in consequence, the traditional 'double bagging' was withdrawn by the Links Trust, which considered it one of the contributing factors in holding up play, especially over the Old Course. The caddies continued their one-day strikes in the hope that the double bags would be reinstated, but it soon became clear that the Links Trust was intractable on this point and furthermore would not consider the caddies' threats to involve visiting golfers by asking them to boycott St. Andrews. Slowly and one-by-one, the caddies came back to work, with the promise that the R&A Greens Committee would in the future listen to any legitimate complaint from the caddies.

A few years later the new grading system became a source of discontent amongst the caddies, because golfers were requesting the lower-rate Silver Grade caddie at the expense of the senior caddies. It was agreed to dispense with the three-tier grading and have only Caddies and Bag Carriers, with upgrading and downgrading at the discretion of the Caddie Manager.

Caddie Billy Gunn on the Swilcan Bridge, 1997. Billy Gunn was a soldier and latterly a policeman by profession prior to becoming a caddie in 1984. In 1990, Bill took a year off from caddying locally to work the European Tour, but came off the tour at the end of the season because he would rather spend the time under "God's good air" in St. Andrews. Bill considers carrying on the links "more like a holiday every day rather than work!" For three years straight, he worked the most rounds of any caddie.

During a Dunhill Pro-Am Tournament in the mid-1990s, Bill's golfer suffered a heart attack. The professional in the match, Ronan Rafferty, immediately ran for help while Bill gave mouth-to-mouth resuscitation to the stricken player. It must have been a combination of Bill's First Aid experience and the 'wee nip' he had before the round which brought the player around briefly! Billy said, "The spirit of the links seemed to work!"

Caddie Profile: 'Tip' Anderson

"Everywhere that Tony went, Tip was sure to know."

Born and bred in St. Andrews with golf in his blood (his father was a caddie before him), Tip did not take up the game until he was 15, but he soon became a single-handicapped player. He later apprenticed as a clubmaker, but this was interrupted with National Service. Upon demobilisation, Tip went back to his trade for two years before becoming involved in caddying. It soon became obvious to him that he could earn more money from carrying than from any 'real job,' so he became a full-time caddie from 1956. Tip's big break came in 1960 when he carried for Arnold Palmer in the Open. This partnership lasted an amazing 35 years longer than any other caddie/golfer relationship. In this time, Tip shared in many of Arnold Palmer's successes, including two Open titles.

When Palmer could not make it to Scotland for the 1964 Open in St. Andrews, he recommended Tip to his friend Tony Lema. Lema had never seen the Old Course, and had only two practice rounds. But in spite of this, he went on to win the Open Championship with Tip, and after his win, he singled out Tip as the reason he had won.

WOMEN CADDIES

Until very recently, caddying in Scotland, like the game of golf itself, was staunchly chauvinistic, with only men and boys employed as caddies. Although women have never accounted for more than a small minority in the caddie ranks anywhere, English Club records mention female caddies from 1890 onwards, and women have worked in this profession for years in other parts of the world. A single nineteenth-century reference to 'girl caddies' in Scotland dates back to 1870, when girls were hired as caddies during a caddie strike at Gullane which lasted some five weeks. When things returned to normal, however, the girls were let go, and it was another seventy-odd years before they resurfaced, this time on the links at North Berwick.

During the early 1970s, a few women were taken on at St. Andrews as bag carriers, a form of junior caddie. But this half-hearted recruitment effort proved to be unsuccessful, and most of the women stayed for only a few months. Not until 1993 was there a serious attempt to attract females to the St. Andrews caddie ranks, and in that year, the first female registered bag carrier appeared on the list. After 15 months as that bag carrier, Meroë Wilson was upgraded to a caddie.

Today there are even more females working at St. Andrews, but in general, recruitment has been hampered by the standard stereotype of the caddie as drunken, foul-mouthed and unkempt. Times have changed, though, with the local image upgraded by the building of a modern Caddie Pavilion and the issue of standard waterproof wear for all registered caddies and some senior bag carriers. The local professional status has benefited by the introduction of the

Caddie Liaison Committee, which was set up to give the caddies a voice in disciplinary and procedural matters. Today, the St. Andrews caddie understands the value of image, and is as keen as his or her professional tour counterpart to develop professional standing. Meroë epitomises this positive image which must surely be a goal for any caddie hoping to work at the Home of Golf.

There are still too few women who want to be caddies but the female profile is coming to the fore and interest from them has increased. Women are fully integrated into the St. Andrews caddie system, and have proven their worth.

Above: Bag carrier armband, 1970-1985.

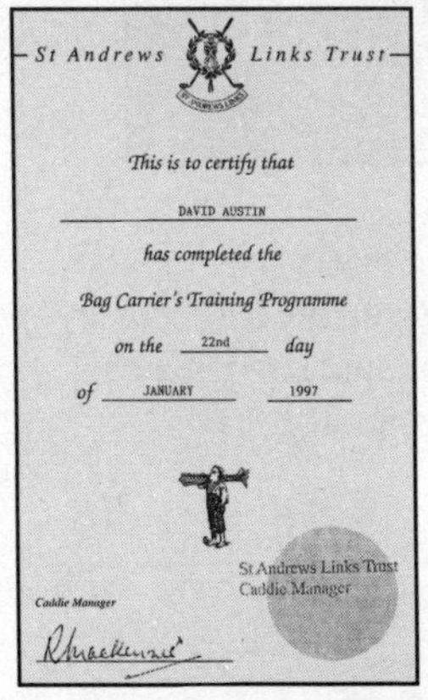
St Andrews Links Trust

This is to certify that

DAVID AUSTIN

has completed the

Bag Carrier's Training Programme

on the 22nd day

of JANUARY 1997

St Andrews Links Trust Caddie Manager

Caddie Manager

Left: The introduction of a Bag Carriers' Training Programme in 1997 for those wishing to eventually become caddies was highly successful. Over 50 young boys and girls completed the training, which included on-course etiquette, understanding golf rules, making up personal course yardage books, and some of the more practical aspects on how to rake bunkers, replace divots, stand by the flag, etc.

Caddie Profile: Meroë Wilson

"Golf *is* life, after all..."

"I would never have dreamed after my first round as a bag carrier in June 1993 that just over two years later I would be caddying on the Old Course in the practice rounds of the 1995 Open, nor that I should participate in games that involved some of the big names in professional golf!

When I started as a bag carrier I did not yet play golf, although my father had urged me for years to take up the game. I enjoyed the outdoor work, meeting people from all over the world and being in a male-dominated environment. I had known many of the caddies for years and they accepted me for *who* I was rather than *what* I was. I listened and learned from them: lines off the tee, yardages from various landmarks, the general rub of the greens, and I marvelled at their abilities. I can still remember the thrill of walking up the eighteenth fairway carrying a bag—there's no feeling quite like it.

The caddie manager encouraged me from the very beginning and urged me to get out, pace the courses, and make up my own books, but I didn't feel confident enough to be 'made-up' to caddie status until July 1994 when I realised I'd spent an entire week being treated and used as a caddie by the golfers I was with. I reckoned it was time to take the offered promotion! Around that same time the golf bug gripped me so I took to playing the game myself, and within a year of getting my handicap I was competing in my Club's Bronze Championship final! Although I had found I didn't need to be a player to be able to caddie, it has helped enormously with my understanding of what I am doing and I feel the golfer is more comfortable in the knowledge that I play the game myself.

I have experienced mixed reactions from golfers when I introduce myself as their caddie, but on the whole I get the feeling that it really doesn't matter as long as you can do the job. There are days when I wonder why I do it: when there's a force 9 gale blowing left to right, when the bag weighs a ton, when the golfer is having a bad day—you can't do anything right then. But all it takes is a single comment like, "she knows your game, great read, good call," to restore faith in yourself. Personally, I can't imagine *not* being a caddie. Golf *is* life, after all..."

Caddies' Nicknames

Most caddies have had nicknames, sometimes reflecting a personal characteristic or trait, and other times to hide the caddie's true identity for reasons best known only to himself!! Some of these nicknames have survived to this day either in local legend or by being handed down in the family from one generation to the other, even when their meanings have long been lost. These humorous and often affectionate names represent a tradition amongst caddies as old as the game itself, and each one has added to the richness and colour of the game.

CADDIES OF YESTERYEAR 'THE WINE OF THE COUNTRY'

The Barrel Dancer: Willie Martin was a bill-poster by trade but preferred caddying on the links.

Pawky Dave: David Corstorphine was known for his dry wit, and Andra' Kirkaldy said that nobody could better him at teeing a ball, according to the weather and the shot required.

Boosy Chas: More often than not, Charlie was to be found at the 19th hole rather than at one of the other eighteen!

Poot Chisholm: Poot was a fisherman and a somewhat disreputably-dressed caddie. When his photograph was taken one day, he looked at it and asked repeatedly whether it was really of himself. On being reassured that it was, Poot gravely said, "It's such a *humblin' sicht.*"

Mathy Gorum: When sober, Mathy Gorum took to caddying, but his name was often used at temperance meetings as "the awful example!" During the winter months, Mathy tried selling razors, singing songs, or *reading heids* to make some money. In his youth, no one could equal him for steadiness of eye, and it was said that he could drive a ball from the top of a bottle. In his later years, the young caddies would get him to attempt this celebrated feat, and much to the amusement of the lads, every bottle put in front of him would be smashed in his effort!

Farnie: College taught, Farnie would fluently discuss most subjects at length, and never failed to remind the other caddies of his six years of studies.

Stumpie Eye: Archie Stump, another of the very colourful caddies, was half-blind. When he took on a job he would say, "I can carry clubs *a'* day sir, but ye'll *hae tae* watch the ball for *yersel.*"

Hole-in-'is-pocket: This caddie claimed never to have lost a ball, but he got his name because when a player for whom he was carrying lost his ball, he would drop one down his trouser leg and declare, "Here it is, sir, an' no such a bad lie *efter a'.*" Actually, this could prove to be expensive, and was only used when there was some money involved between the players!

Plum Melville: John Melville was a local clubmaker and caddie to Jock Hutchinson when Hutchinson won the 1921 Open Championship.

John 'Treacle' Fenton: Treacle was a fisherman said to have a grand face for funerals.

Tee-Ta-Toe: This caddie was a son of fishwife 'Teenie Bell'. When a small boy he was sent to the bakers for 'three half loafs,' and it came out as Tee-Ta-Toe. The name stayed with him all his life.

Bad Lugs: This caddie was a German who, during the First World War, was accused of being a spy. He was later executed in London.

Lang Willie: Caddie Willie Robertson stood 6'2" and always wore *lum hats* and *lang breeks* which were said to be *mither-made.*

Wiggie Ayton: Wiggie later turned professional, and since he was bald as a *coot*, was never seen on the golf course without his wig.

'Skipper' Stuart Fenton: Skipper was a fisherman noted for his big mouth and little nose: make of this what you will!

Trap Door: This caddie had an ingenious system of collecting 'lost' golf balls. He had a hollow sole in the heel of his boots with a metal plate which when opened would trap any of his golfer's lost balls.

Former American President George Bush with his St. Andrews caddie Alan Jones, before teeing off to play a round on the Old Course, 1995. This was Mr. Bush's first time in St. Andrews, and he was "thrilled and proud to play at the Home of Golf." When Alan was later asked what he thought of Mr. Bush's game, he replied, "He's no slouch at the game, although playing off a 20 handicap, he returned a net 73."

THE SPIRIT OF THE LINKS: THE MODERN CADDIE

The Bald Eagle: No one could ever remember Jimmy Beard with any hair.

Jimmy-by-the-way: This caddie always introduced himself as "I'm Jimmy, by the way."

Pete-the-feet: Pete took size 13 in a shoe—whenever he wore them, that is!

Wallop-the-hammer: George Reid, a blacksmith by trade, caddied for Open winner James Braid.

'Paddy' Gallagher: This Irish caddie added a touch of culture to the links by having studied at medical school, and he was always civil to his *man*.

A-la-carte: This was waiter Sid McDonald, of no known address. Sid always slept rough, preferring the bunkers to a bed.

Do-nut: Alex Spence was Sid's buddy and a fellow waiter.

Evil-brew: Caddie Eddie Garland later became known as 'Kick-start' due to a kicking motion made when he got into his stride. When younger, he did time on the stage as a comedian, and he always had a story to tell with his finely-honed wit.

'Ginger' Johnstone: This caddie became Caddie Master during the R&A medal competitions and at most Open tournaments.

Others who are *working the tools* today are Tweedie, Spec's, Putt-Putt, Loppy, Telf, Crocodile, and Balty, to name only a few.

Caddie Chronology

1764	Old Course changed from 22 holes to the present 18.
1771	First mention of St. Andrews caddies: caddie fees set by the Society of St. Andrews Golfers.
1819	Tournament for ballmakers, clubmakers and caddies.
1822	Position of Keeper of the Green given to caddie Geordie Robertson, who was dismissed as incorrigible sometime later after severe *wiggings.*
1823	Caddie David Pirie takes over as Keeper of the Green. First playing-in of R&A Captain-Elect.
1833	Mention of highly-respected David Robertson, earliest recorded St. Andrews caddie/golfer, in George Carnegie's famous poem *Golfiana.* Upon his death in 1836, he was eulogised by Carnegie in another poem.
1840	'Auld' Daw Anderson, senior caddie, takes on the job of Keeper of the Green.
1842	Old Tom Morris, age 21, is the first recognised winner of the Caddie Competition. Allan Robertson, age 27, is prohibited from competing, as his game is considered "superior to all others."

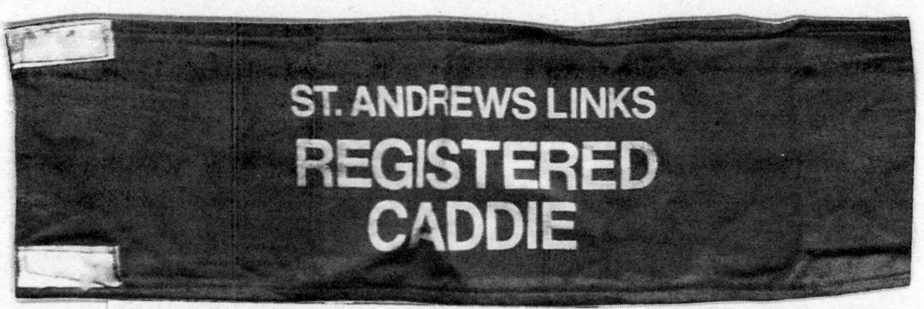

Caddie armband, 1970-1985.

1845 Allan Robertson employs caddies Tom Morris and Lang Willie as feather ballmakers.

1848 Guttie ball played over the links at St. Andrews, much to the immediate displeasure of Allan Robertson and the caddies.

1850 Watty Alexander and Alex Herd take over as joint keepers of the Green on Daw Anderson's retirement. With one barrow, two shovels and a combined wage of £6 a year, they did a good job under the circumstances!

1852 James Wilson, first St. Andrews caddie to work for famous clubmaker Hugh Philp.

1856 'Auld Daw' Anderson retires as Keeper of the Green to set up a ginger beer stall on the ninth green of the Old Course.

1859 Allan Robertson, son of David Robertson and a local caddie who was considered the greatest golfer, goes round the Old Course in 79, becoming the first golfer to break 80. Allan Robertson dies aged 44.

1860 First real attempt to introduce regulations for the employment of caddies.

1864 First official set of Rules and Regulations for caddies is introduced.

1865 Tom Morris appointed Honorary Professional to the Royal & Ancient Golf Club.

1870 Further Rules and Regulations for caddies proposed by the R&A. Caddies strike for higher wages.

1873 Local caddie Tom Kidd wins first Open Championship to be played over the Old Course.

1875 R&A member General Moncrieffe introduces evening classes for the younger caddies at the local Fishers School. Tom Morris is appointed Caddie Superintendent and Keeper of the Green. A revised set of Rules and Regulations are introduced.

1876 First of caddie Bob Martin's two St. Andrews Open wins, the second in 1885.

1877 First of three Open wins for local caddie Jamie Anderson (others in 1878 and 1879).

1883 R&A gives a yearly subscription of £50 plus day-old newspapers to a local workingmen's coffee house by the harbour, for caddies' use.

Caddie Stephen Martin takes time out on the Old Course, 1997.

1890 Dr. Trail's "Canvas Container" makes its first appearance on the Old Course. New set of Rules and Regulations for the employment of caddies. Caddie Benefit Fund set up by R&A Golf Club.

1891 First Caddie Shelter built, for use in wet or snowy weather. Vigilance Committee set up by caddies, headed by Tom Morris, to maintain order and discipline within the caddie ranks. Andra' Kirkaldy comes off the Caddie Register to become a 'professional golfer.'

1892 Twenty-one caddies receive assistance from the newly-established Caddie Benefit Fund.

1894 Caddie Library set up within the new Shelter. Patronage of caddies by the R&A reduced, and discipline of caddies now under the control of the Burgh Court.

1896 Rules for Caddies, Fees and Registration Conditions published in local newspaper. Caddie Benefit Fund is stopped, because caddies have become increasingly unwilling to contribute to the Fund. Special bye-laws for caddies are introduced and implemented by the Town Council and the local Sheriff.

1912 Nicholas Robb's title now becomes Caddie Master.

1920 Caddie fees reduced by 1/- during R&A medal week. Dog licence (Caddie Voucher) worth 7/6d given to registered caddies to help with groceries between December and January when there was little or no work on the links.

1921 Jock Hutchinson, ex-St. Andrews caddie, emigrated to USA. He returned home to win the Open, with local caddie 'Plum' Melville caddying for him.

CADDIES

Only those persons licensed by the Links Management Committee may be employed as Caddies. They shall be engaged only through the Caddie Master.

Charges CADDIES per round £8·00
BAG CARRIERS per round £4·00

Note:- A gratuity may be added at the Golfer's discretion. Any infringement or misbehaviour to be reported to the Caddie Master.

Caddie Fee Board, circa 1980.

1929	Caddie Superintendent Mr. Fyfe introduces a new code of dress and discipline to the Caddie Shelter.
1930	Second Caddie Shelter is built at a cost of £316, sited behind the eighteenth green on the Old Course.
1932	Unregistered caddies taken to court and heavily fined for working on the links.
1934	Andra' Kirkaldy, caddie/golfer and Honorary Professional to the R&A Golf Club, dies.
1938	New rule introduced by the R&A and USPGA limiting the number of clubs carried by any one golfer to 14. Caddie fees reduced. Annual dinner for caddies given by R&A member Mr. Blackwell.
1939	Caddie tournament for those caddies not involved in the war, continuing for three years.
1940	Reintroduction of the Caddie Benefit Fund.
1941	Caddies paid 'double fee' for working over the Eden Golf Course on Sundays. Caddies also offered cheap golf at 2/- a round.
1945	Caddie fees increased from 3/- to 4/-. Reinstatement of R&A Captain playing himself into office (suspended during the war years). Traditional sovereign given to the caddie who returned the Captain's ball.

1947 Return of the Caddies' Dinner, this time hosted by Mr. Blackwell's son.

1948 Caddie Benefit Fund stopped.

1949 Lord Brabazon's cart (trolley) introduced for the first time on the Old Course.

1950 Services of Caddie Master dispensed with as "unnecessary," with caddie demand on the decline. The Old Course starter took over his duties.

1955 Guy Gillespie, local caddie, wins the Open with Peter Thomson.

1956 Trolleys banned from Old Course.

1960 'Tip' Anderson, well-known local caddie, begins longest golfer-caddie association in golf: to date, 36 years.

1964 'Tip' Anderson helps American Tony Lema win the Open.

1974 Links Trust takes over administration of caddies.

Waiting for work in the Caddie Pavilion, 1996.

1984 Series of one-day strikes for higher wages, and introduction of gold, silver and bronze grading system for caddies.

1985 Traditional "double bagging" for caddies discontinued.

1989 Trolleys reintroduced on Old Course, but only after midday.

1992 Caddie Liaison Committee set up to represent caddie views.

1993 Author Rick Mackenzie takes over as Caddie Manager. Inaugural Links Staff vs. Caddies golf match, now played annually over the Strathtyrum Course. Revised dress code, all registered caddies given a set of waterproofs by the St. Andrews Links Trust. First female caddie registered. Old grading system abandoned, caddies and bag carriers are now the two accepted grades.

1994 New Caddie Pavilion opens, containing modern conveniences plus the Caddie Manager's office. Caddie Rules and Advice booklet published and issued to all registered caddies.

1997 Introduction of Bag Carriers (Junior Caddies) Training Programme. Bag Carriers Rules and Advice booklet published, training certificates given to all successful bag carriers

Richard Mackenzie and Rick Gibson teamed up to win the 1994 Dunhill Cup, beating the USA 2 to 1. Mackenzie has caddied for the Canadians since the Dunhill's inception.

Caddie Bruce Sorley, 1997. Bruce is one of the more experienced caddies at St. Andrews. He started caddying in 1974 and that same year, he worked the Open with Ron Caruddo and latterly Tiger Woods in 1995, and Joost Stienhammer at the Open over Royal Troon in 1997.

Bruce has also worked the European Tour, and for many years specialised in the British Amateur events where he first met Jay Siegal in 1979, and took him through the 1980 and 1984 Opens. Bruce exemplifies the bridge that a local caddie can make into the top professional ranks, but more than anything, he enjoys working the links at St. Andrews.

LINKS CADDIE MANAGERS

CADDIE MANAGERS AND CLUB OFFICERS KNOWN AT ST. ANDREWS

Tom Morris was the first Caddie Superintendent appointed by the R&A Golf Club (in 1875) to oversee the discipline of the St. Andrews caddies. Over the years there have been many who followed in his illustrious footsteps. Unfortunately, not all have been recorded, but below is a list of those names known to date.

Caddie Manager Alexander 'Wingy' Taylor at St. Andrews, 1901.

Tom Morris	1875
John McGregor	1890
Nicholas Robb	1891
Alexander 'Wingy' Taylor	1901
James Jolly	1910
David Corstorphine	1920
Alex Fyfe	1926
George 'Grumpy' Grant	1929
William Radley	1935 – 1940
Ted Bodle	1941

From 1950, with the introduction of Caddy Carts, there was a reduction in the use of caddies. The Caddie Manager's services were dispensed with from 1950 until 1973, when the carts were banned from use on the Old Course.

CADDIE MANAGERS WHO HAVE WORKED ON THE LINKS SINCE THE LINKS TRUST TOOK OVER IN 1974

David Christie	1974 – 1975
Joseph 'Bill' Winskill	1976 – 1977
Angus Lang	1977 – 1982
Rick Caffrey	1983 – 1984
Jim Moody	1985 – 1986
Jack Semple	1987 – 1990
John Bradley	1991 – 1992
Richard Mackenzie	1993 – present

Today's St. Andrews caddies in uniform, with author Rick Mackenzie in centre.

Scottish Glossary

Ah'm jist dootin' (page 74): I'm just doubting. Caddie Charlie Thompson was hedging his bets with this remark—he'd be right either way!

aff the nairth (page 74): off the north. On a links course such as St. Andrews the wind is always a major consideration. Even if it weren't, talking about the weather is a major part of any Scotsman's day!

ata' noo (page 66): at all now. Sodger remembers when Hell bunker was deeper than it is today. In those days there was a step which took the hapless golfer into the bowels of Hell!

auld (pages 2, 14, et al.): old; in family relationships, indicating the oldest. In the golfing sense, the prefix *auld* is a mark of respect for an old man's contribution to the game.

auld buddy (page 83): a long-standing companion, who has shared many an agonizing round on the links and afterwards many a *wee nip at the 19th hole!*

awthing (page 8): anything.

baffy (baffies) (page 64): a hickory-shafted fairway wood equivalent to a modern 4 wood.

barras (page 101): barrows.

braw (page 5): brave, fine, splendid.

breeks (or **troosers**) (pages 39, 58): trousers.

bunker (page 5, et al.): similar to sand traps in the USA. Originally dug out by sheep sheltering from the cold north winds, they became one of the accepted hazards in a round of golf.

bunnet (pages 9, 41, 86): a soft, flat, brimless cap worn by men and boys, latterly usually one with a peak. These were an accepted part of the caddies' garb.

cannae gowf (page 78): cannot play golf.

cauld (page 1): cold

chuckie stanes (page 74): pebbles (or occasionally, marbles).

cleek, cleekmaking (pages 61, 79): a golf club (nineteenth and early twentieth century) corresponding to the number 4 iron.

cloot (page 84): a piece of cloth or a rag.

coos (page 74): cows.

coot (page 112): water fowl.

cuddy (page 90): a donkey or horse.

dae (pages 37, 39, 76): do

deaved (page 21): deafened; annoyed with noise or talk.

dinna (page 8): don't.

donnart (page 92): dull, stupid.

Doo Dah verses (page 40): a stylised form of mouth music without words, often practised when a man was the worse for drink but still wanted to entertain anyone who would listen, including himself! This distinctive style of music-making stopped in the middle of this century.

dookin (page 80): a drenching, a soaking.

doon (pages 39, 58, 74): down.

fu' o' ale (page 40): full of ale, drunk and legless as the case may be!

game o' gowf (page 69): game of golf.

gey cauld (page 4): very cold.
gey strang (page 1): very strong.

ghillie (page 34): a sportsman's attendant, usually in deerstalking or angling in the Highlands.

grasshoppin', workin' the land (pages 2, 3): both refer to carrying the golfer's clubs around the links.

haar (page 99): a cold mist or fog, especially a sea-fog coming off the North Sea onto the eastern coastal areas in Scotland. There is an old Scottish pun to the effect that "the *haar* is never mist!"

hae (page 99): have.

heid (pages 8, 64): head

howk (page 72): dig; figuratively: unearth, bring out, extricate.

intae (page 66): into.

ken (page 39): know.

lasses (page 58): young girls.

lang (pages 3, 5, 58, 112): long.

luggin' (pages 8, 90): carrying something.

lum hat (pages 52, 73): a tall silk hat, a top-hat. The word *lum* means a chimney, the smoke-vent or flue of a fireplace, or a chimney-stack. An old Scottish saying runs, "Lang may your lum reek, and lang may you have the wood to fire it," wishing you health and happiness.

mair (pages 66, 74): more.

man (pages 8, 9, 10, et al.): caddies' term for the golfer.

mid-spoon (page 66): see *spoon*

mither-made (pages 58, 112): mother-made. Lang Willie's mother saved money by sewing his clothes at home.

nae (pages 37, 92, et al.): no, not any.

nae mair (page 85): no more.

nae gowf (page 54): not golf.

niblick (pages 5, 66): the golf club corresponding to the number 8 or 9 iron (late nineteenth, early twentieth century). British golf writer Bernard Darwin says that, "When you land in any of the pot bunkers at St. Andrews, there's only enough room for an angry man and his *niblick*!"

och (page 44): a term used to express weariness and exasperation, as in, "*Och*, man, ye cannae gowf, and yer nae likely tae!"

oor (pages 2, 8): our.

oot (pages 4, 92): out.

pawky (pages 2, 5, 85): having a matter-of-fact, humorously critical outlook on life, characterised by a sly, quiet wit.

peerie (page 76): a spinning top.

poke (page 64): a bag or pouch, a small sack; a shopkeeper's paper bag. Used by caddies to mean a golf bag.

porritch (pages 44, 58): porridge, the dish of oatmeal (or rolled oats) boiled in salted water. One of its significant properties is that it does keep you regular!

Provost (pages 8, 38): head of a Scottish town council, corresponding to a mayor.

reading heids (page 111): in the absence of tea leaves and Tarot cards, this was a peculiarly Scottish form of fortune telling in which the reader would feel "the lumps and bumps on a man's heid which were truly a mark of the life he would lead." This was very popular amongst the working people.

richt (pages 39, 44): right.

sartorial dress (page 79): relating to tailored clothes. The fishermen's dark blue 'uniforms' made the standard garb of the traditional caddies look shabby by comparison.

sicht (pages 44, 111): sight.

sillybodkins (pages 74, 75): The term *silly* can mean weak, shaky, or unsubstantial. A *bodkin* is a dagger, stiletto, or small, sharply-pointed instrument. Perhaps the screw nails were prone to fly out of the corks when given a good whack by an enthusiastic caddie!

skelp (page 64): a stroke or blow, especially with a flat object. In this case, a smack with the open hand.

spoon (page 66): a wooden golf club with a slightly hollowed head and backward-sloping face, corresponding to the number 3 wood (nineteenth to early twentieth century). Also known as scrapers, spoons came in short, middle and long sizes.

stumpie (page 80): a short, stocky or dumpy person.

stymie (page vi): difficulty in seeing things; making the best of bad luck. It was said that, "real life had its stymies," and perhaps through golf, we were encouraged to accept them philosophically.

tacket, tackety (page 82): A tacket is a small nail, latterly especially a hobnail, used to stud the soles of shoes, etc.

tae (pages 2, 4, 58, et al.): to.

twa (pages 23 [footnote], 90): two. Jock Hutchinson was given a "twa and six tip," meaning 2/6d or 12 new pence.

wan (pages 35, 91): one (numeral or pronoun).

wark (page 37): work.

wee nip (pages 1, 44, 62): a small quantity of liquor, usually whiskey. The word nip comes from *nipperkin*, a small wine and beer measure containing about half a pint or slightly less.

weel, wel (pages 39, 91): well.

whin (pages vii, 8, 54, et al.): the common furze or gorse; in plural, a clump or area of gorse. The whins have always been a primary hazard on the Old Course, and they provide one of its most outstanding visual features as well, because no matter what time of year, there is always some part of the foliage sporting golden flowers. An old Scottish saying has it that "when the whin's not in bloom, love's out of season."

widnae (page 58): would not.

wigging (pages 14, 15, 22, 115): severe censure from a person in authority; scolding or reprimand. This word might derive from the idea of being scolded by a wigged superior; e.g., a judge.

Wingy (pages 43, 125): To wingle means to hang loosely, dangle, flap or wag. By extension, men who had lost an arm in the war, and thus had a loose sleeve, were called 'Wingy.'

wisnae (page 91): was not.

workin' the tools (page 114): refers to a caddie who can club his man, given any shot.

yins (page 83): auld yins, young yins, wee yins refers to people in an affectionate or compassionate sense. Lang Willie would have been known as the 'Big Yin.'

Charlie Ferguson (left) and Jim Brown, 1997. Charlie joined the department as a seasonal assistant in 1996, and Jim has been the full-time Assistant Caddie Manager since 1995. When asked to rate his game, Charlie says, "Practice, practice and more practice!"

Bibliography

Balfour, James. *Reminiscences of Golf on St. Andrews Links.* Edinburgh, 1887.

Burnett, Bobby, *The St. Andrews Opens.* London, 1990.

Chapman, Kenneth G. *The Rules of the Green: A History of the Rules of Golf.* Chicago, 1997.

Darwin, Bernard. *Golf.* London, 1954.

Elliot, Alan and John Allanman. *A History of Golf.* London, 1990.

The Evening Telegraph, Dundee, 1938.

Everard, H. S. C. *History of the Royal & Ancient Golf Club: St. Andrews, from 1754 to 1900.* Edinburgh, 1907.

Golf Illustrated, 1899-1940.

Herd, Sandy. *My Golfing Life.* London.

Hutchison, Horace G. *Fifty Years of Golf.* London, 1914.

Jarrett, Tom. *St. Andrews Golf Links: The First 600 Years.* Edinburgh, 1995.

Kirkaldy, Andrew. *My Fifty Years of Golf: Memories.* London, 1921.

Lang, Andrew. *Golfing Papers.*

MacKenzie, Alister. *The Spirit of St. Andrews.* Chelsea, MI, 1995.

Mackie, Keith. *Golf at St. Andrews.* London, 1995.

McPherson, J. Gordon. *Golf and Golfers.*

Robertson, J. K. *St. Andrews, Home of Golf.* St. Andrews, 1967.

Salmond, J. B. *The Story of the R&A.* London, 1956.

St. Andrews Citizen, 1890-1925.

Stirk, David. *Carry Your Bag, Sir?* London, 1996.

Taylor, Dawson. *St. Andrews, Cradle of Golf.*

Tullock, W. W. *Life of Tom Morris.* London, 1908.

Photo Credits

The author would like to thank the following organisations and individuals for their kind permission to reproduce the photographs and documents in this book.

Royal & Ancient Golf Club, vii, 9, 12, 18, 19, 25, 26, 28, 29, 30, 31, 32, 33, 35 bottom, 36 (both), 37, 39, 41, 42, 43, 44, 48, 50, 51, 53, 56, 58, 61, 62, 65 (top), 66, 68, 71, 73, 79, 80, 92, 93.

St. Andrews Preservation Trust, cover, vi, 4, 13, 16, 24, 65 (bottom), 125.

St. Andrews University Library, 15 (top), 45 (bottom), 70, 76, 96, 97, 101.

Peter Adamson, 99, 126.

Iain Macfarlane Lowe, 123.

Evening Telegraph, Dundee, 45 (top), 91.

Heiner Kupcke, 89, 102, 105.

All other photographs copyright Richard Mackenzie, 3, 6, 10, 15 (bottom), 22 (courtesy of North East Fife District Council), 35 (top), 40, 46, 49, 63, 75, 77, 81, 83, 85, 86, 88, 100, 104, 107 (top), 107 (bottom, courtesy of St. Andrews Links Trust), 108, 113, 116, 118, 119, 122 (courtesy of St. Andrews Links Trust), 123, 124, 136.

Publisher's note: Although every effort has been made to trace copyright holders, we apologise in advance for any unintentional omissions, and would be pleased to insert the appropriate acknowledgements in subsequent editions of this publication.